THE EQUATION

A Novel by

Judith I Hill

This book is a work of fiction. All names, characters, places and incidents are the product of the author's imagination or are used fictitiously. Any resemblance to actual events, locales, or persons, living or dead, is coincidental. This title is available in both e-book and paperback.

Cover photo credit belongs to Mike P. Nelson

ISBN: 1490313257
ISBN-13: 9781490313252
Library of Congress Control Number: 2013910225
CreateSpace Independent Publishing Platform
North Charleston, South Carolina

IN PRAISE OF

THE EQUATION

A NOVEL BY JUDITH I. HILL

"A superbly crafted novel, *The Equation* is a truly impressive debut effort from an obviously talented author. A complexly woven story populated with memorable and remarkable characters, *The Equation* is a solid entertainment from first page to last and will leave immensely satisfied readers looking eagerly toward Judith Hill's next literary effort."

—Midwest Book Review

"Debut novelist Hill presents a spot-on heroine in Sarah Thompson.... Through straightforward, accessible prose, Hill tells a sweet story of two painfully honorable individuals unwilling to compromise their dreams of true love.... An uplifting, modest tale of algebra and second chances."

—Kirkus Indie Review

For all those souls in whom the flame
of love is kept burning brightly.

PROLOGUE

NEW YORK
APRIL 5, 1959
8:29 P.M.

Thirty miles north of Manhattan on the Palisades Parkway, the headlights of a 1956 Ford Crown Victoria cut through the inky blackness of the stormy night. Ominous clouds hidden in the night sky became intermittently lit by searing blades of lightning as the three young men in the speeding car raced against the clock. Bear Mountain Bridge traffic circle came into view just as the rain began to pour. Torrents of rain engulfed the roadway as the driver turned onto Highway 218 North, paralleling the Hudson River. Within minutes, the windshield became heavily fogged, obscuring visibility.

The driver kept his eyes focused ahead and yelled to the front passenger, "Gunner, find something to wipe the windshield with."

Dutifully, the young man found a rag beneath his seat and did his best to clear the rapidly spreading fog that threatened to totally obscure their vision. The blaring radio's incessant static added to his annoyance as he diligently wiped the glass. Throwing the rag to the seat, he tuned to a station playing Bobby Darin's latest hit, "Mack the Knife."

In the backseat, a third young man reclined half-asleep. Without warning, he suddenly sat upright, bent his head forward, and then heaved loudly, creating an ungodly sound while he vomited on the floor mats.

Turning in surprise, Gunner exclaimed, "Holy shit! How the hell are we going to get Wade cleaned up in time? We'll never make it."

The driver remained focused and continued toward the village of Highland Falls.

"I can't afford another demerit. You've got to speed it up," Gunner pleaded as he turned to shove the sickened man back up against the upholstered leather seat.

Sheets of rain pounded the windshield while the shards of lightning illuminated the car with recurring flashes of eerie blue-white light. Slowing the car in a turn, the driver kept a vigilant eye on the road ahead. "What time is it?"

Gunner strained to read his watch. Immediately after the next jagged shaft lit the sky, he called out, "Twenty-forty."

The driver countered, "We can still make it."

As they neared the village of Highland Falls, picking up speed, a huge bolt of lightning struck the earth directly in front of the car. A thunderous crackling consumed all other sounds as a giant oak crashed across the roadway. The driver did his best to brake and swerve, but the slick surface forced the Crown Victoria to the shoulder, where it hit part of the massive tree, flipping over and down into a ravine. The car continued to roll over and over again down the embankment until it finally came to rest.

Moments later, a four-door sedan ground to a slow stop fifty feet from the downed tree on the right shoulder. Turning his headlights on full bright, an older man donning a sports cap exited his car in the teeming rain and ran to survey the ravine. The 1956 Ford lay on its roof, some hundred and fifty feet from the roadway's surface, wheels still spinning, as "Mack the Knife" blared uninterrupted from the radio. Soaked from head to toe, he raced back to his anxious wife who waited nervously in the car. "We've got to go get help," he told her. "I don't think anyone could have survived!"

Within thirty minutes, red lights were flashing from various rescue vehicles, as well as several police cars. Traffic was being diverted around the fallen tree while an officer directed an ambulance as it maneuvered its way closer to the bank. A slightly balding detective wearing a rain-soaked trench coat and fedora with water dripping from its brim stood watching the rescue team. They placed the second of two bodies on a litter attached to a rope secured at the roadway's surface. The detective reached for an open pack of Camels along with a lighter from his lapel pocket. Tilting the pack, he tapped it against his wrist two times, exposing a single cigarette. Using his lips to secure the cigarette directly from the pack, he cupped his hands and lit it, protecting the flame from the rain. This was not the usual way his Sunday nights on duty turned out. It was a miserable, stormy spring weekend one week after Easter. *The sons of bitches didn't even have a chance with weather like this.*

A third police car arrived on the scene, this one not from the Highland Falls department. A military police officer got out of the car, along with an Army colonel who approached the detective and shook his hand.

"It's a bad night for introductions, Detective. I'm Colonel Nathan Pryor, the Point's command duty officer. What have we got?"

"Well, Colonel, I'm afraid it's bad news. We have two DOA and a third barely alive, if they can cut him out of there before he passes," he said as he handed Colonel Pryor the military IDs found on each of the three men from the wrecked car. The younger military police officer held up a flashlight so the colonel could read the names off the cards as the rain subsided to a light drizzle.

The colonel shook his head. "This is going to be quite a loss for the Academy and the country," he said with shock in his voice.

The final litter was hauled to the top of the ravine as they silently watched. The last man was still breathing but obviously suffered from a grievous wound to his head, as well as several broken bones in his legs and wrist. The colonel moved closer to the litter basket to get a better look at the only surviving man as they prepared to transfer him to the ambulance.

"One minute," the colonel commanded the ambulance team. Bending down closer to the bandaged and blood-soaked head of the surviving man, he whispered in his ear, "You're going to make it, Cadet." After a nod from the colonel, the emergency workers quickly boarded the injured man, securing him in preparation to leave.

Walking back to the detective, the colonel continued, "The surviving cadet was the brigade commander and ranked at the top of the senior class. As first captain, he had the makings of an exceptional officer and had distinguished himself amongst his peers by earning the highest academic scores of his class in his four years at West Point. It's difficult enough to tell the parents of the other two cadets that they have died, but if this one makes it, he won't be able to finish out his last month at the Academy." The colonel wiped the water from the brim of his hat as the detective silently listened, watching the ambulance crew. "With such massive injuries to overcome, he'll more than likely be unable to pass the physical exam and receive his commission." Pausing momentarily, he drew a deep breath before turning to face the detective. "How do you tell one of the brightest and most gifted young men in the nation that everything he's busted his ass for in the last four years means nothing, and that his military career has just ended?" Shaking his head, he added, "To have to deliver such a devastating blow to the best of the best is painful to accept and come to terms with. It's a part of the job you're never really prepared for."

The door at the back of the ambulance slammed shut, and the red lights on top flashed eerily against the misty fog, casting a blood-red tinge to the humid air. The patrolmen cleared a passage for the ambulance. Once underway, the haunting sound of the siren and glowing red lights cast a morbid sense of overwhelming tragedy to those left behind.

The detective turned to the colonel. "They were less than two miles from Thayer Gate."

"Write down the ID numbers of all three cadets," the colonel instructed his aid. Facing the detective again, he added, "If it hadn't been for the accident, they would have made it back to the Point before their passes expired." Extending his hand, the colonel continued, "On behalf of the Academy, I'd like to thank you, Detective, and the Highland Falls police department for your speedy response. One more thing, would you please make sure their names are withheld from release until the Army can notify the young men's families?"

"You got it, Colonel."

Lifting his collar to ward off the chilling dampness, the colonel repeated, "This is not only a blow to the class of 1959, but it truly is a great loss to their families and the nation."

The Highland Falls police detective studied the profound sense of loss on the colonel's face and agreed. "I'll be in touch, Colonel. Please extend my condolences to everyone at West Point Military Academy."

PART I

Some loves blossom quickly and then die hard. Other loves fade away as if planted in stony soil. For very few, there is a love that remains innocent in the depths of the soul, sheltered until time and circumstance brings its infancy to fruition and demands a stage. Confronted by love's great power, the heart opens and learns that wherever the beginning is, there the ending is also on its circular path to completion. Nurtured in good soil, love's destiny is the eternal infinity, first and last as one.

∞

CHAPTER ONE

SEPTEMBER 1962

The windshield of the yellow school bus caught a ray of golden sunlight as it turned the corner on a clear, sunny morning. The temperatures had finally arrived at the midway point between intolerably hot and humid and not cool enough for a jacket. Summer rains had left the manicured yards still lush and green as the Long Island North Shoreline High School students faced their first day of classes in their brand-new school. Bus number seven was right on schedule as it approached the corner of Maple and Dogwood streets. The screech of the brakes brought the bus to a halt as the driver pulled the handle of the door full open. "Morning, Mark," Lou spouted as tall, lanky, somewhat-disheveled Mark Stevens shuffled leisurely on board.

"What's so good about it?" Mark replied, moving on to the rear without waiting for an answer.

Without losing a beat, the dusty-haired, leather-skinned driver countered, "Thought you'd be spitfire glad to be on the downhill side now that this is your last year of high school."

Mark shrugged and continued his way to the back of the bus. "You're in my seat," he shouted loudly to a new freshman who occupied the last seat of the left row.

The younger boy took Mark's word for gospel. "Sorry, I . . . I didn't know the seats were assigned." The boy immediately moved, allowing Mark to sprawl out across the bench seat with a look of smug satisfaction on his otherwise scowling face.

Following close behind, two students boarded, and the driver gave a broad smile and a wink of his eye as if an old friend had arrived. "Morning, Miss Sarah. You're looking lovely as ever. Are you ready for another school year?"

Sarah Thompson moved up the steps effortlessly. Her sun-streaked, ash blonde hair was tightly bound at the back of her head with a strand of aqua blue silk ribbon that mirrored the shade of her eyes. For the first day of junior year, she'd chosen to wear a crisp, white blouse, which hugged her well-proportioned, willowy frame to her waist, tucked neatly beneath a knee-length A-line skirt. Slightly worn but polished penny loafers and stockings completed the well-groomed and casually tailored look. Her ponytail swayed slightly to the left then to the right as she smiled broadly, climbing the steps of the bus. "As ready as I'll ever be, Mr. Lou. How about you? Did you have a good summer?"

In his usual upbeat fashion, Lou managed another toothy and wrinkled smile, exposing his nicotine-stained teeth. "You bet I'm ready, and it was one of the best summers ever, Miss Sarah."

The familiar yet faint telltale scent of cigarette smoke made itself known to Sarah, despite the spearmint gum old Lou perpetually chewed to disguise his age-old habit.

The door jerked shut as bus number seven moved on, negotiating two more turns and another quarter mile to the next stop.

Sarah Thompson was different from other sixteen-year-old girls. Not swayed by fads or the fashion of the day, she wore stockings when everyone else wore anklet socks. Although the latest rage was the shorter Jacqueline Kennedy-bubble-styled hair, Sarah's hair remained below shoulder-length. The majority of girls walked a tightrope to remain popular with the "in" crowd, while Sarah was at ease no matter what group she found herself mingled with; she made no pretext and did not hide behind a mask. With no label, she proved to be no threat.

The truth was she had learned early on what was truly important in life. Her mother was suffering from a long-term illness, and as a result, Sarah carried more responsibilities at home. Her older sister Elizabeth was now a freshman at an institute of art in Rhode Island where she could pursue her dreams. That left Sarah at home with her five-year-old sister, Rachael, whom she loved dearly, and all of the household duties her mother did not have the strength to finish on bad days. Those days were many, and they were growing in number. Money was tight on her father's Nassau County police detective's salary, without much left over for frivolous expenditures. Besides, with her mother's survival foremost on her mind, any other problems paled by comparison.

Old Lou brought the bus to another screeching halt, and an assortment of kids made their way on board. Sarah called out to her best friend, "Nonie, I'm over here."

Naomi Gorman struggled up the now-crowded aisle, laden down with several loose-leaf notebooks, a handbag, a sweater, and a small box in which she kept pencils, pens, and all manner of trinkets. With her arms full, she made her way back to Sarah's seat and practically fell into it.

"Thank God I made it," she said, somewhat breathless. Nonie was a good friend and Sarah had known her since sixth grade. Two inches shorter than Sarah, Nonie sported a more rounded, curvier look. Short-cropped charcoal hair, wide-set brown eyes, and a milky white complexion gave her an attractive appearance without divulging her flighty traits. Somewhat of a scatterbrain, Nonie was always last to get the punch line of any joke. The constant need to wipe the excess lipstick from her teeth lent credence to the perpetual state of confusion inherent in her nature. "I'm just dreading this year, Sarah. I'm loaded up with too many classes that I know I can't pass. I don't know why you have to take all of these classes anyway," she lamented.

Sarah helped hold Nonie's sweater until she got situated. "You'll do okay, Nonie. Just don't worry about it so much."

Nonie shook her head in despair. "A Regents diploma is only for those kids who are heading to college after high school, so what's the point anyway?"

Sarah tilted her face and gave Nonie a stern look. "You have to stop thinking that way because you never know when you might want to go to college, no matter what things look like right now."

Nonie shrugged and remained resigned. "What's the use, Sarah? My dad has it all planned out that I'm going to work in the family restaurant, marry a nice Jewish boy, and carry on the family tradition. Besides, you know I struggle to get a C in every class."

Sarah hated to see Nonie so disheartened. "It won't be so bad, Nonie, you'll see. At least we'll struggle through together!"

Nonie broke a small smile as the bus lurched forward. Mark Stevens had fallen asleep, and the sudden forward motion of the bus brought him to the floor between seats. The thud and look of surprise on his face got the attention of most of the students on board. Nonie and Sarah turned away with hands over their mouths and laughed quietly, hoping Mark wouldn't notice. Several other kids laughed out loud, and Mark was quick to shout back, "What are ya laughin' at?" An artificial serenity fell over the bus for the next few minutes as Sarah and Nonie kept their smiles.

Normally only a ten- to fifteen-minute drive, the route to school took about thirty to thirty-five minutes on the bus, depending on the traffic and students who might keep Lou waiting at each stop. The time gave Sarah a chance to enjoy the view from her window as the bus turned onto Highway 25A, leaving behind the neatly groomed neighborhood of split-level homes with their quarter-acre lots. Turning north again toward Long Island Sound, the gentle rolling hills gave way to a less-populated landscape. The North Shore communities had grown considerably as the sprawl of New York City continued to head east after WWII. The pristine, rolling hills in northern Nassau County became a lure for the growing population. The area once reserved for the rich with their yachts and secluded estates, the middle class was finally on the ascendancy and wanted its share of the good life.

Quaint island towns and villages like Cold Spring Harbor, Huntington, Muttontown, and Oyster Bay all dotted the picturesque landscape. Old growth trees formed canopies over narrow and winding roadways, where an occasional one-room police station could still be found around the next curve. Those small outposts stood as sentinels to an earlier time when life had a more genteel sway. Now, more newly developed neighborhoods were shooting up amidst the once tranquil and privileged communities, as the baby boom continued.

The picturesque serenity of the northern end of the county always put Sarah at ease and allowed her moments of happiness in which she laid all thoughts aside, drinking in the pastoral, old-world landscape. Leaning against the glass pane, Sarah contemplated the beauty of the white fences connected to ivy-covered stone walls, and the pretty, cobblestone driveways lined with hydrangeas and hostas. Most entrances were covered with canopies of old growth trees and shrubs that delighted the senses, especially in spring when the rhododendrons were in bloom and the honeysuckle graced the air with its sweet fragrance. The homes were often hidden by the lush growth and the sheer size of the estates, allowing them a good buffer from the road. She couldn't help wondering what it must be like to live in such grand and beautiful places. The names were bantered about, like the DuPonts, the Vanderbilts, and the Posts. Although those people remained unknown to her, their haunts and playgrounds were real, visible every morning from the seat of her bus. Sarah didn't desire their money or fame, but their stories—and especially the mystery their secluded estates conjured up—were fertile ground for her imagination. She would never tire of those rides to school.

Another jolt of the bus signaled their arrival at North Shoreline High as the wheels rolled over the speed bumps in the circular drive of the newly constructed school. "Oh! We're here already, and we haven't compared our schedules yet," Nonie exclaimed as she tried to gather all her belongings.

The brand-new school was considered avant-garde for its time and replaced a decaying school that had outlived its prime and could no longer support the growing population. A slight tingling filled Sarah as she surveyed the breadth of the sprawling new campus from her window and wondered how in the world they would ever have enough time between classes to make it to the next one. Nonie struggled with her purse, trying to locate her schedule. Sarah excitedly side stepped Nonie, and then tugged on her arm. "Come on, Nonie. I can't wait to see inside."

Twenty or more busses jockeyed for position around the lengthy half-moon blacktop drive. Each pulled up curbside, starting from the farthest point at the auditorium and going back around to the main entrance foyer and administrative offices. The huge arc of the entrance driveway was impressive, as was the modern post-and-beam construction of the school's connected buildings, which were joined by floor-to-ceiling glass hallways. These hallways connected various project areas, referred to as *PAs*, that supported eight individual classrooms. They also joined two gymnasiums, language labs, workshops, as well as a state-of-the-art auditorium with theatre-like, sloped seating. Including the new track and stadium, the sprawling campus must have occupied at least twenty acres. The sense of excitement for all attending the new high school was akin to being pioneers, the first to inhabit this new, architecturally modern space.

The need for more space to accommodate the growing population also brought the need for additional teachers, and more new faculty were listed this year than ever before. As the busses emptied their cargo, the scene at the entrance and lobby looked like a chaotic sea of humanity going in all directions. This was definitely not the orderly plan envisioned by school administrators. Tables with signs had been set up to help guide the students to the correct homerooms and provide extra maps of the school floor plan. Although all the students had been mailed floor maps and color-coded tape was affixed to the walkways in green, blue, red, and gold—indicating freshman, sophomore, junior, and senior homerooms respectively—the massive layout and hallways proved to be too daunting for many. Every counselor and administrator was on hand, but they were behaving more like ill-equipped traffic cops, unfamiliar with the many intersections of the massive new structure. The only word to describe the first day at North Shoreline High was "bedlam."

Two freshmen stepped off bus number seven, looking like kindergarteners abandoned by their mothers. Behind them, several upper-classmen who were not so intimidated and were ready to wear their newfound ranking with pride, couldn't resist the opportunity to mock them. "What's the matter with you two—need your mommies? Or do you need your glasses cleaned?" The boys laughed as they made their way around the new freshmen.

Mark Stevens exited the bus close behind. He pushed one of the younger students forward, knocking his eyeglasses askew. "You're blocking the bus," he shouted. "Get out of the way!"

Sarah glared at him. "Hey, Mark! Who appointed you God this morning?" She patted the younger student on the back as he readjusted his glasses. In a calmer tone, Sarah continued, "Everything will be all right. You'll know where to go when we get inside. Come with me."

Nonie followed, still fumbling with her purse. "Sarah, who do you have first period?" she yelled out.

By this time, Sarah had already made her way through the double wooden doors. Nonie was slow to catch up. Sarah pointed the freshmen to the appropriate table and turned to find Nonie, slightly breathless, at her side.

"Hey, Sarah, let me look at your schedule and see if we share any classes together."

Sarah pulled her schedule from her notebook as they both tried to avoid the traffic milling around them.

On the other side of the massive lobby, a small band of male students was gathered together in a huddle, each wearing a leather jacket in the blue and white school colors. Plainly visible were letters sewn on the front, and the name of the school scrolled over their shoulders in an arch on their backs. With his neatly trimmed sandy blond hair and infectious smile full of pearly white teeth, Kenny Birk was easy to notice. He stood taller than the rest, allowing his letters in basketball and football to draw the attention intended. Kenny was one of those all-around good students who excelled in most of his classes, as well as athletics. The stars were shining brightly for Kenny, whose pedigree joined him to a well-established family in the community. His father was a full partner at the prestigious Lowenstein, Birk, and Hammond law firm. As an honor student and athlete, he was the envy of more than a few at North Shoreline High.

Using his height to his advantage, Kenny turned to survey the crowd and spotted Sarah across the room. Bellowing over the throng, he called out to her, "Hey, Sarah, wait up." He elbowed his way across the lobby.

Sarah waved and turned back as Nonie gave a small squeal of delight.

"Can you believe it? We share second-period algebra class, and we have the same lunch hour. But I guess you'll be working for the dean again this year, so we won't get to share a study hall." Nonie pouted with obvious disappointment.

"That's okay, Nonie. I'm just so grateful I don't have to take algebra alone. I was barely able to get through geometry. You know how math and I don't get along!"

Nodding in agreement, Nonie continued, "Well, don't count on me, because you know both of us will be underwater in that class!"

Kenny Birk nudged his way closer to Sarah and gave a sigh of relief as he arrived at her side. "When do you have lunch, Sarah?"

"Let's see," she said as she looked over Nonie's shoulder. "Looks like fourth period. How about you, Kenny?"

"That's great, me too. Listen, I've got to go, but I'll grab a table and meet you then." Kenny gave her a friendly hug and couldn't hide his delight. With a broad smile, he charged off with several of his friends, all proudly wearing their sports jackets on their way to locate their senior homeroom classes on the gold line. Sarah watched him thinking how confident he always appeared to her. She turned back to her schedule and eyed it a bit closer. "Nonie, do you know Mr. Hall, the instructor for algebra?"

Looking puzzled, Nonie responded, "I've never heard of him before. I guess he's new."

Sarah wasn't given to complaints, but this was not the confidence builder she needed to overcome her aversion to math. "Oh great!" she said. "Getting familiar with a new teacher in a class I'll already have difficulty in isn't what I need—especially since I have to pass this class if I ever hope to get to college."

"You and me both," Nonie agreed. Several more friends joined the pair and compared classes as the first warning bell rang out.

Sarah tugged on Nonie's sleeve. "I guess there is nothing left to do but follow the red line to project area C and meet our fate."

The red line extended on and on as they approached the first project area, which was posted as blue. Farther down they came to an intersection, and a second red line came from that hallway as well. Fortunately, a red arrow pointed straight ahead, and they continued on, Nonie breathing a bit harder. "How much longer till we get there, Sarah?"

"It's got to be the next PA ahead, because I think all the others are behind us."

"I don't know which I like least, these never-ending halls or all those stairs we used to climb up and down all day at the old school." Later they learned four project areas were connected by those long glass passageways, and if viewed from above, they formed a perfect square around a central enclosed courtyard. Anyone walking to project area C could also have taken the other way around, but it turned out to be the farthest PA from the main entrance either way. Another buzzer rang out and a noticeably shaken principal made the compassionate announcement over the public-address system that, due to the confusion of many of the students, they would be extending the time to get to their homerooms for another three minutes.

"Thank heavens! Nothing like a late entrance to start the year out right," Sarah spouted.

Nonie slowed her pace. "You would think they would let the freshmen have this PA and give the upper classmen a break."

"What do you mean?"

"You know, like upper-class privileges or something."

Sarah laughed. "Privileges, ha! Since when have you or I ever been known to have special privileges?"

Nonie broke out in laughter as they finally arrived at the red project area C, designated for the junior-class homerooms.

Once inside the project area, the girls admired the clerestory windows beneath the beams of the vaulted ceiling that added light to the central space. Eight individual classrooms formed the perimeter of the central great room. Lockers ran the length of the walls inside the central space. "This is huge. It sure beats the old school—for looks anyway!" Sarah exclaimed.

"Yeah, but I hope our classes aren't spread out all day between the different project areas, or we'll be worn out trying to get there," Nonie countered.

"We'd better get to our classrooms. I'll meet you back here in ten minutes after homeroom is finished and we can walk together to our first period classes."

"See you in a few."

CHAPTER TWO

Sarah felt right at home in Mrs. Fredrick's first-period English literature class, located in the B project area. Her fascination in discovering the intricacies of life's journey, for good or bad, in those works of literature played out in a kaleidoscope of colors, feeding her fertile imagination. Combined with the reality of the often-tragic police cases her father would occasionally mention over dinner, reading cultivated a deep sense of sympathy and understanding for much that seemed unfair in life. Always attentive, she remained sensitive to the subtleties missed by most. "The devil is in the details," her dad would say, and Sarah looked for them most of the time. The little nuances of a cocked head or the slightest twitch of an eye spoke volumes to Sarah.

Math, however, was her Achilles' heel. Dealing with cold, hard, matter-of-fact numbers was difficult. They appeared somehow sterile, without life, unforgiving. It was almost painful for her as a younger child to memorize times tables and addition tables, all structured like good little soldiers with exact values, unyielding to change. Numbers appeared totally bereft of the feelings and emotions of Sarah's world. Hers was a world of varied words and colorful images that could change and morph on their own; they didn't need specific formulas structured rigidly with neat little lines and hideous equations not easy to decipher, let alone prove. As a result of the disconnect she harbored, she had difficulty adding any two numbers in her head, and memory always failed her as far as numbers were concerned. Unless the subject matter drew a picture, Sarah drew a blank. Nothing in life was guaranteed to be easy, but algebra class might remove the word "easy" from her lexicon altogether.

First period ended as Sarah gathered her books in her arms and made her way out of project area B, stopping to get her bearings once outside the PA. Several more friends joined her as they walked the corridors, each heading in the same direction.

"What class do you have next, Sarah?" one of the girls asked while chewing on a piece of bubble gum.

"I've got an algebra class at C-4. What about you?"

"I've got speech with a new teacher named Baxter in the same PA."

"That makes two of us with one of the new teachers this semester," Sarah added. They continued down the long passageway, waving to several old classmates.

"Don't you think Jackie Kennedy is gorgeous?" A third girl in the group practically swooned as she spoke. "I wish I had her eyes. One day I'm going to have a dress like the one she wore to that recent state dinner."

"At the moment, I'm more concerned with how to get through my next class with a passing grade!" Sarah said.

Standing outside C-4, Nonie was looking frazzled when Sarah arrived. "The teacher isn't here yet," Nonie announced. "Let's get a desk to the rear of the class. Maybe that way we won't be called on or noticed much."

Nodding in agreement, Sarah followed Nonie to the last two rows of desks, and they sat across from one another.

The desks continued to fill when Mark Stevens sauntered in, taking the remaining seat midway up the third row. Leaning back in the chair, he straightened his lanky legs, extending them well beneath the desk in front of his. Arms folded tightly over his reclined chest, Mark had staked his claim.

Nonie leaned to her side and whispered to Sarah, "Wonder why Mark always seems to have a chip on his shoulder."

"I don't know. Maybe he has a reason," Sarah whispered back below the heightened level of the classroom chatter. Little less than a minute remained before the class was to start. The students were taking full advantage of their unsupervised time, and the conversation levels were continuing to rise.

Without warning, the door to the class at the rear of the room slammed shut with a loud thud. All eyes turned to the door as conversation came to an immediate halt. Sarah caught her first glimpse of Mr. Hall. She estimated him to be over six feet tall, well-proportioned height to weight, with close-cropped chestnut hair. His appearance was not in keeping with Sarah's expectation for her new instructor. She had anticipated a middle-aged, slightly graying teacher, someone more in line with the math and science teachers she was already acquainted with. Mr. Hall's well-defined thick brows highlighted deep-set eyes parted by a strong, straight nose. His broad shoulders narrowed to a trim waist. Sarah thought he struck a very attractive, masculine appearance.

She watched as he carried a stack of books to the front of the class and dropped them to the desk unceremoniously with another loud thud. He had everyone's attention. Sarah sat up straighter in her chair. Eyes riveted front, Sarah noticed the slightly wrinkled brown trousers, checkered sport jacket, and off-white shirt with a thin tie that was not particularly well-suited to the sport coat. Although his chestnut hair was cropped close at the sides, it thickened at the crown, forming a slight point in the center of the brow. A wayward patch of shiny brown hair fell to his forehead as he maneuvered the books on his desk. Using his right hand, he ran all five fingers up through the unruly lock, forcing it back into place. She suspected he was right-handed, but the observation brought her little solace, considering it would be the only thing they would ever have in common. The bell announcing the start of second period rang out, and algebra class was officially underway.

"Good morning, ladies and gentlemen. My name is Travis Hall and I will be your instructor this year in algebra. He reached for the chalk with his right hand and printed his sir name boldly in the center of the blackboard. Turning back to face the class he continued, "That will be 'Mr. Hall' to all of you." He moved to the left side of his desk as he surveyed the array of students in front of him. "If there is anyone here who feels they have been assigned to the wrong class, please raise your hand." Sarah almost choked, thinking that was an understatement for her. His voice had a deep, penetrating resonance that felt commanding. An extended silence dominated the room.

"Good," he continued, "then we are all where we need to be, and since you know who I am, I would like to get to know all of you." He moved to the other side of the desk, exposing a faint, white line beneath the neatly cropped hair on his right temple. The line was not prominent, but was still visible beneath the darker shading of his hair—a scar, she imagined. He continued, "In order to do that, I'd like to begin with a simple seating plan in alphabetical order; so, would all of you please stand at the rear of the class until your name is called, and we will start filling in row one." Nonie and Sarah looked at each other with disappointment, realizing their plan to stay under the radar and out of sight had come to an end. This would mean that Nonie would be in one of the first few rows since her last name started with a "G," and Sarah would be relegated to the last row, her surname starting with a "T."

Sarah and Nonie reluctantly left their back-row seats and stood behind several other students in the rear of the room, watching Mr. Hall's every move at the front of the class. He reached into an interior pocket of his open sport jacket and pulled out a roster of names. Starting with the name "Abbot," he called out the student's names alphabetically and they began filling in the first row.

After the first row and a half filled with students, Nonie's name was called. She reluctantly left Sarah's side, making her way to the second row, third seat. Mr. Hall continued calling out the list of names alphabetically, working now on the sixth and final row. The first two desks were seated when the instructor called out, "Mark Stevens next, followed by Sarah Thompson, and Amy Tyler."

Upon his cue, Mark shrugged and nonchalantly shuffled his way to his assigned desk with his usual flair of indifference. Slamming his books on the surface of the desk, Mark Stevens made his own statement. It had not gone unnoticed by Mr. Hall, who made a visual note of each student as he/she was called.

"Mr. Stevens, you seem to be unhappy with your seat assignment. Perhaps we can arrange for something different later if you like." There was no disguising the fact that the teacher's comment was not meant to please Mark, but rather to let him know who was in charge.

Sarah made her way to the desk behind Mark's and quickly took her seat. She brought her eyes back to the instructor standing at the front of the class just as he met her glance. Her immediate reaction was to look away and hope she would fade from his memory. She wanted to be invisible.

That Mr. Hall was a no-nonsense, take-charge instructor was becoming evident. She wasn't sure how old he was, but she estimated he was less than thirty. A masculine line to his square jaw and his thick brows accentuated his deep-set eyes. Not close enough to tell, Sarah detected what might be some freckling, along with a few subtle lines at the corners of his eyes. With his broad shoulders and straight-backed posture, he cut a striking and powerful figure of a man. Sarah pictured him with leadership capabilities, but not so much as a schoolteacher who would spend his life at an eight to four o'clock job, enjoying his summers off in the suburbs. His demeanor spoke of a man who knew what he wanted and would aggressively pursue it. One thing was certain; Mr. Hall had commanded respect in less than five minutes.

Textbooks for the course were the next order of business. Rather than requesting help to pass them out, he carried five books at a time and walked up each row, handing them out individually. He made a point of looking at every student face to face. Sarah thought this was a clear tactic not only to acquaint himself with each student but also to reinforce his authority over the class by making direct eye contact. Sarah recalled her father saying that criminals frequently behaved differently when approached eye to eye, and that some were not willing to commit their crimes on those whom they knew personally—or who could identify them to authorities.

Glancing across the room, Sarah saw Nonie had received her textbook, which lay open on her desk. She wore a vacant look as she stared at her textbook, indicating her feelings of being overwhelmed by the subject. A few muffled groans could be heard as Mr. Hall strode confidently up each row with another armful of textbooks. Returning to the sixth and last row, he handed out the three remaining books, the last one with a bit more emphasis to Mark Stevens. After a momentary pause, the instructor then turned to face Sarah, who was seated behind Mark in that row. As Mr. Hall moved alongside her desk, Sarah lifted her head, meeting the shadow he cast over her. Her heart was racing, and in that moment, they made full eye contact, an involuntary act she immediately regretted. His height and broad shoulders were imposing, especially since she was seated and had to tilt her head up to meet his glance.

"And your name, again, is?" he questioned. Their eyes remained fixed for what seemed an eternity as Sarah fell speechless, caught in time. His green eyes were riveting and she was lost in them. Sarah didn't know how long she remained silent, but he brought the pause to an end without so much as a blink, maintaining his laser focus. "You do *have* a name, don't you?" he said in a commanding tone.

The sound of his voice reverberated in her head, and a wave of embarrassment flooded over her as she struggled to regain her sensibilities. Shaken, Sarah dropped her head and finally found her voice. "Yes, sir, I do. It's Sarah Thompson."

Keeping his attention directed exclusively on Sarah, he rested a knuckle on her desk as he continued, "Well then, Miss Sarah Thompson, if you and this nice young lady seated behind you would be so kind as to return here to C-4 after the final bell today, I'll find two more textbooks." Glancing first at Amy and then returning his attention to Sarah, he asked both girls, "Can you both do that?" Sarah felt the weight of his attention unbearable. Amy and Sarah dutifully nodded in agreement.

"Good," he said. "For today, please pull your desks together and you can share my textbook."

This was definitely not what she had planned. Instead of remaining incognito, she would have to face him twice in one day. He returned to his desk and then brought his copy of the textbook back to Sarah and Amy. With every step closer on his return, Sarah's heart pounded harder.

"Please turn to page five," he said, walking back to the blackboard at the front of the class. Picking up the chalk with his right hand, he drew a straight line on the chalkboard. "Can anyone tell me the definition of an infinite line?"

Those were the last words Sarah could remember with clarity until the bell rang out and he announced pages six through ten for homework. Somehow she managed to scribble the page numbers down in her notebook; although, whatever was discussed between an infinite line and pages six through ten remained a complete mystery.

Sarah asked Amy if she wouldn't mind returning his textbook since Amy was already standing and ready to move to the next class. Amy smiled cordially and then took the book from Sarah's hand. "See ya later, Sarah," she said as she made her way to the front of the room.

Sarah gathered her books, planning to make a hasty exit even though her desk was furthest from the door. She stayed to the rear of the class, hugging the back wall, and then moved down the side wall, intending to go unnoticed. The majority of the class had already made a beeline to the door, including Nonie who, uncharacteristically, had decided to wait outside for Sarah rather than stay in the classroom a minute longer.

Sarah was last to reach the threshold when Mr. Hall called out her name from the front of the room. "Sarah, you won't forget to pick up your book, will you?"

Sarah's heart dropped, believing Mr. Hall assumed she was so inept that she wouldn't remember. She swallowed hard and then turned to face him, doing her best to sound compliant. "No, Mr. Hall. I . . . I won't forget."

Turning again to leave, she heard him say as she exited the doorway, "See you this afternoon, Miss Thompson."

CHAPTER THREE

Nonie stood guard several feet from the math-class door, waiting for Sarah to appear. "What was that all about?"

"Nothing, he just wanted to make sure I wouldn't forget to pick up the textbook later." Sarah kept walking as Nonie tried to keep step.

"I don't mean that, but what happened back there at your desk when he was handing out the books?"

"I don't know. What do you mean?"

"Why didn't you answer him when he asked what your name was?"

Sarah drew in a deep breath. "I did answer him."

"Well, it sure took you long enough."

Sarah felt slightly sick to her stomach. How foolish she must have appeared to everyone, especially Mr. Hall. "I don't know, Nonie. Maybe if I didn't tell him who I was, he would forget I was even in the class."

"How could you have thought that was going to work?"

"That's the thing, Nonie, I wasn't thinking at all except how to get out of there."

"Now that I can understand!"

"Can we just drop the whole subject, please?" Sarah had already made a name for herself in a class where she had hoped to go unnoticed.

"That's okay with me."

Sarah stopped at the next project area to look at the floor map. "This must be where the dean's office is located. I guess I'll see you next hour at lunch."

Nonie gave a sigh. She had a longer hike to go to the green project area. "Hope the next class goes faster than the last one," Nonie exclaimed as they parted ways.

The dean's office was in the center rear of the project area, away from the high traffic at the front. When Sarah arrived, Miss Watson was already busy at her desk, sorting piles of papers.

"Hello, Sarah. I'm certainly glad to see you," she said, standing as Sarah entered. "It isn't the largest office, but at least we do have a little more space than the old one. Come on in and let me help you get acquainted with the layout." The familiar routine was comforting to Sarah, though the dean's stiff professionalism seemed ill-placed considering Sarah had worked for her going on three years now.

"It's a wonderful office, Miss Watson, and the window lets in good light," Sarah offered.

The dean was an attractive woman in her late thirties with fair hair, gray eyes, and an excellent figure. The straight skirt and wide belt she wore served to exemplify her slender waist. Sarah wondered why she remained single.

"There will be more to do once we get settled, Sarah, but I'd like you to take these files of my students this year and put them in alphabetical order, and then return them to the file cabinet, top drawer. Oh yes, and would you please transcribe these phone numbers and extensions to my Rolodex from this master sheet for me as well? I've made up a sheet with our new dress code this year, and I'd like you to run off at least a hundred copies so I can distribute them to all our teachers at the next teachers' meeting. We'll be including the information in the next student bulletin as well." Never seeming to have an extra minute to spare, the dean quickly moved toward the door. "Thank you for your help, Sarah. I'm sorry to dash off so quickly, but I'm a little behind schedule and need to make it to my meeting on time."

Sarah smiled politely and listened as the dean's heels tracked through the project area, making clicking noises in rapid succession on the polished cement flooring. The dean's distinctive gate was habitual, and Sarah could easily recognized Miss Watson's departure or arrival with her eyes closed.

Returning to the desk, Sarah glanced over the dress code. Pants of any kind were not permissible for the girls' school attire. All dresses and skirts must extend to below the knee, and no halters or thin-strapped blouses could be worn during regular school hours. With a few minor exceptions, the dress code for the girls appeared to be the same as last year's, although the penalties were going to be strictly enforced.

Sarah busied herself with the tasks at hand, grateful for the somewhat mindless nature of the office work. Once she finished her assigned tasks, she began reading for her English literature class.

Concentration was difficult as she kept replaying the events in algebra class over and over again. It was unlike her to feel so ill at ease. Something about Mr. Hall was far different from anyone she had ever met before. She couldn't quite find the right word to describe the way he made her feel, though she finally settled on one: "intimidated." Intimidation alone did not account for how she lost control of herself, but it was the best word she could find for the moment.

Sarah did not want to meet his eyes again or suffer another embarrassing loss of speech and thought. No one had laughed at her the first time, but she couldn't risk a second display of such stupidity. Still, not being able to identify the reason why she found him so overwhelming was troubling. The slight cadence in his voice was perceptually different, as well as the way he pronounced certain words—like the word "sit," which sounded more like "set" when he spoke. These slight nuances were hardly noticeable, but Sarah had become attuned to them instantly. He was definitely not from New York. She was familiar with regional differences, since her father was from New England and they had family from the South. The "ah" sound from New England for the letter "A" was well known to her, but she'd heard none of that in Mr. Hall's speech. No, his was a lingo unknown to her, and the accent helped to surround him in a shroud of mystery.

How would she ever prove she was normally quite capable and not given to such a display of empty-headedness? The thought that she had set the stage, allowing the new algebra teacher to have a skewed opinion of her, sickened her. Mercifully, the bell rang, cutting the negative chatter in her head. She could head to lunch and bury herself in conversation with her friends.

The new cafeteria was decades apart from the old school's, and the double serving lines ushered the faculty and students through at a much faster pace. The floor-to-ceiling windows overlooked the central courtyard and offered a spectacular view; however, on nice days, it would be a great distraction for many who would otherwise prefer to be outside.

The scene at the cafeteria was reminiscent of the lobby earlier that morning. Students were scrambling in every direction, jockeying for tables or searching for friends, and Sarah was caught in the middle, doing her best to locate Nonie. A redheaded girlfriend frantically waving a multicolored scarf next to the courtyard windows drew her attention. Nonie stood beside Fran, and quickly raised her arm in unison. "Over here, Sarah."

Sarah did her best to make her way to the windows. Several friends from marching band, including two with whom she shared one of the five slots as majorettes, stopped her along the way to compare their schedules. By the time she worked her way to Nonie, several more girls had joined the group, all giddy with excitement to share their experiences in the new school and discuss who was dating whom.

Francis Johnson always had the latest gossip and could be relied on to share it with anyone who had an ear to listen. Counting Fran's incessant need to talk as a blessing, Sarah wasn't obliged to contribute. Her silence ensured her conversation wouldn't be repeated at the end of the day by another. The *Blue-N-White* campus newspaper was always a day late compared to Fran. The fact that Fran was able to obtain any information at all was a marvel to Sarah, since she never seemed to take the time to listen. With her bright red hair and her heavily freckled face, Fran reminded Sarah of a light bulb, always on and making heat.

"Hey, Sarah, have you heard the latest about Miss Bower?" Francis asked, looking far too eager to tell.

"Why no, I haven't heard a thing," Sarah replied, hoping not to sound too disinterested.

"Well, it seems she got engaged over summer vacation, and the word is she won't be finishing out the whole year here. Do you have her for English lit?" Fran asked, obviously hoping to evoke a shocked response.

"No, I'm afraid I don't have her this semester," Sarah responded in a matter-of-fact tone.

Fran threw a frivolous hand in the air while half-closing her eyes. "Thank heavens," she said. "I feel so sorry for anyone who will have to change teachers mid-course. Don't you?"

Sarah and Nonie both nodded politely.

Kenny Birk spied Sarah across the cafeteria as she made her way to the other girls. Everything about her, especially the way she moved, accentuated a regal carriage Kenny found irresistible. Sarah's classic features and refined cheekbones heightened her elegance. When she wore her hair down, it had a shimmering iridescence with streaks of platinum against a darker ash blonde. Combined with the aqua blue luminosity of her eyes, Sarah's Dresden-like face conveyed a look of purity. Most of the time, the simplicity in her attire appeared pristine, with her hair neatly pulled back and bound, expressing a sense of virtue. No glitz ever distracted from the loveliness in her. She was always poised and graceful, above reproach. A ladylike quality about Sarah often disguised her youth. Perhaps he saw a maturity the other girls lacked, but whatever her special quality was, Kenny had been bitten badly by the bug and wanted to date her. Sarah Thompson was drop-dead beautiful.

She was the one everyone wished they could date but didn't dare ask, feeling much too intimidated to try. It wasn't because she was unapproachable, but because she had the kind of reputation that was hard for many to live up to. First base was off the playing field when it came to Sarah. Although friendly with everyone, she was intimate with none. Her involvement in her many school activities was always in a group setting. Kenny didn't know anyone she had dated, which made her all the more intriguing. Besides, he loved a challenge, especially since she was the only girl at North Shoreline High who didn't show him any interest. Plenty of other guys felt the same way, but Kenny was never deterred from the hope that she would return the feeling. Some boys lacked the courage to ask, and the few who did always came up empty-handed. His own persistence was dogged, and he swore he would never give up trying; a trait in him that allowed for success both scholastically and on the athletic field.

The minute he saw her enter the cafeteria, he was like a racehorse out of the chute to her side. He came up behind her and took her by the arm. "Come on, Sarah, we've got a table already saved over here," he said, hoping to spend as much time with her as possible.

"See you later, Fran. Come on, Nonie," Sarah called out as Kenny tugged a bit, guiding Sarah away from the group. Nonie followed Sarah and Kenny, leaving Fran to spread the news to the growing gaggle of girls.

Kenny led the conversation as they made their way to his table where several other members of the football team were already seated and eating. "I was afraid you might have read the wrong period for lunch off your schedule this morning," he said while still holding on to her arm.

"It's been a full morning; and with so many people not knowing where to go, it just took a little longer to get here. How did your classes go?" Sarah quickly deflected the conversation back to him, avoiding any discussion about her own classes.

"All right," he answered, "if you can call calculus-trig and problems in American democracy fun!" Ken led Sarah to his side of the already half-full table, making sure she took the seat next to him.

Nonie followed and sat across the table from Sarah, relieving herself of the burden she carried. "Come on, let's get in line," Nonie suggested, clearly eager to try out the food service in the new school.

"I'm not so sure I feel like eating," Sarah said, still slightly queasy as she remembered her humiliation during math class.

"Come on, Sarah, you have to see if the food is any better now that we're in the new building."

Kenny stood up and brought his opinion to bear, never missing a meal if he could help it. "Let's go, before they close off the lines." He pulled out her chair, and Sarah went along, deciding on an apple once in line.

Although the food looked enticing, the scents from the daily fare perpetuated the slight upset in her stomach. Nonie paid at the register first and then did her best to balance the meal as she waited for Sarah, who was close behind, rummaging through her purse for the exact change. Kenny was quick to reach across her and pay for the apple, along with his own laden tray.

"That was sweet of you, Kenny. But you really didn't have to do that. I have the change right here," Sarah chided as they made their way back to the table together with Nonie. Once there, she put down the apple and gathered the right change, returning it to Kenny.

He gave her a disappointed look once they were seated. "I didn't buy it to be sweet, Sarah."

"Of course not," Sarah countered. "You would have done the same for any good friend."

Kenny bit his tongue, and then pursed his lips into a tight seal, impulsively pushing some books to the center of the table making more room for his tray.

Sitting on the other side of Kenny, Trent Rogers was busy devouring what looked like two complete plates of spaghetti and meatballs, salad, and four cartons of milk. He was shoveling food in faster than the speed of light, as if he hadn't eaten in days. With his stocky girth, thick neck, and square jaw line, he looked like an iron bulldozer who could easily run over anything or anyone in his path. "Hey, Ken," he mouthed while chewing, "Coach wants us out on the field immediately after classes today. Can you give me a ride home since my tin-can clunker of a car is in the shop again?"

Kenny was surprised he hadn't gotten the message about practice. Football was always the first order of business at the beginning of each new school year, and since Kenny and Trent had already played on the varsity team last year, a slot on the team was pretty much assured. Kenny turned toward Trent with eyebrows furrowed close together. "You bet! I don't want to start out on the wrong foot with Coach Morris by missing practice. How did you get the word about practice starting today?"

Trent finished slugging down one of the cartons of milk, wiping his lips with the back of his hand. "It's posted on both the gymnasium bulletin board and also at the main-lobby bulletin board. It came as a surprise to me too, but coach did tell us during summer practice and tryouts that he wanted to beef up the number of practice sessions as soon as school starts to get a leg up on the competition this season."

Kenny had two great loves; one was Sarah, and the other sports. The second put a kink in his plan to secure a time to see Sarah off-campus. Once he got the coach's schedule, he would work out the plan for Sarah later. For now, he would have to be content to share her company in a crowd. "We better spread the word, or Coach might make us do laps for every man who doesn't show."

"That's what I figured." Trent forked the last remaining meatball and then seemed to swallow it whole.

The familiar routine of the school year was reassuring to Sarah as she listened to all the chatter around her. She turned to Nonie and revealed her thoughts, hoping to release the tension she held inside. "I really made a fool of myself in algebra class this morning. Mr. Hall probably thinks I'm a nitwit. I don't know how I'm ever going to live that momentary silence down."

"You know what I think?" Nonie asked. "I think he deliberately tried to scare you as an example to the rest of us. He's awfully full of himself, if you ask me! It looked like he was half-smiling and enjoying himself as he hovered over you."

"Well, if that was his intention, it worked."

"Forget about him, Sarah. I wouldn't give him that satisfaction."

Nonie was probably right, but something about Mr. Hall, and the way he looked at her, she just couldn't shake. She made the effort to put algebra behind her.

"You know, Sarah," Nonie spoke up while finishing her plate, "it's really not so bad."

Sarah immediately shot back, "Oh yes, it is—it's worse."

With a blank expression, Nonie asked, "How would you know? You haven't even tried the food out for yourself yet."

Sarah laughed out loud; Nonie was not on the same page. Being with friends was good. Lunch always sped by quicker than any other period, and this day was no different. The bell rang while Nonie carried her tray back to the wash area, still pressing Sarah. "What's so funny?"

Kenny brought up the rear and reminded Sarah he would look for her again tomorrow. He leaned into her and whispered, "Like your style, Sarah."

Returning his glance with a cautious smile, Sarah continued on, waving goodbye as everyone headed in different directions.

CHAPTER FOUR

The last half of the school day was relatively easy for Sarah. She pushed through chemistry followed by choir and then history. Music was a joy and choir was the class she loved the most. They would be learning a variety of songs in preparation for the winter Christmas concert, and Sarah's time there flew by much too quickly.

The last class of the day arrived long after the sun had already moved past its apex, allowing the western wall of the American history class to retain its heat as the students filled in the empty desks. Sarah knew the instructor well, having had him a previous year. He knew most of the students by name and had a laid-back style that put the students at ease. Mr. Donnelly was a middle-aged man, somewhat portly, with a receding hairline that seemed to extend further back with each passing year. He rarely got excited, and after so many years of teaching the same topic, his enthusiasm for the subject matter had long ago dissipated to a rather lifeless reading style during his lectures.

His style really didn't matter to Sarah. She found the homework and reading assignments interesting enough and loved to conjure up images of other times and places. This would be an easy class for her. After the students received their textbooks and listened to Mr. Donnelly ramble on, classes finished for the day at the sound of the last bell.

Kenny caught up with Sarah in the hall and walked with her back to her locker in the C project area. "Sarah, I'll be tied up after school most of the week, but I wondered if you'll be at church on Sunday."

"We should be there, depending on how Mom is that morning."

"How is she doing?"

She sighed and then offered what she hoped would be a brighter slant than she was actually feeling. "The doctors say she's holding her own."

"That's wonderful. I'm really glad to hear that."

Once inside the C project area, Sarah went straight to her locker. Kenny looked on, chatting, as he held his books against his hip in one hand and leaned against the lockers to the left of Sarah's. Students were trafficking all around them as Amy Tyler passed by, heading to C-4.

"Hey, Sarah," she said as she passed them. "Maybe Mr. Hall ran out of books," she wishfully suggested with a broad smile.

Sarah laughed, nodding and indicating she would be right there.

Kenny leaned closer to Sarah. "If you ever need anything, Sarah, or if I can help in any way, please promise me you'll call."

Sarah turned to face Kenny, listening to his kind gesture of concern. As she was about to respond to his thoughtfulness, Mr. Hall came walking by carrying several textbooks along with his briefcase. She met his glance as he nodded and continued on to the classroom. A rush of unfamiliar nervousness filled her, knowing she had to face him again in the next few minutes. She quickly turned back to acknowledge Kenny's concern.

"You know how much that means to me, Kenny, and I'll certainly keep that close to my heart. I've got to go pick up a textbook, but I'll see you tomorrow at lunch." She smiled and waved goodbye as she left him standing with a look of longing he could not easily hide. A fleeting thought crossed her mind hoping his look didn't have a deeper, more personnel meaning attached. Kenny always felt the need for playful physical contact. But then, that was just his outgoing nature. Besides, he was notorious for playing the field while they personally had never dated and always remained good friends. The strange thought left her as quickly as it had arrived.

Sarah met Amy as she exited C-4, carrying her new textbook for algebra and hurrying to get to her locker before the busses left.

"It looks like he found them," she offered with a look of disappointment on her face. "See you tomorrow," she said without stopping.

Sarah drew a deep breath and then headed into the class.

"Hello again, Sarah," Mr. Hall greeted her as she entered the room.

She stood halfway between the door and his desk, and for some reason couldn't bring herself any closer.

"I have an extra textbook for you as promised," he said as he looked up from the papers he held above his open briefcase.

Her hesitancy was slight, but he detected it nonetheless. She approached the desk, not meeting his eyes with her own. She stood five feet from him.

Travis read her body language and was taken by her reserved and cautious nature. He placed his papers back in his briefcase, picked up a textbook, and turned to hand it to her. "You can take this one, Sarah," he said as he extended the book toward her. Sarah was still standing a distance from him and he waited for her to come forward and take it from his hand. Again, she hesitated for a second before stepping forward and reaching out. He was surprised that she seemed to want to keep her distance. She certainly had drawn his attention earlier that day. He had been struck by her attractiveness and the way she had drawn him in with the extended lock of their eyes when they first met. He was hoping to meet those beautiful aqua blue eyes again, but wondered why she was suddenly uncomfortable making eye contact. "Your assignment includes pages six through ten," he reminded her as he let go of the book.

Sarah raised her head and politely replied, "I know, Mr. Hall. I have it written down, but thank you for reminding me."

He followed her with his eyes as she turned to leave, fully understanding the interest she generated from the athlete he had noted at her side a moment earlier.

Something about Miss Sarah Thompson was quite captivating. Her reserved reaction to him seemed somehow totally unexpected and misplaced for a girl who could so easily command the attention of the opposite sex. She appeared oblivious to her inherent beauty, and she certainly didn't flaunt or use it in any way for self gain. She held herself with a poise and gracefulness beyond her years, which also seemed at odds with her reaction to him. She struck Travis as curiously innocent, despite her sophisticated carriage, and totally unaware of what others perceived in her. He could easily recall several students' names at the end of the first day, but none with the same vividness that the name "Sarah Thompson" elicited in his mind. This promised to be an interesting year, and he was looking forward to it.

CHAPTER FIVE

The living room of the Thompson's well-kept, split-level home was unpretentious in its appointments with the exception of the mahogany baby grand piano. The keyboard jutted out from the far corner of the room adjacent to the arched entry of the undersized dining area. Neatly displayed silver framed family photos stood across the back of the piano. A comfortable, overstuffed couch beneath the bay window drew the eye to the expansive view of the home's corner lot at the intersection of Dogwood and Maple streets. A long console housing a TV, stereo, and record player stood guard at the front entry, offering a landing for mail or keys. An eclectic mix of furnishings, including a gold-framed mirror, a recliner, an antique wingback chair, and a hexagonal drum table, provided a balanced and relaxed atmosphere in the small but comfortable space.

The arched entry to the dining room revealed more modern-styled furnishings—almost Danish in form, though much darker in color. These included a buffet, a table, and six dining chairs, four around the square table and two placed in the corners for extra seating. Although the furnishings between both rooms bore different styles, the original pieces of oil and pastel artwork allowed the harshness of the conflicting styles to soften and meld as a whole. Positioned over the piano, a large seascape captured the sea foam green of the walls while magnificent magnolia flowers with their rich green leaves added an elegant adornment to the wall above the dining-room buffet.

Sarah climbed the five steps up to the front door, holding her books in one hand and the iron rail with the other. The first day back to North Shoreline High was now behind her, and she was eager to be home. Once inside, she placed her books and handbag down on the console and called for her younger sister Rachael, who would have arrived home from her elementary school long before Sarah. A squeal of delight brought five-year-old Rachael running down the five steps from the upper level, blonde pigtails bouncing all the way.

"Sarah, you're finally home!" she said as she ran into Sarah's arms. Sarah picked her up and twirled her around two times before releasing her back to the floor.

"Did you have a good time at school today, Rachael?"

"Sort of," Rachael replied while still thinking, "but I do like Miss Kelly, my new teacher. She is really pretty and very nice."

Sarah detected a slight note of disturbance in Rachael's voice. "I'm glad to hear you like your teacher, but did something happen you didn't like?"

Rachael brought her index finger to her lips. "Well, remember when we walked to school and you showed me which street to turn on?"

"Yes, I do. Did you forget which way to go?"

"No, I remembered which way to go—it was which way to come home that I forgot."

Sarah smiled broadly. "You made it home, I see, so I guess you did remember."

"Johnny O'Rourke laughed at me and told me which way to go."

Sarah sensed her younger sister's embarrassment and gently took her hand as they made their way up the stairs. "Johnny may have remembered which way to get home, Rachael, but I bet he can't do a cartwheel or a backbend."

Rachael laughed and held Sarah's hand tighter as they made their way into their parents' bedroom where their mother was leaning back on her pillows in a half-upright position, her legs stretched out in front of her.

Several children's books were spread out across the bed, and Lily Thompson sat straighter as Sarah entered the room. "Hi, Sarah. Rachael and I were having such a good time reading together today. Weren't we, Rachael?"

"Oh yes, Mommy. Shall we read some more?"

"Let's save this book for later, and we'll let Sarah tell us about her first day back to school."

Rachael hopped onto the bed and cuddled next to her mother as Lily placed one arm around her daughter. With the heavy gray streaks against her darker ash blonde hair, Lily Thompson could still draw attention. She had a sculpted face with high cheekbones and a long, straight nose. Her brows were perfectly arched but not overly prominent. The silver-gray streaks in her hair helped to soften the darker circles that had recently appeared on her otherwise beautiful face.

"Come sit beside us, Sarah, and tell us all about school," her mother suggested.

Sarah walked to her mother's side of the bed and leaned over to gently kiss her cheek. She straightened the pillows her mother used for support. "The new school is beautiful, Mom. The four project areas are enormous, and each has eight classrooms around it. The only bad part about the design is that it takes more than five minutes to get to your next class once the bell rings!"

Lily smiled as she reached for Sarah's hand. "Tell me, Sarah, do you think the school was worth all the tax dollars it took to build it?"

Sarah nodded. "I most certainly do think it was worth every penny!"

"Good. Now I can't wait to see it myself, perhaps for the winter concert."

Rachael sat up, wanting to be included. "Can I go too, Mommy?"

"Of course you can, dear, if you can be ever so good and sit in your chair through the whole concert. We'll see if we can pick our Sarah out of the choir."

Rachael smiled broadly, happy to be with the two people she adored the most.

Her mother was tiring. Lily reached for Sarah's hand and, with a grateful look in her tired eyes, continued, "Sarah, I've already peeled the potatoes and readied the vegetables for dinner, and the meat needs to be put in the oven in one hour. Would you be a dear and watch the time, and then get it all started so that everything will be done by the time your father arrives home?"

"Don't worry about a thing, Mom. Rachael and I have everything under control, don't we, Rachael?" Sarah picked Rachael up off the bed.

"I know how to set the table." Rachael beamed.

"Get some rest, Mom. We'll take care of everything. Come on, Rachael—let's go outside for a while and I'll teach you how to twirl my baton." Sarah closed the door behind them, bringing Rachael with her to change from her school clothing into shorts and a comfortable cotton-knit shirt.

The girls headed for the yard, taking advantage of the dwindling fall days outside, the extended daylight and weather still in their favor. Rachael delighted in showing off her cartwheels and backbends as Sarah extolled her talent and gave her approval of every move Rachael mastered. Sarah shared the baton and helped Rachael learn how to balance it in her hand and make it spin. The laughter and delight on Rachael's face helped to temper Sarah's concern and constant worry about her mother's health.

Rheumatic fever as a young girl had left Lily's heart damaged. She was able to overcome its debilitating effects in her younger years, but with each of her pregnancies, the damage to her heart had become more pronounced. They had wisely decided, at the doctor's direction, not to have any more children after Sarah, but life often carries risks and surprises; her third pregnancy came quite unexpectedly and, unfortunately, strained and damaged Lily's heart even more, leaving her in a permanently weakened state. Sarah bore the weight of her mother's condition, doing her best to pick up all the household duties Lily was no longer able to keep up with. Sarah never felt resentful; she was moved by her love for her mother, and she bore the burden willingly, wanting only her mother's survival.

The hour flew by quickly and the girls washed up to start the dinner. Rachael set the table and Sarah started in the kitchen. "Let's turn the TV on while dinner is cooking, and you can watch *The Andy Griffith Show,*" Sarah offered.

"Okay," Rachael answered happily.

Charles Thompson pulled up into the driveway, got out, opened the garage door, and then parked his 1958 Ford sedan carefully in the tuck-under garage. His wrinkled brown trousers matched the same color chocolate in the glen plaid sport jacket he threw over his shoulder as he exited the car. His tie already loosened and shirt unbuttoned, the workday had thankfully ended. With his military-styled, short-cropped, light sandy hair, Charley Thompson presented a tight and structured appearance, reflecting the authority necessary at his job. He hoped his five-feet eleven-inch height helped to mask the slight girth holding his mid-frame. Entering the house in the den below, he tramped up the five steps to the kitchen where Sarah was finishing cooking dinner.

"Hi, Dad," Sarah greeted as he reached the final step up to the kitchen.

He walked over and gave Sarah a kiss on her cheek, making sure not to lean in too close, his revolver still holstered in the shoulder strap beneath his left arm. "How's my sweet Sarah today?" he asked as he headed for the living-room coat closet to hang his jacket.

"As good as I can be after the first day back to school," Sarah responded with a note of resignation.

"What's for dinner?" he asked, as he hung his sport coat and removed the revolver and holster from his side. He laid his badge and gun on the console, checking the safety.

"We've got chuck roast, mashed potatoes, and green beans," Sarah answered as she began filling the serving bowls.

"It sure smells good in here. And I'm ready to eat," Charley exclaimed.

Rachael ran to her father's arms, and Charley picked her up, giving her a hug and kissing her before putting her back down. "How did my little pumpkin's first day of school turn out?"

Rachael began to tell him all about her new teacher. She rambled on without taking time to catch her breath.

"Slow down, Rachael, let's save some of the story till later. You can help Sarah put the dinner out, and I'll go get Mom."

"Okay, Daddy," Rachael agreed.

Charley picked up his gun and badge and trekked up to his room. Opening the door gently, he walked inside and placed his revolver and badge quietly down on the highboy before walking to Lily's side of the bed. Standing silently with a stoic expression, he took in Lily's pale complexion as she slept. In that moment, he was unable to prevent wounding himself with questions much too painful to ask. How much time did they have left together and how would he survive without her? She was the love of his life and without her he would be empty. Her loving spirit and artistic nature tempered his structured parameters and brought him to a better place. To lose her would be to lose the best part of himself. He gently ran his hand across her cheek, kissing her as he sat down on the bed beside her. Lily opened her eyes and, with a tender expression, smiled back at Charley, so happy to see him there beside her.

"How yah feeling, Lil?" Charley asked as he reached for her hand.

"Today was a good day, only my energy seems so fleeting."

"Not to worry, Lily, the girls have everything under control. Let's get you up and have some dinner."

Once around the dining-room table, Charley called for prayer; all four Thompsons held each other's hands and bowed their heads, and Charley gave the blessing, adding a special thanks for Lily's good day. Conversation at the dinner table was the Thompsons' daily family time. The girls got to share with their dad the news and concerns of each day. Charley treasured the dinner hour most since it always reminded him of why he joined the police force to begin with.

Charley was driven to make his community a better place for families to raise their children and teach them the values and virtues necessary in a world otherwise filled with hate, violence, and vice. Seeing the gentle smiles and sweet innocence of his daughters gave him the strength and determination to be a better cop. He had the reputation of being a "straight arrow" in his squad at police headquarters. No bribes or favors could ever cross his palm, and his peers knew it. Perhaps his determination was due, in part, to the difficult life he had growing up poor on the streets of Boston. Being exposed to depravity first-hand had given him a nose for all manner of corruption. His reputation was well known, and it hadn't come unearned.

In his military career, Charley had been highly decorated for heroism under fire, taking shrapnel to his right leg while pulling a comrade-in-arms to safety on a small island in the Solomon's during the siege at Guadalcanal. It had earned him the Silver Star and a Purple Heart. His heroism continued when he joined the police force. As a rookie cop, he managed to talk an armed robber out of his gun without the use of lethal force. In addition, during a particularly cold winter, he had rescued a boy from a pond after he had fallen through the ice and almost drowned. Charley had risked his life and then administered artificial respiration until help arrived. Along with his well-earned decorations and citations, his caring side persisted when he headed up the police boys' club, dedicated to keeping wayward teens out of trouble—a holdover from his early teen years on the mean streets of Boston.

With twenty-one years on the force, Charley spent the last fifteen as a detective in the homicide division. Everyone knew he played by an ethical set of hand rules, and he had the right stuff and street-wise experience to back up his higher standards. Because of that, he was up for promotion and might soon find himself the head of the homicide division. The increased pay would certainly help out, but commanding would mean longer days and nights away from the comfort of home and those he loved. He would have to discuss it with Lily; his greatest concern was for her health. Her condition would never improve and at any time might deteriorate. Taking the promotion would also mean that Sarah would bear the extra burden of his absence. It was a decision he would not make lightly.

After dinner, Sarah cleaned up the dishes as the rest of the family sat in the living room around the TV. The familiar sounds of laughter from *The Red Skelton Show* blared in the background as she finished cleaning the kitchen. When she was finished, she headed to her room, taking the next hour to work on her homework. Opening her new algebra textbook, she did her best to decipher the mass of jumbled-looking numbers and equations presented on pages six through ten. No matter how many times she read the instructions and problem examples, Sarah came up blank. She sensed trouble ahead for her in this course and could only do her best in an attempt to work the problems on the pages assigned. The hour she devoted to the subject had not been productive, and she wondered if they would be graded on their homework assignments.

Leaving it behind, Sarah called to Rachael and ran a bath for her. Once Rachael was clean, Sarah helped her into pajamas and brought her back to say goodnight to their parents. Her parents were discussing her father's possible appointment and promotion. It was a big decision to make and Sarah left them, taking Rachael to bed. With Rachael happily tucked in for the night, Sarah drew a bath for herself and was finally ready to end her day. After saying goodnight to her parents, she closed the door to her room, slid beneath the bedcovers as she checked the time, and set her clock. Turning off the light, she lay in the dark, contemplating the events of the day.

Her thoughts wandered back to the brand-new algebra teacher and whether she would ever be able to regain her footing in his class, recalling the fool she had made of herself. No one else had ever caused such a reaction in her. She could think of no reason why she found him so compelling, although something about him had drawn her in; she could still feel the power of his deep-set green eyes when they had met her own. He was extremely handsome, but neither his attractiveness nor height totally accounted for her seeming loss of control and sense of intimidation. He looked at her with an intensity that made her feel as though he could look straight through her and know her thoughts. Something fearsome lay in the realization that her thoughts might not be her own when she was near him, but she found him deeply attractive despite that fear.

Sarah felt vulnerable with him, sensing the feeling of no escape. A slight tremor washed over her while she lay there in the dark, thinking of her first day in his class. She could not forget his face, and it was the last image she held before sleep ruled the night.

CHAPTER SIX

The first two weeks turned the pages of the calendar quickly as the staff and students settled into their routines. Students and teachers were no longer strangers and knew better what to expect from one another. That the new algebra-trig teacher, Mr. Hall, demanded performance became common knowledge, and his classes were considered to be among the toughest at North Shoreline High. Sarah was experiencing difficulty, as she usually did with math, but her academic history didn't account for all her problems in his class.

Concentrating around him was troublesome, and sometimes she would suddenly go blank watching him, feeling an attraction she couldn't dismiss or account for. He was so compelling that, on occasion, she heard only half of what he was saying, while remaining mesmerized by his powerful demeanor. The attraction was partly physical; just being in the same room with him brought all sorts of bodily sensations unknown to her before. They were not easy for her to understand or deal with, and she was often carried away by his presence in ways she had no control over, including sudden, unexpected flushing and an increased heart rate.

He seemed powerful to her on many levels. On the one hand, he was able to make himself clearly understood with his directness, which she appreciated; but on the other hand, his intensity was intimidating and slightly overbearing. She could see he knew exactly what he was saying and his intelligence and knowledge could never be doubted, but at the same time, she had to live up to his expectations. Something about that dichotomy was fearsome, and Sarah struggled to balance the fine line between appreciation and intimidation, afraid she would falter in his class. Wanting to meet his expectations, while feeling uncertain she could, left her vulnerable to failing not only herself but, worse, him. That feeling was especially pronounced when he would call on her, or even if he simply glanced in her direction—the same feeling she had the first day of class when time had stood still in the moment her eyes met his. She was frightened of him and the unknown power he had over her, yet she was drawn to him, regardless of her fear.

She was glad to have his class behind her for the day and was looking forward to seeing Nonie at lunch. Now she could also look forward to her practice after school. The football season was in full swing, and Sarah had marching-band practice several days a week after school to prepare for their home games and practice the routines with the other majorettes. She had to rely on friends for a ride home after the lengthy practices since the late busses ran before they were finished, and Kenny had been there for her—though she frequently had to wait till Coach Morris released them from football practice, which was often long after the marching band dismissed.

The cafeteria was filling rapidly; the chaos of the first few weeks had subsided as mutual friends generally made a point of gathering together, frequently at the same tables every day. Sarah wasted no time locating Nonie, and together they made their way through the line after dropping their books at their usual table.

"Are you coming to the game on Saturday, Nonie?" Sarah asked.

"I don't know. My father thinks I should be at the restaurant on Saturdays since it's our busiest day."

"I wish you could be there. Maybe if you promise to come back home as soon as the game is over, he might reconsider."

"Maybe, but I doubt he will. Business is business to him, you know!"

"Well, I sure hope he'll let you plan on attending the homecoming game. I'd hate it if you'd have to miss that one," Sarah said as they made their way back to their table.

Kenny and Trent were already seated and eating when the girls returned. Kenny slid his chair closer to Sarah's after she took her seat. "Hey, beautiful, do you have majorette practice today?"

"I sure do. I suppose we have to be ready for the big win on Saturday," Sarah answered, bringing a smile to Kenny's face that showed off his pearly white teeth.

"Say, do you need a ride home tonight?"

"If it's not too much trouble, Ken, you know I would appreciate it."

Ken's smile suddenly widened as he slammed his fist to the table in a burst of over animated enthusiasm. "That's my girl," he said, with a quick wink of his eye.

Sarah interpreted Kenny's playful display of friendship as casually as he delivered it. To her, his antics were a fanciful product of over-confidence.

"I'll pick you up at the band-room door once Coach releases us. I hope it won't be as late as last time."

"That's alright, Kenny. I'll just work on homework till you get there. Thanks for offering."

Trent pulled a schematic of several plays the team had practiced from his notebook and brought Kenny's attention back to the game.

Nonie paused from her meal. "Hey, Sarah, how did you do on the quiz we just got back in algebra today?"

"Not very well, I'm afraid. I'm lost in that class."

"You and me both! I guess a seventy percent isn't exactly a failure, but it is pretty darned close." Nonie shook her head in disgust at her poor performance.

"Apparently, we're not alone, because word has it that a lot of us are in the same boat in his class."

"Well, I wish we had a different teacher!"

"It's too late for that now. I'm afraid we're stuck with him," Sarah countered. A scant twitch of conscience compelled her to admit she secretly looked forward to his class, although she had no explanation for her mixed emotions.

Mark Stevens traipsed by drawing the attention of the other students before sitting down at a nearby table. The bulging purple/blue shiner at his right eye was difficult to miss, but no one dared to ask him how he came by the disfigurement fearing his angry rebuttal. A timid freshman quietly moved, offering Mark the space his disposition demanded.

Nonie turned to Sarah and asked in a whispered voice, "Did you hear any rumors around school about how Mark Stevens got that black eye?"

"No one seems to know a thing, but with his short fuse, he attracts trouble all the time. I sort of feel sorry for him. He wasn't always like this when he was a kid growing up. When I was ten and they first moved into the neighborhood, Mark use to play stick ball with all of us. But, as time went on, he seemed to withdraw and didn't come out to play very often. He just seemed to loose the happiness he once had when he was a kid." They sat quietly for a while as they finished their lunch, and then whittled away the remaining minutes enjoying conversation with their friends.

At the close of the lunch period, Sarah turned to Nonie. "Would you please ask your father about letting you come to the game on Saturday, and if not this weekend, then at least for homecoming in November? I'll even drive you back to the restaurant myself since Dad is usually home on weekends and I'll have the use of the car."

"I'll ask him, Sarah, but don't count on it."

At the sound of the bell, Kenny turned and put his arm over Sarah's shoulder and whispered in her ear, "See you later, gorgeous."

Sarah smiled, accepting his nonchalant and familiar ways as casually as he had offered them. "Thanks. I'll look for you then, Kenny."

Classes for the day came to a close quickly after lunch, and Sarah headed to her locker before making tracks to marching-band practice. Tomorrow's game would be one of only three played at North Shoreline High until homecoming in November and the students were feeling a surge in hometown pride.

CHAPTER SEVEN

The cooler autumn weather became a welcomed relief, especially for the North Shoreline High School football team as they continued to practice long hours after school. Coach Morris vowed that the team would go to state this year, and their lengthy and tougher practices were needed to bring about his prediction. By the first of October, the team had secured a 4-0 record and was meeting the challenge effectively. Kenny devoted himself to the game, never missing a practice, while doing his best to see Sarah at every opportunity he could. He wanted to ask her out, but until the season ended, he would have to be content with short visits during school and the few occasions when he could drive her home after her marching band and his football practices. He had managed a visit with her after church one Sunday, but she only accepted his impromptu invitation to go for a burger when several others decided to join them. And Sarah had insisted on paying her own way. Today, he would take her home when practice was finished, but he would extend his time with her as long as possible.

By 4:45, the band room was vacated, and most of the students had already made their way to their cars. Sarah had to wait till 5:30 before Kenny's practice would be over, and she used the time to finish up her homework while she waited. The band director asked her to be sure to turn out the lights when she left. Kenny had suggested picking her up at the southeast exit adjacent to the band room and teachers' parking lot. His thoughtful gesture prevented Sarah from having to walk the long distance to the other side of the school, especially with the cooler weather and darkening skies at that hour of the day.

Checking the time, Sarah decided to head for the exit door early so she wouldn't risk missing her ride. She gathered her books and turned out the lights in the band room, shutting the door behind her. Making her way down the short hallway to the corner, she fumbled with the strap on her purse as she balanced her books and baton. The moment she turned the corner, she abruptly collided against the hardened chest and abdomen of a man of stature as he made his way down the adjoining corridor. The sudden impact of their bodies sent her notebooks, textbooks, and papers in all directions. Sarah found herself face to face with Mr. Hall while all her books and papers lay strewn across the floor. Dumbfounded, she remained immobile, staring back at him. He appeared to be surprised as well as he towered over her. A gripping pause punctuated the awkward moment.

"Well . . . I'm certainly surprised to see you here, Sarah," he finally said, bending down slightly and setting his briefcase to rest on the floor. "Are you all right?" he asked, looking back at her as she stood frozen in place, holding her handbag tightly.

"I'm so sorry, Mr. Hall. I didn't hear you coming."

"There's no need for you to apologize, Sarah. I'm afraid I'm the one who owes the apology. I didn't expect to see anyone here at this late hour." he said, while staring at her intently. He cleared his throat as if catching himself and continued, "Let me help you pick up your things."

He bent down to help gather her papers, and Sarah knelt beside him, scrambling to collect as many papers as quickly as she possibly could. She did her best to stack them while her heart raced at the nearness of him. At the same time, they both reached for the last piece of paper from her notebook. He held the opposite corner from Sarah and then looked back up into her face as they slowly lifted the paper from the floor together. Time moved in slow motion, and Sarah didn't know how to respond to the clumsy situation. This was the closest they had ever been to one another, and the awkward moment remained suspended as their eyes locked for a second time.

She was overcome by him and the strange effect he had on her, and the subtle sense of panic crept over her that only he was able to instill in her. Holding the stack of papers in her left arm, Sarah continued to grasp the opposite corner of the last sheet of paper with him, as they simultaneously rose.

He was slow to release the edge of her paper, while holding her aqua blue eyes.

Sarah tilted her head down slightly, embarrassed under the weight of his stare. "Thank you for the help," she offered. She hoped he would say something.

Her attempt to break eye contact with him along with the blush of her cheeks caused him to smile as he obliged her taking the lead. "What's kept you after school this late, Sarah?"

Attempting to balance the wayward papers, handbag, and baton, Sarah nervously responded, "I had band practice. The majorettes were scheduled to work together with them today."

"It seems late for practice to end," he said. "You seem to be the last one here."

"I stayed behind to finish up some homework." She attempted to shake some papers into place while answering him.

He looked at the door and then back at Sarah. "It's nearly dark out. How are you getting home?"

The awkwardness for Sarah, standing so close to him, sent chills up her spine. "I . . . I have a friend coming to pick me up."

"It's pretty late, are you sure they're coming? Perhaps you need to call someone, or may I offer you a ride home?"

"Yes . . . I mean, I'm sure they're coming, and no, I don't need a ride. I'll be all right, Mr. Hall," Sarah blurted, trying to disguise her unease at the prospect of his offer.

He slowly nodded, watching her closely. "All right then, but I suggest you remain inside till your ride arrives. That way, you can return to the lobby and the pay phone if your ride doesn't show up. The doors all lock behind you at this time of day when you exit them." Mr. Hall searched her facial expression, but Sarah remained silent. "With the colder temperatures, you'll stay warmer that way," he offered with a smile, in a less instructive tone.

Sarah did her best to respond, trying not to show the tension she felt. "I'll be sure to do that."

They started walking together to the exit door, neither speaking as they made their way down the hall. Arriving at the exit, he stopped, resting his hand on the crossbar of the glass door glancing outside at the dwindling day light, and then checked his watch before turning to face her again. He paused briefly before speaking. "Are you certain your ride will be here? It's approaching six o'clock and I'm not comfortable leaving you here alone at this late hour, Sarah. It wouldn't be any trouble for me to drop you off at home," he asked again, with a concerned expression.

"Yes, I'm certain, but it's very kind of you to offer," she managed quickly.

Mr. Hall gripped the cross bar as he hesitated, then nodded before he spoke. "All right, then I'll see you Monday morning. Have a good weekend," he said, displaying a clear reluctance at leaving her there alone.

"You too, sir."

He pushed the door open and walked across the parking lot to his car. Sarah stood inside the school alongside the door, watching him as he walked to the far side of the lot, her heart still racing at having been near him. Walking around to the driver's side, Mr. Hall opened his car door and slid his briefcase across the front seat to the passenger side. Before getting in, he brought his head up, looking back at Sarah standing by the door inside the school. She watched him and knew he was staring back at her. She wondered if he were reconsidering leaving, causing her pulse to race faster.

Kenny slowly turned the corner of the building and pulled up to the exit door where Sarah stood guard. His arrival brought Sarah's attention away from Mr. Hall, and she pushed the door open without further delay, hoping to leave quickly without drawing Mr. Hall's continued attention or concern. Just to be near him caused an unexplained anxiousness and feeling of insecurity. He left her unnerved and slightly shaken, as if she were a captive totally under his spell. He was the only person who had ever caused her to have a litany of sensations and emotions all rolled in one with a single glance.

Kenny reached across to the passenger side and pushed the door open as Sarah approached. "Hey, Sarah, how's my girl?" he asked as she quickly sat, then closed the door behind her.

"Glad to be headed home. How are you, Kenny?" she answered, all the while watching Mr. Hall as he finally got behind the wheel of his car, closing his door after watching her get into Kenny's car.

"To tell you the truth, I'm beginning to get tired of getting the stuffing knocked out of me."

"I guess it was a rough practice then?"

"You could definitely say that."

They left the parking lot as she watched Mr. Hall head out the far side in the opposite direction. Sarah wondered what his night would be like and where he lived. In that moment, she wished she were in his car and not Kenny's, but it was only wishful thinking that she dare not dwell on for long.

"Sarah, I really need something cold to drink. Do you mind if we swing by the drive-in on the way to your house—if it's not too late?"

"Sure, Kenny. I don't want the star quarterback to be anything but healthy and happy before the big game!"

Kenny smiled his consummate smile as he turned on to the highway. Sarah looked at her watch and hoped their stop wouldn't take long since it was already getting dark.

"You know Sarah, homecoming is coming up in November and since we're both going to be at the big game, I was hoping you'd like to celebrate by going to the homecoming dance with me that Saturday night?" His question immediately conjured up a situation Sarah was not willing to leave herself open to. Although she valued their friendship, she didn't want to complicate it by accepting a date, giving Kenny a false signal encouraging more physical contact. On the other hand, she didn't want to hurt his feelings when declining. Before she answered, Kenny pulled into the drive in. "How about- something to drink?"

"Thanks anyway, Kenny. Not for me."

"Come on, Sarah. I can't drink alone. Have something."

Not wanting to offend him, she finally agreed, "Al right, a small coke would be fine."

Kenny got out and placed his order at the walk up window. After paying for both sodas, he walked back to the car and handed them to Sarah before getting in.

"Thanks for the coke." Sarah said, as Kenny took his seat behind the wheel.

Starting the car, he drove to the back end of the lot, away from the brighter lights in front. He turned off the ignition and turned to face Sarah. A sudden grimace distorted his face that took Sarah by surprise.

"Oh, Kenny, are you all right?" she asked as she rested the sodas on the dash and moved closer to him.

"It's nothing. I'll get over it," he said. She could see that he was doing his best to hide his pain.

"Are you sure it's nothing?"

"I took a few hard hits this week. That's all," he said. It was obvious to Sarah that he was trying to maintain his usual upbeat behavior. She watched him closely and then reached for his drink, peeling a straw and punching it into place before handing him the cup. Extending his arm to take his drink from her hand, Kenny once again held his side as a look of pain lit across his face.

"It's not all right, Kenny; maybe we should have a look at it," Sarah said firmly. Kenny finally agreed, putting his drink back down on the dash, and then slowly removed his coat.

"Where does it hurt?" Sarah asked as she watched him.

"It's my left side."

"Can you open your shirt, and I'll have a look at it?"

"Okay, but I think it will be all right by tomorrow." Kenny unbuttoned his shirt and lifted his T-shirt as Sarah slid closer to his side to get a better look. She was shocked to see a purple-blue and magenta bruise larger than a football across his lower left rib cage. She gently brought her hand across his side to feel for any protrusions, and in that moment, Kenny forced his hand over hers and leaned into her, kissing her suddenly with a forcefulness that took Sarah by surprise. She pulled away from him, shocked at his unexpected and aggressive behavior.

"Come on, Sarah—you look surprised when you shouldn't be." he told her as she brought her hand to her lips, feeling them as though they were hurt. Sarah slid away from him, retreating to the far side of the bench seat.

"What's wrong, Sarah? You must know how I feel about you, and you can't expect me not to want to kiss you when you touch me that way!"

"My touching you wasn't an invitation." she frowned at him in disgust. "I was concerned about your injury, but I see you're better than I thought."

"Listen, I'm crazy about you, and all I really need to know is how you feel about me," he said, holding his side once more.

Sarah forced her lips together remaining silent, trying to decide what to tell him that would allow their friendship to continue without a committal to a deeper relationship.

Taking in her tightened expression, Kenny spoke up quickly. "Wait, before you answer, please don't tell me we're just good friends. We both have plenty of those, and you and I know our friendship is more than that!"

"What do you want me to tell you, Kenny? Because no matter what I say, you won't accept it if it's not what you want to hear."

He wanted to reach out and pull her next to him but knew she would not accept that from him in the moment, and it would only serve to push her away. He reasoned half a loaf was better than none, at least for now. "All right, Sarah, but don't tell me we're just good friends. Let's just keep it as it's always been, 'more than good friends' for now, fair enough?"

"Fair enough," she said, breathing a sigh of relief.

"You still haven't answered my question. What about the homecoming dance?"

Sarah drew a deep breath watching him as he rubbed his left rib cage. "I can't go, Kenny. My parents have planned a birthday party for me and have invited my aunt and uncle to the house that night to help celebrate my seventeenth birthday." Kenny tilted his head looking half dejected and partly angry as though he hadn't expected that answer. His expression compelled Sarah to soften his disappointment. "This doesn't mean that we're not still friends, but you know that none of us knows how much time God has left for Mom, and I won't disappoint her." Sarah watched him closely from her side of the car. Kenny closed his eyes and then hit the steering wheel with the palm of his hand in frustrated resignation. After a momentary pause he turned back to face her again reining in his emotions.

"I suppose I understand, Sarah, and I wouldn't want you to disappoint her either." He finally responded. He couldn't accept the fact that he might never have a chance with her, and hoped he hadn't made his move too soon. At least he had bought himself more time to win her affections. After all, she hadn't agreed to go to the dance with anyone else, and there wasn't another girl he knew who didn't want him. He still couldn't fathom why Sarah was the only one who didn't accept his interest with open arms. *She'll come around.*

"You'd better get me home now," Sarah said as she reached for her soda. Kenny buttoned his shirt, slowly tucked it back in, and put on his jacket. He turned the key in the ignition and, before backing out, looked over at Sarah one more time.

"My side really does hurt, Sarah. I didn't lie to you."

"I know you didn't. You should probably get in the shower and let the hot water run over it for a while tonight when you get home," she suggested.

Kenny regurgitated that thought in his mind; what he really needed was a cold shower, and the sooner the better.

CHAPTER EIGHT

Travis Hall entered the teachers' lounge and put his briefcase down on a nearby table. He had the next forty-five-minute period between classes to himself, and he would use the time to correct assignments collected from his last class. He opened his briefcase and pulled out the papers and a red pencil, which he used to make his corrections. While Travis moved through the assignments, Mrs. Helen Fredrick and the dean of girls, Ms. Betty Watson, entered the lounge and took the couch not far from the table where Travis sat. He looked up and politely greeted them before returning to his task.

The two English teachers smiled courteously and continued their discussion regarding a recent writing competition their students had been encouraged to enter. "I'm afraid we can only send ten entries from our school, and we'll have to limit the five English teachers to choose only two submissions apiece from all their students," Betty Watson said.

"That's too bad, because several students of mine have noteworthy work, though none is as well-written as Sarah Thompson's," Mrs. Fredrick continued.

Travis couldn't help but overhear their conversation and was surprised to hear Sarah's name come up; he came to an abrupt halt, placing his pencil down.

"Excuse me, ladies, for the interruption, but I couldn't help hearing one of my students' names in your conversation, and I wondered if you might tell me about Sarah Thompson's writing?"

Mrs. Fredrick smiled. "Sarah is one of my best students and has an enormous talent and gift for writing. She seems to have a way of expressing shared emotions and feelings in a way unlike any of my other students. If she is moved by a cause, her writing is exceptional."

"If you don't mind my asking, what was the nature of the assignment?"

"I don't mind at all, and I happen to have her paper with me if you care to read it." Mrs. Fredrick began thumbing through a large shoulder satchel while explaining the specifics of the challenge. "The assignment was to write a paper explaining either governmental or societal obligation to its people, while focusing on finding areas of need or failure. It had to include examples of specific ways that society or government could improve its function once the need was identified."

"What was her specific topic of concern?" Travis asked, now more intrigued.

"Here it is!" Mrs. Fredrick pulled out an eight-page paper from her bag. "It's titled 'The Minimal Role of Women in a Non-Democratic Society and the Resulting Consequences to Children and the Population at Large.' She is a bit idealistic, but it is quite an exposé on the plight of women in Third World countries and is very well researched. I think you will agree that it is well written. With her maturity, it didn't surprise me. " Mrs. Fredrick handed the paper to Travis and then added, "Sarah's short stories are where she shines, though. So much of her writing has a lyrical quality to it, and it's usually filled with eloquent metaphors that delight the reader. She seems to be deeply moved by injustices that most girls her age would turn a blind eye to. I think she has a possible journalistic or writing career in her future."

Travis thanked her for sharing and set about reading Sarah's assignment. He spent the remaining thirty minutes engrossed in Sarah's writing. Travis was struck by her eloquence in describing such heartbreaking conditions while incorporating vital factual statistics to substantiate her case. The construction of such a detailed bibliography added weight to her efforts, and her writing was convincing. The entire paper was organized and written so well he was taken aback by her ability, considering her age. He handed the paper back to Mrs. Fredrick. "Thank you for letting me read this. I have to say, it is quite impressive to see that level of maturity in writing for a junior in high school."

"I've known Sarah going on three years now, and she definitely is more on-the-ball than her peers. I don't think she's ever missed the honor roll since I've known her," Ms. Watson added.

Travis smiled politely, but couldn't help but be puzzled why Sarah was struggling in his class. One thing was certain, after reading her paper, he was once again thinking about Sarah with more interest than he should. Something about Sarah Thompson resonated with Travis, and to read her words and thoughts touched him in surprising ways difficult for him to admit.

He had to ask himself how it was possible for her to capture his constant attention and attraction. She drew him with her striking beauty, but he found her unpretentious and self-effacing demeanor captivating; she acted as though she was completely unaware of the image she presented. She wore her quiet sophistication and intelligence like a cloak, covering an innocence that kept its roots in deep moral ground. The unexpected evasiveness in her glance when he looked at her, countered by the way she could hook him in an instant with a few well-chosen words and force his thoughts to a standstill—it all captivated him. He'd never detected any malice in her when she spoke, and perceived her to be genuine at all times. She was intriguing to him in every way, and he had the desire to learn all he could about her. Sensing many more thoughts lay hidden in the depths of her aqua blue eyes, he wanted to be the one to discover them. For whatever reasons, he looked forward to seeing her every day, with an eagerness he could not explain—or fully justify.

When the period ended, Travis thanked Mrs. Fredrick again as he made his way to the door. He walked the long hallways on his way to class, disturbed by the fact that Sarah Thompson was struggling to maintain a passing grade in algebra. It bothered him that his class was the only one that Sarah might have trouble passing, and he didn't want her to fail. He knew she had the capability, and he resolved to find a way to help her.

CHAPTER NINE

The days moved slowly in the first five weeks back at school, and Sarah continued to struggle in algebra class. The last two tests found her average going down from a less-than-modest 82 percent to a 79 percent, and her understanding declined as the weeks went by. She found herself adrift in Mr. Hall's class, unable to keep up and constantly distracted by him in ways that were difficult to explain. Her stomach tied in knots if he called on her, and meeting his glance brought about an inability to reason. Something about the intensity in his eyes when he looked at her would stop Sarah cold, as if she were a bird in a cage wanting to fly away but powerless to do so.

Today was no different as she sat in his class hoping for the bell to announce its end. Many of the other students disliked being assigned to his class, but their reasons were primarily because he demanded performance and took no nonsense from anyone. He frequently used surnames while teaching, although with the girls, he was less formal. Sarah assumed this practice was his way of reining in the often-raucous conduct of many of the male students, and it helped keep in check any outbursts before they started. He was always fair, and the strict governance of his classes alone did not account for the slight edge of fear she frequently felt when around him.

Sarah tried to pay strict attention when he was teaching, but her mind would eventually wander, thinking about him in ways she knew she shouldn't. He presented a certain strength that could not be crossed or challenged. Frequently, he would copy an equation on the blackboard, and though he never looked back at it, he could announce the value of "x" without working the problem—doing all the calculations in his head. When the need to add, divide, or subtract large numbers or columns of figures presented itself, he could calculate their sums without missing a beat as quickly as he could jot the figures down. His abilities in math were remarkable, including his recall of everything he wrote on the board at the start of class. Sarah was unable to add three or four double-digit numbers without the aid of paper and pencil.

At the same time, she was drawn to him like ink to a blotter, totally absorbed by him in an instant. Not just his remarkable abilities and intelligence or his compelling good looks; she found herself wondering what he was like outside the role of teacher. She wanted to know everything about him—his history, what part of the country he was from, what his interests were, and if he had many friends, especially any female companions. On the one hand, she couldn't wait to get out of his class, but at the same time, she found herself longing to see him again.

Minutes before the bell, Mr. Hall called the class to his attention one more time. "For the benefit of those of you who would like to pass this class or keep your standing, I will be offering a help class beginning Monday. I strongly advise attending these help-class sessions if you are having any difficulty. We will be moving on to fractions, which require a solid foundation and understanding of the material covered up till now. Although they are strictly voluntary, I'd like to remind you that it is better to prepare now than be sorry later." He finished just as the bell rang.

Sarah gathered her books and began to make her way to the door along the back wall, specifically avoiding the front of the room where he stood straight-backed, holding their recent assignments in his hands. "Sarah, may I please have a word with you?" he called out before she reached the door.

Sarah's knees buckled slightly at hearing him, and she slowly turned, making her way forward to his desk. He watched her as she walked toward him and she stopped a short distance from him, keeping the desk between them.

"Sarah, I've reviewed your last two exams and see that things are not progressing as well for you as I would like," he said as he directed his attention toward her with the same burdensome intensity. "I think you might profit from the help-class sessions, if you could make the time to come. I don't want to see your grade-point average drop any further."

Sarah remained silent, wanting desperately to remove herself from his singular attention.

"I'm told that if you don't pull your grade up in this class, you'll miss the honor roll for the very first time. Is that true?"

"Yes, it's true," she answered immediately, her pulse racing at being left alone with him. She couldn't wait to get out from under the weight of his knowing eye and leave behind the awkward tension he instilled in her. Yet, she would be unable to stop herself from thinking about him as soon as she left.

Before Mr. Hall could continue, a tall, thin male teacher poked his head in the room, halting their conversation. "Excuse me, Travis, am I interrupting anything, or do you have a minute?" Robert Baxter peered through his black horn-rimmed glasses, which contrasted the shaggy blond hair at his forehead. The new speech teacher stood at the door waiting to enter.

"I'm just finishing up, Bob. Come on in." Turning back to Sarah, he continued, "Would you please try to be there?"

"I'll try to work it out, Mr. Hall," she answered him softly.

She appeared anxious as their eyes met, and immediately looked down, biting the corner of her lip. It was obvious to him that she was still reluctant to engage him. Travis wanted to help her bring her grade up, as well as learn more about her, and he hoped the smaller help-class setting would afford him the opportunity to be able to do that. He couldn't keep himself from watching her as she turned, making her way back to the door, passing

Bob on the way out. She moved effortlessly with an air of sophistication at odds with her reaction to him.

Bob made his way to the front of the classroom, eying Travis's face. Looking back over his shoulder, he paid more attention to Sarah as she left the room. "Is she one of your students?"

"Yes, she is," Travis answered, returning to the papers on his desk.

"Well, that's a bit of trouble if ever I've seen any!" Bob approached the desk.

"How's that?" Travis asked as he looked back up at his friend.

"Come on now, Travis, I'm not blind and I can see you're not either!" Bob shook his head, a grin spread across his face that Travis was well acquainted with.

"She's not what you're thinking, only a student who needs some extra help."

"Hell, Travis, who wouldn't want to help her! What's her name?"

"Her name is Sarah Thompson, and she's not your student, so enough of the wisecracks. I'm sure you didn't come in here to critique my student's physical attributes," Travis chided him.

Bob scratched the side of his head and continued, "Oh yah . . . I almost forgot why I came." He pushed his heavy glasses back up his thin, pointed nose as if recapturing his thoughts. "Do you remember I told you about a friend of mine who has season tickets for the NY Giants? Well, he gave me two seats for this weekend. Do you want to go?"

"You bet! Count me in," Travis replied as he closed his briefcase and headed for the door. "Listen, Baxter, I've got another class in four minutes, so I'll catch you later and you can fill me in. I'll see you this afternoon. Thanks!"

Bob remained behind, still smirking, reflecting on Travis's denial of interest in Sarah Thompson. He knew Travis Hall better than anyone. Their friendship went back seven years when he had met Travis at a small pub up state New York. Travis was there to check out his new college campus at West Point for the weekend along with a rowdy bunch of other eighteen to twenty year old Plebes. That was the same summer Bob had graduated from high school. Along with a group of buddies from Long Island, Bob decided to take a day trip up state for a scenic joy ride along the Hudson River. They happened to stop at the same burger joint/ pub along the way. The outing was their last planned get together before Bob had to depart for college at ASU that fall.

Travis and Bob hit it off immediately during their chance meeting. They identified common ground when they each discovered the other was attending college in his home state— Travis moving to New York from his home state of Arizona, and Bob soon heading to Arizona State University. From that point on, they kept close contact exchanging places of interests for the other to check out, and frequently joining up between school semesters when only one of them had opportunity to return home. Four years latter, Travis returned home to Arizona with a degree in mechanical engineering, supported by a cane, but minus his coveted Army commission and uniform. Bob was still at ASU starting work on his masters. Although teaching wasn't the direction Travis intended for himself, he needed a radical change to take his mind off the painful loss of his promising military career. Bob had suggested the door was wide open on Long Island where they were actively recruiting for math and science teachers. Some schools were offering large signing bonuses, especially for someone with Travis's accomplished math background. He knew Travis might bite on the idea since going back to N.Y. would keep him within shooting distance of the school he loved. Besides, they were both already familiar with the turf, Bob being born and raised there, and Travis by this time was well acquainted with the Hudson Valley. One year after he returned home and after he had completed physical therapy, the two of them were sharing an apartment together and Travis Joined Bob at ASU pursing his teaching certification. By May of 1962 Travis applied for a job at the same high school where Bob had recently applied and been hired for the 1962-63' school year. That summer they were both headed back to New York, teaching contracts in hand.

Their long time friendship allowed Bob to understand Travis in way no one else could, and that look in Travis's eye spelled trouble regardless of what he told him. Shelving that thought, Bob headed to his own classroom.

~~~~~~~~~~

Sarah caught up with Nonie and they walked together to their next class.

"What did Mr. Hall want to talk with you about?" Nonie asked.

"He asked me to think about attending his help classes since my average has dropped."

"Well, are you going to attend?"

"I don't know. I don't think I can be around him twice in one day. What about you; are you going?"

"I don't think so. I won't pass his class with or without help!" Nonie hunched her shoulders with an air of resignation.

"It might be worth our time, Nonie. I can't go there alone. If you go, I'll go. Okay?"

"I don't know. Besides, you'll do just fine without me," she answered with a bit of an edge.

"What are you talking about? We've always been together when the going gets tough," Sarah promptly countered with her brows slightly furrowed, surprised by Nonie's provocative tone. "Exactly what are you suggesting?"

"How come he called you up to see him about help class when your grades are better in his class than mine are?" Nonie asked, accusingly.

"I don't know, except that he found out I won't be making honor roll this semester because of his class."

"Do you know what I think?"

"No, but I bet you're going to tell me anyway."
~~~~~~~~~~

Nonie lowered her voice. "I think he likes you, Sarah, and I don't mean with a teacher's concern. I think it's more than that with him."

Sarah laughed out loud. "Don't be ridiculous. I can tell you exactly what he really thinks of me, and that's the furthest thing from his mind. He decided I was an unintelligent little twit on the first day of class when he practically scared me into permanent silence. Besides, if I fail his class, it might seem like a reflection of his teaching skills, and I don't think his ego could handle that," Sarah replied, forcing sarcasm.

Nonie shook her head in disagreement. "That's not it. Haven't you noticed the way he takes longer with you when he calls on you during class? Or the way he looks at you, holding his attention on you a little longer than with anyone else?"

"No, I haven't noticed that, and I can't believe you're even suggesting it." Sarah glanced around to be sure they hadn't been overheard, her face heating. "Even if that's true, it's probably because he has taken pity on me, and he thinks I need the extra help. All I know is that I'm just trying to hold it together long enough to pass this course and get out of there."

Nonie paused as she considered Sarah's thoughts. "Well . . . I have to admit he is very attractive but also a bit of a slave driver. He sure scares the heck out of me, and I don't think I want go to his help-class sessions."

"Please, Nonie, he scares me to death also, and I just can't go alone. Besides, we both need to pass this course," Sarah pleaded.

"Well . . . we have till next week to decide. Let's think about it for a while first. Okay?" "All right. But at least think seriously about it between now and then."

CHAPTER TEN

Small pellets of rain were striking the C-4 classroom windows as Sarah arrived a few minutes early to algebra help class. She placed her books on a desk closer to the windows and stood with her back to the door, enjoying the sound of the rain. By mid-October the skies were turning darker earlier now, and with the rain, the overall grayness of the skies was a portent of the approach of winter.

She had prepared for a cooler day by wearing a baby-blue sweater ensemble that reflected the blue in her eyes. The matching top sweater draped loosely over her shoulders, fastened securely with two silver clasps connected by a silver chain. As was often the case on Long Island during those long fall weeks in the march toward winter, the humid air still clung to the surface of the ground, lending a sultry stuffiness to the now-empty classroom. She removed the clasp from one side of her sweater and slipped it off, setting the top half of the ensemble aside. Her hair was neatly pulled from her face with a decorative hair clip set slightly to the rear of the crown of her head, allowing the rest of her sun-streaked hair to fall free to her shoulders. Wisps of silver and ash blonde tendrils were feathered randomly around her face as the humid air lent a slight curl to the loosened ends. She gently lifted the hair from the back of her neck with one hand and fanned the dampened air toward her face with her other hand. Standing for a moment, facing the windows with eyes closed, Sarah allowed herself to become absorbed in the cadence of the rain as it struck the glass panes of the windows. The strains of "Clair de Lune" moved through her mind as she visualized her fingers moving across a keyboard, keeping time with the tapping refrain of the rain as it beat against the glass. Lost in the moment, Sarah was jolted by the rumble of distant thunder accompanied by a slight flickering of the lights. She turned to check the clock above the door.

It was now ten minutes after three, and an uncommon silence settled over the room since most of the students had vacated the project area and the busses had left for the day. She wondered where Nonie was—and the others who said they were coming to help class. A sudden wave of fear crept over her at having to face Mr. Hall alone. Checking the time again, she wondered if she might have misunderstood which day the class was scheduled to take place. A sense of relief crossed her mind at the thought.

After assessing the situation, Sarah resigned herself to staying in the classroom until the late busses returned for the last pick up at 4:00. She could finish all her homework by then and be able to spend more time with her sister when she returned home. Reaching for a folder from her books, she used it for a fan and lifted her hair as before. Turning back to the windows, Sarah closed her eyes again in hopes of recapturing the welcomed escape.

A moment later, Travis Hall entered the classroom and startled Sarah; she dropped her hair and turned to see him standing at the entry door watching her. Sarah's long and slender silhouette curved noticeably beneath the neatly fitted sweater, drawing Travis's silent attention. "Good afternoon, Sarah," he said after an appreciable pause as their eyes met. He turned and took several long strides to the front of the room, placing his briefcase on the front desk. "Please accept my apologies for being late."

Sarah remained frozen in place.

He removed his sport coat and placed it over the back of his desk chair, then looked back at her motioning with his hand. "Come on over, Sarah, and take a desk in the front row."

Sarah managed to swallow, and then retrieved paper and a pencil from her notebook and took a seat in a front desk, watching him closely.

"I see the others couldn't make the class," he commented in a matter-of-fact way, loosening his tie and unbuttoning his shirt at the collar. He walked to the windows and opened several at an angle, allowing a breath of cooler air into the stagnant room while preventing the rain from entering. The dress shirt he wore was cropped at his biceps and emphasized his muscular arms and well-defined chest, adding to the feeling of power and authority he projected. Opening his briefcase, he removed a textbook and turned it to the appropriate page.

Sarah watched him intently, trying to remain calm inside.

Picking up a piece of chalk, he looked at the blackboard and then suddenly paused, turning back to Sarah again. "Since it is just the two of us, there's no need to use the board." He replaced the chalk on the ledge. Reaching for his sport coat, he pulled out a pencil from the lapel pocket and then pulled some blank sheets of paper from his open briefcase. To Sarah's surprise, he slid another student desk adjacent to hers and sat down.

She had never been so close to him before, and she couldn't control the flush that cascaded from her head down to her toes as his desk touched hers.

"Let's start with some basics to get a feel for where we are," he said, as he slid into the empty desk now adjacent to hers. On a clean sheet of paper, he wrote down an equation:

$$2L + 49 = 177.$$

Sarah took note of a long scar on his right wrist, extending to his palm, as well as a small scarring above his right upper lip, as he wrote the equation. She wondered how she had missed seeing them before, although the way he held the chalk when writing on the blackboard did seem out of kilter. With his desk now firmly abutted to hers, Sarah could no longer exit her desk, and her slight sense of anxiety grew stronger with her newfound confinement.

He turned the paper toward Sarah, leaving it on his desk, and then brought his eyes directly to hers before continuing. "All right, Sarah, what is the first step we need to take in order to solve this equation?"

The commanding sound of his directness made her ill at ease. Nervously, she leaned closer to his desk in order to read off the paper. Doing her best to concentrate, she understood that the *+49* should be moved to the other side of the equation, but had to be made a negative in order to do so.

"Write it down on the paper, Sarah," he said as he moved closer to her, repositioning the paper to face her more directly.

She took her pencil in hand and reached across her desk to his, hoping to avoid touching his arm, which he still had resting on the desk. Sarah carefully wrote the first step as directed.

$$2L = 177 - 49$$

"What is the value of 177 minus 49?" he questioned, waiting patiently for her response.

Sarah quickly brought her pencil to her scratch paper, jotting the numbers down to calculate the answer. "One hundred twenty-eight," she nervously answered.

"Now, what do you do next, Sarah?" he asked her.

"I have to divide both sides by two in order to be left with the value of L," she answered softly.

He nodded a slight gesture of approval. "Every step must be made plainly visible to see how we arrive at the solution, so write that down also."

Again, Sarah was careful not to touch his arm, although the position she was in made writing with her right hand crossing over to his desk on her left side difficult. She struggled to prevent her hand from shaking while holding the pencil. Cautiously,

She wrote down the next step as well as she could, praying he wouldn't move any closer to her.

$$\frac{2L}{2} = \frac{128}{2}$$

He brought his pencil to her last attempt at the proper step and crossed out the 2s on the left side of the equal sign above and below the dividing line.

$$\frac{\cancel{2}L}{\cancel{2}} = \frac{128}{2}$$

"Can you understand why we do that?" he asked as he met her eyes directly.

Heat radiated from his arm against hers, bringing on a complete cessation of thought.

"Sarah, you do know why we do that, don't you?" he repeated with more emphasis.

Her heart was racing, and she needed to say something, anything, so she could be free of his stare. "No," she said, "I can't remember why." The look of disbelief on his face was heartbreaking, and she felt totally inept.

"What do you get when you divide two into two?" he asked her with a look of incredulity.

"One," she answered immediately.

He scratched his head and then showed her on the paper again how the two numbers cancelled each other out. "Now," he asked, "what does that leave?"

"It leaves 1L," Sarah replied, her heart still pounding at the nearness of him.

He continued, "Then the equation should read, *L equals* . . . what?"

A long silence stretched as Sarah stared down at the paper, absolutely blank. The pounding in her chest was all she could hear as a complete mental fog descended upon her. The only thought her mind produced was that she would completely melt away if he moved any closer—or if their arms should touch one another. The problem could have been any numbers at all. It simply didn't matter, because her response would have been the same.

Travis leaned back in his desk chair and stretched his legs out in front of him. He brought the eraser side of the pencil to his lips and looked at Sarah as he tapped the eraser against his teeth. He said nothing for a moment. His eyes scanned her face as if he knew nothing made any sense to her, and Sarah looked back at him convinced he had read her thought. His pause indicated to Sarah that he was searching for the right thing to say. "Sarah, I happen to know that you're making excellent grades in all of your other classes. What makes you freeze up when it comes to math?"

Shocked that he asked her that, she wouldn't tell him that, in great part, he was the distraction making her feel intimidated and overwhelmed. She opted to tell him only a partial truth—that she had always been disconnected from math. "Numbers are rigid, cold, and unforgiving. The only thing they express to me is confusion."

Travis suddenly raised his head with brows pulled tightly together. It was clear that something else was going on. The tension and surprised look on his face slowly eased as he leaned forward supporting his chin against his closed fist which was braced by his elbow now resting on the desk top. He watched her a moment longer before speaking. "Okay, Sarah, look at me," he said as he adjusted himself in the seat to face her more directly. She raised her head from the paper and turned to face him. "I want you to tell me some of the things you love."

In a matter of minutes, the whole conversation had changed. "What do you mean exactly?"

"I mean just what I asked. Tell me what makes you happy and what you love to do." He put the pencil down on the desk, folded his arms on his chest and leaned back in his chair.

Sarah sat slightly more erect, with her head held higher in order to meet his glance directly. She turned her upper body in his direction. "Well, I love my family, music, and reading, and sometimes I like to write."

He suddenly smiled as if suddenly struck with new insight. "Do you play a musical instrument?" he asked her.

Her tension gently faded as he made an effort to speak to her about something other than algebra. Sarah wondered where all of these questions were leading but continued to comply. "Yes I do, though I don't play the piano as well as I would like. What has any of this got to do with algebra?"

"Sarah," he started out slowly as he ran his whole hand up through the falling strands of his shining chestnut hair. "When you read music, it is written in a language of its own. When you read the words of a book, it too has its own language. Algebra is just another language that is expressing something in a different way than the words of a book or the notes on a piece of sheet music. You can express almost anything, if you know the language of algebra, just like the letters in a book or the notes in music. So long as you have the right equation and numbers, it expresses something also."

Sarah continued to meet his gaze, wanting to be able to explain exactly how she felt. For the first time, she saw in his face a willingness to meet her halfway and an openness that had been lacking in his demeanor as a result of the authoritative role he played as teacher. "Mr. Hall, algebra may be saying something to you, but it doesn't speak to me. It is so exacting that it doesn't allow for a different interpretation or even a correction. Math is either right or wrong. When you play a musical composition, part of yourself is in it, and the music is open to interpretation. The music itself evokes a sensation in you. In math, there is no movement outside the pencil on the paper. To me, it is dead."

He listened intently with an earnest expression that led Sarah to believe he wanted her success and was willing to consider her point of view. "You may be partly right, Sarah, but you have to admit that even music is first written on paper and is dead, as you describe it, until you put the notes into effect. All of these are symbols for the thing; they are not the thing itself."

"I don't believe that's completely true," she said rather assuredly.

Travis brought his legs back and tucked them under his chair. He leaned forward. "It is true," he told her, fixing his piercing green eyes on hers.

With her chin held higher and displaying more courage she asked, "All right then, if it's true that you can express anything just as you can in writing or music, then teach me how to write an equation that expresses love. I want to know exactly what the equation is, and in the moment when I read it, I want it to evoke the feeling of love in me just as the words in a novel or the notes of music when you play them can do. If you have to alter it in order to feel and comprehend it, it will still be two steps away from my understanding."

He leaned back in his chair again, remaining speechless. He folded his arms, then bringing his hand to his chin, he looked at her as though he were totally amazed. He didn't take his eyes off of her. Sarah wondered how he would answer her. Travis drew in a deep breath and paused another moment, scanning her face, while Sarah waited patiently to see what he would write or say.

After a lengthy pause, he finally straightened himself again in the chair. "Almost anything can be expressed in an equation, Sarah. I didn't say that I was personally capable of knowing how to write an equation for everything, only that it is theoretically possible to do so."

Unhappy with his attempt to sidestep her question, she added, "Mr. Hall, would you please tell me why I should try to learn the language of algebra if that language doesn't enable me to express what is most important to me? If even you can't write an equation expressing love, why should I pretend to feign interest in an empty exercise of the mind that is always devoid of feeling and forgiveness?"

His eyebrows suddenly furrowed in perplexing fashion as he stared back at her slow to respond, as if lost in thought. Sarah sat quietly returning his stare when he suddenly clenched his jaw tighter. She thought he was struggling for an answer. Another moment passed before he drew a deep breath raising his broad chest and then exhaled.

"Okay, Sarah, you can't play football on a tennis court," he finally countered, tapping the pencil on the desk more forcefully. Still facing one another, his expression slowly softened, a slight smile forming on his lips. "I have the best reason of all for you to want to know the language of algebra," he answered with a glint reflected in his eye.

"I'm listening," she said.

"It's called final exams!"

Sarah's shoulders dropped slightly as she broke a small smile, still meeting him eye to eye. She realized they had reached a stalemate, and, for now, he was still very much in control.

They returned to the problem at hand, and he continued to try to teach her all she could absorb in the remaining minutes of the help class. At the end of the class, Sarah gathered her things to leave and Travis watched her from behind as she left the classroom.

Travis sat at his desk alone in the classroom for a while after Sarah left and he couldn't stop thinking about her poise and the gracefulness in her movements when she made her exit. It intrigued him that she was finally able to bring herself to meet him eye to eye as he recalled their aqua blue radiance. The feeling he had of swimming in a warm, crystal blue sea he didn't want to get out of, was tantalizing. And then, he thought of her straightforward inquiry in which she chose the emotion of love, rather than sorrow or hate or any other, to want to express. She had captivated him in a way he was hell bent to explain. When she had posed her startling question wanting him to write an equation expressing love, he shocked himself with his immediate thought. In that moment he wondered how she would express the feeling of love in the language of words, music, or better yet. . . physically. As quickly as the unrestrained thought had arrived he caught himself, but was astonished at having such a strong sexual feeling regarding a student. The fact that it came out of nowhere when it hit him with such force was jolting. He asked himself instantly, *What in God's name am I thinking?* Although he managed to yank back hard internally, his failure to discipline his thinking regarding Sarah was both shocking, and at the same time disturbing. He didn't know how he had gotten so far off course with her or how he had crossed from his world to hers, in which she seemed so masterful. The truth was, he didn't have the answer she was seeking. No one had ever posed a question remotely like hers, and he felt the danger in going any further. Being with her had dragged him to a place he couldn't conceive going regardless of her beauty. There was something about her that got the better of him and he struggled to identify exactly what it was.

She was never confrontational but was always strong in her convictions, which he suspected enabled her to hold her virtuous comportment. It never occurred to him, until now, that what was meaningful to her was something he had avoided most of his life. He could see in her something missing in himself. She thought with her heart and he thought with his head. She looked for ways to express love while he looked mostly for ways to succeed in every challenge for the sake of achievement.

The irony wasn't lost on him that the reason he excelled in math was not just for the challenge, which he thrived on, but also because he needed the high even the smallest victory provided. Sarah, on the other hand, was more concerned with purpose and what the face of the numbers could convey that would allow her empathy and understanding. Achievement for the sake of winning and being right didn't move her. Words and feelings were her medium, while the facts and the mission were his. That he couldn't give her an equation that actually expressed love only spoke to the fact that he wasn't looking for it, while she sought to find emotional meaning in everything. Her way of thinking was foreign to him, and yet, he found himself seductively attracted to her in more ways than one. He had watched her intently when she left the classroom, perceiving in her a symphony of elegance and class supported by those beautiful long legs. He also sensed the danger in feeding the flame that watching her aroused in him.

Travis was looking at her differently somehow, and although he had been struck by her natural beauty the first time he laid eyes on her, he was now drawn to her at a deeper level than he would have thought possible. Sarah was stunningly beautiful, uniquely intelligent, and at the same time, totally innocent, a combination he found painfully difficult to ignore. The question she posed continued to plague him long after the help-class session ended. Travis smiled to himself while he toyed with the idea of whether or not it was truly possible for him to write an equation that could express his unfettered interest in Sarah Thompson.

CHAPTER ELEVEN

Monday morning arrived on the heels of an especially pleasant and sunny last weekend in October. Students were piling into second-period algebra class, and Sarah sat at her desk, sorting through papers before the period began. A huddle of male students across the room were involved in a discussion, easily overheard, before Mr. Hall arrived.

Sidney Cooper was one of the brighter students at North Shoreline High and was involved in a discussion with Johnny Medford in the center of the group.

Johnny raised his voice above the others', "I haven't heard any of you come up with another plan to bring Hall down to size. Besides, we all know Sidney is the regional chess champion, and Mr. Hall knows nothing about that."

"I'm not so sure about challenging him to a game—he might not even accept," Sidney offered in rebuttal.

"What's wrong with you, Sidney? Don't you think you can win?"

"I didn't say that. I just thought there might be some other way we can humble him, other than a chess match."

A third boy in the group piped up, "Well, he sure demands a hell of a lot out of us, and I, for one, would love to see him fail at something!"

With a few more students siding with him, Johnny took the lead. "I don't think there is a guy in the school who would go head to head with him in any kind of physical match. Besides, the principal already gave his approval for the chess match to be held in the auditorium after school today, that is, if Mr. Hall accepts our challenge. This way, more of the students can be there to watch him go down. What do you say, Sidney, are you up to it?"

With only a few minutes left before class was to start, and at the prodding of the other boys, Sidney finally agreed. The group decided to let Johnny suggest the match to Mr. Hall, since he was the most gregarious and the most outspoken.

Shortly thereafter, Travis entered the room, accompanied by Robert Baxter; they were engaged in conversation as they walked to the front desk together. Johnny approached the two teachers. "Excuse me, Mr. Hall; I wonder if I might have a word with you?"

Travis placed his briefcase down on the desk as Bob folded his arms to listen in on the conversation. "What's on your mind, John?" he said, turning to face him as the other boys made their way up to the desk to listen.

"A few of the students have taken up the game of chess, and we were wondering if you would be interested in a friendly match after school today? You know, students versus teachers, with you representing the teaching staff."

Mr. Hall remained expressionless as he listened, but Bob shook his head slightly, looking right at Johnny. "Johnny, you uh . . . you don't want to do that." A quirky little smirk formed on his lips.

Travis gave Bob a stern look with a quick cock of his head, raising an eyebrow to show his disapproval of the advice to the student. "Let the young man finish his proposal, Mr. Baxter. He's inviting me to take up the challenge, so how about you stay out of the conversation?"

Bob's expression became quizzical as he tightly folded his arms over his chest. Remaining silent, he waited to see what Travis would say.

Turning back to face Johnny, Travis continued, "Now, tell me more about the challenge. Where and when would the game take place, who would the match be played against, and what, if any, are the stakes?"

Johnny Medford smiled broadly, as if he could already feel the jaws of victory clamping down around the dreaded Mr. Hall with their soon-to-be win. "We've already got approval from the principal for the use of the auditorium today after school, if that's agreeable to you, but we do have another teacher lined up who would agree to play if you're not willing to take up the challenge. Sidney Cooper will play for the students while you would play for the teachers. If the students win, you would have to agree to a five-day reprieve from homework for all students in all your classes." A smug smile spread across Johnny's face as he finished.

After listening carefully to the challenge, Travis replied, "That takes care of the 'whom,' 'where,' and the 'when,' but what if I win and you lose? What are you offering me, John, should I be the victor?"

Johnny Medford furrowed his eyebrows together, acting surprised at Mr. Hall's question as he attempted to answer. "Why you'd get bragging rights that the teachers won!"

"Bragging rights won't take a man anywhere, gentlemen, and I wouldn't have any reason to play the game for such a paltry and shallow victory. I think you need some skin in the game, boys."

Johnny turned to Sidney, looking dazed by the question. "Well, we haven't thought that through just yet, sir," Johnny answered.

"A man ought to know what his risks are and what he intends to gain before he gets into the game," Travis countered. "If I understand you correctly, you stand to win one week's freedom from homework in all of my math classes. If I might suggest, since a win for you represents five days' reprieve from homework for everyone, I would like to propose a five-point higher test-score requirement to pass every quiz in all my classes for a period of one week following the competition. It would have to apply to all my students, with no exceptions. That would mean a passing grade would be seventy-five percent, not the usual seventy percent. Five days for five points. Do we have an agreed-upon challenge?"

Johnny and Sidney looked at each other, surprised at the proposal. "May we have a minute to discuss this?"

Travis looked at the clock and then answered. "That's exactly the time left before the bell. Take a minute and then I'd like your answer."

Johnny and Sidney turned their backs to both teachers and formed another huddle with several other students. Two of the boys seemed hesitant, but Johnny held sway, sure that Sidney Cooper could easily defeat Mr. Hall. After all, Sidney was the regional champ.

The sound of the bell signaled the start of class, and Johnny turned to announce they had an agreement as stated. Robert Baxter just shook his head one more time, grinning silently to himself as he headed next door to his class, not saying another word.

Travis nodded. "As agreed, gentlemen, I'll see you this afternoon in the auditorium immediately after school. Take your seats."

~~~~~~~~~~

At the conclusion of class, Sarah caught up with Nonie outside the classroom. "What do you make of the chess match?" Nonie asked first thing as Sarah caught up and walked with her to their next class.

"I don't know. It sounds risky. I'm already struggling in his class, and if I have to make better than seventy-five percent, I may not pass at all; I'm hanging on at seventy-five percent right now. What do you think?"

"It's the same for me. I'm already on the borderline, but just think how great it would be not to be saddled with any homework in his class!" Nonie shared, practically salivating at the prospect.

"To be perfectly honest, Nonie, I don't think losing is something Mr. Hall would ever open himself up to, and I'm not as confident as John and Sidney are. He made it easy for them to agree, seeing that neither of them is making less than a B in his class. I
~~~~~~~~~~

suppose it's his way of making all of us work harder. But, with my grades, I can't afford to give away another five points. By the way, are you coming to help class this week or not?"

"I can't. I'm needed at the restaurant after school all week since one of the waitresses quit. Are you planning on going to the chess match?"

"You haven't attended any of the help classes, Nonie, and I'm not comfortable being left alone with him. I wish there was a way you could be there too. As far as the chess match goes, I have practice after school today, but if I get finished early, I'll swing by the auditorium to find out who won the match." Sarah was frustrated inside dealing with the feeling of abandonment, and couldn't understand why Nonie refused to come to help class with her. There was always a convenient excuse. The still small voice from within countered immediately, reminding Sarah of the secret truth she dare not share—she would go, despite Nonie's absence and couldn't stay away.

"I don't know why you're going back to his help class anyway, considering the punishment you take from him when you're there. He's too strict and he scares me to death."

"Well . . . I've asked myself that a few times, and it keeps coming back to my mind that I've got to pass his class if I ever want to get accepted to college. You should consider that also." Sarah paused a moment, considering her next thought before speaking.

Nonie caught her speculative expression. "What are you thinking, Sarah?"

"Have you ever wondered what he might be like outside of the classroom? There's a chance he might not be as intimidating as he appears when he's teaching. He actually surprised me and showed an interest in hearing about the things I enjoy. Although, I think it might be his way of trying to put me at ease dealing with algebra. When we were alone together, he seemed to have a different temperament. There's just something compelling about him I can't explain. He seems different to me than how everyone else perceives him."

"God no, I've never wondered what he was like outside of the classroom! Leave it to you to find something good in everyone and everything you come in contact with. I guess I'd sooner repeat this course with a different teacher next year than to spend ten extra minutes a day near him! Have you ever thought that you're just a glutton for punishment since you're the only one showing up there?"

"The thought has crossed my mind, but I don't think I have another choice. Besides, he really isn't as mean as you think he is," Sarah added.

"That's news to me!"

They continued to walk to their next classes together, oddly silent, mulling over each other's thoughts. Nonie raised an eyebrow slightly appearing vaguely suspicious of Sarah's softened tone regarding Mr. Hall.

Sarah felt isolated in her compelling attraction for the teacher everyone else feared so much. She shared some of that same fearfulness, but it could not overcome her attraction and secret longing to know him fully. "Listen, Nonie, I'll call you tonight if I find out who wins the chess match this afternoon. Keep your fingers crossed that Sidney can pull it off!"

"I will. Talk to you later."

~~~~~~~~~~

The news traveled fast, and the whole school was buzzing with anticipation to see Mr. Hall go down in defeat at the upcoming chess match. An air of confidence filled the student body as word got out concerning the match.

At the close of the school day, a cadre of fifty students, many of whom were familiar with the game of chess and others who were just anxious to see Mr. Hall taken down, slowly filed into the auditorium. Johnny Medford, Sidney Cooper, and a handful of other chess-club members were busy on stage, setting up the table, chairs, and chessboard for the anticipated match.
~~~~~~~~~~

Sarah headed to the band room for practice with the other majorettes, glad the auditorium was in close proximity, which would allow her a possible chance to catch part of the chess match after her practice.

By 4:00, Sarah had changed back into her school clothes, gathered her books, and headed straight for the auditorium. She took a seat halfway down the center aisle doing her best not to disturb the audience. Sensing the quiet tension in the atmosphere of the auditorium, Sarah wondered how the match was progressing. Sidney was moving slightly in his chair and looked as though he were anxious to make his next move, while Mr. Hall sat erect with his hand beneath his chin, eyes focused intensely on the board. Johnny Medford stood at the ready to call out the next move played to the waiting crowd. Even if the chessboard were visible to Sarah, the board's configuration would have little meaning to her. She was unacquainted with the game and its many pieces, as well as its objective. The outcome was her primary concern. The male student seated to her left whispered to her that Mr. Hall had drawn white and was about to make his next move.

Within a minute after Sarah took her seat, Mr. Hall exercised his turn. Johnny called out the move to the audience. "The white queen moves to b8 and puts the black king in check." A collective sigh of disappointment came from the crowd at the call. Within sixty seconds, a buoyant and confident Sidney quickly brought his hand to the board to make his next move, showing white teeth beneath widely parted lips. Johnny relayed Sidney's move to the audience with an equally jubilant expression, unable to contain his excitement. "Black knight captures the white queen at b8." A sudden burst of excitement and clapping rumbled in the crowd at the call.

Sarah watched as Sidney Cooper moved restlessly in his seat, wearing a presumptive expression, as he awaited Mr. Hall's next move. Mr. Hall remained expressionless, his right hand still resting beneath his chin; he raised his eyes toward Sidney without the faintest hint of apprehension.

The young man to Sarah's left clenched his fist in animated joy at Sidney's last move and leaned into Sarah, commenting in a whisper, "It looks like a student victory is almost assured now that Sidney captured Hall's queen. Sidney ought to have this wrapped up very shortly now."

After the excitement in the auditorium died down, Mr. Hall made his next move, without so much as a twitch in his action, and announced a checkmate. A sudden look of disbelief fell across Sidney's face as Johnny Medford looked down at the board, and then scratched his head, trying to decipher what just happened. After a minute analyzing the move, and with a look of utter shock on his face, Johnny finally grasped the significance. Shaking his head in disappointing realization, he turned to the crowd and remorsefully announced Mr. Hall's move. "White rook is moved to d8, and with the white bishop on g5, the black king is checkmated." The groans echoed throughout the auditorium, and Sarah was perplexed at the outcome.

"What just happened?" Sarah asked the boy sitting next to her.

"Beats the heck out of me, but it looks like Mr. Hall deliberately forfeited his queen to set up the checkmate. I don't know who could have seen that one coming. I thought Sidney was supposed to be the champ, but it looks like we've been had!"

"Does that mean Mr. Hall has won the game then?"

"I'm afraid so. The match is now over with the checkmate called."

Sarah's heart sank, realizing she would have to work even harder the next week to prevent a failing grade on all tests in algebra class. She looked back up on stage as Mr. Hall stood and extended his hand to Sidney, thanking him for the match. Sidney shook his head, accepting Mr. Hall's handshake, still wondering what had hit him.

Sarah listened to the others talking around her about the outcome. "Seems like all he did was sit back and let Sidney get too confident while he waited patiently to make the kill." "You just couldn't read him throughout the whole game." "He's fearless and calculating, and he must have ice water running in his veins because he never trips up—even when you think you've got him cornered!" "Who else would have had the brass to forfeit a queen deliberately just to make a setup? I'd hate to play poker with the SOB."

Sarah made her way out of the auditorium, listening to their comments and wondering if she was the only one who saw in him something extraordinary despite the students' loss. She dreaded having to call Nonie with the bad news later that night.

~~~~~~~~~~~

By 7:30 p.m., Sarah was nearing completion of her day. The scent of roast chicken still lingered in the air as she washed the last of the dishes and pots after dinner. Charley Thompson entered the kitchen and picked up a dishtowel on his way to the sink. He walked to Sarah's side, reaching for a pan to dry.

"Do you think North Shoreline stands a chance at a win Saturday?" he asked.

"Everyone thinks it will be close, but Kenny Birk seems to believe we have the edge."

"Glad to hear it. Kenny is a dedicated and responsible young man. I see his father around the courthouse in Mineola every now and then. JD is a damned fine attorney."

"Kenny says he intends to go to law school, too, depending on his LSAT scores. He plans to apply to Columbia. I'm excited for him, though I'm not sure he seems as happy as I would be."

"Your mother tells me Kenny has been kind enough to drive you home from practice the last few weeks. Good people, those Birks!"

"Yes, I suppose they are," Sarah offered quickly.

"Listen, Sarah, I've got something I want to share with you," Charley said as he finished drying a pot and put it away.

"What is it, Dad?" she asked as she continued to work.
~~~~~~~~~~~

"Your mother and I have reached a decision concerning my possible appointment to head up the homicide division, and we feel it might be the right thing for me to do. We don't want you to feel tied to the house as a result of my time away, Sarah. I'll be putting in longer and more erratic hours, but you won't need to play nursemaid to me, keeping dinners warm for me. I'll fend for myself, and probably will be eating away from home much more often. We want you to involve yourself with all your usual school activities and friends just the way you normally would do. Rachael is getting older now, and she is in school a full day. Besides, with Mrs. Reed next door leaving her job, she is home full-time and has offered to watch Rachael if need be."

Sarah pulled her hands from the water in the sink and gave her father an unexpected hug, unable to hide her elation at hearing the good news. "I'm so happy for you Dad!" she told him smiling broadly. "You don't have to worry about anything. We'll handle everything on the home front. It will all work out just fine, you'll see. I'm just happy you decided to take the post. After all, they couldn't have picked a better man for the job!" Her smiling eyes revealed her genuine happiness for her father and she never gave a thought about her responsibilities at home.

"There is a silver lining to all of this, Sarah. I thought you should know that along with the pay raise, the county will be providing me with a car for my permanent, full-time use. That means, of course, that you'll be able to drive to school and won't be relying on others for a ride home from practice anymore." Waiting for her response with a hint of a smile, Charley's pride in Sarah beamed in his expression.

"Oh, Dad, you're kidding, aren't you?" Sarah's sudden broad smile shared the same sparkle now lit in her crystal blue eyes.

"That's the upshot of it, but don't get too excited. Along with the set of wheels, you'll need to run some of the errands around here, like picking up a quart of milk and bread once in a while."

"You know I can do that, Dad. When do you get the car?" she asked excitedly. The sudden realization of the new found freedom and the relief of not having to depend on others for a ride was exhilarating to her.

"First thing Monday morning! Detective Crowley is picking me up for work that morning, and I'll drive the unmarked county car back home that night."

"You mean I can start driving to school starting next week?" she asked, thrilled inside at the prospect.

"That's the plan."

"Oh, Dad, I'm so happy!" Sarah exclaimed, embracing her father in another happy hug.

Her thoughts began to race as she and her father finished up the dishes together. It would be a relief not to have to rely on Kenny. He was always glad to drive her home, but Sarah hadn't liked feeling indebted to him. He would eventually get around to making another play for her, and she was grateful to be able to avoid that situation. With transportation of her own, she could pick Nonie up for football games and other activities she might otherwise miss—that is, if Nonie's father allowed.

After wiping the counters clean, Sarah made a beeline to the phone to give Nonie both the bad news about the chess match and then the happy news of her newfound transportation.

CHAPTER TWELVE

After a tiring week, Sarah was anxious for the weekend. Sidney Cooper losing the chess match had been a disappointing blow, and the students were now subject to a five-point higher test score to pass all exams in algebra. The new rules were especially painful for Sarah; she had failed a recent quiz with a score of 74 percent on Thursday, a score that would have been passing but for the chess bet. She sat alone in the C-4 classroom Friday afternoon, awaiting his arrival for help class and feeling more anxious than ever, having to deal with both her attraction to him and, now, her failure. The resentment she felt toward him for the new grading system was simultaneously, tempered by the awe and admiration of his intelligence and skill. He was a force to be reckoned with leaving Sarah on shaky ground.

He strode into the room with his same, confident air, glanced in her direction, and offered a greeting as he prepared himself to sit beside her. "I'm glad to see you here today, Sarah."

He had to be indirectly referring to her recent failing grade, and she responded immediately. "I suppose congratulations on your chess-game win are in order, although I'm not exactly feeling overjoyed at the moment."

He glanced back at her with a faint smile. "Thank you, Sarah, but I think we can overcome this setback. I hear congratulations are in order for you as well. I read in the news bulletin that you recently won a writing competition."

"Yes, sir, I did. It was actually written earlier this semester. But I'm afraid my writing-competition win won't help me escape the consequences of your win."

Sliding a student desk next to hers, the corners of his mouth turned slightly upwards revealing an expression just shy of a smirk, and Sarah wondered what he was thinking. He took his seat and then opened the textbook, writing down an equation and still sporting that telltale smile.

She suspected he deliberately chose to ignore her last comment as she fought back the temptation to tell him exactly what she thought. She did her best in attempting to solve the equation he presented her as he looked on. After completing the first two steps, Sarah paused, her mind blank.

"Sarah, this isn't rocket science. If 2x equals 756.8, what does 1x equal?" His face had a strained look of disbelief at her inability to figure such simple numbers in her head.

Sarah fell silent and couldn't bring herself to look at him, knowing how feebleminded she appeared to him. She brought her hand to her forehead, leaning on her elbow while supporting her head with her hand, embarrassed at her crippling capacity to calculate the numbers at the speed he demanded and finding it difficult to concentrate around him. With a sigh of embarrassment and frustration, she looked down at the paper on her desk. "I can't think of the answer with you sitting here telling me what I should be able to do!" she said, upset with both herself and his exacting expectations of her. She knew how gifted he was, and how quickly and easily he could calculate figures in an instant. His off the cuff comment had upset her causing her to freeze up. That, along with the new test score requirement to pass, seemed an unnecessary burden he wasn't even willing to reconsider. Sarah refused to look back at the disbelief in his face one more time.

Travis didn't say anything as he watched her. He brought a hand to his mouth and then traced around his lips as he slid his hand down his chin taking on a more moderate expression. He drew in a deep breath and put his pencil down, dropping any sign of his frustration with her lack of capability. "Okay, Sarah, when you fall off a horse, you get back up in the saddle and ride him again until you conquer your fear and you get the hang of it. Never let the horse ride you. You do the same in math until you succeed. You've got to keep pushing forward Sarah; just don't quit."

Sarah shook her head. "That may be true for a horse, but I don't know how to ride either. I wish I were as capable as you seem to be with everything you do, but I'm not," Sarah responded with exasperation.

He tilted his head focusing on her through sympathetic eyes. "I see I've used the wrong analogy for you again, Sarah!" he said as he ran his fingers up through the falling hair at his forehead. Appearing disheartened, he spoke with less forcefulness and a little slower, "Listen, when you practice a new piece of music, you repeat it over and over again until your hands get used to the feel of the pattern and the sequence becomes second nature to you. It's the same way in math. I suspect you let the numbers intimidate you when you're not sure of the process. You need to force yourself to work the math out on scratch paper if you can't figure it out in your head. Don't stop till you reach the finish line. If you keep pushing through the problem, it will eventually make it easier for you as you become familiar with the process, just like memorizing addition or multiplication tables." He stared at her, sensing her disappointment and recognizing that she didn't even want to look back at him.

"Mr. Hall," she began again, finally raising her head. "How do you force the mind to do what it doesn't want to do?"

"Discipline, Sarah!"

Frustrated, she found her voice, despite his disappointment in her. "May I ask you something?"

"That's why I'm here."

"Did you like math when you were in school?"

Travis broadened his tentative smile. Looking back at her with a softened expression he answered, "Yes, I guess I've always had an affinity for math, but it wasn't always easy, and I disciplined myself to accomplish what needed to be done in order to master my classes. And you could too."

"Ah . . . I think I can see this a little more clearly," Sarah said while nodding. "You said you liked it even though it wasn't always easy. It's the same for me with music. It isn't always easy, but because I love it, I force myself to practice for the reward of hearing something so beautiful. What's different for me in math is that I don't love it the way you seem to do. I don't see or hear the music in it or feel the satisfaction you must feel when you've solved a math problem. I'm as empty when I finish solving an equation as I was when I started, not any happier with the right answer than I would be with the wrong one. What appears to be missing for me is the fact that I don't love math."

She faced him with a sincere and imploring look in those pools of luminous blue in her eyes. He became lost in the sweet vulnerability and beauty of her expression as Sarah struggled to continue.

"I.... I truly do admire you for your skill in math and the love you seem to have for solving equations, but I wonder if it's possible that while you try to teach me, you might also have a small amount of patience with me for my lack of ability and fondness for the subject that you seem to care so much about? I promise to try harder to discipline myself, if you'll accept the fact that I may need more time to do what is second nature for you." Dropping her eyes and shaking her head slightly as if disheartened, she paused before continuing, "I'm . . . I'm so sorry if I'm disappointing you."

He was silent, enamored by her openness and humility with him. Why did he always have to treat everything as a challenge he had to win? The last thing he wanted to do was hurt her and Travis knew he would never be able to help her by voicing his dismay at her insufficiency. Those tactics might have worked very well on him, but projecting his observations and judgments would make it more difficult for her to learn anything. She had a way of disarming him not only with her physical beauty but with the sincerity of her words. Sarah was accepting of her failures, and while they might not be welcome to her, she was able to embrace them because they couldn't rob her of her center. He, like a driven taskmaster, refused the notion of failure and had always pushed himself harder than anyone else. Sarah, on the other hand, was able to bring everything back to what mattered most to her. For her, all things had meaning if they mirrored some good, a good that she could know through feeling. With every disappointment she found a way to see the good in it, fashioning a castle out of mud pies and replacing disillusionment with joy. She rested in a place somewhere deep inside, and that place acted as an anchor, a rock from which she never strayed, yet she came to his help class regardless of her dislike for the subject and her repeated feelings of failure when the other students wouldn't venture there. In that moment, he wanted to share in her world, to know it. Yes, he was very good at many things she never would be, but Sarah was intimate with whatever she loved. Her writing, her music, the sunrise, the rain, all of it had value to her and she gave herself fully to what she loved. He could master most anything he set his mind to, and in the mastery found satisfaction, but he wondered if he had ever been intimate with any of what he'd mastered. For the first time, Travis felt empathy for her in a way he might not have recognized with anyone else. The look in her eyes and the open honesty of her words were so genuine they took a direct route to his heart, bypassing his reasoning capacity on a fast track uninterrupted. "Sarah . . . I can assure you that you've never disappointed me."

She stared directly back into his eyes with a sad tentativeness.

"I want you to be able to pass this course. I may not be able to get you to hear the music in it, but I promise when you pass, we'll both be able to smile." Looking intently into her eyes an imperceptible longing crept into his heart, not openly invited but secretly desired.

Robert Baxter entered the classroom a short time later, just as Sarah made her way to the door, heading home after the long day. "Hey, Travis, are we still on for dinner together?" he asked, following Sarah with his eyes as she left the room.

"You bet! I'm free the rest of the night," Travis answered as he filled his briefcase to leave.

"I see you're still spending time with Sarah Thompson," Bob said with a slight raise of his brow. "Haven't you been able to help her out by now? This is about the third or fourth time you've given her one-on-one private tutorial, isn't it?"

"That's right. What's it to you anyway?" Travis shot back at him.

"That's not the right question, Travis. The real question is what is she to you?"

Travis slammed his briefcase shut and then turned to face Bob directly. "She's a student who needs my help. Anything else you need to know?"

Bob threw his shoulders back sporting a generous smirk. "I don't know why that beautiful young lady comes back here to take your abuse. If she only knew how pigheaded you can be, she'd quit coming!"

"Thanks for the vote of confidence. Now, where are we headed to eat?"

"I'm in the mood for Chinese tonight," Bob answered as they walked the long corridors back to the teachers' parking lot. "Tell me something, Travis—I know you still have that chip on your shoulder because you'd rather be somewhere else than here teaching right now, but I wonder, with your background and training, if you might be scaring the hell out of some of these kids. That girl Sarah looks intimidated by you."

With a surprised look of disbelief Travis quickly answered as he felt the sudden sting in Bob's assessment. "You don't know what the hell you're talking about, Bob."

"Unlike these students, you can't pull rank with me. I know you too well for that. I've been with you too many times and dragged your ass out of too many tight spots, especially when you've let the liquor do your thinking for you. Remember that little *señorita* you met in La Jolla Verde Cantina just a few miles east of Nogales? You caught her trying to steal your wallet, and when you confronted her, she brought the wrath of an extended Mexican family down on us. If it weren't for me, you would have killed every goddamned one of those SOBs, not to mention the damage caused in the fight. Fortunately, I was there to stop you before the *federales* arrived, and I got us the hell out of there."

Travis kept walking feeling quite amused. "Is there a point to any of this, Baxter, or do you just enjoy annoying the hell out of me? As I recall the incident, it was your idea to go there, and it was me who saved your ass, or did you forget the *señorita*'s brother, Miguel, who wanted to use you for carving practice?"

"Okay, so that was just one example. I could have used twenty-five others. The point is, Travis, I know how determined you get when you set your mind to something. Nothing stops you. You're used to getting what you want, but this excursion could be fatal, my friend! I've seen the way you look at that girl, and you're headed for trouble. I don't think you need to be spending any more time with her alone after school. There ought to be some other students in that help class besides just her."

"For your information, Baxter, that help class is open to all of my students. It just so happens that Sarah is the only one willing to avail herself of my help, so quit drawing conclusions about me that you don't know anything about. Besides, she really does need the help."

Bob shot Travis a look of disbelief. "That's part of my point. You've got the whole lot of them so damned intimidated, not one of them would show up for another hour in the day to spend with you."

Travis kept walking, halfway tolerating his friend's perceptions. "So, you don't think I've got the right goods to teach?"

"To command, yes, but teaching is another story. Listen, just because you're one tough SOB and maybe the most intelligent person I know, doesn't necessarily translate into excellent teaching skills."

Travis looked back at Bob out of the corner of his eye. "It may not be where I want to be, but it's a good place for now, until I decide what's next. Besides, the students will learn to like me just like you did!" Travis said with a grin. "I'll agree not to remind you about the rest of that story, if you agree to quit drawing false assumptions—especially about Sarah Thompson."

Travis found Bob's inference that he might entertain making a move on one of his students disturbing. The notion was ludicrous. Although.... as difficult as it was to admit, if Sarah hadn't been his student and he had met her outside a school environment, he would have felt very differently, never guessing her young age. But, just because he could appreciate her beauty didn't make him guilty of any crime. She was a student, albeit a very attractive one who needed his help—that was all. He wanted Bob to believe that. He gripped the handle of his briefcase a little tighter feeling grazed by Bob's question. A disquieting thought crossed his mind as he clenched his jaw. Did he really need to convince Bob that his interest was strictly professional, or did he need to convince himself? Whether Bob had guessed correctly, or whether his assumption was wrong, the disturbing truth still remained—Sarah Thompson was never far from his thoughts.

CHAPTER THIRTEEN

Homecoming day was made-to-order with its crisp, cool, and sunny weather inviting a bigger crowd than usual. The morning was filled with activities, including a small parade down Main Street in celebration of the coming afternoon game. The North Shoreline High School marching band performed admirably along the parade route. They were followed by the pep squad and several open convertibles, each carrying local dignitaries, including three town councilmen, the homecoming queen with her attendants, as well as a congressional representative. The streets were lined with families eager to cheer the hometown team on, waving their blue and white streamers as the band passed by. Local businesses always welcomed these events, counting on the increased foot traffic in town to deliver more sales and add to their bottom line in profits. The rivalry between the two opposing teams had been building for most of the season. The usual outbreaks of minor scuffles occurred when the South Shore team arrived in town, but most confrontations were innocuous and limited to a few hotheaded teens in need of tighter discipline, not incarceration.

The game later that day did not disappoint, highlighted by several long, completed passes thrown by Kenny Birk—two for touchdowns and a third that provided a good setup for the ensuing score. It was a thriller of a game right down to the end, with North Shoreline ahead, 21 to 20. The last few minutes of the final quarter had found South Shore in possession of the ball with just two yards to go on fourth down. Sarah thought they would go for a field goal, but instead they faked the kick, trying to plow into the end zone for a touchdown. Fortunately for the home team, Trent Rogers managed to prevent the charge by tackling the carrier and then forcing him back, staying their drive and assuring the win for North Shoreline High. The stadium went wild, and homecoming turned out to be the best game of the season.

The stars were definitely shining brightly that day, and Nonie Gorman couldn't have picked a better time to be in attendance. Sarah was so glad Nonie's father had finally relented and allowed her to attend, with the understanding that Sarah would bring her back to the restaurant right after the game. They agreed to meet at the southeast corner of the bleachers when the game ended and Sarah would be free to leave the band. Clusters of students and fans milled about, with spirits riding high, and in their excitement many stopped Sarah on her way back to find Nonie. Still wearing her uniform with its shorter skirt and fitted bodice, Sarah couldn't wait to change into something warmer to cover her legs. She was doing her best to work her way through the crowds when she was unexpectedly grabbed around her waist from behind.

Turning her around to face him, Kenny picked Sarah up and then slid her down his well padded chest beaming from ear to ear, sweat still dripping from his brow. "We did it, Sarah!"

"You were the best, Kenny," Sarah offered as his arms still embraced her.

"What, no kiss for the winner?" he bravely asked while maintaining his hold on her.

Sarah shook her head as she fashioned a slight smile, finding his persistence with her both surprising and slightly endearing. Not wanting to dampen his hard-won victory celebration, she replied, "A kiss for the win is a fair exchange."

Kenny brought his lips to hers, taking his kiss boldly from Sarah's tender, sweet lips. Sarah pulled away quickly as several more students and friends surrounded Kenny, some slapping him on his back, reliving his great passes over again, much to Kenny's delight. Sarah started to walk ahead to go find Nonie when Kenny called out to her again, "Hey Sarah, I'll miss you at the homecoming dance tonight, but say hi to your mother, and have a Happy birthday!" He yelled over the crowd.

Sarah turned to face him and called back, "Thanks, Kenny. I'll be sure to do that, and I'll share all the great passes you made today at the game with her as well." She could tell by his broadening smile that his disappointment regarding her not attending the dance was lifting with her recognition of his stellar performance during the game.

She'd been successful at declining his invitation to the homecoming dance while keeping their friendship in tact, but she wondered when he would tier of asking her out. She had grown accustomed to his caring and it almost felt natural. She hurriedly turned to go find Nonie, leaving Kenny to his adoring fans.

Sarah finally caught sight of Nonie, who was happily chatting with several other girls as she pressed through the crowd to join them. Susan Anderson, who was a pretty girl and quite popular as well, was speaking candidly, "You know, Nonie, I'd do anything to get a date with Kenny." A sudden look of surprise crossed Susan's face as Sarah approached. "Oh! Sarah, I didn't see you coming," she said, embarrassed at being caught admitting to what half the female class all felt. "You know I'd never move in on Kenny, Sarah, if you're dating him," she said, wondering if Sarah had overheard her speaking.

The question caught Sarah off guard as her face tightened. "You don't have to be concerned about that, Susan. Kenny and I are just good friends."

"It's just that I see you two together a lot, and I just assumed you two were an item."

Sarah hadn't considered that anyone would have thought she and Kenny were dating, let alone being an "item". Susan's comment was irksome, but then again, even if it were true that she was dating Kenny, it wouldn't have prevented Susan from seeking comfort in the arms of someone already spoken for. There was a host of names already on that list. "It was thoughtful of you to think of me, but I'm afraid I have no intention of being an item with anyone, least of all with a good friend."

"Well, since you put it that way, I'm going to go find out where Kenny and the other guys on the team are going after the dance tonight. Maybe I'll see you two there? Catch you later."

"Have a good time tonight, Susan," Sarah called back as Susan left the group.

"I can't believe you, Sarah!" Nonie exclaimed.

"What do you mean?" Sarah asked as they made their way to the car.

"Why, Kenny Birk is absolutely mad about you, and you act like you don't care."

"I didn't say I don't care. I only said we weren't dating."

"Well, why aren't you dating him? It's not because he doesn't ask you. I don't know anyone who wouldn't give her eyeteeth to go out with him, so what are you thinking, girl? You practically gave him away to her!"

Sarah kept on walking as she tried to formulate her thoughts. "Can we talk about this later?"

"All right, Sarah, but we better get you out of here in a hurry before you offer him up to every girl in the school."

"He's not mine to give, Nonie," Sarah shot back as they arrived at the car. She stuck her key in the door and quickly unlocked the car placing her baton on the seat. Turning back to face Nonie, Sarah brought the conversation back to the game. "I'm so glad your dad let you attend the game today. It was a great game—the best one of the season," She pulled a pair of jeans from the backseat and then took off her majorette boots as she sat in the car with the door open.

"The game was terrific, in more ways than one, and I can't thank you enough for bringing me," Nonie added excitedly, with a dreamy expression across her face.

"Okay, what's up?" Sarah asked as she slipped into her jeans, pulling them up under the short skirt of the one piece majorette's uniform.

"Well, it's a long story, and I want to tell you all about it when we get back to the restaurant. I sure hope it isn't real busy yet so we can have some time to talk."

Sarah zipped and fastened her jeans and then slipped her feet into a pair of flats, feeling much warmer and ready to drive. Both girls relived the highlights of the game as they followed a long line of cars out of the school parking lot.

Beneath the idle chatter, Sarah kept her feelings for Travis Hall a secret, unable to share it with anyone. She questioned why she couldn't feel the pangs of love for Kenny when everyone else thought she should. She did like him, and being with him was comfortable, like slipping into a pair of well worn shoes. You know what you're getting and what to expect. But, that type of convenient love was swiftly swallowed up, disappearing in the face of a heated cauldron of desire she couldn't prevent whenever Travis Hall came to mind. All other types of love seemed like the prattle of a child wanting to hold a teddy bear, soft and comforting, but not real, presenting no gain and coming with no risk. Many were moments like this when she examined her emotions questioning what it was that compelled her to a man she could never hope to have or fully know.

They arrived at the restaurant at 4:30. Fortunately, the rush on dinner didn't usually start till later on Saturday nights, when movies let out and the non-workday extended later into the evening. Once inside, they were greeted immediately by Nonie's grandmother, who stood vigil at the hostess stand. Her short, rounded appearance gave her a somewhat matronly look that matched the thinning gray hair. She wore a broad smile on her deeply lined face while gesturing animatedly with her hands for them to come closer. Bubbe wasn't difficult to recognize.

"Come! Come on in here, Sarah. Let me get a good look at you. Oy-yoy-yoy! What are they feeding you at home? Still no meat on your bones! So pretty, but so thin you are," she exclaimed as Sarah and Nonie entered the restaurant.

Sarah bent slightly to give Nonie's grandmother a hug. "Hello, Mrs. Gorman. I'm afraid I eat too much most of the time. And how have you been feeling lately?"

"Oy vey!" Bubbe threw her hands up in the air and rolled her eyes. "It isn't easy, this growing old, Sarah, but the young shouldn't want to know about such things!"

Nonie gave her grandmother a loving kiss on her cheek and then made a quick scan of the restaurant. "I see we're still not too busy, Bubbe. Do you think Sarah and I have time to talk a few more minutes?"

"So, with that look on your face, Nonie, it could only mean it is important and probably about a boy chick!" Nonie smiled broadly as Bubbe winked back with a twinkle in her eye. "I must have known to keep my booth open for you two." Bubbe pointed to the last booth against the wall in the rear of the restaurant. "Don't worry, Nonie. I'm the chairman around here, and I lend my booth out when I want to. You two head back for a while longer and talk!"

Nonie tugged at Sarah's coat and they walked to the back of the restaurant, taking their seat in the "chairman's booth."

"Okay. Now you can tell me what's up." Sarah rested both arms on the table and leaned forward, anxious to hear what Nonie had to share.

"Sarah, do you remember the guy my parents wanted me to meet who belongs to a different synagogue on the south shore?"

"Vaguely, who is he?"

"Well, his dad owns a supply company with several warehouses around the county, and they distribute restaurant supplies, some to us. My father has been trying to convince me to meet him, but I just wouldn't agree, fearing the worst as usual."

"Don't tell me you met the guy?"

"Oh, Sarah, he is wonderful!" Nonie swooned.

"Tell me all about him, starting with his name." Sarah hadn't ever seen Nonie with such a sparkle in her eye before.

"His name is Abe—Abraham Kaplan to be exact. I was sitting at the end of a row of girls with Fran Johnson and several others in the bleachers when three guys from the other school sat down next to me. At first, I was uncomfortable cheering for our team while they were cheering for theirs, but this guy Abe, all of a sudden, out of the blue, started talking to me. Oh, Sarah, he was so kind and acted like he felt bad when his team scored, on account of it being a homecoming game for me. Anyway, after we got to talking, we found out that his dad was trying to get him to meet me too! Can you believe it? He isn't the best-looking guy on the surface, but he has the most wonderful dark eyes and just seemed to know what to say to put me at ease. You know, the conversation wasn't strained or unnatural the way I usually feel with most guys. Best of all, Sarah, my father already approves, and he has no idea we've met each other!"

"I'm so happy for you," Sarah exclaimed excitedly as she reached out and squeezed Nonie's hand and then leaned forward to hear more. "Tell me, did he ask you out?"

"Not exactly, but he promised to come by the restaurant next weekend when he and his friend will have a car to use on Saturday. Besides, he wants the chance to introduce himself to my father first. He thinks that's the way things should be done. He's so sweet and a little old-fashioned."

"This is wonderful! I'm so glad you were at the game this weekend."

"Me too, Sarah! Now, why in the world did you tell Susan you weren't dating Kenny?"

Sarah immediately pulled back from leaning on the table. Nonie's question brought back the subject she had hoped to avoid. "I'm not dating Kenny!" She replied forcefully.

"Why not? He's crazy about you, and everybody knows it." Nonie snapped back with eyes wide open, a look of disbelief in her expression.

Sarah turned her head to the side, sighing before answering. In a softer tone, she continued. "It's not that I don't like him. I do like him, but I don't know exactly what it is. Maybe it's the idea that he and everyone else thinks I should feel privileged to have him like me or something. Besides, I don't want to ruin a good friendship with that whole dating thing."

"God, Sarah, I don't think there is a girl I know who wouldn't want to date him. He's drop-dead gorgeous, a good student, drives a great car, and his family is wealthy. So what's wrong with him?"

"That's part of the problem. Kenny is so used to getting everything he wants. I would eventually be just another girl he dated, and he would end up moving on to the next catch. I want to keep his friendship and leave it at that," Sarah finished, seemingly unaffected at the prospect of Kenny getting involved with someone else.

"Well, if I loved someone, I couldn't bear the thought of him being in the arms of another," Nonie replied, obviously confused at Sarah's explanation.

"I really don't love him that way. I sort of feel sorry for him in some small way because he's always gotten everything he wants without having to work very hard for it. Oh, I know he truly does care for me as best as he's capable of, but there should be a passion between two people who are in love. I don't feel it for Kenny, and to be honest, Kenny seems to have a passion in life for whatever he can't have, which isn't very much, and he mistakenly thinks that's love."

"You always were more mature than the rest of us Sarah, but I'm still having trouble understanding why any of that is a problem." Sarah remained silent. After thinking a moment, Nonie leaned on the table, and then brought her hand up resting her chin. "Well, I think you're being too hard on him, and besides, who else would you want to date?"

The question hit Sarah hard and it pierced her heart touching the secret flame she carried for Travis Hall. She drew a long, deep breath shutting her eyes briefly giving herself time to formulate an answer. Wetting her bottom lip she answered, "I really haven't given that much thought, but I suppose someday the right one will come along, and I'll know it right away."

Nonie twisted her head with that familiar questioning look across her face and then proceeded, "Well.... I for one am not willing to wait forever. Besides, the prom is just around the corner!"

Sarah suddenly laughed out loud at Nonie's anxious thinking releasing the tension she held at trying to explain her thinking without revealing her heart. Nonie grasped the silliness' in her comment and started laughing along with Sarah. Sometimes Nonie could read Sarah like a book, and sometimes she was far, far away from the truth. Interrupting their laughter, Bubbe returned to the chairman's booth with two bowls of her famous matzo-ball soup.

"So . . . tell me, girls, did you solve the world's biggest problems yet?" she asked in her Yiddish accent, smiling slightly and deepening the creases in her heavily lined face.

"If I could do that, Bubbe, I don't think I'd be working here!" Nonie answered as all three of them laughed in unison.

"I can't help you with that, girls, but I can keep you healthy. Sarah, stay a little longer and nosh a little. You need more flesh on your hips to make healthy babies someday. Besides, any problem seems smaller after soup. Eat, nosh, girls, nosh a little!"

By 5:30, business was starting to pick up, and Nonie and Sarah had happily finished their soup. Sarah thanked Mrs. Gorman again for her hospitality and hugged her and Nonie goodbye.

The quiet moments by herself always brought her thoughts back to the one man she could never hope to know or have, and Sarah wondered how Travis Hall was spending his weekend. She found herself lifted to a place of sweet joy, contemplating his longed-for touch, regardless that thinking such things was scandalous. There was no past and there would be no future with him, yet that couldn't prevent her from visualizing his face. Her desire was improper on many levels, yet Sarah could find her passion nowhere else.

~~~~~~~~~~~

Robert Baxter put his feet back up on the coffee table in front of the TV set at his apartment. "I guess that was another less-than-stellar performance by the Jets again this season. Now there's no chance of a place in the playoffs," he said, reaching for his open bottle of beer.

Travis hadn't had a lot to say during the game with the Houston Oilers. With a staid expression, he responded to Bob's disappointment, "You've put your money on the wrong team again, my friend!"

"Well, at least I'm consistent," Bob sarcastically shot back, half-poking fun at himself. He placed his beer on the table. "Something's on your mind today, because you sure haven't been interested in the game. Do you want to talk about it? And don't give me that BS about it being a boring game and the Jets losing. There is only one team you ever gave a damn about, and the New York Jets aren't that team. Something else is floating around in that mind of yours."

Travis took a few gulps of his beer and shrugged. "Nothing I'd care to talk about," he answered with a look of indifference.

Bob took one glance at the faraway look in Travis's eye and continued, "You're not planning another trip back up to the Point, are you? The last trip up there put you in a sour mood the rest of the month. I don't know why you torture yourself by reliving the accident over and over again. That's over three years now since the accident, and it's high time you put it to bed and forget about that place."

"No, I'm not planning on another trip back upstate, and for your information, I don't go back up there to relive the accident."

"Well, why do you go then? I know the scenery attracts a lot of tourists, but what the hell other reason is there for you to put yourself back at the scene so often?" Bob questioned as he got up and flipped through the channels on the TV. "Look, Travis, you had
~~~~~~~~~~~

an unbeatable run and proved everything you needed to about yourself finishing at the top, but you need to move on and forget about that place and the military career. Besides, you'd get tired of having all those enlisted men saluting you all day long, kissing your sorry ass!"

Travis's parted lips formed a straight line showing teeth. With a tightened jaw he provided more information than he was normally willing to share. "You're right; I left a big part of myself there and still haven't found a new direction to go yet, or at least something that I'm willing to expend the same amount of drive and energy on. West Point is the one place I go that puts all the pieces of myself together and makes me feel whole again, but I'm not pining over it, and that's not what's on my mind."

Bob changed the channel one more time, checking the scores of another team. "Listen, you're the smartest, toughest son of a bitch I know, and you could pretty much write your own ticket anywhere; so why you're teaching high school is still a mystery to me with the offers you've already had—and with your math background."

"Teaching is a comfortable place for me to be right now in the interim, until I decide what's next."

"If it's not the military career or the accident, then something else has been distracting you lately. Whatever happened to ninety-proof whiskeys and hundred-proof women you could never get enough of? I'm not sure I like your new mood."

Travis was slow to respond. "Have you ever noticed that too many women wear their skirts too short and the religious ones talk too much?" He leaned back into the cushions of the deep-set couch, looking straight ahead into empty space.

"None of that ever concerned you before. That is, of course, until that baby doll showed up in your class."

Travis turned his head slightly in Bob's direction peering out of the corner of his eye, lips pursed. "If you mean Sarah Thompson, you're missing the big picture."

"What picture are you talking about?"

"Sarah doesn't fall into either category. The others are all 'wannabes.' She's the real deal. You and I, we keep running and pushing, looking for something she's already found."

"What the hell are you talking about? She's seventeen years old, and you're on the downhill side of your twenties," Bob quickly tossed back.

Travis finally turned to face him directly. "I'm not talking about age. I'm talking about her way of knowing things, the way she looks at life, and what's important to her, the things she finds happiness in. She's got something bulls like you and I don't have, and the parade of 'pretties' we keep running after are all missing it."

"Yeah, you mean like another year and a half to go before she finishes high school, don't ya?" Bob expelled a puff of air threw his lips turning his head.

"If I took the next ten years, I couldn't conger up what she has."

"What are you talking about?" Bob asked, totally perplexed.

"I can't put my finger on it exactly, but she's the only girl I've ever known who can immerse herself in the miracle of a flower, the color of the sky, or just the sounds around her like the rain, as if there is some awesome beauty in all of it that the rest of us have no knowledge of. Call it happiness born of some inner goodness or even peace, but whatever the hell you want to call it, Sarah Thompson has it, and I want it."

Bob just shook his head, throwing his hand up waving at the air. "That's not what she has that you want, and if you think it is, you're deluding yourself with your own propaganda in the hopes of making it acceptable to your conscience." He halfway laughed at Travis, wondering who he was trying to convince.

Travis slowly turned his head to face Bob with lips curved into a restrained smile. The intense eye contact, along with the well-concealed smile, told Bob that he wasn't all wrong.

Bob reached for his pack of cigarettes and lit one. "I'll give you one damned thing. You always did shop at the top of the beauty meter when it came to women; but although this one may be a Grace Kelly look-a-like and right up there, she sure is off-limits, so I suggest you drop the whole thing and get back to reality. You of all people know you don't buy anything at the company store. The little details like age difference and position ought to be floating around in that brain of yours somewhere! Besides, what in the hell could you possibly have in common with a girl that age?"

"First of all, I didn't say anything about wanting to date her, and secondly, you're not hearing what I'm saying. She's not like the others, and it's not just the fact that she's beautiful to look at. She's the same outside as she is inside—no pretense, honest, and genuine. She's not out to impress anyone, and she can admit to her failures freely. Sarah is beautiful inside and out. She's the real thing."

"Who do you think you're kidding, Travis? This is your old friend Baxter you're talking to. Since when have you been interested in the real thing, whatever the hell that is?" Bob took another drag of his cigarette and expelled a long puff of smoke from his lips.

"I never knew the real thing before, but I'm telling you, this girl is unique, mature, and has a different perspective on life. She's smart in ways you don't test for."

"I thought you said she's close to failing your class?"

"She's got some kind of mental block about math and doesn't relate to the subject, but if you ever read anything she wrote, it'll make you feel something you never felt before."

"Stop right there, partner! That young lady is already making you feel things you have no business feeling."

Travis cocked his head back up, raising one eyebrow but remaining silent.

"Tell me something, just for the record, what the hell ever happened between you and Tracy?"

"She *wasn't* vested in a meaningful relationship," Travis responded tersely with a twisted smirk.

"What are you talking about? You told me yourself that Tracy was crazy about you back then. Besides, when were you ever interested in a meaningful relationship?"

"Tracy was crazy all right . . . but not about me. She loved the uniform and the rank, along with the notoriety it brought her. When the shit hit the fan and the uniform came off, she headed for the hills."

Bob ran his fingers through his straw-like hair, stunned into a momentary silence, reflecting on the wound Tracy must have inflicted on his friend. *That was then,* he thought to himself, but his friend might be getting ready to walk through a landmine now. "Okay, but what was wrong with the host of others, like that good-looking brunette, Pamela at ASU, and all the others standing in line behind her? You can't tell me that they were all crazy as well."

Travis took his time to answer, gulping down the last of his beer. Turning his head slowly in Bob's direction a second time, he answered deliberately, "I never liked an easy ride!"

Bob rolled his head back, resigning himself to the impenetrable nature of his longtime friend, while still hoping he could get Travis to think about someone other than his student. Although Travis never confided his heated interest in Sarah directly, Bob knew him well enough to read between the lines. It was the key to understanding and keeping their friendship. "I suggest you start playing on a broader playing field and leave the schoolhouse behind. What you really need is a good dose of reality, so how about the two of us head on over to the Long Beach Pub and find a real deal that's touchable."

"That's what I always like about you, Bob. You hear only half of what I tell you, and you're always ready for a good time! Yah just can't beat a friend like that!" Travis stood and grabbed his coat off the side chair. "Let's get out of here, unless that advice was just for me!"

CHAPTER FOURTEEN

Sarah arrived home from school and hung her coat in the front closet after setting her books down on the console. The weather was colder now, and the heavy stillness of nature's rest mirrored the silent brooding and heaviness in her heart. Travis Hall was never far from the forefront of her thoughts, and there seemed no escaping the longing he created in her. To have him come close to her or bring his eyes to rest on hers brought waves of palpitations to the point of fainting. He was the incessant flame that burned deep inside, feeding on all she assumed herself to be, swallowing whatever carefree happiness she had once carried before knowing him.

Thoughts of him were constant, and she could barely keep up with her daily responsibilities without the weight of him distracting her. Sarah was lost in a wilderness without a compass, hoping—no, praying for direction. She had nowhere to go and no one to ask for help. With each passing day, her love for him grew stronger, and she could not imagine what would be left of her at the completion of the school year.

To be next to Travis Hall filled her with the torment of desire, wanting to know his touch. The painful state she found herself in added a sense of guilt for desiring what was not to be tolerated or accepted. "Good girls" would never cross such a protocol, even if there were any suggestion of mutual agreement. To want him was bad enough, but even for a fully matured and responsible seventeen-year-old, the fact that she had eleven more months to go before she were eighteen made it unthinkable. Sarah knew full well the lawful punishment for fraternization with a minor, and she was familiar with many of those stories from her father's police work. The whole situation was impossible, and the longer it played out in her mind, the more painful it became to live with. She needed this course, but how could she ever survive it? Besides, she had another year to go before graduation, even if he felt the same way the day she turned 18; his position as an instructor and authority at her school, was another strict impediment. All of this was leading Sarah to a dead end, and she saw no way out of her torment.

Sarah made her way up the stairs to her parents' room, where her mother sat in a chair, reading a book. "Sarah, I didn't hear you come in," she said.

"How are you, Mom?" Sarah asked, still forlorn.

"I'm feeling much better today," Lily insisted.

Sarah went to her mother's side and kissed her cheek before sitting on the foot of the bed. "Where is Rachael?" she asked, just noticing her absence.

Lily put her book down in her lap and looked over her glasses at Sarah. "She's visiting with her friend Kitty today. They promised to have her home by six p.m. Did you forget?"

"I completely forgot about that," she replied, tapping her forehead with her hand.

Lily was always able to pick up on her daughter's thoughts and had a sixth sense when it came to reading body language. Something had been troubling Sarah for quite some time. Having these few moments alone together gave her the opening she needed. "Sarah, I couldn't help but notice that you haven't been yourself lately. Is there anything you would like to share with me?"

"No, everything is fine, Mom," she replied with a false promptness that Lily keyed into immediately.

"You know, I remember being your age, and if the truth were told, I had difficulty disguising myself from my mother when I was hurting also."

"Is it that obvious?" Sarah asked, raising her head while squeezing her hands together tightly as they lay in her lap.

"It's not difficult to see something is troubling you and that it has been for a long time now. It might help if you would like to talk about it."

"I'd rather not, Mom." She turned her head to the side, away from facing her mother.

"I see. I suppose this must be a bit more serious than I thought. Are you in any trouble, Sarah?" Lily removed her glasses from her head and folded them, laying them down on the table next to her chair.

"Oh no, it's nothing like that," Sarah countered instantly.

Lily took in Sarah's face and the way she was rubbing her arm. "Sarah, does this problem have a name?"

Sarah met her mother's eyes. "How did you know that?" she asked with a slight look of surprise on her face.

"I suppose it seems familiar to someone who's been there." Another long pause stretched between them as Lily waited, hoping Sarah would open up to her.

"All right, Sarah, let's not use any names. Just how big a problem is he?"

Sarah dropped her head as if gathering her thoughts, then slowly lifting it again she continued, "Have you ever loved someone who couldn't love you back?"

Lily thought a moment and contemplated the word "couldn't" in Sarah's question. Whoever Sarah felt something for was restricted from expressing the same sentiment toward her. Lily assumed it could not be one of Sarah's peers or classmates. She knew her daughter, and with her maturity, the young men her own age would not hold Sarah's interest. Either this man was married, or he held a position of authority in her school. "Before I answer you,

I need to ask you if you are sure this isn't just an infatuation or a crush."

"Glen Ford is an infatuation, Mom, and yes, you know I do know the difference."

Lily could see in her daughter's eyes the truth in what she said. "Does he feel the same way?"

Another long pause opened between them as Sarah's eyes began to glisten. "I'm not sure."

"All right then, Sarah. Love isn't always easy and can't always be explained. It can take your heart captive once in your life and never let go, or it can falter and fade, leaving only a memory. Sometimes it can live in one person's heart and not the other's. But I do know this—love is never wrong. So don't be too hard on yourself."

Sarah wiped a tear from her eye. "What if it hurts too much?"

"Real love doesn't always come wrapped in happiness and perfect packages, but if it is real, it will call you back to its light over and over again. The mystery of love is that it never returns back to you empty, and it sometimes returns in a way you least expect." Lily leaned forward in her chair and then continued. "Love is that little light that burns inside of you, and if you keep it close to your heart, it will bring you strength to go on to face another day; love will give you the hope you didn't know you had. The light can even make you happy when you're sad, recalling the quality in him that makes you love him." Sarah fashioned a small smile while lifting her head as she listened. "Whether his love is ever returned to you or not, Sarah, your love is a lifeboat you can enter when the waters of life become turbulent." Lily paused as Sarah wiped a tear from her cheek. "Right now, love has a face and a name for you, but something in him has allowed you to see a goodness that has called you to notice him. Even if your lives go in different directions, the gift he has given you to be able to see those wonderful attributes will live on in you, thanks to the love you bore for him." Lily drew a breath as Sarah bit her lower lip slightly.

"And what about the pain? How do you deal with that?" Sarah asked.

"Sarah, the pain does the greatest work in you, making you stronger in every way. I can't stop the pain you are in right now, but there is one thing I do know. Always keep that love in your heart, and I promise you it will carry you through no matter what life has in store for you; it will never be wasted. If you feed the flame, Sarah, it will keep you in its warm arms and help to ward off the darkness and the chill that life delivers to all of us at some time in our lives."

Sarah was not given to childishness, and of all her children, Sarah was the most level-headed, with wisdom well beyond her years. She never knew Sarah to take part in the childish pastimes of the majority at her age. Whoever this was Sarah was drawn to, he must be someone worthy of Sarah, or she would find no interest in him. That there was so little she could do for her daughter wounded Lily, and she hoped with time Sarah's pain would diminish. Lily was certain of one thing—Sarah was deeply in love.

CHAPTER FIFTEEN

"Good afternoon, Sarah," Travis acknowledged as he entered the classroom with measured stride. "Glad to see you were able to make help class this week," he said in a matter-of-fact tone, bringing his briefcase to the top of his desk in one fell swoop without breaking his gait. After removing his sport coat, he pulled paper and a pencil from his case. "It looks like it will be just the two of us again this week."

Sarah's eyes followed him as she sat at her desk with hands gripped tightly together in her lap. He stood confidently never missing a beat, riding the crest of the moment with ease. A small shock of his shiny, brown hair fell to his forehead as he removed a few sheets of paper from his case. He checked the clock on the wall and then slid another student desk adjacent to hers. Sarah jerked suddenly as his desk bumped hers and Travis sensed her tenseness.

Bringing his free hand to his head, he forced the errant strands back into place, running all five fingers back up through his shining hair. Sarah looked back up at him, her breath quickening as he stood above her.

Before sitting down, he loosened his tie, just as he had done so many times before. Looking back down at Sarah, he stopped short, pausing for a moment as she sat silently, her crystal blue eyes looking back anxiously into his. He quickly asked himself what it was about this girl that could draw his interest with such force by simply looking at her. Her sweet vulnerability played against her sophisticated carriage and communicating skill, creating an enigma he couldn't get a handle on. Gritting his teeth, he forced his renegade thought to the back of his mind, disciplining himself to the task at hand. "There's no better thing to do with your time, Sarah, than to strive for perfect grades," he told her as he concluded his lengthy stare and protracted pause.

Sarah took her eyes from his, instantly bristling as her lips pursed forming a look of mild decent.

"Apparently, you disagree with me," he said with a slight cock of his head as he pushed the desk snugly next to hers and slid into the seat. His closeness to her brought him the subtle awareness of her sweet, delicate fragrance, and it stirred him unexpectedly.

Sarah flipped her loose-leaf notebook open and answered him emphatically without looking back. "Yes, sir, I most certainly do disagree."

His appreciative gaze turned into one of question with a raise of a brow as he continued, "Really . . . and exactly what other things are more important to you than good grades at your age, Sarah?"

She kept her tightened expression as she pulled paper from her notebook, busying herself in an obvious attempt at avoiding facing him directly. "I don't think you really want to know, nor would you agree with me, Mr. Hall, if I told you," she said, moving her loose-leaf aside.

He sat back in his chair, surprised at Sarah's sudden burst of confidence with him and her strong reply. He hadn't anticipated that response, but then everything about this girl was unexpected to him. "Why don't you tell me what those other things are and let me decide if I think they're important or not?" he countered, still studying her in hopes of reading her thoughts.

Sarah lifted her head slowly and brought her eyes back to his. "And if I share them with you and you don't agree, that still won't make them any less important to me, so I guess it really doesn't matter," Sarah answered him, half-facing him with a turned head.

Once again, he was caught off-guard by her answer. She was suggesting that he probably cared very little about her thoughts, and that was the furthest thing from his mind. Raising his eyebrows slightly, with a twist of his head he continued. "You're probably right; my opinion really wouldn't matter," he confessed with a less-hardened expression. "But I'd still like to know what's important to you if you'd care to share." He leaned further back in his chair, totally taken with her beauty, and brought one hand up to support his chin, waiting patiently to hear what she would say.

Sarah looked down, considering, and then slowly raised her head again, turning her body to meet him face to face.

"All right, there are a thousand things I can think of that are as important to me, if not more so, than making perfect grades, starting with time spent with people I love or maybe offering a helping hand to someone who might be sick. It isn't just the good feeling that benevolence brings to my life, Mr. Hall; it's taking the time to find happiness in a million small ways also."

"Like what, Sarah?"

"Oh . . . I don't know exactly. It could be any number of things. Maybe standing on the beach in the morning and feeling the sea mist brush across my face, or that first walk in the rain in springtime when everything smells so sweet and new. Perhaps it could be just listening to the kids playing ball on a dusty field on a hot summer's night. Even reading a good book or just playing the piano. All of these things bring me happiness, and not one of them is less important to me than making 'perfect grades.' To me, my time is *well* spent on each of them."

She stared back at him with those bewitching, aqua blue eyes. He reveled in this moment, since she didn't often keep his gaze, and the contact pricked him with a feeling of deeper intimacy than he had been able to experience with her before.

Sarah continued, unafraid, "But, I suppose you, too, have other things that you like to do that make you happy, and I doubt very much that you would call them less important than academic perfection." She answered him with a certainty he found impressive.

He sat alongside her, contemplating her gentle yet sophisticated nature, feeling totally seduced by her crystal blue eyes set above her sculptured, high cheekbones. Her delicate, porcelain skin hinted a soft pink glow, begging his touch.

Sarah seemed to have roots reaching deep inside, as though she were connected to some invisible majesty he had no knowledge of. In some odd way, her words made him wonder if he had sacrificed the things that made him happiest with his driving need to finish ahead of the pack. He hadn't expected such a simple or sincere answer, or one dressed in a wisdom belying her virginal beauty. Travis Hall found himself spellbound by her and her way of seeing the world. No duplicity existed in her. Sarah viewed the world through the prism of her heart, and it matched her loveliness. She drew happiness from intangibles, while he sought accomplishment in the visible world. He worked hard and he played hard, driven by action, while she was moved by simple and subtle things, drawing from them a joy unknown to him. She saw beauty even where there was none, because she was beautiful—inside as well as out. Sarah brought the world into herself while he pushed against it, moving mountains to change it. She continued to surprise him with perceptions that inspired his interest and a sense of longing to touch and know the essence of her.

He wondered how she managed to avoid the shallowness most of her peers were generally caught up in. Sarah was the sole author of herself, drawing on an inner wisdom free from whatever storm surrounded her. When the rug had been suddenly pulled out from under him and his reward had been snatched from his hand, he found no place to land and knew nowhere else to go to derive the same happiness Sarah Thompson saw everywhere. He found leaving thoughts of her behind after their time spent together at school difficult, and moments like this one only heightened his intensifying interest. He wanted to know all he could about her but a line loomed between them he dare not cross.

But she was so unlike most women he dated who were often struck on themselves and overtly flirtatious or without sense.

Sarah wore a quiet intelligence unexpected for her age. The subtle feeling that she often knew far more than she let on excited him somehow. In unexpected moments the gossamer veil she wore, rose slightly, as if lifted by a gentle breeze, exposing tantalizing hints into her heart. Although he longed to part that veil, he could only contemplate her elusiveness with far more interest than any game of strategy he had ever engaged in. Tactically, he'd always loved the hunt; the prize was secondary. With Sarah, the prize became the lure and the hunting remained off-limits—like holding a tightly strung bow without any arrows.

The idea that she might find him unyielding and not accepting of her disturbed him. He exerted his will to dampen the driving urge to touch her and pull her tender body against his own. He could easily subjugate his thoughts and not allow them to interfere with his objectives, but the reoccurring impulse to want to know her intimately was becoming difficult for him to control. The stark contrast played in his mind of how women always made themselves readily available to him and he could easily take his pick. Yet, Sarah sat innocently beside him, never suspecting his heated interest or the irony that she would be the one he desired but was restrained from possessing.

Everything about her fueled his simmering passions. Sarah was strikingly beautiful, authentic, unspoiled, and unequivocally off-limits to him.

"Yes, I suppose I do have other interests that are important to me, but I'm afraid daydreaming about them won't allow me to enjoy them." He smiled at her, understanding the boundaries and responsibilities that had to be kept, and he finally asked Sarah to turn to page fifty in her textbook. His surety and control took center stage and Sarah obediently complied.

"Remember, Sarah, I want to see you write down every step when we work these equations," he instructed her, donning the teacher's mantle he had momentarily set aside while listening to her.

At the completion of their help-class session, Sarah walked the long corridors back to the front of the school on her way to her car.

She couldn't prevent herself from thinking about him, and she found herself wishing their roles were different somehow. It wounded her to think of him in the arms of another, particularly a more experienced woman familiar with the ways of love. If only he didn't look at her as though she were just another adolescent in his charge. She was wildly attracted to him physically, but there was so much more about him, which she contemplated on the ride back home.

There was the funny little half-smile that would cross his face quite unexpectedly. He could take her heart in an instant when she found herself avoiding his glance, and he would tilt his head down with one eyebrow raised slightly and then the corners of his lips would turn upward as if to say, "Come on, Sarah; I'm still here." In those moments, she was caught by him, a cage she couldn't resist entering. With few adjectives or words for dressings, his meaning was always clear and inescapable. His strength was intimidating but, at the same time, so compelling it drew her to him without resistance. The idea that everything in life could be brought to its common denominator was foreign to Sarah, who always saw life's intricacies and mysteries as multifaceted, making up a tapestry of many colors. His ability to distill every situation was often a shock to Sarah's sensibilities and compassionate heart. Something direct and tacit to his nature caused a sense of mild fear. A reason always existed why someone behaved badly, and she searched endlessly for those mysteries; Travis Hall dealt with the obvious in the present moment, with no inquiry to muddy up the waters. Hers was the way of burden and his way was free, unencumbered in dealing with whatever situation arose before him. In so many ways, she thirsted for the freedom and control he had mastered in his life. Ironically, being with him gave Sarah the strange feeling of being both captive and free simultaneously.

When they were alone together in help class, they appeared to be on opposite sides of a fulcrum. Together they were balanced, yet when she was alone, Sarah's life felt out of sync. He was teaching her the proving of numbers and solving of equations, but she was hearing something far more profound and liberating. If only she could tell him what she was really thinking.

CHAPTER SIXTEEN

Charley and Lily Thompson readied themselves to attend the North Shoreline High School Christmas Concert. "You look marvelous, Lily," Charley said as Lily helped to straighten his well-worn tie. She wore a deep-kelly-green suit with a crystal Christmas tree pin on her right shoulder. The red and white hues of the crystal stones reflected a splash of color across her face missing from her complexion of late.

"Thank you, Charley, and what a dashing escort I have!" Lily called to Sarah as she glanced at the time, "Where is Rachael?"

"We're in here, Mom—we're just finishing up the braids in Rachael's hair," Sarah called back to her mother.

"Would you like the red or the green bows tied on the ends, Rachael?" Sarah asked.

Rachael paused to think and couldn't make up her mind.

"How about we use one of each?"

"Oh yes, that would be perfect."

"There. You look very pretty," Sarah said as she surveyed Rachael's green and red plaid dress, white pinafore, and patent-leather pumps. "Maybe we should take your picture."

Lily entered the room and looked at the girls. "That's a splendid idea! Rachael, go ask Daddy to get his camera, and tell him we would all love to have our pictures taken by the Christmas tree."

"Okay, Mommy." Rachael ran back to her parents' room.

"You look beautiful, Mother," Sarah said.

"Thank you, Sarah. Now let's have a look at you."

Sarah stood up to face her mother, waiting for her verdict. She was wearing a simple, floor-length, empire, black sheath with capped sleeves and a mandarin collar. A small, circular opening, cut out beneath the standup collar in the front, offered a delicate suggestion of womanhood, revealing no cleavage, but exposing a small patch of the milky white, smooth skin at her chest. Cinched beneath her breasts, the sheath hung fluidly to her ankles. Her hair rested in a French knot high on her head with wisps of tendrils at the sides that looked as if they'd been dropped by a gentle breeze. Sarah's porcelain skin highlighted the blush of her cheeks, and the black thin-strapped sandals she wore kept the dress at just the right height above the floor. Sarah was the picture of refinement.

"You know, Sarah, I think pearl earrings would add just the right touch. Don't you agree?"

"Oh no, Mother, I couldn't possibly borrow yours. I know how special they are to you."

"Don't be silly, dear. What do you think they are for if not to use them?" Lily went to her room and returned with her pearl earrings that had been her mother's. She placed them in Sarah's hands gently cupping her hands around Sarah's. "Go ahead Sarah, put them on."

"Thank you so much, Mom." Sarah turned to her mirror adjusting the earrings as she put them on.

"That's exactly what was needed!" Lily said approvingly. "Let's have your dad take a look at you to see what he thinks."

Charley met them in the hall and immediately came to a stand still at the sight of his daughter. "My God, Sarah, when did you get to be such a beautiful young woman?"

Sarah gave her father a hug and whispered in his ear a gentle thank-you, adding, "You know I'll always be your girl, Dad."

Charley cleared his throat, hiding his pride and love behind his crusty façade. "Well, let's not stand here gawking at each other. Better get these pictures before it's time to leave."

Charley was proud of all his children. He'd had difficulty in switching gears from work, where he dealt with the criminal elements and lower echelons of society, back to his home with the sweet, innocent young daughters who were untouched by crime and the cruder side of life. A dichotomy of two different worlds, and he did his best to make those daily transitions the only way he knew how, often falling short of the right words when needed.

Once the photos were taken, Charley did his best to corral the girls and head to the car. The ten-minute drive heightened their Christmas spirits as they took in the festive decorations and lights that adorned the homes along the way. Rachael delighted in the grand and spectacular displays with every home they passed, and her bright blue eyes widened at every turn.

As the car approached the school, the parking lot was filling quickly. Charley dropped his family at the front entrance to the auditorium and went to park the car.

The early evening air was colder than normal and Lily coughed, holding her scarf over her nose and mouth until they arrived in the lobby. The Thompson girls joined the already-growing crowd at the entrance hall in front of the theater. Many of the parents were gathered in small groups interspersed around the grand vestibule, visiting with friends and neighbors while taking advantage of the forty minutes before show time. Sarah took off her coat. Rachael took Sarah's hand in hers and smiled up at Sarah, expressing her joy at being included in the evening. "You will remember to be good, Rachael?" Sarah asked as they stood together, holding hands, letting Lily converse with friends.

"Oh yes, Sarah. I promise to be still, and I'll look for you in the choir."

"Good girl," Sarah said.

Charley made his way through the growing crowd of people and finally found his family. "It certainly looks like a larger crowd than last year's concert! The lobby is grand, Sarah, and I bet the new theater seating will be more comfortable than the old school's seats were."

"I think you can count on that, Dad. I see that Mr. and Mrs. Gorman have just arrived with Nonie. I better go say hi and then make my way back to the music room before they dim the lights. I hope you enjoy the concert." Sarah kissed her father and hugged Rachael, turning to make her way to the Gorman's.

Lily took hold of Charley's arm and brought him into the conversation. Once Charley became engaged with their neighbors, Lily turned to look back for Sarah and skimmed the crowd. On the far side of the lobby, a tall, rather handsome young man with a shock of shiny brown hair falling forward at his forehead stood alone, leaning against the wall. He focused his attention intently toward a group of people at the entrance doors. Lily couldn't help but notice how attractive he was, and she wondered what held his interest, since his gaze seemed quite intense. Glancing in the direction of his stare, Lily was surprised to see Sarah standing near the door, visiting with Nonie and her parents. Sarah was the picture of loveliness and elegance, and Lily had to admit her daughter was arrestingly beautiful tonight and appeared to be a woman in her own right. Looking back at the attractive man at the side of the lobby, Lily's curiosity became heightened as she suspected he was staring at Sarah. He looked too mature and too well-dressed to be a student.

One of Sarah's classmates passed Lily's side. She called to the girl, "Carol, do you have a minute?"

"Hi, Mrs. Thompson, how are you?" the teen replied immediately.

"I'm doing well. Thanks for asking. I wonder if you might tell me who that gentleman is over on the far side of the lobby, leaning against the wall."

Carol leaned a little to her left and then rose up on her toes, trying to see over the crowd. "Oh . . . you must mean the dreaded Mr. Hall!"

"What do you mean 'dreaded,' and who is he exactly?"

"Mr. Hall is the new algebra-trig teacher this year, and he's very strict. He's a bit of an ogre! Most everyone who has him dreads his classes because he's so tough, and you can't get away with anything in his class!"

"I see!" Lily replied. "I suppose he demands performance and runs a tight ship, keeping to the rules?"

"Yes, that's it exactly, Mrs. Thompson," Carol replied.

"Perhaps he's so unpleasant that his wife decided not to join him this evening!" Lily jokingly added.

"Oh no—that's probably why he's not married!" Carol concluded with playful sarcasm. Lily was hoping for the answer to her unasked question without being direct, and Carol had obliged her perfectly.

"Thank you, Carol. Merry Christmas, dear, and send your parents our best wishes for the holidays."

Glancing back in his direction, Lily studied Mr. Hall more closely as he remained focused exclusively on Sarah. With her attention now heightened, Lily took in his open face and his broad, sweeping shoulders and chest. His long legs led up to a trim waist. Overall, he was an exceptionally handsome man who presented the appearance of self-confidence and vitality. He suddenly stood up straight as Sarah made her way toward him on her way to the choir room. Lily watched as he stopped Sarah several feet from him. He stood at least a half-foot or more taller than her. They stood facing one another for a moment, and Lily wished she knew what he was saying; Sarah appeared nervous as he spoke to her. Lily continued to watch them until Sarah turned to walk away from him. She took several steps and suddenly turned back to face him again, as if called by him a second time. Once again, he said something to Sarah, and Sarah wore a tentative and small smile beneath her lowered eyes, as though she were unsure of herself. Sarah nodded her head slightly before turning once more to leave him. He watched her as she walked away.

Lily regarded something about their interaction with one another as telling. She suspected Mr. Hall's interest in Sarah was more reminiscent of an attraction than a cordial friendship between teacher and student. Although subtle, Lily did not overlook his attentiveness to Sarah. Sarah's slight uncertainty around him might be due to his imposing and somewhat intimidating appearance, or, if Lily was correct in her interpretation, Sarah might have feelings for him and would be unsure of herself in his company. He certainly was strikingly handsome with his masculine features, including a well-defined, square jaw. Lily could see how his look of determination and strength might intimidate the students, but on the other hand, she could easily understand how Sarah might be attracted and drawn to him. She reminded herself that with Sarah's natural beauty and maturity, she could easily attract the attention of a man, even a teacher.

She and Charley had relied heavily on Sarah over the past few years, especially during Lily's confinement on bad days. They had been leaning hard on her, delegating responsibilities a girl Sarah's age would not normally have, including the daily care of Rachael, and it had tempered Sarah, giving her a level head. Even when her older sister Elizabeth had a problem to deal with, it was always Sarah to the rescue. Lily understood Sarah's uniqueness. She had the soul of a lion and the heart of a lamb. They always turned to Sarah when something needed attention, and she always proved responsible. An inner strength and virtue somehow mingled with a caring and tenderness, producing a perfect temperament not often found in a girl so young. Her sense of justice often moved her to action where others conveniently turned a blind eye. Sarah was able to organize everything from a closet to the annual school food drive for the homeless. Others might esteem those qualities in her as well; when combined with Sarah's pristine beauty, she did stand out from the crowd.

Sarah was a young woman, and she and Charley could not keep her tied forever to home with all the responsibilities running the household entailed, regardless of the needs they may have as a result of the burden Lily's health placed on all of them. She considered the fact that she had married Charley at the age of eighteen when he had returned home from the Pacific theatre in 1942. Charley was nearly eight years her senior. It wasn't a stretch to assume that Sarah would be attracted to someone older, just as she had been at that age.

Nevertheless, times were changing, and Sarah was still just seventeen years old and had another year of high school to complete, with more years of education ahead of her. Lily could not prevent others from admiring her daughter, though she knew Sarah well enough to know she would always stay between the lines of moral and ethical behavior. Sarah had her own exacting inner compass, a far superior guide than either Lily or Charley could have ever hoped to instill in her. Sarah was born with Charley's high standards and values in her soul!

Lily shelved her suspicions but was relieved to have a possible glimpse into Sarah's heart. In some strange way, a sense of approval filled her for the characteristics and traits in the man Sarah might be attracted to. If Mr. Hall was anything like Carol portrayed, he sounded too much like Charley. Lily smiled to herself as she turned back to the conversation with their neighbors and took Charley's arm, holding it tight once more.

The Thompsons made their way to their seats in the theater with a few minutes to spare before they dimmed the lights. Rachael's eyes were wide with anticipation as the orchestra began playing a medley of Christmas favorites. The new cushioned theater seats brought a smile to Charley's lips as Lily took his hand. With her family at her side, life was still good.

CHAPTER SEVENTEEN

JANUARY 1963

Christmas break was quickly drawing to a close and Sarah's sister Elizabeth would be leaving in the morning to return to college in Rhode Island. Reining in Elizabeth had always been difficult for Charley; her free-spirited ways were foreign to him. She was nineteen years old now, and although he did his best to give her the benefit of his experiences, Liz always cut her own path and dared to push against the lines of societal norms. Perhaps her artistic nature and her need to express her individual freedom were responsible, but many were the days Charley thought her temperament would have been better suited had she been born a boy. At least he might not worry about her daring to experiment with every new fad and trend if she were a son, obligated to a draft which always matured the most rebellious of the nation's youth. Elizabeth attacked life head-on and didn't mind shocking people with her clothes and appearance, despite the more conservative bent of her family. Her first few months away from home had added to her eccentricity, and Charley could only look on with concern and surprise as his eldest daughter continued to test boundaries, including the new bright red hair coloring, which added to his shock.

Liz and Sarah made their way down the stairs to the kitchen where Lily and Charley sat sharing a cup of coffee. The girls were laughing happily as they entered the kitchen together, clearly anxious to head out to be with friends this last Saturday night before classes started back up again on Monday.

"Where are you headed tonight, girls?" Charley asked.

"We're going to Rene Peterson's house, and then we might go for a pizza later," Liz offered as she kissed her mother goodbye.

"Well, don't stay out too late. You've got a long drive ahead of you tomorrow," Charley reminded her as he placed his coffee mug back down on the table.

"Don't worry, Dad. We'll be back by eleven," Sarah promised as she kissed her mother goodbye.

"Come on, Sarah," Elizabeth called out as she headed for the front door, grabbing her coat on the way out.

"Don't let her talk you into doing anything foolish."

"I won't, Dad." Sarah kissed Charley's cheek, whispering in his ear, "I love you." Sarah turned to catch up with her sister, yelling back to her parents as she made her way out the front door, "See you later tonight."

Charley shook his head. He would be wide awake until the girls were home safe in their beds.

"They're young women now, Charley, and you have to learn to let go," Lily reminded him.

"I'd be a lot happier if Elizabeth gave up on the art career and found a good husband to settle down with!"

Lily just laughed and reached out to pat his hand. "Come on, Charley, let's go put our feet up and watch *The Jackie Gleason Show*."

~~~~~~~~~~

Liz took the driver's side and Sarah slid into the passenger side of the old '56 Chevy Elizabeth now used as transportation to and from school. It had been the old family car for years, and although it wasn't the car that Liz would have wanted, it
~~~~~~~~~~

was at least better than no wheels at all. No one loved freedom and independence more than Elizabeth Thompson, and she was only too glad to acquire more of it, no matter what package it came in.

"Sarah, you really do have to brighten up your wardrobe and start stepping out with a bit more style!" Liz exclaimed as she started the car and headed to her girlfriend Rene's house on the other side of town.

"What's wrong with what I'm wearing?" Sarah asked.

"Nothing much, if you like looking ordinary with no way to separate yourself from the crowd."

Sarah glanced down at her nicely fitted pair of wheat jeans with a neatly tucked in, white button-down oxford, open at the neck. Over the oxford, she wore a pale pink V-neck sweater that gently hugged her frame without any bulkiness to hide the curves of her torso. A small pair of pale pink, faux pearl earrings accentuated the blush color in Sarah's porcelain skin. Her hair was swept back in a ponytail, tied with a strand of pink ribbon, personifying a sense of feminine virtue. With her polished, burgundy penny loafers and neatly pressed seams of her jeans, Sarah held the same refined, tailored look she always presented. She threw her hands in the air with a quirky smile, one eyebrow raised as if she thought Liz's suggestion was comical.

"I guess all of us weren't blessed with your sense of color and style, Liz, and this will have to do for tonight," She playfully answered with a touch sarcasm. Sarah wasn't troubled in the least by her own appearance as she eyed what Elizabeth was wearing. Liz's bold and outlandish outfit contrasted Sarah's much preferred conservative guise. Her black toreador-styled pants and knit sweater were covered halfway over with a large, triangular orange-and-red-print scarf. It draped over one shoulder and was cinched tightly at the waist with a wide, patented-leather belt. Liz made a bold fashion statement that even Audrey Hepburn would have been proud of. Her black, flat Capizio shoes were still the rage, and Elizabeth swore they were the best to dance in. With her newly colored bright red, shorter hair, Liz would definitely stand out in a crowd.

Rene Peterson always had difficulty being on time, and she was still dressing when the girls arrived at her home.

"Hello girls, come on in. What have you done to your hair, Elizabeth?" Mrs. Peterson asked with a shocked look on her face.

"Isn't it wonderful, Mrs. Peterson? I thought I'd give Ann Margaret some East-Coast competition!"

"Well, you've certainly accomplished that!" Turning toward the stairs, Mrs. Peterson called out, "The girls are here, Rene."

"Come on up. Maybe you two can help me decide what to wear tonight," Rene yelled back.

Liz and Sarah climbed the stairs to Rene's bedroom. Rene Peterson was a long-time friend of Elizabeth's, and all three girls had practically grown up together. She and Liz were in the same graduating class at North Shoreline High, two years ahead of Sarah. Rene was a business major and she shared Liz's need to be daring. She found Elizabeth's ability to go against the flow just the influence necessary to give her the courage to do the same. Sarah was always there to pull Rene back to the center when Liz tugged too hard.

With her shiny auburn hair and speckled greenish-brown eyes, Rene was an attractive girl. She was of average height and carried a little extra weight through her hips, emphasizing her slender waist. Her perfectly coiffed hair was cut shorter in the rear and then lengthened down the sides to just below the jaw line at the front, helping to keep her well-groomed appearance. The only detraction from her otherwise pleasant look was the thick lenses of her glasses, which she did her best to avoid wearing whenever possible. Unfortunately for Rene, she could see very little without them.

Once in Rene's room, all three girls examined the various articles of clothing spread out across her bed. Liz wasted no time discarding any item that might have a hint of conservatism to it and grabbed a paisley-print blouse with a long sash around the neck. The deep chocolate and umber colors of the blouse would highlight Rene's shining hair, and Sarah was quick to pair it with the khaki pants lying across her bed. Turning to Rene's jewelry box, Liz pulled out a pair of large gold hoop earrings, and the matter of what to wear was settled within minutes.

"I found out Tim Burns and Eddie Johnson are going to be at the Red Windmill tonight," Rene mentioned as she began dressing.

"No kidding!" Elizabeth replied with a sense of excitement. "I haven't seen Eddie in six months. Is he still going to NYU?"

"I don't know, but I hear Tim is as cute as ever and is still working at his father's construction company. What do you say we head over there for a pizza and beer?"

"Sounds good to me, but we don't want to be too early. What do you think, Sarah?"

"I'm just along for the ride. Besides, this is your last night at home, and I'll be here in the same old town for a long time to come. So your choice is fine with me. It will take us a few extra minutes to drive over to Huntington, and we better factor in the extra time to make sure we're home before eleven."

"That makes sense to me. It's already going on eight. Let's head up there now so we don't miss seeing Tim and Eddie," Rene added anxiously.

The parking lot at the Red Windmill Pizzeria in Huntington was almost full, and the girls agreed it was a good thing they had left when they did or they might not have been able to get a table. Once inside, the casual atmosphere afforded self-seating, with carryout available at the bar, as well as bar-side pizza service when the limited booths and tables were full. A postage-stamp-sized wooden dance floor occupied the back end, where many of the patrons gathered as the jukebox played the latest songs on the daily hit parade. Wine and beer were available, and tonight the Red Windmill attracted a diverse crowd, including several families with children, a few locals sitting at the bar, and plenty of young people who kept the jukebox busy most of the time. A half-wall with modest latticework on top separated the front room from the rear with open passages on either side, while the bar straddled both rooms to one side. Booths occupied the perimeter of each of the rooms, and a few scattered tables and chairs filled in the remaining space to accommodate larger crowds. The jukebox took up part of the passageway between the front and back rooms on the opposite wall from the bar. The red and white checkered tablecloths, as well as the scent of garlic lingering in the air, were inviting after a long holiday season of turkey and ham leftovers that, right about now, had the same appeal as a plate of spinach to a four-year-old.

Sarah spotted a newly vacated booth in the front room next to a window where a waitress was busy clearing the table. The three girls made their way to the booth and hung their jackets on the coat hooks attached to the side of the booth.

"Help me look and see if Eddie and Tim are here," Rene suggested as they slid into their booth. Even with her glasses on, Rene always seemed to be straining to see clearly what most folks took for granted. The same waitress approached their table again and asked what they wanted to drink. Liz ordered a beer on tap, and Rene followed suit. Sarah ordered a coke and scanned the room briefly, looking for their friends.

"I don't see them, but it is pretty crowded, and the back room looks full also. I'll go check it out," Liz said. "Let's order half the pizza with pineapple and sausage."

"Okay, Liz. We got you covered," Rene agreed immediately.

Elizabeth slid out of the booth and made her way to the other side of the restaurant as Sarah and Rene waited for their drinks to arrive so they could order their pizza.

"You know, Sarah, you ought to wear your hair down more often. It looks rather plain pulled back all the time," Rene commented as they waited for Liz to return.

"What is this, pick-on-Sarah night?" After her sister's comment on her clothes earlier and now Rene's critique of her hair, Sarah couldn't help but ask feeling annoyed.

"Oh, no, I only meant that your hair is so beautiful, you should show it off more often," Rene said half-apologetically.

"Okay, okay, I hear you." At her suggestion, Sarah reached back and pulled the ribbon and binder from her hair and shook her head from side to side, letting her hair fall free. Threading the ribbon under her shirt collar and then tying it in a bow beneath the collar, she looked back at Rene. "How is that?"

"Perfect—you look great," Rene happily replied.

~~~~~~~~~~

Robert Baxter stood at the end of the bar taking a long drag of his cigarette. Travis Hall stood at his side with eyes fixed straight ahead. "What are the odds that, of all your students, sweet Sarah Thompson would show up at the same joint you decided to drag our sorry asses to tonight?" Robert Baxter asked with a bit of skeptical amazement in his voice.

"Is that a question, or do you think I had advance notice?"

"You've done crazier things!" Bob shot back as they continued to watch the trio of girls from the back room. "Who are the other two girls with her?"

"Now I'm supposed to know all her friends as well? I guess you think I'm clairvoyant, too."

"I don't recognize them and don't think they're students at North Shoreline High. Besides, they look older than Sarah, don't you think?" Bob took another long drag of his cigarette, waiting for Travis to reply.

He didn't answer immediately but remained focused, his eyes on Sarah as she pulled her hair down. She was stunning, and seeing her wearing jeans with her hair now down, in a setting other than school, was more than alluring to him. A budding tug across his jeans reinforced her tantalizing and compelling appeal. "I have no idea who they are, but they can't hold a candle to Sarah," Travis finally responded.
~~~~~~~~~~

"Oh . . . now the truth comes out, and you're finally admitting she's more than a bit of eye candy to you!" Bob exclaimed.

"What's that suppose to mean, Baxter?" Travis turned his head and gave Bob an intense look that demanded a response.

"Hell, Travis, you've been struck on that girl from the first day of class. I don't blame you. I can't think of a guy who wouldn't give a week's wages to be with a gal as good-looking as she is, so why won't you just admit it?" When he received no immediate response, Bob continued, "She's really gotten to you, hasn't she?" Travis's silence told Bob what he already suspected. "You better watch yourself, buddy. Like I told you at the start of the school year, she could be trouble." Bob lifted his draft to his lips and wet his palette, watching Liz as she headed back to the table, returning from the back room.

Travis kept his attention on Sarah, making no attempt to move, but finally responded to his friend's suspicions. Under his breath, he replied, "You don't know the half of it."

~~~~~~~~~~

Sarah and Rene had already ordered their pizza when Liz finally returned to the booth. "You were right, Rene. Tim and Eddie are here."

"No kidding? Are they alone?" Rene asked excitedly.

"Yah . . . I think Eddie is picking out a few songs on the jukebox," Liz added.

"Here they come now," Sarah said as the two young men approached their table.

"Hey, Rene, how in the heck are you?" Tim Burns asked. His five foot eight inch frame was shorter than average, but his muscular arms and shoulders detracted from that fact. A result of his physical labor in the construction trade, Sarah thought.

"I'm doing great, Tim. It's good to see you guys again."

"Hi, Sarah. How's school going?"

"Just the same as always."
~~~~~~~~~~

Tim turned to Rene. "Would you like to dance, Rene?"

"Sure I would—just like old times." Rene slipped out of the booth and followed Tim across the room back to the rear dance floor, and Eddie held his hand out to Liz.

"Come on. We can't let the two of them hog the floor."

Liz nodded and then turned to Sarah as she exited the booth. "Go ahead and eat without us if the pizza comes before we get back."

Eddie took Liz's hand and then looked back at Sarah. "Hey, Sarah, would you go pick out the next three songs on the jukebox for us?"

"Okay, I'll do that," Sarah agreed as Eddie and Liz negotiated their way through the tables on their way to the dance floor.

Sarah reached into her purse for loose change, and then headed to the jukebox. She leaned forward slightly over the well-lighted display, her lengthy hair framing her face as she read the titles. Taking her time in choosing, Sarah finally made her selections and placed the correct change into the box. She pressed the appropriate letters and numbers for the Four Seasons' latest hit "Sherry," "Twist and Shout" by the Isley Brothers, and for her sister, whom she knew would appreciate a slow dance, "I Can't Stop Loving You" by Ray Charles.

As she finished making her selections, a young man approached her from behind. "What do you say you and I kick the dust around the floor, sugar?"

Sarah glanced at him briefly, struck by his presumptive and crass introduction. His slicked-back, DA-styled dark hair, thin pointed nose, and tight-fitting T-shirt with a pack of cigarettes rolled up in his sleeve blared his wishful tough-guy persona. "Thanks, but no thanks," she said as she attempted to walk past him.

The unkempt and greasy looking youth took her arm. "Come on, you didn't pick out that music for nothing!"

He caught Sarah by surprise, and a sudden sense of unease closed in as his hand gripped her arm. "Thanks for the offer, but I'd rather sit this one out," Sarah said more forcefully, hoping he would release her. Sarah pulled her arm, but he continued to tighten his hold.

"That's still not the right answer," he said with a threatening attitude.

Coming from behind her, the next voice Sarah heard was Travis Hall's. "I believe the young lady said she doesn't want to dance, so I suggest you find another dancing partner."

With a surprised look on his otherwise brazen face, the pushy young man released Sarah's arm and turned to face a much taller Travis Hall. "Yeah, well who the hell are you?"

Without flinching, Travis answered, "I'm a very close friend who's known to get very disagreeable with those who can't accept 'No' for an answer."

The James Dean–imitator reflected a brief moment as he sized Travis up.

Travis continued, "I'd hate to have to be formally introduced after the fact."

"Yeah . . . introduced after what fact?" the young aggressor asked with a heated attitude.

"That would be the fact that you are about to be served up like butter on toast if you don't bug off," Travis calmly stated, as he stood with legs parted, feet slightly offset, arms by his sides, fists held loose, restraining himself from action but ready to move any direction.

The swagger and bravado of the young man immediately gave way to a more temperate posture after assessing the situation, noting the intensity in Travis's eyes, as well as his formidable stance. "Listen, I didn't see you come in with her and didn't know you had a vested interest. Yah can't blame a guy for trying!" he said with both hands slightly raised, palms showing as he slowly backed away.

Sarah was still holding her arm, leaning back against the jukebox in a state of disbelief at what had just occurred. To see Travis Hall standing there—defending her—was more of a shock than being confronted and grabbed by the stranger. She stood frozen, unable to remove her eyes from his face.

"Are you all right, Sarah?"

His sudden appearance stunned her and she remained tongue-tied. Travis took her arm and asked her a second time if she was all right.

His gentle touch sent a shock wave through Sarah's body, and she answered immediately, as if charged by a bolt of lightning. "Yes . . . yes, I think so," she stammered, trying to regain her composure.

"Let's get you back to your table," he said, letting go of her arm and then accompanying her back to her table. Sarah slid into the booth, taking note of his more casual clothing, which was so different from the sport jackets and suits he normally wore at school. His relaxed attire included a pair of blue jeans and a casual, cotton-knit sport shirt open at the neck, revealing a few stray hairs at his chest. The shorter sleeves tugged around the bulge of his biceps, and the knit fabric clung to the sculpted muscles of his broad chest, accentuating the look of power he always presented to her. She shook inside at seeing him out of the role she was so accustomed to seeing him play.

He stood at the side of her table, looking down at her for a moment before speaking. "You should be more cautious, Sarah, especially when you're out in the evening."

"I try to be most of the time," she said.

"Do you know that idiot?" he asked with a stern look on his face.

"No, I've never seen him before."

"Do you come to this place often?"

She felt the weight of his authority but was uneasy with his line of questioning, wanting to be out from under his examination. "We visit this place once in a while," she said and then wanted to temper and clarify her answer in order to deflect the direction his line of questioning was leaning. "Tonight is my sister's last night home before she has to return to college, and her friends were going to be here."

"I see," he said as he stood staring down at her. He drew in a breath and took on a calmer tone. "May I sit down?"

Sarah nodded extending her hand and then added, "Excuse me for not offering."

Travis sat down opposite Sarah and gave an exasperated huff. His restraint was on full display showing a creased forehead and tightly clamped lips. "Maybe you should consider staying closer to home, especially at night, if you don't have an escort."

His attempt at parental advice struck Sarah as totally misplaced role-playing. He already held the authority of being her teacher, and the last thing she wanted from him was fatherly advice, especially because her secret thoughts of him were of a far more carnal nature. "Mr. Hall, I didn't come here by myself and I never would."

Travis scratched his head, and then approached the touchy subject differently. "Look, Sarah, your sister wasn't with you when that guy took hold of your arm, and I doubt seriously if she or any other female friend would have had much luck convincing that punk to put his attention somewhere else."

He was placing far too much significance on the incident than Sarah thought it deserved, and she was somewhat surprised at his strong reaction to her—as if he thought her behavior was at fault. That he still thought of her as a young girl in need of instruction and not yet old enough for any nighttime excursions with her friends wounded her. After all, she would be eighteen at her next birthday. "Are you suggesting I should take my father along with me wherever I go, Mr. Hall?"

Her question was direct. Travis didn't answer her immediately, but pulled his head back slightly, forming a deep furrow between his brows, appearing shocked at her response and question.

After a moments pause, Sarah brought the back of her hand to her lips, hiding a slight smile as she considered the absurdity in her suggestion and the situation in general. Travis caught her smile beneath her hand. His tightened expression suddenly softened, as he scanned her smiling face.

A slight surge of heat blushed Sarah's cheeks as he stared at her and she tilted her head down toward the table to free herself from his knowing eyes. The loosened strands of her hair fell across the right side of her face, and Sarah quickly pushed it back behind her ear. She looked back up at him once more and swallowed, managing to break their short silence. "Well . . . I should thank you for rescuing me from a dance I really didn't want to dance, but I think you may have given that fellow the wrong impression, Mr. Hall."

Ray Charles's recent hit, "I Can't Stop Loving You," was nearing completion in the background, and Travis stood to leave her table. Looking back down at her intently, he responded, "Did I?"

Sarah shook at his words, her lips parted slightly as she drew in a small breath. He stood, towering above her, their eyes locked in a timeless freeze. He drew in the corner of his lower lip and slowly moistened it, sliding his tongue from one side to the other. He was about to leave when Sarah summoned the courage to speak up again, "Mr. Hall . . . thank you for helping me out," she said unsure of herself, but especially of him. He never spoke many words, but to Sarah, his silence was always charged with meaning, despite her inability to correctly interpret it.

"Don't stray too far from your friends, Sarah. See you at school on Monday," he said and then walked back to the bar.

Liz and Rene passed by Travis as they returned to their table.

"My God, Sarah, who was that?" Liz quickly asked, not trying to hide her obvious approval.

"No one you know," Sarah quickly replied, her eyes following Travis as he returned to the bar.

Liz and Rene glanced at each other and then back at Sarah, both with slightly shocked and anticipatory looks. Liz continued, "Maybe I don't know him, but that doesn't mean I wouldn't like the chance to. So . . . do you know who he is or not?"

"You could say I know him too well!" she countered with sarcasm.

"What on earth are you talking about? Who the heck is that, and how do you know a good-looking man like him?"

Sarah shrugged slightly. "He's the new algebra-trig teacher at North Shoreline High School this year, and you might change your mind if you were in his class."

Rene's jaw suddenly dropped open. "You've got to be kidding me! Things sure have changed a lot since we went to that school," she exclaimed.

"Yeah, they've gotten a lot harder with enforcers like Mr. Hall," Sarah said facetiously.

"Who would have ever guessed a hunk like that would be a teacher! What a loss to the real world." Liz shook her head as she looked back in his direction.

The pizza finally arrived, and Sarah checked her watch. "We only have about twenty more minutes if we hope to make it home by eleven o'clock," she reminded them. Liz and Rene quickly grabbed a slice. Sarah slowly wiped her palms down the side of her jeans before reaching for her pizza.

~~~~~~~~~~~

Back at the bar, Robert Baxter shook his head as Travis walked up, flanking him. "Well, are you satisfied now that you cornered her?" Bob asked.

"You saw what was happening over there, and I didn't exactly corner her."

"Maybe not this time, but you better get a grip on this thing," Bob said, lighting another cigarette. "So, who are the girls with her?"

"I think the red head is her older sister, and the brunette, her sister's friend."

"Maybe her sister is available. At least she's of age."

Travis leered back at him. "Drop it, Bob. I'll handle my life and you handle yours. If I need your advice, I'll ask for it." Travis reached for his beer and glanced back at the Thompson girls and
~~~~~~~~~~~

their friend, wishing the situation could be different concerning Sarah.

"Maybe it's time to get the hell out of here," Bob suggested.

"Not until those girls get in their car and head home. I don't want that punk to get anywhere near Sarah again."

"Jesus, Travis, you're not going to be around the next time she has some sap fall all over her."

"Maybe not . . . but I'm here tonight," Travis said with steely-eyed conviction. He looked back at Sarah's table, and then gulped his beer. Sarah had managed to diffuse his lecture with humor. She wasn't a child, he thought, and she would only continue to attract attention she might not want. She had, after all, gotten his. How, he had to ask himself, could this girl bring him to an utter standstill in thought so swiftly with such ease and grace? She had the maturity of a woman twice her age but was without the experience, and yet how quickly a stalemate was again reached between them.

Bob glanced at Travis shaking his head slightly before raising his shoulders. Drawing a deep breath, he exhaled a long burst of air through pursed lips. Turning to the bartender again, he ordered another round for both of them, adding, "Jeeezzz, it's going to be a long night."

CHAPTER EIGHTEEN

Spring finally took its stage as the long winter's night took its bow, leaving behind the shorter and colder days of January, February, and March. April brought to life colorful daffodils and forsythias now dotting the driveways and yards along the roadways to North Shoreline High School. Tulip magnolias, redbud, and dogwood trees put forth their pastel colors with outstretched arms, along with crocuses and tulips displaying waves of magnificent color. The lilacs and honeysuckle would soon be in bloom, adding their heady scents as another layer of sensory delight to the season. The fresh newness of springtime glories pushed men's hearts to their fancies, and along with it came the renewal of attraction for all things loved. Final exams were overshadowed by proms as the student body buzzed with plans in preparation for the long-awaited events.

Sarah had successfully staved off a number of requests for the honor of her company at both proms by junior and senior classmen and would instead devote herself to her studies for finals as well as her part-time work at the local public library. Unlike her peers, she hadn't the faintest remorse at not attending the prom and would never consider sharing the staged event with anyone just to say she had attended. To Sarah, it would be considered a date and a "date" to the prom was always reserved for those who shared more than casual friendship, or at least hoped to. Once coupled together at the prom, the label would stick starting a feeding frenzy for Fran Johnson and friends. The distinction between a friend and a boyfriend was missed by many of her classmates. Chief among them was Kenny, who was quick to interpret affection for love, unable to nuance the difference. Besides, only one person in her life held such a special place, and a relationship with Travis Hall, sadly could never become a reality.

She had resigned herself to both facts and did her best to avoid thinking about either. Being near Travis Hall had become too difficult, and she had stopped attending his help-class sessions the last few weeks. She did her best to avoid him whenever possible. The very thought of him came with a sense of guilt for desiring him so desperately. As a consequence, her grade and understanding in algebra class was teetering on failure, but to fail was less painful to her than to risk being in his company any longer. The Regents exam was next week, and she would submit to it, suffering the consequences without any further contact or help from Mr. Hall outside of normal class time. Her job at the public library was a blessing, and exactly what she needed to distract her from constant thoughts of him. She looked forward to time spent there, and especially loved reading to the children on Saturday mornings during storybook hour.

Sarah's graceful decline of their invitations hadn't come as a surprise to any of her suitors, but it was a rejection Kenny didn't take lightly. The fact that she hadn't accepted any other offer didn't lighten the blow, and he would have to ask another classmate whose company he hadn't sought or particularly wanted. He couldn't come to terms with Sarah turning him down when any other girl at North Shoreline High would give anything for his attention. She held the whole package. Sarah was one of the few girls who could hold an intelligent conversation and never allowed her opinions to diminish another's point of view. No doubt she was drop-dread beautiful, but her refusal to date anyone else only added to Kenny's hope he would be the one to finally kindle her passions. He couldn't let her be the one who got away forever, and he couldn't bear the thought that someone else might have the honor of being her first love. Kenny wanted, no, needed that distinction for himself. Her refusal only served to strengthen his resolve. She remained the only thing Kenny wanted that Kenny couldn't get.

Second-period algebra class began at the bell, and Sarah did her best to keep from looking up at Mr. Hall, not wanting to draw his attention. While he was writing down several equations on the blackboard, Mark Stevens attempted to use his persuasive powers to enlist another young man into providing his last homework assignment to him. His request went unanswered before the bell, and Mark Stevens had refused to take "no" for an answer. After the start of class, Mark had quietly exited his seat and then bent over the adjacent desk, extending his hand in a gesture of demand. The honor student stood his ground, not responding to Mark.

Another student, seated in the rear of the class, laughed out loud, watching the scene play out, and his laughter brought Mr. Hall's quick attention. Turning in time, he caught Mark out of his seat.

"What are you doing, Mr. Stevens?"

"Nothing, I dropped my pencil and went to pick it up," Mark answered, unaffected by the question and still wearing a casual expression.

"Take your seat, Stevens," Mr. Hall firmly stated, watching him. Mark narrowed his eyes glaring steadily toward the honor student and slowly returned to his desk. Once Mr. Hall turned back to the board, Mark Stevens made one more attempt to coerce the student into handing over his homework assignment by stretching out his hand toward him, gesturing with his fingers. Still not persuaded, the youth chose to ignore Mark a second time, fueling Mark's anger. He stood up one more time to approach his chosen prey. Mr. Hall quickly took several long strides down the aisle, catching Mark between both desks, and stood in front of him, blocking his path.

"Now, tell me exactly what you think you are doing, Mr. Stevens."

Mark sarcastically replied, "I had a leg cramp and needed to stretch. So what's the big deal?" His brazen display of rebellion to Mr. Hall's authority shocked the class into utter silence.

"You seem to be under the misapprehension that this classroom is your playground. This is not a physical-education class, and you are not entitled to leave your seat at will. Do I make myself clear?" Mr. Hall maintained an immovable stance and unblinking eye contact, which would convince most anyone not to test him. The entire class sat motionless, aghast at the scene playing out in front of them, shocked that Mark would try to confront Mr. Hall—of all teachers.

A sudden flush washed Sarah's face as the tension escalated.

Mark Stevens was not like everyone else. With his chin held high and lips somewhat distorted, Mark suddenly shot back, "You can't tell me what to do!"

Maintaining a steely-eyed expression without flinching, Mr. Hall brought his finger to Mark's chest with a strong thrust. "Sit down, Mr. Stevens!" he said in a very slow, methodical voice, sending chills up Sarah's spine.

Mark fell back slightly with the force of Mr. Hall's deliberate motion, stumbling as he tried to maintain his stance. Once Mark regained his footing, he stood facing the teacher in a standoff until Mr. Hall took one more step toward him without saying another word. Mark finally caved and slowly slid back into his seat. The class gave a collective sigh of relief, while Sarah sat motionless, her heart racing.

Still standing, immovable, next to Mark's desk, Mr. Hall placed the knuckles of his right hand down on the desktop, keeping eye contact with him, and then spoke after a slight pause. "You have one month left in this class, Mr. Stevens, and unless you care to take another year to graduate, you'd best not even think about doing anything disruptive that would prevent that from happening, and I do mean *anything*. I suggest you choose your battles more wisely, or at the very least pick the ones you might have a chance at winning!" He stood over Mark's desk, tapping his knuckle on its surface twice, emphasizing his statement. A few more seconds passed as he maintained the piercing stare before he finally walked back to the blackboard. Mark did not leave his desk again, while Sarah and the rest of the students sat straighter in their chairs.

The tempo of her pulse increased steadily watching the display of wills and at Travis's ability to maintain control and respect in every situation. The entire student body knew Mark Stevens was a rebellious tough guy, and as time went on, he isolated himself from the other students, tracking a loner's path. Sarah wondered what had hardened Mark.

Sarah never had doubt in her mind about Travis's ability to handle whatever life threw at him. This latest display only solidified her opinion of him all the more.

Travis Hall was everything she was not. She worked at avoiding conflict and confrontation, and while he might not look for it, he faced trouble head-on when it presented itself to him. Everything about him pulled Sarah deeper into the place of love she held for him. The pain of having to be in his company without the hope of ever being able to share that love wounded her deeply. Her love for him was a one-way street fast approaching a dead end.

Toward the close of the class, the students were directed to hand their last homework assignments forward, and Sarah was anxious for the period to end. Mr. Hall made his way to the head of each row, collecting the papers, and when he arrived at the last row of desks, he looked back at Sarah and asked her to see him after class was over. Her heart sank, and she couldn't remove the knot in her stomach. She wished she were invisible, just as she had wished at the beginning of the school year, only this time for completely different reasons. She was no longer afraid to be near him, but now it was painful, precisely because it would be the closest she would ever come to him, with no hope of any future relationship—a relationship she desired with a passion she could barely contain. He was to Sarah what the flame was to the log, the source and substance of its burning.

At the sound of the bell, Sarah gathered her books and waited till the classroom emptied before making her way forward.

Travis walked around to the front of his desk and sat on the edge, watching Sarah as she approached the front of the room. She avoided meeting his eyes directly and strained to keep her emotional balance. She stopped a good distance from him. "Come on up here, Sarah, I'd like a word with you."

She held her books in her arms and came within six feet of him, then waited for him to speak.

"You haven't come to help class the past few weeks." His voice was tender, and expression questioning.

Sarah look down, nodding slightly by way of confirmation.

"Is there a reason why you haven't been there, Sarah?" he asked as he tilted his head down slightly to get a better look at her expression.

Sarah bit her lower lip and raised her head, bringing her eyes to his. "I . . . I haven't been able to come since I'm working part-time at the public library after school now." Equivocating slightly, she hadn't divulged the whole truth.

"Perhaps you could change your days around in order to attend this week since it will be the last class before the Regents exam. I think you need the extra help, Sarah.

She suddenly answered without checking her emotions, "It wouldn't make any difference, Mr. Hall. I won't pass it with or without your help."

He tilted his head with a quick jerk as his lips suddenly parted and then clamped tightly again before he spoke. "Sarah, that's just not true. You can do this," he said with all the sincerity he could muster. He watched her closely as she turned her eyes away from him again, closing them momentarily while shaking her head.

"No . . . you don't understand. I can't. I can't do this anymore." Sarah suddenly turned and walked away as fast as she could toward the door, never looking back. She wiped a tear from her cheek as she left.

He watched her, crushed inside as she quickly left him behind. He sat on the edge of his desk, feeling a deep, emotional cut. He was incapable of moving as he struggled to make sense of their situation. Sarah was the one who didn't understand. She had always taken him at his word and could never have guessed what he really thought of her. He had told her the truth that he wanted her success, but mostly, he wanted to be with her, even under the guise of helping her with algebra.

It suddenly hit him with the force of that downed tree that he had been right all along. Sarah *was* attracted to him as well, and she couldn't deal with her emotions. Like a fool, he insisted on playing with fire working with her one-on-one. Was he guilty of encouraging their futile attraction? Had his compelling need to be with her at any cost wound the one he loved the most, and what good was winning his mission if he lost the war? He had never wanted anyone the way he wanted Sarah Thompson.

To see her hurt sickened Travis, and he found himself in the awful and painful position of not being able to do a damn thing about it. He had known being with her was impossible from the beginning and this thing between them would end before it could ever start, yet he didn't want it to end, especially not like this.

~~~~~~~~~~

Sarah struggled the rest of the day, tormented with the knowledge that Travis Hall would never be a part of her life. To be so close to and yet so far from him was a cross she could no longer bear. Concentration was difficult as she moved through the evening hours by rote memory, finally retiring to bed, still tortured by their last meeting. She had done her best to put thoughts of him aside for most of the day, but as it happened nearly every night, Travis Hall invaded her consciousness, preventing sleep. The quiet stillness pulled Sarah within as she lay on her bed in the darkness, recalling their time spent together over the past eight months. He refused to give up on her, and Sarah sensed his motivation
~~~~~~~~~~

was more than his wanting her to pass. In moments when their eyes would suddenly lock, she felt as if he were whispering, "I know you and feel you, Sarah, without having to touch you, and you know me too." Deeper meaning lay behind every protracted glance; she sensed it intuitively.

He was strong and disciplined, but within his eyes, she saw in him the capacity to love powerfully. Sarah was convinced his love would never constitute a willowy empathy or sugary kindness dripping with sentimentality. Those things were no part of him. To be falsely kind because it was expected or to win favors was not his suit. His brand of love would keep deep company with his nature and would remain closed from public view. Sarah suspected if he were ever in love the passion would be real, encompassing all of him with no dressings to prop it up in appearance. Whatever battles he faced in his life had toughened him, teaching him to waste no time on infantile platitudes and superficial expressions of love unsustainable and weak in a storm. He was capable of a love that took no part-time prisoner. Love from him would be all or nothing, which reinforced the edge of fear she had felt from the beginning with him, even though she understood it differently now. To think he would feel anything but pity for her after she ran away in tears like a child unable to check her emotions was a useless fantasy.

His face and form drifted through her memory as Sarah lay there, longing to know his touch. The momentary thrill such visions conjured up was always fleeting, and the sweetest joy was invariably followed by the impossibility and wrongness of her deepest desire.

She was naïve to the ways of love and certainly knew how unsophisticated she must seem to him by comparison to women his age. How utterly ridiculous of her to assume she would even cross his mind in that regard! No, she was just another student to him and not a very astute one as far as algebra was concerned. She refused to allow him the notion that she was just another silly teen with a childish crush on a teacher. He had always remained professional, never crossed the student-teacher divide, never given voice to indicate he cared. Although, she had nearly convinced herself there were moments he was speaking of love between them without speaking the words. Only in her own thinking did she indulge in such a possibility.

Still, there were moments when his glance seemed more extended and his patience unending. He never gave up on her, even when she gave up on herself. She saw so much more in him than the others ever could. His strengths were her weaknesses. But what were his interests, his likes and dislikes, what made him happy, and especially, what did he find attractive in a woman? She longed to know the essence of his heart, and she lay there in the darkness, recalling one moment with him burned in her memory because it captured the emotion and feeling he could easily instill in her.

Toward the end of the fall football season, very late in the afternoon after a lengthy majorette practice session, she had needed to return to her locker to retrieve a forgotten paper and textbook. Still dressed in shorts and tennis shoes, she returned to the project area and laid her baton, notebook, and school clothing on a chair at the side of the now darkening and wide-open space. By that late hour of the day, the lights were already out, making it difficult for her to sort through the books and papers inside her locker. It took more than a few minutes to find what she needed and replace everything neatly. After searching and struggling, her hair was coming undone. She removed the binder from her hair, shaking her head back, hoping to recapture the wayward strands to secure them back in place.

In that moment, she sensed she was not alone. The feeling was so pervasive she turned abruptly to survey the quiet and empty space, only to see him there across the wide expanse in the deepening shadows. The shimmering strands of her lengthy hair cascaded back down across the right side of her face as she peered through the unkempt locks, hesitating to move. Leaning against the far wall with both arms folded across his well-defined chest, one knee bent with the sole of his foot pressed against the baseboard, Travis Hall stood silent and motionless. She was certain it was him, recognizing the silhouette of his tall and muscular body in the darkening shadows. No words were exchanged, but Sarah sensed he had been watching her the whole time. She stood perfectly still, facing him across the great expanse in the brooding shadows and stillness, breathless while her heart raced. The tension was agonizing, and she felt lost, not knowing if she should speak. He never said a word as Sarah grappled with indecision, unsure of herself and uncertain of him. It was the most paralyzing pause of her life.

Without thought or reason, she instinctively turned back to her locker, quickly finished binding her hair, then collected her books and left the project area with her heart still pounding in her chest. She hadn't looked back or dared to guess what he would have said or done if she had stayed. A wave of unease had crept over her as she suspected he had known exactly what she had been thinking. It was a mutual mental movement with no movement that kept repeating itself over and over again between them.

He never referred to that afternoon with her. Almost as if they both knew better than to speak the unspeakable, lest the roles they played become corrupt. Later, when she replayed the incident in her mind, she asked herself if the paralyzing fear was of him, or whether she was afraid to fully believe the strong sense that he too, felt the same compelling desire for her. No matter how many times she replayed the incident in her mind, she found no plausible explanation for his total silence, which had held her captive for those lengthy, unbroken moments.

Sarah fought back the enveloping emotions as she remembered that incident and struggled yet again to interpret its meaning. She reminded herself she might have misinterpreted moments like that one and they might be products of her wishful thinking—but that particular encounter haunted her nonetheless. Trying to express the inexpressible between them left her repeatedly without words. No matter his motives or thoughts, Travis Hall remained the love of Sarah's life.

CHAPTER NINETEEN

The Ferris-wheel lights reflected on the smooth surface of the bay, twinkling and dancing at the water's edge in the town of Glen Cove. The giant spokes of the carnival ride turned slowly over the midway, casting intermittent light toward the dock and small marina adjacent to the fairgrounds. It had been a perfect Saturday afternoon in early spring, teasing residents and city visitors alike with a taste of summer in the North Shore Long Island community.

The sun was setting on a relatively calm day with little wind as Travis Hall and Robert Baxter leaned against the weathered wooden railing of the marina's dock, taking in the sunset and array of boats now moored for the evening in the bay. Sailboats and skiffs gently bobbed up and down in the wakes of passing boats. Bob took a drag of the cigarette he held in one hand and, after exhaling a long puff of smoke, brought the cup of beer he held with his other hand to his lips.

Travis wore a pensive expression and had remained relatively quiet most of the afternoon. He drank down the last of the beer he had been nursing for the better part of an hour. "Let me have one of your cigarettes."

Bob stood up, turning his back to the water while leaning against the rail. "Since when did you take up the habit?"

"Since when did you decide to look out for my best interest? Give me a damn cigarette," Travis countered, a slight edge to his voice.

Bob tapped out a cigarette, leaned the pack toward Travis, and then handed him the lighter. "You've hardly had five words to say all afternoon. So, do you want to tell me what the hell is going on with you, or do you want me to guess?"

Travis lit the cigarette and took a long drag, still leaning on the rail silently facing the water.

Travis was not one to talk openly about himself. Although they had known each other for seven years, there was a line Bob could never cross unless Travis allowed it. He attempted, once more, to get Travis to open up. "Just in case you forgot, this was supposed to be a cut-loose weekend. We were going to have some fun, but so far, it feels like I'm keeping company with the walking dead!"

Three young women walked past them on their way to the end of the dock, drawing Bob's attention as he acknowledged them with a nod of his head. "There goes opportunity," he said wistfully, following the young ladies with his eyes. "Don't you even want to see what you're missing?" he asked, hoping to elicit a response.

"I know exactly what I'm missing, and that's not it."

"No, no, no. Don't tell me we are back to that again? I thought you understood that's a 'no brainer' and you have no business entertaining any thoughts about that girl. I've got to talk some sense into you before you make the one mistake you won't be able to recover from. Do I have to tell you again that one wrong-headed move with her could put you in jail and label you a pedophile for life—forget the fact that you wouldn't have a job. What is it with you anyway? For God's sake man, look around you and see what else is out there. Drop all thoughts of her before you do something foolish. She's seventeen, Travis! You can't have her and that's the end of the story."

Travis took the last drag of the cigarette and flipped it from between his fingers, propelling it out into the water away from the dock. Standing to face Bob, Travis answered, "You don't have the faintest idea what's right for me, and you sure as hell don't know anything about Sarah Thompson or what I might or might not do concerning her."

"For all you know, she probably hates your guts because you've established yourself as a hard-ass with the student body, and any one of them would like nothing better than to see you hung out to dry. Besides, you told me yourself she never says any more than she absolutely has to and never even offers you a smile."

Travis ignored that comment and started walking back toward the midway while Bob kept step, doing his best to quell Travis's interest in his student, an interest that went beyond the lines of ethical standing.

"For Christ's sake, Travis, her dad's a cop!"

They kept walking as they dodged the crowds of people, listening to the barkers soliciting patrons to test their luck for a prize and go home a winner. The smell of corndogs and cotton candy wafted in the early evening air. A shooting-gallery vendor caught their attention as he waved a Kewpie doll in the air, trying to entice them to try their hands and prowess.

Bob laughed loudly after taking one look at the blonde, blue-eyed baby doll being waved in front of them and couldn't resist the opening it afforded him with Travis. "You might as well try your luck winning this one, because that's as close as you'll ever get to the other baby doll."

Travis turned and took the bait. "Oh, really? Well, I guess I'll Quite Positively win this 'Q-P' doll, and Miss Sarah Thompson as well," he said with forcefulness and a steely-eyed look directed at Bob.

Bob chuckled at the play on the words and recognized Travis's focused determination.

Travis laid his money on the vendor's bench and picked up the air gun. Raising it to his shoulder, he took aim at the revolving ducks passing in front of them down the gallery. He squeezed the trigger ten times in rapid succession and brought all ten of the moving ducks to a downed position within seconds.

A small crowd had gathered around the shooting gallery, watching with interest as each of Travis's shots hit its mark decisively. Two young boys stood in awe of Travis's accuracy as they leaned against the boards, gawking with jaws wide open. "That's ten out of ten! How'd you do that, mister?" One of the boys asked with a shocked look of wonder in his eyes.

Travis looked down at the boy and answered in his usual style, using as few words as possible, "Practice and concentration!"

"Where did a city boy like you learn to shoot like that?" the vendor asked with a look of surprise on his heavily lined and unshaven face.

"Mister, I'm no city boy!" Travis replied with a slight huff.

"Wherever you're from, you can take your pick of any item off the top back row!"

"No, thanks; I'll take the Kewpie doll," Travis answered with a smirk on his face as he turned to look at Bob.

"Suit yourself," the vendor said as he handed Travis the blonde, blue-eyed Kewpie doll.

Bob just shook his head. When Travis Hall put his mind to something, there was no stopping him. Just as they turned to leave, a young girl and her female companion stepped forward from the onlooking crowd and approached Travis. She was wearing a tight-fitting pair of shorts and a provocative halter-top, snapping her chewing gum loudly.

"So, where are you from, mister?" she asked as she edged her way closer to him.

Travis eyed her from her feet up to her ruby red lips and teased-out hair, and politely replied, "I'm from a place where nice young ladies like you never talk to strangers, especially at a carnival."

The girl was duly chastened, and her face turned a bright shade of pink as she abruptly turned to walk away, her female companion in close tow.

"Now why did you have to go and do that?" Bob asked. "They might have been two perfectly nice young ladies to pass some idle time with!"

Travis glanced back at Bob with a look of total disbelief on his face. "Are you kidding me? Aren't you the one lecturing me about robbing the cradle?"

"Hell yes, I am, but those girls aren't your students, and they might be eighteen," Bob suggested with an air of redemption.

Travis jerked his head in disgust. "Baxter, you've got to stop lecturing me when the rules don't apply to you. You're using some kind of twisted standards. You need to get real and stop looking for a good time in all the wrong places."

"Listen, Travis, there was a time not so long ago when we both had the same standards, before little Miss Kewpie Doll showed up."

Travis kept walking down the midway, creating a short period of silence until Bob spoke up again. "How about I buy you and Miss Kewpie here another beer, although you do know she's not old enough to drink yet?"

Travis shot a look of disgust at Bob out of the corner of his eye as they returned to the beer stand, each holding their positions in the discussion without wavering.

They made the rounds that Saturday night, finding common ground in their drinking, one to ease the pain of his unrequited love and the other to assuage his defeat in influencing his friend. By 1:00 a.m., both were sufficiently numbed to their respective concerns, and Bob dropped Travis off at his Huntington apartment. Still holding the Kewpie doll, Travis pulled himself up out of the car and fumbled for his keys.

Bob gave one more try at changing his friend's thinking. "Travis, I'd hate to think you'd give it all up for the kiss of death. She's going to grow up one day and probably change. At least the one you're holding will always be a sweet baby doll, ready for bed whenever you are!"

Travis kept a straight face as he said good night, adding before he shut the car door, "Thanks for the beer, but you can keep the free advice."

Bob shouted back as the door began to close, "See you back at the puppy mill on Monday!"

Travis unlocked the apartment door and pushed it open. Heading straight to the bedroom without turning on the lights, he threw the Kewpie doll on the bed, and stripped down to his boxers and sleeveless T-shirt, exposing his muscular arms. Once undressed, he lay across the bed on his back with his arms tucked beneath his head, staring up at the ceiling. The bedroom window caught the light of the streetlamp from the parking lot, and its reflection crossed the bed with a blue-gray light resting over the Kewpie doll lying at his side.

Travis was in an untenable situation and understood everything Bob had argued. But Sarah was filling his thoughts and desires with an unquenchable passion that was getting more difficult to live with each passing day. The fact that she still had another year of high school to complete only highlighted the impossibility of the situation, and he understood it would never turn out right for either of them. His desperateness regarding her had only increased when she decided not to attend his help classes any longer. Yet, despite the outward absurdity of his attraction to her, deep inside, Travis knew this was a mutual desire that went beyond the physical—regardless of what anyone else thought or said.

He could have never imagined himself drawn to such a young girl, though he saw in her a maturity and wisdom completely lacking in most of the other women he'd been with. In fact, the only thing they had over Sarah was more age, which hadn't garnered them much wisdom and certainly not any more virtue. Her refinement and natural virtue was unique even for a seventeen-year-old who, somehow, was able to remain unaffected by her ability to attract the opposite sex. She didn't seem to be tainted by frivolous desires so prevalent with most young women. Something genuine lay in her and the way she found meaning in the smallest things. Sarah didn't have a superficial bone in her body. What was outwardly apparent in her was just an extension of the beauty she held within. She was the gemstone already chiseled and polished into a flawless jewel. Each facet of her character was radiant and reflected back in the light of his awareness when he was alone with her. He longed to be with her and to spend time getting to know each facet intimately.

So many others littered his past, but now they lay in the long-forgotten ash heap of "good times," when he'd played hard, always to win—but to win what? Another night followed by the need to start all over again, chasing another "high" that invariably came crashing down in the morning's light? Women had always come easily to him. The others had been good at the games they played, and he had to admit he loved the chase and the winning, but Sarah was different. The pursuit wasn't about winning with Sarah but more about being, and trying to derive happiness or understanding in the moment, not looking to see who would win the next volley. She found happiness and goodness in places where he never took the time to look. Sarah wasn't the child others would suppose. Her writing and thoughts could arrest his thinking in an instant, and she often knew far more than she was willing to share, choosing silence over showy dialog when they were alone together, as if waiting for him to take the lead. Her words were always well chosen, laced in the refined wisdom of her pure heart.

What he couldn't admit to either Bob or to himself until now was his absolute certainty that she felt the same way, and he could sense her struggling against the same overpowering desire he also lived with. They were communicating in ways he hadn't known were possible before he met her. His mind replayed their encounters and time spent together for the last eight months, and although neither he nor Sarah had ever said or done anything to suggest or encourage the attraction directly, when their eyes would meet, a million words couldn't contain all the meaning. More was said in one moment of silence with Sarah Thompson than twenty-four hours' worth of conversation with any other woman on earth.

He could sense her insecurity around him, and he attributed that to her naivety and inexperience with men in general, but that would be an easy barrier to cross with her if their roles as student and teacher were somehow different. He would have no difficulty teaching her that course, and he wanted desperately to be there for that graduation.

Travis was well acquainted with the flirtatious overtures used by many women, often punctuated with the batting of eyelashes and direct eye contact. Sarah took no part in those types of games. She always avoided meeting him eye to eye, as though she knew not to give herself away. At first, he had attributed that to her inherent modesty, but over time, he began to understand her avoiding his eyes was the only way she had to protect herself from inviting an emotion she had difficulty dealing with. If they had met one another outside of school just a year from now, none of the same constraints would be involved. Even the age difference of eight years would lose its stigma if they were two consenting adults. But the question still remained as to how he could work through this and find a way to be with her. There was no easy answer.

He lay there looking at the Kewpie doll, knowing no force of heaven or hell could ever make him lose the love he held for Sarah and the desire he had to share his life and his bed with her. He was successful in everything he'd ever set his mind to, but Sarah was the one prize he couldn't lay claim to, even though he would gladly relinquish all others to possess her. She had asked him once to write an equation expressing love, but until he could find a way to bring them both to the same side of the equation, completing it remained impossible, just as their chances of ever being able to express the love they both shared. He picked up the "Q-P" doll and vowed he would **Q**uite **P**ositively one day have Ms. Sarah Thompson.

CHAPTER TWENTY

At 4:49 PM the telephone at the second precinct station house in Woodbury, New York, rang loudly three times before it was finally answered. "Homicide division, Detective Crowley speaking." The detective grabbed a pencil from the desk and started writing. "Can you repeat that address, Officer Tufano?" Checking the address a second time, Detective Crowley continued, "Has the coroner arrived yet? No one moves that body until we say so. We're on the way." Slamming the receiver down, Detective Crowley reached for his sport coat hanging on the back of his desk chair and then stuck his head into the office of Captain Charles Thompson, commander of the homicide division. "Hey Charley, don't you live up on Dogwood Street?"

"Yeah, what have you got, Crowley?"

"Looks like somebody murdered one of your neighbors at number twelve Dogwood. They haven't secured the scene yet. We're on our way," Crowley called back as he made rapid tracks out of the office.

Without missing a beat, Charley Thompson rose to his feet, moving quickly to the door of his office, calling out with a loud, commanding voice, "Markowitz, you're in command till I get back." Returning in heated stride to his desk, Charley picked up the phone and speedily dialed.

"Hello," the soft-toned voice answered on the other end.

"Sarah, where is Rachael?"

"Hi, Dad. She's in the living room watching TV. Do you want to talk to her?"

"Listen very carefully, Sarah, and do exactly what I tell you. I don't have time to explain, but I want you to close all the windows and lock all the doors. And pull the shades down tight. Don't open the door for anyone, no matter who knocks. Do you understand me?"

"Yes, I will, Dad, but what's happening?"

"Not now, Sarah. I'm on my way up there, and I'll tell you more when we get a handle on the situation. Lock the doors NOW!"

Sarah suddenly understood the importance of her father's call as she heard the hard click of the phone in her ear. Going to the front door first, Sarah locked it, then went to the basement and locked both the back door and the entry door from the garage. Racing back up the stairs, Sarah did as her father instructed, closing the drapes and then continuing upstairs to the bedrooms. Once in her room, Sarah could see the flashing red lights from two police cars halfway down the street from them. Although she was curious, she shut the shades as her father directed, unnerved at not knowing what was going on. She made her way into her mother's room where Lily Thompson sat up in bed, her tired, gray-blue eyes wide with question.

"Who called, Sarah?" she asked as she watched Sarah draw down the shades.

"Dad. He wants all of us to stay inside away from the windows and to keep the doors locked. He didn't say what was happening, but I saw two patrol cars down the block with their lights still flashing." Sarah moved to the second window.

"I certainly do hope it's nothing too serious. Could you tell whose house it was?" Lily propped herself up with her pillows.

"Not really. One of the patrol cars was parked crosswise across the street."

"Let's not alarm Rachael. We'll just go about our tasks as usual," Lily suggested.

"Okay, Mom. I'll go get dinner started, and if Rachael tires of the TV, I'll send her up to see you."

"Good girl, Sarah. I'm sure your father will let us know as soon as he can what's going on down there."

Sarah kissed her mother on the forehead and returned to the kitchen. Her father would not be called to a simple domestic dispute or a petty larceny. If Dad was on his way here, there had to be a murder involved. As head of the homicide division, Charley Thompson worked no other type of crime. A chill moved up her spine as she headed back down the stairs. Continuing to prepare dinner while thinking there might be someone on the prowl in her neighborhood was difficult, but she did her best to assemble the tuna noodle casserole for the oven.

~~~~~~~~~~

Within ten minutes of his call home, Charley brought the unmarked police car to a lurching halt alongside the yellow tape cordoning off Dogwood Street from further traffic. Several officers gave Captain Thompson a quick salute as he headed to the house numbered twelve, halfway down the block on the opposite side of the street from his own home. He already knew whose house it was as he entered the front door and was immediately joined by Detective Frank Crowley. From the gripping look across Detective Crowley's already heavily creased face, the captain anticipated what to expect.

"This one isn't pretty, Charley!" Crowley commented as Charley entered the living room of the split-level home.

"What do we know, Frank?" Charley queried as he surveyed the surroundings of the modestly furnished and somewhat disheveled rooms.

"Looks like the father decided to end the marriage in a drunken rage, using an eight-inch butcher knife. The wife's on the bed in the master bedroom. She'd be too difficult to identify if it weren't for the kid."
~~~~~~~~~~

Charley shook his head in disgust. "Don't tell me Mark Stevens was home at the time?"

"You got it, Charley. We've got him in the kitchen, taking his statement until the ambulance arrives. He's cut up pretty bad himself, probably trying to stop the drunken SOB from attacking his mother."

"Where's the perp now?" Charley continued to question.

"The old man is still lying on the floor in the bedroom alongside the bed. Apparently the teen hit him pretty damned hard over the head with some sort of a heavy iron doorstop. The kid's got a set of balls on him to muster the courage to take the bastard on with nothing but grit on his side. The old man's got to be at least six two, and about two hundred fifty pounds or more. Looks like the kid knocked him out cold for a while. He's still alive, but totally incoherent, drunk as a skunk, and unable to be questioned. From the initial looks of everything, it won't take much to make a case. The officers found him lying alongside the bed, with the butcher knife still in his right hand, when they arrived."

"Who notified the cops?"

"The kid called, using the phone in the kitchen. There's blood all over the damned house. It must have been one hell of a horror show around here for a while today!" Crowley finished, shaking his head in disgust as he glanced at the blood-spattered wall along the stairs.

Charley climbed the five steps up to the bedrooms, being sure not to step in the bloody footprints, and headed straight for the crime scene. Another detective and a police photographer were already busy photographing the room and marking the body position. Charley stood back out of the way, sickened at the horrific nature of the crime, especially because he knew the Stevens family personally. *Why did the weapon have to be a knife?* Charley asked himself disparagingly. The bedroom looked worse than a bloody slaughterhouse on meat-packing day, and his jaw and neck tightened as he surveyed the gory site. Knifings were always the worst crime scenes, and his thoughts went immediately to Mark, who would suffer this memory for the rest of his life.

Blood spatters covered the walls, particularly heavy above the headboard. The bed covers were stained with the blue-black tinged crimson blood coagulating in pools beneath the body of Trudy Stevens, who lay face up, unrecognizable with the disfiguring slashes across her face, arms, and chest. On the floor to the side of the bed, Patrick Stevens lay mumbling between loud outbursts and moans, oblivious to a large gash across his skull that covered the left side of the back of his head in blood. The detectives had already removed the murder weapon, placing it in a plastic bag and marking it for evidence, while another cop wrapped a bathroom towel over the incoherent man's head wound until the ambulance arrived.

"Keep him in here, and if he tries to get up or move, cuff him."

"Yes sir, Captain," the young officer promptly acknowledged.

After surveying the scene, Charley turned around to make his way back down to the kitchen, where the ambulance crew had arrived and were tending to Mark Stevens's open wounds on his hands and forehead. The table and counters were strewn with empty beer bottles, while the phone on the wall was covered in blood. Mark remained seated, his head resting against the wall as one attendant applied pressure to a thick wad of gauze held to his head. A second crewman was kneeling at Mark's side, wrapping his right hand with layers of gauze to help slow the bleeding. Mark was shaking steadily, partly from the rush of adrenaline and partly from shock after losing such a large amount of blood. Charley pulled up a chair beside Mark as the ambulance team continued to work.

"You're doing just fine, Mark, and we're going to get you through this." Charley reached over and gently laid his hand on Mark's leg, in the hopes of helping to calm him. "Before we get you boarded and on to the hospital, son, I'd like to ask you a few more questions. This isn't easy for either of us, Mark, and I know you've had a hell of time here tonight, but we've got to get to the bottom of this to be done with it. The best way to handle this is to start with the truth as best you can remember it. Can you tell me exactly what started all of this tonight?"

Mark's eyes scanned Charley's face from beneath the bulky bandage now wrapped around his blood-soaked head. "It was the same tonight as it always is. He just got an earlier start, that's all. How is my ma?" he pleaded, still shaking.

"They'll be taking her on to the hospital, Mark, so we don't know just yet." Charley chose not to tell him the whole truth. Trudy Stevens was already dead.

"He killed her, didn't he? The bastard finally did it, just like he always said he would!" Mark spoke through clenched teeth.

"Has your father threatened to kill her in the past?"

"Yeah . . . for as long as I can remember, he'd say the same damned thing every night after he'd have enough beer." "What would he tell her, Mark?"

"He'd tell her she should be killed because she had an affair with some Joe bloke he knew. Every night Ma would tell him the same thing over and over again, that she never knew the guy, until he'd finally fall off into a drunken stupor and sleep it off."

"What happened tonight that was different?"

Mark jerked in his chair as one of the ambulance workers began working on Mark's other hand. "He came home from work earlier than normal and started in on her when she was still in the kitchen fixing dinner. Usually, he didn't get that bad till later, when he'd be in front of the TV and he'd finally fall asleep; but he must have been drinking before he got home. Most of the time, he'd go after her and slap her around or punch her out, but he never got his hands on a knife before. I couldn't let him do it to her anymore."

Charley leaned in toward Mark, once more. "It's okay, Mark; he won't be hurting her or you anymore."

"I hate him and hope he gets what's coming to him for what he did to us."

A second ambulance arrived, and the workers headed up the stairs to tend to Patrick Stevens.

"What happened when he got the knife, Mark?"

"He went after her, but Ma tried to get away from him. God . . . he'd already slashed her face once, and she ran up the stairs. Jesus . . . the blood was everywhere. When she got to the bedroom, she tried to lock the door, but he smashed it in, and by the time I ran up there, he was on top of her on the bed just calling her a whore and stabbing her over and over again. I tried to stop him twice, but he turned around and started swinging the knife at me too, until I tripped and fell down." Mark started sobbing and heaved a deep, shaky breath before continuing, "I . . . I couldn't make him stop, and he went back to her on the bed. She started screaming again, and I couldn't stand to hear her anymore. I had to stop him. . . ."

"What happened next?" Charley prompted.

"I saw the doorstop by the door and crawled over to pick it up. Then I got behind him and brought it down as hard as I could over his head. He fell off the bed to the floor, and I ran back down the stairs to the kitchen to call the cops as fast as I could. I . . . I . . . couldn't go back up there. Sweet Jesus . . . I never saw so much blood." Mark began to shake more violently as the tears rolled down his face. Charley rubbed his shoulder as the medic loaded him onto a gurney, readying him for transport.

"You did the right thing, Mark. Everything will be all right." Charley told him as the medics carried Mark out the back door.

Detective Crowley walked into the kitchen as a second gurney was being carried down the stairs on the way to one of the two waiting ambulances. Patrick Stevens was strapped down with hands and ankles tightly cuffed to the sides of the gurney as he jerked, still mumbling incoherently.

Charley stood in the archway between the kitchen and living room and caught the crazed look in Patrick Stevens's eye, as well as the spittle drooling down the side of his blood-stained face. The medics strained, negotiating their way out the front door under the weight of their burden, challenged in their balance with every twisting jerk Patrick Stevens generated.

The tense, ice-cold expression across Captain Thompson's face indicated his contempt and disgust at seeing his drunken, murdering neighbor. "We've got the name of the nearest relative, a Mrs. Anita Fitzgerald, who lives in Mineola," Detective Crowley informed the captain. "She's the sister of the deceased, and we've already notified the fifth precinct to send someone over to her house. The coroner is upstairs finishing up." Crowley folded his small notepad and tucked it back into his sport-jacket pocket. Loosening his tie, he shook his head; he would never get used to the violence inflicted on people at the crime scenes they were called to. "So what's the story on this guy, Stevens, boss? Did he have any history in the neighborhood?"

"He was known to be a boozer, but nobody had too much trouble with him other than a few cross words when he'd sometimes park his car in front of the wrong house. As far as I knew, no domestic disputes were called in on them. You know, Crowley, as long as I've been at this job, it amazes me that none of us really knows what goes on behind closed doors. I guess with Stevens driving a beer-delivery truck for a living, everybody just turned a blind eye to the drinking, assuming it was par for the course. The son, Mark, was always a bit of a hot-headed kid with a chip on his shoulder, but he never said anything to anybody, and everybody figured he was just going through his rebellious teen phase. The occasional black eye he'd show up with was attributed to his bully status in the neighborhood. It looks like his father might have been using him for a punching bag also. It's too damned bad the kid never said anything before this.

"Listen, Crowley, I've got to get back over to my house and let the family know everything is all clear now. You finish up here and I'll meet you back at the station in half an hour."

"You got it, Captain." Detective Crowley headed back up the stairs to finish up with the coroner.

Charley drove the unmarked car back up the street and parked in front of his house. Instead of entering through the garage as he usually did, he got his key out for the front door. Climbing the five steps up to the door, he knocked several times before inserting the key. Sarah ran to the window next to the door. Pulling the drape to the side slightly, she peeked out the window and saw her father under the porch light. Charley unlocked the door as Sarah stood in the living room to greet him. "Oh, Dad, am I glad to see you! What's happening down there?"

Charley put his arms around Sarah. "Let's not discuss this in front of Rachael," he whispered in Sarah's ear.

"Okay, Dad."

"Sarah, I have to return to the station house, but I want you to go ahead and eat without me tonight. I'll be working late.

"How's my girl, Rachael?" Charley beamed as Rachael ran to his side.

"Want to see what I made in school today, Daddy?" Rachael asked as she hugged Charley's leg.

"Well, I guess I have time to see that, and then I'll go say hi to your mother before I head back to work."

"Okay, Daddy," Rachael said as she ran to the kitchen, her blonde pigtails bouncing as she retrieved her pasted picture of butterflies.

"They're beautiful, Rachael! Why, they almost look real."

Rachael smiled broadly, proud of her work. "I'm going to tape it to the fridge so everyone can see it."

"Good idea," Charley offered, always moved by the innocence of his young daughter, who was the exact antithesis of the individuals he was subject to dealing with daily in his line of work. The stark reality of good and evil existing side by side were never more evident to him than in moments like this one after he had left the scene of such a brutal crime.

Rachael ran back to the kitchen and Charley took Sarah's hand, walking with her toward the stairs. "Come on up with me to see your mother for a minute before I leave." Turning to the kitchen, he called to Rachael, "I'll be right back, pumpkin to see how the butterflies look on the refrigerator."

Lily sat in her bed, reading a book. She quickly removed her glasses as Charley and Sarah entered the room. "Close the door, Sarah, and come sit down," Charley directed as he sat next to Lily and kissed her. "Girls, I'm afraid I have some bad news to share with you tonight."

Lily Thompson took Charley's hand in her own. "We suspected it wouldn't be good. Who was it?"

"Trudy Stevens."

Sarah brought her hand to her mouth feeling her stomach turn over in shock.

"My God, Charley, how did it happen?" Lily asked, a stunned look across her pale face.

"Until the inquest is over, what I'm about to share doesn't leave this room. Do I have your word on that, Sarah?" Charley asked.

Sarah swallowed understanding the gravity of what took place. "You can be sure of it, Dad. I'll tell no one."

"All right then, it looks like Mark's dad, Patrick, got into a drunken rage and killed Trudy tonight. Mark tried to stop him, but not in time."

"Where is Mark now?" Lily asked sadly.

"That's the bad part, Lil—Patrick attacked Mark also. Hopefully, Mark will recover, but I doubt very seriously if he'll be returning to finish out the remainder of the school year."

"How did he kill her, Charley? Did he have a gun?"

Charley drew in a deep breath before answering, "I'm afraid he used a butcher knife, and Mark's wounds won't be just those left on his flesh. The images of what he witnessed tonight will never fade. This information is not to leave this room, but I wanted you to know no one else is involved or out there for you to be concerned about."

A tear rolled down Sarah's cheek as her father explained the awful circumstances of Trudy Stevens's violent death, and without another word or question, she sat down on the bed next to her father and embraced him. "I'm so sorry you and Mark had to witness such a terrible thing."

Charley hugged Sarah, kissing her forehead. Standing back up, he leaned over Lily and kissed her tenderly, then cupped the side of her face with his hand. "I love you, Lily." Without another word, Charley headed back out the door to return to the station house.

After they took a moment to compose themselves, Lily said, "Dry your eyes, Sarah, before you go back downstairs. We don't want Rachael to sense there is something wrong. I'll be down in a few minutes, and we'll have dinner together just as we always do."

Sarah nodded as she stood back up. After taking a quick look at herself in the mirror and patting under her eyes with a tissue, she headed back down the stairs.

CHAPTER TWENTY-ONE

The school year was drawing to a close and finals were now behind them as Sarah walked the long halls with several friends to algebra class on this last day of school. Sarah held tightly drawn lips listening to Fran Johnson's opinions regarding Trudy Steven's murder. She found it difficult to hide her distain. Fran's words only added another layer of sadness, in addition to thinking about the upcoming three months' separation from Travis Hall for the summer.

"I heard Mark Stevens never returned to school because he might have been the one who murdered his mother," Fran announced quite casually, looking out of the corner of her eye, as if she were expecting a shocked response.

A second girl accompanying them couldn't help but add her opinion, "Well, it wouldn't surprise me one bit! He was always getting into trouble and pushing people around like he was Cassius Clay."

"I don't think it would be fair for anyone to believe that without knowing the facts," Sarah interjected.

"Maybe he wasn't the one who killed her, Sarah, but all we're saying is no one would be surprised if he did," Fran remarked, quite sure of herself.

Mark had alienated many with his hostile behavior, but no one considered the reason why he might have behaved the way he did. Keeping true to her father's request, she added nothing else to the conversation. Although the newspapers did run a short article concerning Trudy Stevens's violent death, it held a relatively inconspicuous byline buried toward the back of the news pages; it was limited in detail and claimed a domestic dispute. No one knew Mark had been badly injured, or the fact that he had tried to save his mother, and Sarah bore her silence with a heavy heart when she heard such harmful and hate-filled judgments. She had always suspected Mark behaved badly for a reason, and to know he had suffered in silence at the hand of an abusive, alcoholic father for so many years caused her pain. The Grand Jury was soon to be seated, but if more information came out, it would likely be long after school was recessed for the summer, and everyone would be too involved in their own pursuits to care about the truth. Rumors had a way of taking on a life of their own, lingering when they shouldn't, and by then the falsity would be remembered as if true. That terrible dark shadow would follow Mark with whispers and gossip in his own hometown. She did her best to ignore the ignorance of others, holding to her father's request to remain silent about what took place. For now, she had pressing concerns of her own that begged her full attention.

She was not anxious to receive the results of final exams. She could rest easy concerning most of them, but the news would not be good on the Regents algebra final. The strain of having to walk into Mr. Hall's class this last day of school and feel the sting of failure and embarrassment in front of the man she loved so deeply was too difficult to stand. How could she possibly face him when he had put forth so much time and effort with her to prevent that from happening? Sarah had avoided him over the last month, hoping that limiting her contact would help the pain of her secret desire to fade. Instead, her yearning continued on, insistent. His face and smile were never far from thought, and even to see him in the halls the last few weeks brought waves of intense longing she could not escape.

But seeing him now was more difficult than anything she had ever done in her life. She would be embarrassed by her failure but mostly by her secret desire to know him intimately. To have him lock his eyes on hers was to expose her longing, and Sarah could no longer risk the possible outing of her true feelings about him. She didn't want his sympathy or pity for being a mere teenager with a childish crush on a teacher, and she was unwilling to give him the opportunity to draw that conclusion.

When Travis Hall entered the class, several groans arose as he made his way to the front desk, carrying a stack of papers along with his briefcase. Everyone knew his or her test results were moments away from being revealed. Sarah's heart sank as she watched him from the back of the class.

She had spent nearly a year of her life desiring him, thrilling to his nearness and coming to know him in a way the others never could. Beneath the fearsome and disciplined facade, Travis Hall lived his virtue quietly. His greatest challenges in life would likely be only those he imposed on himself. He was a self-governed, strong-willed, and self-disciplined man of few words whose deeds and actions alone spoke for him. To have been near him was to be his captive. The summer would bring a painful separation and parting. Sarah was already wondering how she could exist without seeing him until next fall and the start of her senior year. Even then, it would only be glimpses of him in the halls, unless she had to repeat the course and she were lucky enough to be assigned to one of his classes. If not, she would never again feel the thrilling ravishment their time alone together had always instilled in her.

"Good morning," Travis Hall began as he stood in front of the class. "I say it is a good morning for most of you because it is the last day you will be subjected to this course." Several outbursts of laughter wrapped in nervous anticipation rippled across the room as he continued. "Finals are complete and the journey into algebra has ended. For most of you, it was a successful year, and although fraught with ups and downs for more than a few, your efforts have paid off. As you already know, the State exam is not recorded with numerical scoring, and you will receive either a pass or fail evaluation, allowing you to advance in mathematics and fill the requirements for college admittance. Your last classroom exams count toward your final grade for the quarter, and also count toward your final average overall in this course. Those will be mailed to you in several days."

Johnny Medford suddenly called out. "Do you know exactly what day so I can be sure not to be home?" The class broke out in an uproar of laughter as Travis smiled broadly shaking his head in amusement. He returned to the front of his desk and sat on the edge straddling the corner still smiling as he waited for the laughter to die down.

"If you had put as much thought into your homework as you gave to that idea John that bridge wouldn't need to be crossed." he said half jokingly, punctuating the humor. Another round of laughter echoed in the room as he sat casually still sporting his relaxed smile. The tension in the room had eased and Travis continued. "Before I hand out test results, I would like to say that I'm glad to have had the opportunity to instruct all of you this year, and I want to wish all of you the best of luck in the future, with clean calculating ahead. Anything worth having is worth working for," he said, suddenly pausing, and then looking back at Sarah. Without taking his eyes from her, he continued. "I encourage you to keep that in mind as you continue with your educations."

The pause and his glance caused Sarah to close her eyes briefly, and then readjusted her position in her seat. Travis watched her momentarily and then brought himself to a stand walking to the opposite side of his desk keeping an earnest expression.

"I will be giving you both the State Regents results and your class exam results at the end of class today. The State exam results are sealed in envelopes. You may open them now or later, at your discretion. The form inside will indicate either a pass or fail grade. The Regents exam is the property of the State, so you will be unable to discuss with me any possible difference of opinion you may have with the results. The sealed envelopes do not contain the exam—only your pass or fail status. If you have questions regarding the regular class final, I will be available after school today to discuss that exam with you and to address any other concerns you may have." His serious expression and tone lightened with his smile as he reached for some papers lying on his desk.

"Now that we have that out of the way, and just to keep the smiles on your faces, I hold in my hand your next and last quiz."

A collective groan with a few shaking heads changed the happy mood of the class as Mr. Hall continued.

"A series of equations contained on this quiz might jog your memory from this past year. I'd like you to complete these; however, you will be happy to note there will be no grading on this final quiz. Take all the time you wish to solve them, and when you are finished, bring your paper up to the front desk. I'll hand you your recent test results at that time. If you finish early, feel free to use the extra time to read or do other work for the duration of the period. Please bring your textbooks up to the front of the room to turn them in with the quiz when you are done."

He made his way to the first row of desks closest to the door. "I have one more word for those who were not able to master the course this year. Don't look upon this as a failure, but consider this year as preparatory work for next year. You will be that much further ahead next year as a result of your efforts this semester. I encourage you not to quit, but to persevere, knowing algebra will be easier for you now that you have a basic understanding of the material. Don't be discouraged. Concentrate on the feeling of accomplishment you will have when you do succeed." Mr. Hall handed the appropriate number of papers to the first student in each row, instructing them to hand back copies of the quiz to the students behind them.

Sarah's heart sank. She would be among those who would have to repeat this course, and it wounded her to think his remarks might have been directed specifically to her. At least he chose not to hand the last quiz out individually. She was relieved not to have to come face to face with him till the end of class. She watched as he approached the last row and counted out the correct number of papers, handing them to the first student in that row. He brought his head up, scanned the row and directed his attention momentarily on Sarah. She could not bring herself to meet his glance, and she quickly lowered her eyes.

Turning back slowly, he walked to his desk. The young man seated in front of her handed Sarah the remaining two copies of the quiz. Sarah took the tests from his hand and passed one back to Amy. Sarah looked down at the test and was barely able to concentrate enough to work the equations. Somehow she managed to fill in her name and forced herself to push through the problems, but with her inability to concentrate, her efforts were taking much longer than most of the class. One by one, the students made their ways to the teacher's desk, handing in their papers and books and receiving their test results.

The bell finally rang out, and Travis Hall wished the students a good summer, adding, "Stay safe!"

Sarah managed to scribble down an answer to the last equation, realizing she was the last to complete the quiz. When she looked up, Travis sat at his desk, watching her while all the students were quickly vacating the classroom.

Sarah swallowed hard, gathering her books and quiz, and approached his desk. He never took his eyes off her; Travis Hall sat with an unreadable expression that unnerved Sarah as she moved ever closer to him. She handed him her paper and textbook. He sat behind his desk, saying nothing as he took them from her hand. His intensity burned as though she were under a spotlight, unable to escape what was coming. He brought his right hand to rest on top of the desk, watching Sarah as she stood nervously in front of him on the opposite side of his desk.

"How is your job working out?" he asked.

She drew a quick breath. "Very well, thank you, sir . . . I think they may work me into a full-time position for the summer." She hoped he wouldn't draw this out any longer.

"I'm happy for you, Sarah," he said, holding his intense stare. After a brief pause, he continued, "How do you think you did?"

She answered in a rush, to get it over with. "Mr. Hall, I know I didn't pass, and there is no use discussing this any longer. I'm sorry if I let you down, but no one could have helped me relate to a subject I just can't connect with, so please don't think I didn't appreciate all your help and effort with me. I blame myself."

He made no attempt to respond, and his lack of expression gave none of his thoughts away. His lengthy silence added to the heavy feeling that time was moving in slow motion. Moving slowly, with seemingly deliberate caution, Mr. Hall handed Sarah the class-exam paper first, keeping his attention fixed on her face.

Sarah's hand trembled as she reached out to take it from his hand. Looking down at her score, she was amazed to see a passing grade of seventy-seven written across the top of the page in red ink. She caught her breath and was happily surprised at the results. Shocked at her unanticipated good fortune, she looked back up at him. "I don't know what to say!"

"You don't have to say anything, Sarah. You earned your score."

Still in a state of shock, she knew the news would not be as good on the Regents final. And the Regents exam was the one she had failed; it mattered little whether she passed the class semester or not because the college admittance required the Regents results, not classroom scores.

Reaching back into his briefcase, he removed the envelope containing the Regents results and slid it across the desk toward her, never removing his hand from its edge.

Sarah was frozen in place, unsure if she should take it, not wanting to read its contents.

"This one belongs to you," he said.

He hadn't taken his eyes off of her since she approached his desk, and the intensity was becoming unbearable. After a hesitant pause, Sarah slowly reached out, resting her hand on top of the envelope, biting her lower lip slightly, and then brought her eyes back to his face again, unsure of herself, agonizing at the knowledge this would be the last time she would see him for at least the next two and a half months.

Travis spoke again in whispered tones, "You don't have to open it now."

He said it so faintly she was taken aback at his words and hushed delivery. Without looking down, Sarah slid her fingers across the surface of the envelope, hoping to find its edge. Travis brought his hand to gently rest over hers, then wrapped his fingers tenderly around hers, pressing down slightly as both their hands remained united on top of the envelope. Sarah's heart stopped at feeling the heat from his strong hand now enveloping her own; she remained frozen, startled, and unable to move or fully understand his gesture while, at the same time, thrilling to his gentle and unexpected touch. She had been transported to a different place and time, and nothing mattered, not even the test results. She found herself locked once more in his deep green eyes in a fleeting moment that felt eternal; she finally closed her eyes, praying not to shed a tear or expose her heart.

Slowly, he slid his hand tenderly off the top of hers, caressing her delicate soft skin, not speaking another word. Sarah lifted the envelope from the desk, bringing it to her chest and clutching it tightly as she took in his face, her eyes wide open once more. He smiled faintly, and then nodded once, ever so slightly. "Have a good summer," he said with unbroken attention.

Sarah forced a small smile, nodding back, but could bring herself to say nothing more. She turned and walked away. Looking back would be too painful.

Her pulse raced as she made her way out of his class, heading to the dean's office for the third period of the day. Still gripping the envelope tightly, Sarah's mind scrambled to understand his unanticipated gesture, assuming he had probably felt sorry for her. In his kindness, he would give her the space and distance from him to open the results, knowing it would be too painful for her in his presence. To have touched her was, perhaps, his only way to express his sympathy without having to say the words she couldn't bear to hear. To have failed in his eyes was heartbreaking, but to have loved him so much, with no hope of ever having her love returned, trapped Sarah in a torturous cage of her own building. His touch was far more than she could bear, especially because she believed it was given in sympathy to the same young, inept, and inexperienced teenage girl who had entered his classroom on the first day of school almost a year ago.

He had changed her life in an instant with a glance and taught her more about love and perseverance than he could guess, and in ways neither she nor he could have imagined. Travis Hall had engraved an imprint on her soul, and Sarah Thompson left his classroom leaving a part of her heart behind.

CHAPTER TWENTY-TWO

Clutching the envelope with the results of the State Regents exam, Sarah made her way to the dean's office. What caused her to tighten her grip wasn't the fear of the test results but the need to extend the feeling of Travis Hall's gentle touch; the envelope was the tangible reminder keeping that moment alive in her aching heart.

Dean Watson's office felt stuffy and closed-in as Sarah put her books down on a cabinet next to the door. Propping the door open, she pulled a tissue from her purse and wiped the corner of her eye, doing her best to rein in her emotions. The dean would soon be there, and she did her best to present a normal appearance before her arrival.

"Good morning, Sarah," the dean offered as she entered the office with her usual speed.

"Good morning, Miss Watson."

"It hardly seems possible another year has come and gone by so quickly!" Miss Watson dropped the books and papers she carried onto her desk. She took her seat and pulled another stack of papers from her canvas bag. "I'll need the desktop today, Sarah, to transcribe my students' test results to my log. When I'm done, I'd like you to file all of these exams in the students' files. In the meantime, please deliver these three notes to the teachers addressed on the front of each envelope. Let me identify the correct classrooms to deliver them to during this period."

Sarah waited patiently for the dean to finish, lost in the thought of her last moments with Travis Hall. Holding the back of her hand, Sarah lingered in the memory of his tender touch.

"That should do it," the dean announced as she put the correct classroom number on the last envelope. "Before you leave, I have something for you. It's just a token of my appreciation for all your help this year. I hope you'll be able to give up a study hall next year to work for me again." She reached into her bag and handed Sarah a small rectangular box with a ribbon wrapped around it.

"Thank you very much, Miss Watson. You really didn't have to do this for me. I enjoy working for you and would be happy to help next year also, if my schedule will allow it."

"Why wouldn't it?"

Sarah was embarrassed to share that she might have to repeat her algebra class but Miss Watson would find out soon enough. "Well, I may have to retake a class I had trouble with this year, and it would probably eat up my study-hall slot," Sarah admitted sorrowfully.

"Why you've never failed anything in all the years I've known you, Sarah. What class are you talking about?"

"I'm afraid algebra and I didn't get along well this year."

"Have you received your test results yet?"

"Yes, although I haven't opened the Regents results. But I know I did poorly on the exam." Sarah sighed.

"Go get the envelope and open it," Miss Watson directed.

Sarah didn't want to open it, but at the dean's request, she took the envelope off the top of her notebook. She held it in her hand a moment as Miss Watson came to a stand at her desk. She then motioned for Sarah to open it. Sarah pulled up the tab on the back side and slid her hand inside the envelope, pulling the paper out. Slowly, she unfolded the paper and read her name across the top of the page with the name of her school and class instructor. There, in the center of the page, was the word "PASS" in bold print. Sarah read and re-read the word again several more times. "That's impossible!"

"Perhaps it would have been impossible had you had another teacher, Sarah," Miss Watson told her.

"What do you mean?"

"It seems Mr. Hall was able to go back over your exam when he asked for his right of second review and was able to garner a few more points. Your arithmetic mistakes caused your initial failure, but, as he argued, you were clearly able to demonstrate your knowledge of the proper steps involved in solving the equations. At Mr. Hall's request, the additional points were granted in order for you to receive a passing grade."

Sarah was speechless, overwhelmed at what Mr. Hall had done for her. Unable to prevent another tear from falling to her cheek, Sarah was gripped with a sense of shame, thinking of the way she had treated him the last few weeks of school, avoiding him and turning away if he approached her in the halls. He had worked tirelessly for her to succeed, and now to discover that she was able to pass on account of him was almost too much for her to accept. Why would he have gone to so much trouble and then ask for a second review when she had ignored him and his repeated request for her to attend his last few help classes? She couldn't live with herself not thanking him, knowing that only what he did for her allowed her to pass.

Ms. Watson continued, "I happened to be at the meeting where he made his case for you and one other student, otherwise no one else would ever know about this. I thought you should know what happened. Go ahead and open your gift, and then you can stop at the ladies' room to dry those eyes on your way to deliver these notes."

Sarah smiled beneath her tears and quickly removed the ribbon from the box. Upon opening it, she found a matching pen and pencil set. "They're wonderful!" Sarah exclaimed. "Thank you, Miss Watson. I'm sure I'll put them to good use."

"All right then. You better head out and get these notes delivered before the end of this period. If I'm not here when you return,

I'll say thanks for another great year, and I'll see you back here again this fall. Hope you have a good summer."

"I will, and I wish the same to you." Sarah turned to leave, stopping before she got to the door. Looking back, she spoke up again, "Miss Watson, thanks for telling me what Mr. Hall did for me."

"I just thought you should know," Miss Watson reiterated as she sat back down at her desk to work, motioning for Sarah to go on.

Sarah made her way through the project area on her way to the ladies' room, carrying the notes to be delivered. She pushed the door of the lavatory open and stood in front of the mirror, looking at the reflected image, filled with an overwhelming sense of remorse and sorrow at the way she had handled the situation with Mr. Hall. If she hadn't been so in love with him, she would have conducted herself altogether differently and would have made a concerted effort to continue with his help-class sessions. Running away from him had only made the problem worse for her, and now she could add guilt to her consuming heartache, knowing she had hurt him despite the fact that he only wanted her to succeed. Sarah hardly knew the person in the mirror staring back at her anymore.

Travis Hall had turned her world upside down. She couldn't let the year end without seeing him one more time to tell him how grateful she was for what he had been able to do for her. It would take all the courage she had to see him again, but she couldn't live with herself if he didn't know how grateful and humbled she was by his effort on her behalf. Remembering that he would be in class after school if anyone wanted to discuss the final test results, she would muster the courage to bury her pride and find a way to undo the hurt she must have caused him.

She kept asking herself why he had done so much for her.

She was heartbroken she could never be more to him than a needy student. She loved him so desperately and didn't want his sympathy or patronizing, only desired to know his love, which she could never hope to have. Sarah prayed the words would come out right when she faced him one last time at the end of the day.

~~~~~~~~~~~

The '62– '63 school year drew to a rapid close. The student body was eager to greet the newfound freedom of summer. Sarah made her way down the hall, heading back to her locker in the C project area. Kenny, along with two other boys, caught up with her as they all walked together. "How's my girl?" Kenny asked as he threw his arm over her shoulder.

"I suppose I'm happy to have my junior year finished. Are you glad to be graduating?"

"I'm damned happy to be moving on out of here. I can't wait to start at Columbia, my father's old alma mater. What school are you headed to, Harry?" he asked one of the other boys.

"I got accepted at Lehigh, but my parents can't afford the tuition, so I guess I'll stay local and attend C.W. Post College for now. Besides, anything is better than the draft."

"What do you mean?" Sarah asked.

"There's a lot of talk out there that the Vietnam conflict is about to blow wide open. If you don't have a college deferment and keep your grades up, there's no hope of avoiding the draft when the Selective Service calls you," Harry shared.

The third boy suddenly responded, "Well, I can't afford the tuition anywhere, but I've got a good job lined up with my uncle's plumbing company. Maybe they won't call my number. What the hell—if I don't like the plumbing trade, I might even join the military and see the world myself. It couldn't be any worse than fixing toilets!" All three boys laughed heartily as they continued their way down the hall.

Overall, the atmosphere was filled with happy expectancy, despite the looming dangers. Kenny was beaming from ear to ear since he had been accepted to Columbia, assuring him the ability to come home frequently and see Sarah. Dating her was the only thing he hadn't been able to accomplish while attending North Shoreline High, and he was compelled to expunge that failure from his record.
~~~~~~~~~~~

Sarah's hair was pulled neatly into a ponytail, and it swayed gently from side to side as they continued down the hall together. The feathered ends brushed lightly across Kenny's arm, and the feel of her hair on his skin was tantalizingly seductive. The delicate caresses teased him with every step, heightening his desire for more of her.

Taking Kenny's familiar ways as typical of his nature, Sarah learned not to react shocked or offended at his need for physical contact. She had grown accustomed to his overt displays of friendship and affection, and she always knew it had to be Kenny when she would feel his arms around her before he made himself known.

"Are you coming to graduation tomorrow, Sarah?' Kenny asked.

"I'd like to, but I'm not sure I can."

"I'd really like you to be there. My parents are having an open house tomorrow night after graduation, and it would mean a lot to me if you could at least come by the house to help celebrate with us, even if you can't make the afternoon ceremonies. A lot of the others will be there, including Trent and most of the guys from the team, and many of the girls from the cheerleading squad too. It might be the last time all of us will be together for a while."

Sarah felt the pull of Kenny's plea, and she didn't have it in her heart to disappoint him. Besides, there would be plenty of others there, and it wasn't like a date alone with him, which she was always careful to avoid. Graduation was a special one-time event that needed to be acknowledged and celebrated by family and friends alike. Kenny was a good friend, and she could hardly allow his graduation to go unnoticed or uncelebrated. He had gone out of his way to help her all year long. Kenny had been there the first part of the year to drive her home, allowing her to keep her practices when transportation was a problem, and he managed to help deliver boxes of canned goods for the annual food drive Sarah had organized before Thanksgiving. He hadn't repeated his attempt at intimacy again since last fall, although Sarah had done her best not to give him an opportunity to do so. It didn't seem right not to honor his day when he had always done whatever she asked of him.

Smiling broadly back at him, she responded, "I'll try to be there, Ken. What time is the open house?"

"Commencement ceremonies should be over by three-thirty, and with most all the others having family obligations of their own, we thought anytime after six p.m. tomorrow night would be appropriate. Mom's catered the food for the party, so there'll be plenty to eat if you want to skip dinner at home. Just, please, try to come whenever you can break free."

"I'll do my best to be there, although it might be later, after I help get dinner out of the way at home."

"Great! Don't worry about the late hour. The celebration should last pretty late into the evening—the guys always like a good party. I'll be looking for you then, Sarah. I've got a million things left to do before graduation tomorrow, so I better get going. I'll see you tomorrow night." He turned quickly and headed back to the gold project area, beaming from ear to ear leaving Sarah behind.

She stood in front of her locker, reflecting on the past school year. Kenny had remained present in her life, but always in the background, even knowing what his intentions were. He was the one all the other girls pined over, and yet, she couldn't bring herself to fully accept him in that role. How misplaced her affections were since the man she really loved could never be hers. Travis Hall's face alone haunted her dreams. A sudden flurry of nerves washed over her as she thought about seeing him one last time before heading home for the summer. She was still unsure of exactly what to say to him, embarrassed by the fact that she had avoided him the entire last month of school, and unsure why he had gone to bat for her.

She gently touched the top of her right hand with eyes closed as she stood facing her locker. The memory of their last moment together, when he slid his hand over hers and then pressed against it, drifted back as she reveled in its feel once more. The recollection of his touch lingered but was quickly followed by the downward spiral in thought that his actions were only a kind, congratulatory gesture with a hint of sympathy for her struggles in his class. They had spent so many hours together, and to be without his company now meant she would be without the high of love that only he brought to her. The thought of his absence in her life was devastating, and Sarah quickly dropped it. She had to see him before he left the school.

She cleared her locker of the remaining papers and disposed of the accumulated notes that held no more purpose at the close of the semester. Nonie joined her, holding a large bag filled with an assortment of items she had felt compelled to store in her locker that year, most of which went unused and had now become extra baggage for her to carry back home.

"Well, I guess we made it through another year! Looks like I'll be taking algebra again, and hopefully it won't be with Mr. Hall."

"Don't worry, Nonie. It will be easier next semester." Sarah tried to soften her friend's disappointment.

"Did you get around to opening your results yet?"

Sarah didn't want to share the news that she miraculously passed both exams but Nonie would find out sooner or later. "I don't know how it's possible, but the envelope containing the Regents results says I passed."

"My God, how did that happen?"

"I'm not exactly sure. Listen, I've got to take another minute to find out if this is a mistake or not. How about you take the keys to the car and go put your things in the backseat while I go back and see Mr. Hall one more time about my grade. Hopefully, this won't take too long."

"Okay, but if it was me, I'd take the grade and run without looking back! Mr. Hall's class was the toughest class I've ever taken, and I personally don't care to come face to face with him again. Don't stay too long in there or he might change his mind about your grade! I'll just wait in the car for you."

"Okay, thanks. I'll see you in a few minutes then." Sarah gathered her notebook and remaining papers, turned, and walked back to the C-4 classroom.

Two students were exiting the class, followed closely behind by another as Sarah lifted her chin, catching her breath before entering. She walked quietly into the classroom, trying not to draw Mr. Hall's attention away from the student he was speaking with at the front of the room. She watched him as she waited. He sat on the corner of his desk with his left leg hanging freely off the edge, the other leg braced firmly on the floor for support. Still listening to his student, he brought his eyes to the door where Sarah stood patiently waiting. His sudden change in expression let Sarah know he was surprised by her appearance. Looking at her out of the corner of his eye, Travis continued to listen to the young man standing beside him. The student lifted his test paper to Travis making note of a particular equation, and Travis returned his attention to the problem pointed out on the test. Reacting unconsciously to the impact of his glance, Sarah shifted her stance.

"I'm sorry, Peter, but even here in this problem, you repeated the same mistake a second time. Your test score will remain the same. One thing about this, if we share a class next semester in Trig, I'm sure you won't be making that mistake again now that you understand your error. Have a good summer, and I'll look forward to seeing you in class next fall," he said firmly to the student.

Peter took his paper back, looking slightly forlorn as he headed for the door.

Sarah slowly walked to the front of the room as Travis Hall watched her. They were alone now, and Sarah was trembling inside, unable to read his expression as she approached him.

"I . . . I was hoping you would still be here," she said, in almost a whisper, as she came to a halt several feet from him.

"Sarah," he tilted his head slightly, by way of acknowledging her. His seated position allowed him to meet her face to face with their eyes at equal height. "I'm surprised to see you back. I suppose you've opened your Regents results by now."

His expression and eyes were riveting as he kept steady watch on her. Sarah's heart pounded faster as she struggled to come up with the right words to say to him. "Yes. . . . Yes, sir, I did. I'm still trying to make sense of my passing grade when I know I shouldn't have passed."

He suddenly smiled that small half-smile that always captured her heart. "You're the only student I know who would come back to see me after passing to convince me otherwise."

The corners of her mouth edged up slightly at his comical assessment of the reason for her return and then she lowered her eyes before continuing. "That isn't exactly why I'm here," she spoke nervously. "The truth is, Mr. Hall," she continued, bringing her head back up, "I know what you did for me, and I'm very grateful, although I probably didn't deserve your effort on my behalf." She waited to see if he would say something, but it was as if he were engrossed in thought. Sarah struggled, making an effort to go on. "It . . . It was Dean Watson who shared with me what you were able to do for me," she told him, feeling unsure of herself and strained in expressing her thoughts correctly with him.

He moved slightly, changing his position as he continued to straddle the corner of the desk, before finally speaking. "That was a judgment call I was charged with making, and it wasn't misplaced. You earned your score, even if it was a bit difficult to obtain. You were clearly able to show how to solve the equations by demonstrating all the correct steps needed to do that."

"I can only thank you for that," Sarah responded, searching his face. She became caught in the depths of his emerald green eyes, but they looked different somehow. The moment lingered between them. A sudden shock wave hit her as he held her eyes, locking them in fixed attention to his own. The boldness and protracted intensity emanating from them shook her, and she pulled her head back slightly. His gaze was more a communication than a glance. She recognized something powerful in his expression, but what was it? Unable to speak, she watched him, waiting for him to say something.

He cocked his head slightly to the right, holding her gaze closely. Taking his time, he continued, "You know, Sarah, there are always two sides to every equation. The key is finding the value of the unknown by keeping both sides equal, reducing and merging them where you can, until you are left with as few factors as possible and one side becomes a reflection of the other in its simplest form." He was speaking as though he was deliberating, pausing briefly, still formulating his thought. He raised his chin slightly and brought his hand to his lips, parting them a bit, and then barely brushed his lower lip with his index finger before proceeding. "On first glance, you might be intimidated by the fact that parts of the equation are unknown to you, while other parts have known value. Both sides appear to be totally different, dressed in different letters and numbers and symbols. With attention and effort, you work the equation out, integrating, reducing, and refining it—first on one side, then on the other, keeping its equality. If your calculations are correct, what was once unknown to you is eventually revealed and its value made plainly visible as a result of the interaction of both sides. The final equation bears no resemblance to the original, yet the answer was contained in the original equation from the start." Pausing, he searched her face before continuing. "You lose the nonessential along the way, until only the essential remains. When the moment comes that you discover the hidden value, the revelation is . . . is a perfect fit, and is the answer you were looking for all along. In that moment, you know your efforts were well worthwhile, and all of it makes perfect sense."

He stopped again, staring intently at her. Sarah made no attempt to respond, but was shaking inside not sure of his meaning and guessing at his expression. Drawing a breath, he went on, "I like to think of it as two hands clasped together, joining like minds. The hands represent the equal sign connecting what appear to be two very different things, but the minds those two hands connect are the same, regardless of the expression or form they take. Like so many problems in life, some equations are just much more difficult than others to solve, and they require more time. I have no doubt you're able to understand these principles in algebra."

Travis Hall searched Sarah's face, looking to see if she understood. His look seemed so direct and unambiguous in its intention. Sarah held fast, stunned at the sudden realization that he was speaking to her on two levels simultaneously. He was usually so direct, using few words and keeping to the facts when making a point. This was the first time he had ever spoken to her using metaphors that communicated indirectly to her heart. Her mind reeled at the implication, trying desperately to comprehend his analogies, and she wasn't sure how to react, or even if her shocking supposition were truly correct.

Could it even be possible he knew she was in love with him? Or more startling, could she dare to think he, too, felt the same way?

A tidal wave of embarrassment washed over her. Her ivory complexion gave way to rising heat, tinting her cheeks in a deep crimson blush. She had to say something but refused to trust her instincts, thinking it inconceivable that he might hold the same desire for her. The likelihood was too shocking to believe. Not wanting to play the fool for assuming such a thing, she struggled to answer him. "If . . . If I was able to understand or learn anything at all this year, it was only because of you. I . . . I couldn't possibly have passed this course without your help, and I didn't want to leave today for the summer without thanking you, and to apologize for missing your last help classes. I should have made the extra effort to be here."

He folded his hands together, keeping them in his lap as if he were still holding something back, and then drew in his lower lip, slowly wetting it with his tongue. "There is no need for you to apologize. I understood, Sarah."

His words were not unexpected, but beneath their outward meaning, Sarah couldn't shake the feeling he was once again implying something more. The tension between them was palpable as Sarah grappled with the subtext, her emotions rising and falling with every breath, trying to extract his full meaning. She didn't want to leave him, but at the same time, emotionally exposed and vulnerable, she wondered whether he did indeed know her heart or if she was the victim of her own misinterpretations. "Well, I've got to get back to the car. I have someone waiting for me. I hope you have a good summer, Mr. Hall, and I suppose I'll see you back here again this fall then."

He nodded slightly. "I look forward to that, Sarah. Enjoy your summer and your work at the library."

Their eyes held court longer than customary as the same subtle feeling returned, strengthening Sarah's suspicion that his discussion of algebra was a veiled attempt at disguising things of a much more personal nature between them. She was so certain in one moment and then vacillated the next, knowing what a devastating scandal such a reality would be for both of them. No, it just couldn't be possible. He never gave her any clear indication he might have feelings for her. It was simply out of the realm of possibility, and she had to be reading into the moment only what she desperately wanted to believe.

She took two steps back from him and swallowed, unable to take her eyes from his as her pulse raced. The telltale sign of suppressed tears suddenly tainted her eyes. She forced her last words, "Thank you again, Mr. Hall. I'll see you next fall."

Sarah turned and started walking to the door, struggling to make sense of the well-disguised undercurrent in his conversation. The sting in her heart at their parting caused the tears to well up in her eyes.

"Sarah," Travis Hall called out to her as she reached the threshold.

She turned around to face him once more, eyes glistening, now full on the verge of spilling over. He brought himself to a stand, facing her with a steady, unbroken stare. She waited for him to speak, uncertain of him, blinded by her secret longing and imprisoned by her doubt.

"I won't forget you," he finally said, and slowly smiled at her.

His words pierced Sarah's heart. She managed to smile in return but wasn't able to respond. She nodded slightly, accepting his unexpected and endearing words with bittersweet sadness. She quickly wiped the tears from her eyes as she turned and walked out of the classroom, thinking to herself that she would never love anyone the way she loved Travis Hall.

CHAPTER TWENTY-THREE

Nonie caught a glimpse of the tear in Sarah's eye as she threw her notebook in the back of the car and got behind the wheel. "Well, from the look on your face, I guess you failed after all! I told you, you shouldn't have gone back to see him about your grade."

"No, the grade was correct. I didn't fail." Sarah backed the car out of its allotted space.

"What on earth did he say to you that's got you so upset?"

"He didn't say anything except that I earned my score."

"What is it then?" Nonie asked

"It's not him, Nonie, it's me. I behaved badly toward him the last half of this semester, and he managed to save me from failing, despite the fact that I avoided him the entire last month of school. He pulled extra points out of the Regents exam for me, allowing me to pass."

"I don't know how you were able to pull that one off, but I suspected he always had a special interest in you, and I guess that proves it."

"No, it doesn't prove anything, except that he felt sorry for me all along and knew I needed the help. I don't want to talk about it."

"That's okay with me, Sarah, but I'd forget about him and put on a happy face about the passing grade. I for one am just glad to have this year over with, and you should be too. Hopefully, I'll get to see more of Abe now that school is out." Nonie paused a moment. "I saw Kenny a minute ago, and he asked if I wanted to come to his graduation party tomorrow. I told him I had to work. Are you going?"

"I guess I'll go after dinner for a while since I owe him that. Besides, there'll be plenty of others there too," Sarah answered in a nonplussed tone.

"He's still mad about you. You do know that, don't you?"

"He'll soon forget all about me when he gets to college."

"You say that like you want him to forget you. Is that what you really want?"

Sarah didn't answer immediately, realizing how harsh she must have sounded, and contemplated Nonie's question with more thought. "I guess I didn't mean that the way it sounded. I suppose I'd miss his friendship."

"For God's sake, Sarah, don't burn your bridges with him if there's the slightest possibility you might want his company. You know, that 'hard to get' attitude can't last forever—besides, you don't want to destroy the possibility if you're still not sure how you feel about him." Nonie raised her eyebrow as she looked at Sarah.

"I'll try to keep that in mind," Sarah responded with sarcasm in her tone. Kenny Birk was the last thing on her mind, and she would see him tomorrow. For now, all she could dwell on was that Travis Hall would be gone for the summer, which would leave a terrible void in her heart she couldn't share with anyone.

~~~~~~~~~~

For the rest of the evening, Sarah replayed every word of her last few moments together with Travis Hall. Her heart implored her repeatedly he had meant something more than his words alone implied, while her head pulled her back to the absurdity of such a shocking assumption. The emotional and mental game of seesaw over the next day and a half was consuming.
~~~~~~~~~~

She managed a trip to the store on Saturday morning to pick up Kenny's graduation gift. A week earlier, she had decided on a keychain with a round brass medallion bearing the scales of justice insignia on one side, and the opposite side inscribed with his initials "K.R.B." and the words "Friends Forever, Sarah."

After dinner was finished, she readied Rachael for bed, and then got herself dressed to leave for Kenny's party. She wore a sleeveless sundress with a deep, open back extending to her waist. The front bodice angled sharply from beneath her arms up to her neck, where it tied in back. Delicate blue and lavender spring flowers dotted its sheer gossamer fabric, and the bodice had a flattering fit, flaring at the waist and draping delicately to her knees. Her thin-strapped white leather sandals bore baby-blue flowers covering her toes and mimicked the print on her sundress. With her hair spilling to her shoulders, Sarah portrayed an enchanting, fresh, sweet look of springtime reflecting her virtuous, feminine aura. The pastel colors enhanced the blueness of her eyes, and her father took notice of her refined and elegant beauty.

"You look lovely tonight, Sarah," Charley told her as she made her way down the stairs.

"Thanks, Dad, especially for buying me the dress." She kissed his cheek as he sat in his reclining chair, sporting a proud smile of admiration.

"Be sure and drive straight home, and keep the doors locked in the car. Your mother and I want you to be sure and give our regards to Kenny's parents and our congratulations to Kenny as well."

"I will, Dad. I should be home by eleven-thirty, but you don't have to wait up." Sarah gave Rachael a hug and kissed her mother goodbye as Lily reclined on the couch.

Lily Thompson just smiled at that remark, knowing the suggestion would go unheeded. "Have a good time, dear, and you can tell me all about the party in the morning."

"I will. Thanks, Mom." Picking Kenny's gift up off the console, Sarah tucked it into her purse and headed out the door.

"You know, she really is quite beautiful, Lily; and we would be fools not to be concerned about her when she goes out."

"I know, but at least Sarah always tells us where she intends to be, which is refreshing and so unlike many young people these days! You needn't worry about her the way you do. She has a level head on her shoulders and knows what's right and wrong."

"It isn't Sarah who worries me, Lil!" Charley leaned back in his recliner once more. The same conversation repeated itself each time their daughter left home.

~~~~~~~~~~

Sarah headed north, winding her way through the wooded roadways, passing the smaller incorporated villages and quaint towns of the north shore. Kenny's family had always held a place of prominence in the community, and their home and surroundings exemplified that fact. The smaller two-lane roads were less trafficked than the more heavily populated areas along Jericho Turnpike. Towns like Cold Spring Harbor, Huntington, Laurel Hollow, Lloyd Harbor, and Oyster Bay graced the shores of Long Island Sound. This area was predominately reserved for those more affluent who could afford the pricier real estate and taxes. Old money reigned here along the secluded and often privately owned shoreline. It was a world apart from the vast majority.

Although Kenny's home wasn't situated directly on the water, its concealed site in the wooded hills overlooking the Sound was a prime location. The massive, two-story federal limestone was surrounded by ten acres and added to its considerable value. The grounds were meticulously cared for, and with the in-ground pool, tennis courts, and panoramic views of Long Island Sound from its elevated vantage point, most would consider it a paradise. The Birks' stately home left an impressive mark when viewed from the water, but it remained hidden along the heavily wooded roadway. The ivy-covered stone wall with bronze address plaque identified its entrance and foretold its grander presence.
~~~~~~~~~~

Sarah hadn't been there in the evening before, and she was amazed to see the in-ground lighting illuminating the gate as well as the winding blacktop driveway. The lighting continued around the sweeping curve of the circle drive at the front of the majestic home. At least twenty cars were parked along the arc of the driveway, and she could easily see into many of the well-lit floor-to-ceiling windows. The glass conservatory attached to the right side of the majestic home sparkled beneath the clear night sky. How wonderful it must be to view the stars at night from inside the glassy enclosure.

Parking her car behind the last car in the long lineup, she locked the doors and started walking to the grand front entrance. The telltale scent of cigarette smoke drifted in the still night air as the sound of music mingled with the chirp of the crickets and the croak of frogs, so common to early summer. The sweet, heady fragrance of honeysuckle overshadowed the cigarette smoke, and Sarah found its delicate fragrance tantalizing. The blinking lightning bugs brought back youthful memories of summers past as she continued up the hosta-lined driveway.

Two of her classmates leaned against a car fender opposite the roadside, each with cigarettes in hand. "Hey, Sarah," the girl called out as she got closer to them. "It's a great party, but I didn't think you'd be here tonight." Sarah recognized Susan Anderson and her male companion, a member of the football team.

"I wouldn't have missed Kenny's celebration for anything. I'm glad everyone is having a good time." Sarah continued on as Susan took a drag of the cigarette she held, keeping a skeptical eye on Sarah as she walked by.

She climbed the broad, limestone steps to the veranda with its stone balustrade across the entire front of the stately home. Parts of the stone façade were shrouded by creeping ivy, and its heightened growth added to the feeling of the home's enduring presence. Two massive stone urns supporting well-manicured green topiaries stood guard on either side of the front door and played sentinels with their permanent placement. Sarah rang the bell, admiring the hefty lion's-head doorknocker beneath the arched, beveled glass fan lights sparkling at the top of the oversized door. She waited patiently for the door to open and was soon greeted by Kenny's mother.

"Sarah! How wonderful to see you, my dear. I know Kenny will be so glad you could come." Katherine O'Hara Birk always held herself with poise and dignity. A certain air about her exuded a confidence born of privilege, and her calmness was a natural heritage of her breeding. She wore a well-tailored navy blue suit with an off-white silk tie blouse beneath the perfectly fitted waist-length jacket. An opera-length set of luminous pearls complemented her graying hair, which was twisted in a knot at the back of her head. Although her face was of medial attractiveness, its kind expression drew one's attention. Katherine Birk's trim figure, dignified carriage, and pleasant demeanor allowed her to stand out in a crowd.

"Good evening, Mrs. Birk. I'm so glad I could be here."

"Do come in, Sarah, and come join us in the living room for a moment and say hello to Mr. Birk." Katherine led Sarah down the marble foyer, turning left into the elegant living room where a group of distinguished-looking guests gathered in groupings around the well-appointed room. The formal living room with its high ceiling and crown moldings was marked by tall, arched, palladium-styled French doors leading to the front veranda. Finely crafted woodworking and a hefty mantle surrounded the fireplace, over which hung a regal portrait of Mrs. Birk in sovereign pose. Two blue and white porcelain Chinese vases stood resolutely to the sides, framing her portrait. A richly polished, antique, parlor grand piano was positioned cattycorner in the room, adjacent to the French doors, and its heavily scrolled legs rested on top of an exquisite, ornately sculpted Chinese rug.

As Katherine and Sarah entered the room, John Douglas Birk turned to face them and excused himself from the company he held. JD had a distinguished look with his dark brown, slightly graying hair and steel-blue eyes. He was a tall man, in the habit of holding his chin up, which encouraged in others the need to take him seriously—unlike Kenny, who had a much more genial and relaxed nature. Sarah had the sense much of Mr. Birk's conversation was well-thought-out and covered a hidden agenda, no doubt a product of his many years in the practice of law.

"Sarah, it's wonderful to see you tonight," he offered immediately as he took her hand. His deep, resonant voice was steady and direct. "How are your mother and father?"

"They're both doing well, Mr. Birk. It's kind of you to ask. They've asked me to send you their regards, along with congratulations to Kenny, of course."

"I haven't seen your father in a while, although I suspect his new post keeps him busy and away from the courthouse."

"Yes, sir, it does."

"I must say you grow lovelier each time I see you, Sarah, and I don't understand how you've managed to keep those rowdy young men from your doorstep!"

"Thank you, Mr. Birk, but I suppose lots of schoolwork has something to do with that." She also considered that none of those "rowdy young men" held a candle to Travis Hall, a fact she could not escape in her thinking at his remark.

"Now that school is out, perhaps Kenny will bring you around a little more often."

"I'd like that, thank you, sir."

"I'm sure Sarah doesn't want to hear you ramble on, John Douglas, so we ought to let her go visit with her friends," Katherine interrupted, taking Sarah by the arm and leading her back to the hall. "I suppose you recall the way to the family room, Sarah, and if not, just follow the sound of the music, and you'll find everyone."

"Thank you, Mrs. Birk. I remember, and thanks for having me."

"It is always our pleasure, Sarah. Be sure to take a plate. The chocolate-covered strawberries are delicious!"

"I will."

Sarah headed down the long hallway, past the grand, sweeping, and ornate iron-railed staircase, then past the paneled study and formal dining room. At the end of the long hall stood two arches, one leading to the gourmet kitchen where the caterers were busy filling trays, and the other leading into the sizable family room. The music was playing loudly with quite a few people occupying the space. A long table at the side of the room supported an array of foods, all displayed with eye-catching appeal on tiered pedestals, garnished with colorful greens, fruits, and even flowers. The blue and white tablecloth draped to the floor, highlighting the school colors of North Shoreline High, while a small ice sculpture of a bulldog, representing their school's mascot, took center stage. The ice sculpture sat on a shiny silver tray, which was elevated prominently in the center of the long table; a congratulatory banner to the graduates was hanging above.

"Hey, Sarah, glad to see you could make it tonight," Ginger, one of the girls standing near the arched entry, called out to Sarah as she entered the family room.

Sarah joined the group of girls and tried to listen in on their conversation over the volume of the laughter and music playing in the background. "I got a late start, but I'm glad I could be here," she said, raising her voice in an effort to be heard.

"You look terrific, Sarah! What do you think of this little number?" Ginger asked in a loud voice, and then twirled around twice to show off her new blue party dress. "I bought it on sale at Abraham and Straus last week, just for the occasion. I couldn't resist, since it matched our school colors."

"It's beautiful, Ginger, and it fits you perfectly," Sarah responded, as she strained to be heard.

"Well, maybe Trent Rogers will think so too, if he can tear himself away from his team-mates long enough to notice. If I'm not competing with the team for his attention, then it's the food!" Ginger said loudly, as she pointed to the lavish spread of food to Sarah's back across the room.

Sarah laughed slightly, and then looked back over her shoulder. "I think I'll go find something to drink. It's good to see you, Ginger," Sarah replied, and then turned toward the opposite side of the room. She smiled to herself recalling that Ginger had been crazy about Trent Rogers most all of her junior and senior years. Liking Ginger, Sarah hoped Trent would notice how lovely she looked as well.

Small groups of friends and graduates formed separate huddles throughout the large space, while several couples danced to the music in a cleared area to the rear of the open room. A set of French doors at the far side of the family room led to the conservatory, lit by two massive chandeliers hanging from the framing at its peak. Sarah could clearly see the plants and ferns through its open doors. She scanned the spacious family room for Kenny and found him amongst a group of team members who formed a semicircle alongside the pool table. Ken's added height made him easy to find. They were engaged in a boyish game, counting the number of grapes each could throw into the air and catch in their mouths without eating them. Sarah smiled, thinking how their games were another reflection of their competitiveness, which Kenny basked in most of the time.

She made her way to the bar and helped herself to a soft drink while she surveyed the elegant presentation of foods displayed on the table to the side. A large, copper vessel containing beer on ice at the corner of the bar caught her attention, and she read the small placard resting on the bar in front of it. The card politely requested that beer was only for those over eighteen. Many of the graduates had already met that criteria, but with some friends still younger, it was an appropriate message. The enforcement of such a polite urging would remain difficult if not impossible, as the already rollicking crowd was proving.

A second set of French doors led to the back veranda. Its elevation gave an excellent view of the lighted pool with its statuaries spouting streams of water. The large, rectangular pool was centered on an expansive grassy lawn. The spacious limestone decking and potted plants surrounding the pool offered an attractive setting for the many lounge chairs, tables, and umbrellas. Half a dozen or more young people entertained themselves outside under the starlit heavens. They made themselves comfortable on cushioned chaise lounges, some unable to restrain themselves from their youthful urges, and their public displays of affection went ignored. How easy it was for them, she thought. They never gave a second thought regarding such intimate exposure in front of a crowd, nor did they consider the feelings of anyone there whose own affections went unanswered. Sarah sighed to herself, then turned to view the garden.

Sarah stood alone for the moment, admiring the beauty of Kenny's home, cognizant of the affluence needed to support such a charmed lifestyle. She was facing the backyard, reflecting on what the future held and where they would all be years from now, when life would be less carefree.

With all the finesse of a charging bull, Kenny came up behind her and wrapped his arms tightly around her waist. Resting his head close to her ear, Kenny spoke loud enough for Sarah to hear him. "Why didn't you tell me you were here?" He maintained his hold on her and inhaled deeply at the nape of her neck.

Placing her drink back on the bar, Sarah managed to turn while still in his embrace to face him. "You had your mouth full of grapes when I arrived, and I didn't want to interrupt the competition," Sarah offered, half-teasing him.

Kenny's white teeth shone like Chiclets as he smiled. Releasing his hold, he took both her hands in his own and stood back several feet, eyeing her from head to toe. "Sarah, you look fabulous! I'm so glad you were able to be here tonight. Did you get a chance to see Mom and Dad?"

"Yes, your mother met me at the door and was kind enough to bring me in to see your father as well. They both look wonderful."

"So, I guess you went into the lions' den—the old man never misses the chance to make every occasion an excuse to do some politicking. It doesn't matter if it's birthdays, anniversaries, graduations . . . they're all the same to him" Kenny said, while huffing and showing more teeth than usual. But enough about Dad; listen, Sarah, I was hoping, now that classes are finished for the summer, you might have some extra time so we could get together."

Two boys haphazardly bumped into them as they stumbled out to the back veranda, beers in hand. The noise level was continuing to rise, and Sarah could hardly hear Kenny speaking. He took her by the hand and headed for the conservatory, which remained free of traffic. He closed the glass doors behind them.

Sarah was thrilled to visit its interior, and now had the chance to view the stars through its glass roof. "Oh, Kenny, this is spectacular; but it isn't as easy to see the stars as I thought it would be."

"That's because the lights are still on." He turned to the wall and flipped the switch, turning off the sidelights and the chandeliers that hung from the framing.

"Oh, it's so beautiful! If I lived here, I would spend a lot of time in this room and gaze at the stars every night." She placed her purse on a nearby table and walked further into the space, her head tilted up in wonder at the alluring view of the twinkling stars above.

Kenny followed close behind. The open back of Sarah's dress exposed her smooth, soft skin along the delicate curve of her back. She was gorgeous, and Kenny's passions rose. "Sarah, dance with me." He put one arm around her waist and took her hand in his a second time.

Accepting him on his terms in that moment, Sarah relied on the security the close proximity of the others provided, and followed Kenny's lead.

"You know, I'll be heading to Massachusetts the last part of the summer. We always go up to my grandparents' place on the water so the family can get their sailing time in. I'd like to spend some time with you before we leave."

Sarah felt his arm tighten as she answered him, "I'll be working at the library full-time, Kenny, but I suppose we'll see each other before you leave."

"How about planning on next Saturday night?"

Sarah wasn't sure how to evade him this time and made a feeble attempt to answer as the music to the song "Go Away Little Girl" drew closer to an end. "I'll have to check to see what's going on at home before I could say for sure." Heat radiated from Kenny's perspiring hand as he slowly traced across her exposed back.

With very little subtlety, he slid his hand beneath the delicate fabric at the side of the open back of the dress, feeling the soft smooth skin of Sarah's ribcage. She pushed back slightly against him in quick rebuttal.

Kenny responded in frustration by putting both hands in the air at her reaction. He had made his play too quickly. "I'm sorry, Sarah, it won't happen again—I promise." She stood back from him a moment. Kenny had to keep her from overreacting, or risk not seeing her, and he had to prevent that at all costs. "I don't know what came over me. Maybe it was your perfume."

Sarah was grateful he recognized she didn't want his intimate physical contact, and she breathed a sigh of relief. "I accept your apology. I hope you know our friendship means a lot to me, Kenny, and I don't want us to ruin it."

"You make it damned hard to be just friends, Sarah, especially when you look so beautiful, but I'll try hard to live up to it."

A pause stretched between them as Kenny stared back at her, rubbing his heated palms against his trousers. Sarah knew what he was feeling but didn't want to hurt him. She went to retrieve her purse and pulled out the gift she had brought for him.

"What's this?"

"It's your graduation gift, Kenny."

He took it from her hand; a look of surprise crossed his face. "I think you're the only one who brought one."

"That's probably because most of the others here tonight graduated also. I, on the other hand, still have another year to go."

Kenny walked over to the French doors to catch the light of the family room and examined the small box looking eager to reveal its contents. He pulled the ribbon loose, and removed the lid, smiling broadly at Sarah. Kenny pulled the shiny brass keychain out of the box. Looking at it closely, he rubbed his fingers over the engraved image of the scales of justice and then glanced happily back at Sarah. "It's perfect! Now I suppose I'm locked into attending law school in order to use it."

"Call it a good-luck token then. Turn it over and read the other side."

Turning the brass medallion, Kenny tilted it toward the light of the family room once more and read its inscription. Along side of his initials, he read the engraved words "Friends Forever, Sarah." Facing her with a longing he could not hide, he confided with heartfelt sincerity, "I'll keep it with me always. Does the graduate at least get one kiss?"

Sarah smiled, shaking her head in conciliatory fashion, then drew a small breath as Kenny brought his lips to hers, taking from them eagerly the sweetness he longed to possess, this time without the use of his hands.

Returning to the family room, Kenny walked Sarah back to the table and offered her a plate, still holding his cherished key ring in hand. Several male friends yelled across the room for Kenny, one holding up an empty beer bottle and pointing to it. Kenny excused himself, returning to the rowdy group and bringing four more bottles of beer with him.

One of Kenny's teammates couldn't help offering his considered opinion as Kenny returned to the group. "What's the matter with you? Haven't you given up on Sarah Thompson yet? We've all decided she must be frigid, and you're just wasting your time on her, even if she is the best looking 'knock-out' this side of heaven. If you're not good enough for her, then she's the one with the problem. I'd forget her, if I were you, and move on."

Kenny looked back at Sarah wistfully, taking the ribbing of the group as he put his hand in his pocket, touching the key ring one more time. Not one among them wouldn't jump at the chance to date her if she ever gave them the slightest hint of possibility. As it was, they wouldn't dare move in on Kenny's territory until he gave up trying with her. Unlike the others, he had her close friendship, and he didn't intend to let that or the summer go to waste. For now at least, plenty of other girls were all too anxious for his company, and his attentions would be willingly received.

PART II

The Puppet

Life, said the puppet master, *is mine alone to scheme.*
But I am here, said puppet and know that I can dream.
Your fate is mine alone to give,
To fall or rise and die or live.

His hands may move my body sure,
But in my thoughts I truly soar.
What fate is his alone to give,
When in my mind I surely live?

In life I toil and find no peace,
But in my dream I soundly sleep.
To take my stand, this puppet dreams,
A vision held, I cut the strings.

Who will move me where I stand,
If puppet master has no hand?
I am awake in reverie; who then, master,
Has charge of me?

CHAPTER TWENTY-FOUR

The last of the teachers' meetings were finally finished for the year as Travis and Bob left the conference room behind and headed for their cars.

"How in the hell could the superintendent waste so damned much time on BS? For a while there, I thought we were back at ASU in one of those boring lectures with that philosophy professor who loved to hear himself talk," Bob complained.

"That's the privilege of rank," Travis reminded him.

"Well if that's what rank allows, you know what he can do with it."

The long hallways were empty now, and the school had an eerie silence unlike its usual hustle and bustle. With the class of 1963 graduated and the endless meetings finished, the long-awaited summer was finally at hand.

"So, what's your plan for the summer, Travis?"

"I've decided to head back to the ranch to give my dad an extra hand around the place. He's not as young as he once was, and my mother tells me he's slowing up lately. After that, I haven't got anything else planned. I'd like to get some fly-fishing in when I'm there. How about you? What have you got lined up?"

"You know me—I can always find something to keep myself busy. I've got a family reunion the end of July I've been roped into helping with, and I have my name down on the substitute teachers list for summer school. Other than that, it's just a matter of beating the women back off my doorstep! You think you'll be back by the end of July?"

Travis shook his head slightly as they walked. "I don't know. I guess it depends on what things look like at home after I get out there. It's actually been a while since I've spent any time helping out back home. As it is now, we already need to be back to Shoreline High no later than the second week of August, so you know I'll be back by then, maybe by the first of August if I can cut loose any sooner. Knowing my father, he'll have plenty lined out for me to do."

"When are you heading west?"

"The sooner I get out there, the sooner I can return, so I figured I'd tidy up some loose ends and get myself packed and ready to leave no later than Thursday morning of this week."

"The way I see it, the change in scenery will do you a lot of good. It's high time you put to rest that 'pie in the sky' dream you've been chasing concerning little miss baby doll, and the more distance you put between you and her, the better."

Travis wasn't amused. He shot Bob an intense and harsh expression with lips tightly pursed. "Count yourself lucky that I only take half of what you have to say seriously, my friend, or you might find yourself on your ass. I'd appreciate it if you wouldn't bring Sarah Thompson's name up with me again, and if you should somehow slip up, don't refer to her as a 'baby doll.' Got that?"

Bob knew he had just touched a nerve and understood he'd better back off. The fact that Travis hadn't carried out his impulse was clearly a happy ending to an otherwise touch-and-go situation. Travis had it bad, and he knew it wasn't going to be good for him if he acted on his desires. Leaving well enough alone, Bob changed the subject. "Are we still on for seafood before you leave?"

Travis threw his briefcase across the front seat of his car. "How about heading to the south shore? I've heard about a great little clam-bar in Freeport where they say the bartender makes some mean drinks."

"Have you ever known 'the man' to turn down a deal like that? Suppose we plan on Wednesday, say about four o'clock?"

Travis slipped into the driver's seat and turned to face Bob. "You're on. That will give me time to finish up before I leave on Thursday."

Baxter nodded, standing beside Travis's car with his hand on the roof. "Since you know where it is, why don't you pick me up at my place?"

"I'll be there. See you then." Travis shut the car door and headed north out of the school parking lot, checking his rearview mirror as he left the high school behind.

He wondered where Sarah Thompson was and what the summer held for her. He couldn't prevent the thought that both of them carried an unspoken longing, yet the impossibility of the situation loomed along with thoughts of the coming fall semester, how he would be able to get through it. The last year had been painfully difficult; seeing her day in and day out for another year would be equally trying. She was the one who tore at his heart, and only Sarah filled his senses with longing and passion. His interest in her was far more than a physical attraction; never before had any female drawn him with such voracity.

Even at her tender age, Sarah didn't run with the pack. Hers wasn't a forced identity, when so many were experimenting to see who they wanted to be and what cloak they wanted to wear. Self-guided from within, her easy naturalness produced an authentic nature never scripted or forced. Beauty lay in the mundane to her, a spark of life hidden beneath every façade lit by the act of her witnessing. He had been busy attacking life, molding it to conform to his expectations, demanding himself to be the very best, while she partook in life as a grateful member, happy to share in it the way it was delivered. Where pain existed, she brought empathy and effort to regain harmony. She could see beneath the surface, the cause rather than the effect, while he righted what was obvious in each moment, standing in harm's way if necessary. He left others to question "why," while he concerned himself with the outcome alone. They were as different as night was from day, he the warrior and she the peacemaker, yet their attraction had an overpowering, magnetic pull. Her lack of experience made her unsure, but he could see the obvious. What each of them lacked, they found in the other, compelled to a union worthy of both.

It would have been an easy seduction for him, but he cared far too much for her to settle for that and risk everything. Sarah brought him to a place inside himself long-neglected, a place he badly needed to help overcome the loss he had suffered. Being with her made him feel alive again, and he couldn't settle for anything less than all of her. He needed her gentleness, her joy in life, and he needed to know he was someone she could love, minus the vestments of his honored past at West Point. He had lost everything, including who he was and who he should become now that he was without the distinguished military career his achievement had promised. Sarah knew nothing of his past or the coveted first captain rank he had attained, and yet, she found in him someone worthy of her love. Her love was without condition, needing no dressing or promise to support it. She saw beneath the strong man and courted only his heart.

There had been a parade of others through his earlier college years. All left him wanting. Some were beautiful to look at, but their flaws always overshadowed them. Many were struck on themselves to the point of narcissism while others were totally needy; and in some cases, they were both. Far too many bore the hallmarks of easy virtue, while a host of others claimed their hallowed affections reserved for the future through tightly clenched lips. Their conversations matched the chains that bound them—cold, chatty, and empty. They were all looking for men with money, position, and power. It mattered little to them if polish replaced principle or if good looks took precedence over intelligence, so long as it brought them fortune. With time, he recognized the truly ambitious among them who wanted to pin their hopes and dreams on his shirttails, knowing his past achievements and, consequently, assuming his bright future.

In the end, good times were just that, good times that never lasted and always begged to move on to the next good time. Sarah presented something lasting he could not escape, and no matter the endless possibilities for him, her face was the one he returned to time and again.

With one glance of those compelling translucent aqua blue eyes, Sarah was able to read him, and only her lack of experience with men and the position he held over her caused her insecurity. Her decision not to attend his help classes any longer wounded him, even though he now understood that as her only way to cope with an impossible attraction.

He didn't have the means to tell her how he felt about her without risking harm to both of them, and he couldn't do that or he would forfeit everything. For the first time, he understood what it was to love someone and ask nothing in return. Selfless love was a lesson he could learn from no one else.

Sarah was a born lady in every respect, with an instinctive wisdom that refused deception. He never experienced the psychological gap in their age difference when alone with her, even though he was well aware of her inexperience and naivety with men in general. Intellectually, he grappled repeatedly with their eight years difference in age and struggled to reckon that fact. She could use words with eloquence, yet the quiet between her words allowed their unspoken conversation to soar. She excited him in their silence together. Travis recognized her passion in the way she could become lost in simple things like a bird in melodic song or a few well-written words in a novel. He easily expected to find the same thrilling level of womanly passions disguised beneath her virtuous and ladylike covering as well. It wouldn't take money to make Sarah happy, and he doubted she would ever be a fortune hunter. No, she would be the one hunted, the prize that made men enviable. Sarah was the perfect woman—arrestingly beautiful, intelligent, kind-hearted, and passionate. The only thing she wasn't was eighteen and graduated.

His needed restraint clamped down hard inside him like a bow stretched to it limits. Without a much-needed separation, they would be tempting fate. An impossible task both of them were doomed to fail. One more time, he was watching what he desired most slip through his fingers like water through a fisherman's net, leaving nothing but an empty dream.

Maybe Bob was right. A change of scenery would do him good, and with Sarah's absence, the unrequited desire would relent. One thing was certain; he didn't think he could endure another year as agonizing as this one had been for him.

By early Thursday morning, Travis Hall passed through the Holland Tunnel, landing on New Jersey's shore on his long trek west.

CHAPTER TWENTY-FIVE

SUMMER OF 1963

By the end of July, Kenny had managed to see Sarah at least four times. Unfortunately for him, his time with her was limited to friendly excursions that always included several others and was predominately during daylight hours. She and Nonie joined Kenny and a group of friends at a private beach along the north shore several times. It was a beautiful and well-tended beach in a secluded cove where many sailing boats and yachts were moored. The gently rolling, tree-lined hills graced the shoreline to the water's edge. Lush green lawns carpeted beneath towering oaks, providing clear passage to lengthy docks that protruded like slender fingers into the picturesque cove. The small, well-manicured beach formed a silver-white arc that reflected the radiance of the midday sun, beckoning boaters on the sound to tarry a while and enjoy its tranquil location. The partially concealed site, with its white sandy shore and off-shore diving raft, made the private beach an oasis, but with the others as company, Kenny grew thirsty for time alone with Sarah.

Although he knew she wasn't dating anyone else, his yearning to claim her for his own was not dampened. Everyone thought he was crazy to continue his pursuit, while Sarah did her best to walk a fine line with him. As a result, he was free to date whomever he pleased, and he always had plenty of others to choose from when his passions needed to be met.

The month of August came quickly, and Kenny left for Martha's Vineyard with his family. The Birks had much to celebrate, including the fact that Kenny had been accepted to Columbia. His course was now firmly set toward law school, which pleased his father—something that wasn't always easy to do. It was a direction he had been groomed for all his life, but he wondered what his father would have done had he decided on a different path. It was a scenario he never tested, knowing that his father wasn't a man whose objectives and purposes could be easily redirected. Kenny went along to get along. He wasn't particularly looking forward to college, but he would be close to home and would be able to make it back on weekends and holidays when he would see Sarah again. In the back of his mind, the only decision that was truly his own was to one day capture Sarah's heart.

Sarah kept her job at the public library that summer and soon managed a small following of youngsters who delighted in her readings at storybook hours. The staff recognized her love of literature, along with an excellent work ethic, and they conferred on her the chance to continue working part-time during her upcoming senior year. She gladly accepted the offer. As a result of her work with the children, she recognized the impoverishment of some. Sarah initiated the placement of a children's clothing drop box alongside the after-hours book return in order to meet the clothing needs of the poorer children in the area, and she organized a group of women to help sort and distribute the clothing in the community. That project was dear to her heart, and she was glad to have had a busy summer, which kept her thoughts from drifting continually back to Travis Hall.

Her quiet moments alone were the sweetest moments of each day. She would relive precious time spent with him, especially his words at their parting on the last day of the school year. Regardless of the fact she was nothing more than another student, Sarah couldn't shake the feeling that she might have meant something more to him and that he had been attempting to share that with her during their last few moments alone together. Sarah counted the days till the fall semester would start, longing to see him again.

Lily Thompson had rallied the last two months, partially because the extreme humidity that was usually part of their summers hadn't accompanied the warmer temperatures. With the dryer air, breathing was easier for Lily, and she didn't tire as quickly as usual. Liz had taken a job waitressing for the summer at one of the trendy beach resorts in Rhode Island, keeping her off-campus apartment with several other girls, and she ventured home only once that summer for a short visit before returning to Rhode Island. With the help of Mrs. Reed next door, Rachael was looked after without Sarah having to be at home full time, but Sarah still managed to handle dinners, with her schedule at the library releasing her by 4:00 most afternoons. Her father was dining away from home two out of three nights, which made fixing meals relatively easy.

Charley had adjusted well to his new post heading up the homicide division. He proved to be quite the diplomat when it came to keeping the elected politicians happy while enforcing the laws. His record was proof of his stellar service; he helped to secure more convictions in the homicide division than any of his predecessors had in the same amount of time. The Grand Jury had convened earlier that summer and found probable cause to indict Patrick Stevens for the murder of his wife, and the trial was set for September. Mark Stevens healed from his wounds and remained in the custody of his aunt in Mineola. He would become the State's witness against his father at the upcoming trial. His story became a footnote to history as neighbors moved on, but Sarah felt the awful reminder of his pain-filled life each time she backed out of her driveway and caught a glimpse of the for-sale sign firmly fixed in the unkempt yard.

Classes were slated to begin immediately after Labor Day. September third couldn't arrive soon enough for her. Travis

Hall's memory had become her silent companion the last two and a half months. She was constrained from talking about him with anyone; ever mindful of the harm such talk would cause both of them if her suspicions and longings were taken seriously. Many were the hours she wondered where he was and how he was spending his summer. Thoughts always beckoned to know if he held company with another, and invariably, such thoughts proved depressing when she again realized the age difference between them and the impossibility of any relationship. Sarah came to think her understanding might have been incorrect, and with each new day, her doubts grew stronger. Still, the flame of love burned on in her heart with or without such assessments. Sarah fed the flame, knowing their moments together had been real, regardless of their future. No amount of time would ever erase his memory.

~~~~~~~~~~~

AUGUST 19, 1963

Holding a glass of iced tea in his hand, Robert Baxter jumped as the telephone unexpectedly rang out. Bob readjusted his black horn-rimmed glasses and rose from the couch. He turned the volume down on the TV before he headed to the phone. "Baxter here," he answered, expecting the caller to be from the school with a request for him to substitute.

"I wasn't sure I'd find you home, Baxter. Hasn't the school called you for duty yet?"

"Hell, Travis, you ought to know all this time off keeps me in circulation. So where are you, and are you heading back? It's beginning to get boring on the chase without you around here," Bob answered with a smile at hearing Travis's voice.
~~~~~~~~~~~

"That's the reason I'm calling. The good news is you won't have any competition from me anytime soon, my friend. The bad news is I'm not coming back for the fall semester either."

"Are you serious? What the hell's going on, Travis? School prep and teachers' meetings start next week."

"I know this is a surprise, but we've had a setback out here. My father took a stroke two weeks ago, and I'm afraid it's worse than we first expected. He's completely paralyzed on his right side, has difficulty speaking and even swallowing. We thought he might regain some mobility by now, but it doesn't look good. He's going to require full-time care, and my mother insists on bringing him home. She's not going to make it without me, Baxter."

"Damn, Travis! I'm sure sorry to hear about your dad. Is there a chance that with rehab and physical therapy he can ever get back on his feet again?"

"They aren't very optimistic, and the doctors tell us the damage to his brain is extensive and permanent. It's similar to severe head trauma where parts of the brain are lost and can never be restored. Once we get him home, the county nursing service will make weekly visits, but there's no way my mother can handle his care alone, not to mention the daily running of the ranch. To make matters worse, I've been going over the books, and my father never told anyone how much debt he'd taken on the last couple of years. I haven't said anything about it to my mother, and I'm sure she has no idea. Besides, she has enough to deal with as it is right now."

"Is there anything I can do on this end to help out?"

"I've already notified the school, and they still have time left to find a replacement, but there is one thing you could do for me."

"You name it," Bob immediately replied.

"My apartment is paid in full through the end of August, and since I won't be back anytime soon, I need to ask if you'd mind clearing what little is in the place out. Just keep whatever you want and give the rest to Goodwill. There are a few papers lying around the place I might need, but other than that, do whatever you want with the rest of it."

"Will do, my friend. I'll give you a call in a few weeks to see how your dad's making out. If something else comes up, just give me a call. I wish there was something else I could do or say to help."

"Thanks, Baxter, I appreciate the offer. Until I get a handle on things out here, I'm not exactly sure what all the needs are going to be just yet. Listen, I've got to go, but I want you to know I appreciate the help."

"You got it, Travis. Talk to you soon, buddy." Bob hung up the phone, keeping his hand on the receiver. He shook his head, feeling the weight of the problems his friend had to contend with. He picked up the phone again to call another friend to muster some help in clearing Travis's apartment. Bob couldn't help but think the troubles came one after another for Travis, and he wished life would cut the guy some slack.

CHAPTER TWENTY-SIX

SEPTEMBER 1963

Travis threw the mail on the counter, including a medium-sized box wrapped in brown paper. Reading the return address and sender's name, he tore off the paper and quickly opened the parcel. He pulled out an assortment of papers, including old utility bill stubs and other notes that had remained scattered around his Huntington apartment. A small, handwritten note accompanied the papers.

> *Travis—I didn't know how much of this stuff you needed and decided to forward all of it. Mission Clean Out is completed and all went well. I had the apartment cleaned before leaving the key with the landlord. Hope your dad is making progress—will call later in the month. Baxter.*

From beneath the old papers and mail, he pulled out a copy of the 1963 North Shoreline High School yearbook. Several pages were marked with bits of paper and Travis turned to each of the marked pages. On page 110, the North Shoreline High School marching band was pictured on the football field with Sarah Thompson prominently centered in uniform at the front of the band, smiling broadly. He stared at the page for a moment before turning to the second marker. The second marked page was highlighting one of the junior homeroom classes; Sarah Thompson sat beside her classmates in a ladylike pose with her hair neatly pulled halfway back as she wore a slight smile across her delicate pink lips. Travis kept his eyes fixed for a protracted moment on the page while forming a crease along his lower lip with his teeth. After a moment, he moved the book aside, leaving it open as he reached back into the box and pulled out a wad of newspaper lying on the bottom. The paper was wrapped firmly around something. He quickly removed the layers of newspaper, and the blonde, blue-eyed "Q-P" doll fell to the counter. Travis smiled knowingly; Bob knew his heart, despite the constant harassment and warnings he sounded throughout the school year. True to Travis's request, Bob hadn't mentioned Sarah's name, but he wanted Travis to have his keepsakes. He stood silently collecting his thoughts, running his hands first over the open yearbook and then across the face of the wide-eyed baby doll. No time or distance could separate him from thoughts of Sarah, and after a few minutes he drew a dejected breath.

Discarding most of the papers, Travis put the doll and yearbook back in the box, covering it with the lid, and then carried it to his closet where he stowed it on the top shelf for safekeeping. Sometimes he felt like a passenger on board a high-speed train that allowed for no stops, and all he could do was hold on tight for the ride. The life he wanted was out there as he viewed it from the windows, but he wasn't able to walk the streets of the towns as the train sped by.

~~~~~~~~~~

Sarah Thompson and Nonie Gorman held their allotted places as seniors in September of 1963. Much to the relief of the majority of returning students, word traveled fast that Mr. Hall was no longer teaching at the high school, relieving many from being assigned to one of his math classes. Nonie took the news with an added sense of relief, but his absence came as a devastating blow
~~~~~~~~~~

to Sarah, and her despondency went unexplained. The utter emptiness she carried in her heart produced a perpetual malaise that dragged on for most of the year. Even Fran Johnson, the school gossip, hadn't been able to discover the reason for his departure, and all anyone knew for sure was that he wasn't coming back for the '63–'64 school year. Her eighteenth birthday meant nothing that year. What good was turning legal to her with the absence of Travis Hall?

When even the dean hadn't heard a word about the reason for his departure, Sarah remained disheartened. She managed to keep busy with her job at the library after school three days a week, and most of her classes were relatively easy, proving to be a lighter load in her senior year. The fall semester kept its melancholy with the horrible murder of John F. Kennedy late in November, and Sarah's despondency was soon shared by the student body as a whole.

Kenny kept busy his freshman year at Columbia, although he never missed a chance to see Sarah when he would return home over holidays. A few members of the old gang were always still in the vicinity, and Sarah gathered with them, often at Kenny's home or out for pizza when they were all in town. She never missed the chance to visit with Kenny's mother on such occasions, since both shared the same love for worthy charitable causes; Katherine O'Hara Birk could always entice Sarah to volunteer for one thing or another with the many charity events she helped coordinate.

Nonie made time during holidays for Abe Kaplan, and she wasn't shy about sharing the fact that she considered her future bright with him. Even her grandmother approved. What Nonie could never understand was Sarah's lack of interest in dating and how Sarah still considered Kenny only a good friend when everyone else knew Kenny considered her much more than that. Nonie thought if she had been blessed with Sarah's good looks, her calendar would be full most of the time and, more than once, told Sarah she wasn't using her considerable physical attributes to her advantage. Her pleas always fell on deaf ears.

Hidden from the world, Sarah lived in the hope that Travis Hall would return by graduation when she would be eighteen and neither of them would be subject to the laws constraints. No matter the length of time since his departure, Sarah returned time and again to his memory, where the sweet burning embers kept alive the hope of his return.

CHAPTER TWENTY-SEVEN

FEBRUARY 1964

The black hearse parked adjacent to the cemetery near a row of pinyon pines that were dusted in a light blanket of snow. The limousine waited not more than seventy-five feet from the funeral canopy where Travis and his mother, Clara, sat protected from the gently falling snowflakes. The gray and dreary skies added a depth of chilling sadness to their loss. Cordell Hall's death came as no surprise; he had lingered in a crippled state for more than eight months before his demise. Clara leaned against her son's chest; her eyes filled with tears, unable to hide her grief.

With the service ended, the mourners filed past them, extending their sympathies as they returned to their cars for the warmth and shelter the modest canopy could not provide. Edgar Sims, a tall, wiry-looking man wearing a wide-brimmed black Stetson, dark cowboy boots, and a fleece-lined suede jacket, made his way to them from the end of the line of mourners. His neatly trimmed, full mustache traced a downward path around his lips but was unable to hide the sadness reflected in his heavily lined eyes. Leathery skin and callused hands identified that he was well-acquainted with hard work. Edgar took Clara's hand with a gentleness that somehow belied his rugged exterior.

"Clara, I know you already know how deeply sorry I am, and how we'll all be lost without Cordell, but we've been friends for far too long for you not to call on me if you have the need to. You know this old cowboy is as close as the next spread from your place, and I'd be in a heap of pain if I couldn't start helping out." He turned to Travis. "Travis, I don't know what your plans are now, son, but I think we need to talk when things settle down. Give me a call when you can." He shook Travis's hand.

"You've been a good friend and neighbor, Edgar, and we are beholden to you. I'll be in touch in the next few days. Thanks again for the support," Travis gratefully replied.

Edgar tipped his hat toward Clara and then turned, heading back to his jeep in the gently falling snow.

No better horseman lived in this part of the country than Edgar Sims. Although years younger than Travis's father, Edgar's friendship with Cordell Hall went way back as far as Travis could remember. Together, Cordell and Edgar were able to save each other's houses and barns when a Rim fire threatened them up in the high country during the long dry spell years earlier. Cordell and Edgar were not only the best of friends but played an integral role in the success of the annual rodeo that attracted nationwide competition and brought the spotlight to this part of the country for three days every August. Cordell Hall was primarily a cattleman and Edgar Sims a horseman. Cordell provided the calves for the rodeo each year, while Edgar trained, bought, and sold cutting horses. People came from all over the country to buy one of Edgar's horses, and he was known to many from the rodeo circuit on a first-name basis. Together, Edgar and Cordell formed a strong bond and friendship that had only strengthened with each passing year.

Edgar would probably be aware of Travis' father's financial losses since beef prices took a nosedive in recent years. Travis could count on Edgar for the help he would need to recover some of those losses. Because of the added debt incurred at the ranch, Travis recently took a job down in the valley with the Honeywell

Corporation working in research and development of weapons systems. Travis hoped to turn things around with the added income. He was determined not to tell his mother the seriousness of the situation, and worked down in the valley during the week and returned to the Rim on weekends to keep up with the ranch's demanding workload.

Once back home at the modest ranch house with his mother, Travis cleaned the remains of the dishes piled at the sink from the various casseroles and salads left behind by neighbors and well-wishers. Clara sat in the living room, wrapped in a plaid blanket, a cup of tea at her side as she peered into the fire. The touches of gray in her strawberry-blonde hair feathered around her freckled face while the bulk of hair rested in a knotted braid at the back of her head. Her light green eyes and fair complexion hid her fifty-five years with a more youthful appearance. After cleaning the kitchen, Travis joined her on the couch, touching her hand tenderly as he sat beside her.

Clara turned to face him with a sad and weary expression. "You don't have to stay, Travis. You are young and have to make a life for yourself of your own choosing."

"What makes you think this isn't what I would choose?"

Clara brought her hand to Travis's cheek, and her love showed clearly in her eyes. "Your father wanted more for you than this, Travis. He was so proud of you and all your accomplishments. He never graduated and only knew hard work from sunrise to sunset. Can't you understand he wanted more for you than just that?"

"There's nothing wrong with hard work, Mom, and there is plenty of honor in that for any man. Besides, this is my home, too, and working the ranch will always be in my blood, just as it was Dad's. I'm staying, and you can't talk me out of it," he said emphatically.

"What about your teaching back in New York?"

"You know teaching wasn't my first choice, and if I really wanted to teach, I could do that here as well. But there is no money in that either, if that was your concern. Besides, I was beginning to miss this old place anyway."

"You're a good son, Travis. Your father was always proud to have you bear the Hall name, and so am I. It's been a hard, long day, and I think I'll turn in. I want you to think on your decision. Don't make up your mind too quickly. We'll hash this over again later, son, when we have clearer heads to think it through. Today isn't the time to make such a decision." Clara stood up, kissed Travis good night, and then headed to her room, still wrapped in her blanket.

Travis sat by the fire, engrossed in his thoughts, feeling the loss of his father and concern for his mother as well as the family ranch. He was all she had after the untimely death of his older sister ten years earlier. Her death, along with his accident and now his father's death left his mother broken with no where else to turn. Straightening out her affairs and saving the ranch from foreclosure would be up to him. It was a responsibility that he knew rested squarely on his shoulders. With his decision already made, his thoughts drifted back to Long Island and to Sarah Thompson, wondering when he would ever be able to see her beautiful face again. At the time of their parting, he expected to return the following school semester in the fall. Life was pulling the rug out from under Travis for the second time, and he was determined not to give up on seeing Sarah again, although how and when he would be able to do so still remained unknown. Sarah was his last thought as he fell asleep on the couch in front of the fire.

~~~~~~~~~~

The months after his father's death moved slowly for Travis, and the strain of keeping up the constant work pace between the ranch and Honeywell levied a toll both physically and mentally. He had another five weeks before the rodeo in the third week of August, and the herd had a good birthing rate this past spring, with a couple of hundred calves born between April and May.
~~~~~~~~~~

He would have plenty of calves at the right weight of 220 to 280 pounds for the upcoming rodeo, and the addition of so many healthy new calves was a nice increase to the existing herd. Edgar Sims remained the stalwart neighbor and friend, without whose constant help and oversight Travis would be unable to keep up. Without the added income of Travis's salary, the needed repairs and higher costs to run the ranch would have been impossible. Still, it would be quite a while before the debts would be paid off. Cordell Hall had taken out a second mortgage shortly before his stroke and had been falling behind in those payments. For now at least, Travis was able to keep up with the payments but knew he could make the ranch self sustaining with enough time. The long drive every weekend back to the ranch gave him plenty of time to think, and those thoughts would eventually take him back to Sarah Thompson. There was no way he could spare the time or expense of a trip back east, especially with the cost of maintaining an apartment down in the valley, where he stayed during the workweek. That additional expense subtracted from the bottom line of his expendable income. The more his thoughts rested on Sarah, the more despondent he became.

This Friday afternoon brought such thoughts to mind. It had been a pressure-filled week at Honeywell as Travis tried to meet deadlines in the department where he worked. The long hours both at work and at home were coming to a head, and tonight Travis was feeling the stress heavier than ever before. Missing Sarah with a craving and desire that he was unable to keep in check, he needed a way to dampen those obsessive thoughts. On his way back to his apartment after work, Travis spontaneously pulled into the Hacienda Bar and Grill, hoping to drown out the yearning desire. He needed relief, and a quick drink might help to numb his senses.

Travis headed straight to the bar and, instead of his usual beer, ordered a scotch on the rocks. He wasted no time downing it, hoping for its intended effect. It was already 6:00 p.m., and he decided he could wait until the following morning before heading back to the ranch. With his plan now set, another scotch would help to tamp down his thoughts and feelings, since he wouldn't have to face the two-hour drive tonight.

Still nursing his second drink, Travis glanced at the mirror in front of him and caught sight of a woman approaching the bar. Wearing a low-cut, sleeveless black dress with bright red flowers printed randomly across the tightly fitted bodice, she took a seat adjacent to his at the bar. With his head tilted toward his glass, Travis slowly chased the ice around in a circle with his finger, using the mirror to keep an attentive eye on the woman now seated to his right. Her short brown hair framed her face with sharpened points and helped accentuate her light brown eyes and slightly turned-up nose. She placed her purse on the bar, and then leaned forward on her elbows and arms, attracting the middle-aged bartender who did not try to hide his glance at her provocative and revealing pose.

"Vodka tonic with a twist," she said slowly. The bartender was all too eager to respond and went about the task at hand. She reached into her purse and pulled out a cigarette, holding it casually between two fingers of her right hand. Travis watched in the mirror as she rummaged through her bag and finally cast it aside in frustration. Turning to Travis, she asked, "I don't suppose you might have a light?"

Travis was mildly entertained, thinking this was obviously a ploy she had used more than once to solicit the attention she craved. He reached for a set of matches in a bowl on the bar to his left and struck a match as she leaned into it, bringing the cigarette to her lips while meeting the flame. He estimated her to be about twenty-five, although the makeup she wore made her look older. Her hairstyle and petite figure gave her a pixie-like appearance, though she could not disguise a somewhat-hardened look, especially around her heavily made-up eyes. Taking a long drag of her cigarette, she blew the smoke to the side.

"I'd like to thank you, but I try to make a point of knowing who I'm thanking first," she said.

Travis scanned her more closely, facing her directly. A slight creasing to the corners of his mouth did not reveal his thoughts about how well rehearsed she really was. "Who wants to know?" he asked, still holding an unreadable expression and discarding the match in a nearby ashtray.

"Mary Cavanah," she answered, holding her chin up meeting him face to face.

"The name is Travis Hall, Miss Cavanah," he said, his eyes held steady on her.

The bartender returned with her drink, and Mary raised her glass with a nod of her head and a twinkle in her eye. "Thank you, Mr. Travis Hall, for the light."

Travis brought his drink to his lips, and then returned it to the bar. Feeling quite entertained and amused at her rather bold and overt manner, he wondered why she was alone and just how often she played the obvious chasing game. Managing a polite smile, he turned back to his drink, deciding to leave well enough alone.

"I don't suppose you'd care to share some conversation since we're no longer strangers?" She finally asked when the pause became extended and he made no further attempt to engage her.

Travis was slow to answer, though he gave her an "A" for persistence. "Miss Cavanah, I don't know why you're here tonight, but I didn't come for the conversation, as nice as that might be with you, so perhaps you should find someone else to engage in chatting."

"Why are you here then, Travis?"

Travis raised his glass with a cock of his head as he met her glance out of the corner of his eye, hoping she would understand the only companion he sought was the liquor.

"Well then, it seems we're both on the same mission," Mary confided as she held her glass to her lips in the same hand she used to support her cigarette.

Travis finished his second drink, and the bartender received his nod, mixing a third. With no words exchanged, the bartender placed the drink down in front of him.

Mary Cavanah took another long drag of her cigarette. Too anxious to wait any longer for him to offer further conversation, she continued, "There is no crime in drowning ourselves in our troubles together, is there?"

"It's a free country," Travis replied. He was feeling the effects of the alcohol, and it mattered little what his uninvited companion did or said. The pain of leaving Sarah Thompson behind was diminishing as his senses numbed.

Mary Cavanah ordered another vodka tonic with a smile on her face, eyeing her catch, and vowed to herself to hang in there with him drink for drink. She couldn't help but admire the masculine physique and handsome square line of his jaw, as well as the intense green eyes of her newfound friend. Her luck, she thought, was about to change.

By 9:00 p.m., Mary had downed several more drinks than the three consumed by Travis, and he could see she was in no condition to continue. "The fun is over for tonight, Mary," he said to her. "I'll call you a cab."

"Is that any way to treat a friend?" she protested. "I don't think I like the idea of getting into a cab with a stranger who might be inclined to take advantage of a lady in my condition."

Travis shook his head and shrugged, realizing his leaving as well was long overdue. "All right, Mary, grab your purse, and I'll drive you home," he finally agreed.

Together, they made their way to his car as Mary clung to his arm for support. Once inside the car he asked, "How far is it to your place, and what's the address?"

Looking back at him with a devilish smile, she replied, "It's within a mile, just north of McDowell on North Fortieth Street." She leaned back in the seat and began singing along playfully with the music from the radio during the ride to her apartment.

Travis parked the car while Mary searched in her bag for her keys, fumbling in her inebriated state. Travis got out and went to her door to help her out. She would need his support to negotiate the flight of stairs to her apartment. Taking her keys from her hand, Travis wrapped his arm around her and helped her up the stairs to her door and then used the key.

Once inside, Mary directed him to her room. Travis helped her to her bed and then turned to leave, when she suddenly grabbed his arm and pulled him back to her.

"Travis, can't we pretend to be more than friends for just tonight?" she pleaded, with a longing in her glassy, bloodshot eyes. Without moving, he watched as she began undressing herself, obviously hoping to entice him to her bed. Her small but firm breasts were now fully exposed as she forced the dress from her curvy body, revealing the black bikini panties she wore beneath. From the start of the evening she had been working tirelessly for just this ending, and in that moment, he decided to oblige her, not giving a damn about her objectives and motives and only wanting to release his own frustrations and pent-up anger. With no more thought than that, he got undressed and slid next to her, taking her with the force she demanded.

For a short while after, Travis lay there without feeling, empty inside and no closer to the answer of how he would ever get to see Sarah Thompson again. He left Mary sleeping soundly, no more relieved than when he had ordered his first drink. He could mask the pain temporarily, but nothing would remove it except to be with Sarah again.

CHAPTER TWENTY-EIGHT

By June of 1964, Sarah and Nonie were finally high-school graduates. Sarah enrolled in a local community college and had decided to stay close to home, knowing her mother's condition could turn for the worse at any time. There had been several setbacks the last year, but Lily managed to rally after her last hospital stay. She was treated with a round of diuretics that helped remove the fluids built up around her heart. Everyone understood that her heart was failing, and Rachael would be the one to suffer the most if her mother did not survive. Without Sarah at home, there would be no one else to fill the void in Rachael's young life.

Sarah continued to work over that summer and into the fall that year. Although she did manage to date on several occasions, it was usually with friends, and she made sure never to accept a date with the same person twice. She found it far easier that way, ensuring her freedom from any relationship other than friendship. Mirroring her junior year, Sarah had politely turned down invitations to the senior prom as well, citing her mother's deteriorating health as reason for her decline. To have done anything else would have meant living a lie; Travis Hall was the only man she could bring herself to think of in a more meaningful and intimate way. Kenny was always there, and Sarah became comfortable with him as he learned to hold his distance. Together with several others that summer, she and Kenny took in the New York World's

Fair. He was always happy to have Sarah at his side, even if hand-holding was the best she could offer him. It was no different this day as they sat across from one another at a local diner after a full day with their friends at the Fair.

After Sarah had placed her order for a coffee with a muffin and Kenny had ordered a burger and fries, Sarah asked him, "How is school going this semester?"

"It's all right, but it's tougher than I thought it would be, and my classes don't allow a lot of extra free time."

"You know you can handle it. Besides, it's all headed toward a great goal."

"A great goal for my father, you mean!" he scoffed, with a sudden downward slant to his lips. "I get enough pressure at school without him reminding me every time I come home that I need to keep my grades up." A slight bulge of the veins in his neck as well as the flaring of his nostrils highlighted his change in tone.

"He only wants the best for you." Sarah tilted her head to the side, eyes wide open appealing to him to see the best in his father's prodding. Kenny drew a deep breath.

"I suppose you're right. Besides, Columbia is as good a place as any to be right now, since Congress just approved the Gulf of Tonkin Resolution. Dad seems to think that it gives the green light for President Johnson to wage a wider war in Vietnam. Even without a declaration of war, I'm still glad to be in school to keep my deferment," Kenny reluctantly admitted.

"Maybe it won't be as bad as the news media makes it out."

Kenny looked out the window pensively for a moment, caught between the devil and the deep blue sea, and then suddenly turned back to Sarah with a wide smile, immediately discarding his previous seriousness. "So, what's new at the library? Do you plan to keep that job now that you're attending C.W. Post?"

"They've been good to me there, and they continue to work around my schedule. I really need the money, although my time will be spread thin enough, especially not knowing if my mother might take a turn," Sarah answered. "Are you headed back to Columbia tomorrow?"

"No, Dad's got some kind of a political fundraiser tomorrow and insists on taking me along. I guess I'll have to tolerate the meaningless handshakes and all the B.S. the bigwigs throw around at these things. I'll do whatever makes my father happy to keep him off my back." Shaking his head, he looked out the window pausing, before facing Sarah again. "Mom tells me you two are working together on another project. Want to tell me about it?"

"It's really quite exciting, Kenny. Her foundation was looking for another cause they could contribute to. She took my suggestion to build an after-school children's center located near the center of town. It would provide a safe place for many of the kids to congregate after school until their parents arrive home from work. The building could be used for a variety of other uses as well, like a local community center, but with an emphasis on the kids."

Kenny reached out and took Sarah's hand, holding it across the table. "It sounds great, and between the both of you, I know it will be a great success." He fashioned a smile as he looked into her eyes.

"Thanks, Kenny, that means so much to me," Sarah responded with sincerity. After a pause, she gently pulled her hand out from beneath his, placing her hand back in her lap. They finished eating, and then Kenny drove Sarah home, making plans to see her, along with their other friends, over Thanksgiving break.

Kenny continued to believe Sarah would one day see in him something more than a good friend. Sarah working closely with his mother allowed him to keep careful tabs on her. In between visits home, he happily entertained several other girls at Columbia on the sidelines, and the list of those available to him was long and varied. He didn't mind the sampling, so long as Sarah remained unattached.

By the end of the fall of '64, Sarah began to realize her constant thoughts of Travis Hall's return were only wishful fantasy of a nonexistent reality. She recalled that before her high school graduation, Fran Johnson had also queried Mr. Baxter regarding Mr. Hall. Much to Fran's chagrin, he would only share that Mr. Hall wasn't returning to school. No one was able to learn anything more about him, although Sarah had lived in hope. With his memory in her heart, Sarah visited the old Red Windmill pizza joint with friends several times during that winter and following summer, and at each visit, she relived the moments shared with him there more than a year and a half ago. She was well aware her interest and longing were now useless and wasted. Still, that understanding never prevented her from running to the hidden place inside that held his memory. She had loved him, and she couldn't let it go.

CHAPTER TWENTY-NINE

OCTOBER 1964

Travis sat at his desk in his apartment, finishing up some figures on the papers he had brought home with him from work. Glancing at the clock, he made note of the hour, 10 p.m., then stacked the pile of loose papers to the side of the desk next to several thick manuals. The workweek was almost completed, and he planned on making a speedy departure for the ranch immediately after work tomorrow for the weekend. Turning the desk lamp out, he made his way to the kitchen, opened the refrigerator door and grabbed a bottle of beer. Just as he walked back to the TV to catch the late news, the phone rang.

"Hello," he answered on the second ring.

"Travis, I . . . I was hoping I'd catch you at home."

Travis remained silent as he listened to the female voice on the other end of the line. Her voice was vaguely familiar, and he remained silent, trying to place the caller in mind.

With his extended pause, the caller continued, "It's Mary . . . Mary Cavanah. We met at the Hacienda Bar and Grill last July."

The sudden memory gave him a start as he stood perplexed. He hadn't had any contact with Mary since their encounter three months earlier. "Mary, this is indeed a surprise!"

"I know it's been a while, but a . . . I've . . . I've been thinking about you lately and thought maybe we could get together."

Travis listened but wasn't anxious to enter the conversation. Although receiving calls from women he knew wasn't unusual, ten did seem late to get a call on a work night. He couldn't help but notice a wavering in Mary's voice, and he suspected more prompted the call than the need to catch up with a one-time acquaintance. Travis was surprised she had remembered his name, since his recollection of their brief time spent together had Mary in a less-than-coherent state. He wondered if she were drinking tonight when she placed the call, and he also wondered how she had gotten his number since he never shared it or his address with her. She must have spent time searching the city directory to locate him. "It's a little late for house calls, Mary, and my schedule is pretty tight."

"Listen, Travis, we had a good time together, and I think we could again," she countered with a bit more distress in her voice.

"Mary, as nice as it was to whittle away a few lonesome hours together last July, I think we both know that's where it ended. I really would like to leave it on that happy note if it's all the same to you."

"Well, it isn't all the same for me, and we need to talk. And I don't mean next week. We need to talk tomorrow, so where can we meet?" she answered him angrily.

Travis was taken aback at the sudden, heated tone of her voice. He didn't like the sound of this; his brain took a one-way race to critical mass. Holding himself together long enough to regain his composure, he finally answered, "All right, Mary. Where is the nearest coffee house to you? We'll meet for coffee as soon as I get off work tomorrow." His thoughts were scrambling, and beads of sweat formed at his brow as he took a pencil in hand. He wrote down the name of the coffee shop she suggested. "It'll be five o'clock before I can get there. Don't hold me to the exact time since there's always something that comes up late on Friday afternoons."

"I don't think you can afford being late for our meeting, and you might want to make a point of leaving work earlier to be there. I'll look for you at five."

Mary hung the phone up with a slam of the receiver as Travis stood in a state of shock, still holding the phone. The sudden sickening, gripping feeling that he was about to be taken on a bumpy ride, destination unknown, tore at his heart once again. Tomorrow was coming too soon.

CHAPTER THIRTY

CHRISTMAS 1967

It had been over three years since Sarah had graduated from high school. Those years had been marked with repeated hospital stays for Lily Thompson, whose damaged heart took its last beat on August third of that year. Although everyone lived with the expectation of her eminent death, it still came as a blow to all who knew and loved her. Sarah made the decision long ago to remain close at hand throughout the long ordeal, and she was the one who her younger sister leaned on for support and love during those difficult days. This holiday season was lacking in luster as everyone went through the motions for Rachael's sake, trying to keep some degree of normalcy in her young life.

Charley Thompson knew Sarah's abiding love for her family and wasn't surprised that she decided on attending a local community college rather than the other colleges where she had gained acceptance. He knew she would be successful in any literary field, especially if she had accepted a post with one of the smaller news outlets in Manhattan where she was offered a summer internship, but Sarah chose instead to stay closer to home. He remembered, with anguish, Lily's parting conversations regarding Sarah. Lily had reminded him he had to let her go and give Sarah the chance to lead a life, without making her feel responsible for their care. Sarah had deliberately lightened her course load at college this past year to be home longer hours to help care for Rachael and Lily before her passing. Unlike Liz, Sarah made every decision keeping those she loved of primary concern. By contrast, Liz had graduated this past summer and had taken a job with a clothing design firm in California that seemed to meet all the requirements of the eccentric lifestyle everyone came to expect from her. As a result, she wasn't available to offer any help at home with the care of Rachael. Charley now struggled with such thoughts as he was coming to terms with Lily's parting.

With Kenny home for the holidays from law school, he was anxious to see Sarah and had invited her to see *The Graduate*, which was now playing at the local theater. After the movie, they went to a diner for coffee where they lingered in conversation together, catching up with the latest news.

"You know, Kenny, I never really had a chance to thank you for your concern and for attending Mom's funeral last August. I know you're usually up in Massachusetts at that time. It really meant a lot to me having you there."

Kenny reached across the table and took Sarah's hand in his. "Don't you know by now that what concerns you concerns me too?" He looked directly into Sarah's eyes and squeezed her hand in sympathy.

"Yes, I suppose I do know that. We've shared a lot of history," she said, lifting her head and staring back at him with her melancholy blue eyes.

"It's been a good history, hasn't it?"

"Of course it has. We've been the best of friends," Sarah offered in return.

Kenny slowly slid his hand back from hers, his face serious and drawn. It was an expression needing explanation and foreign to his usual happy demeanor.

"What are you thinking?" she asked him.

"I hadn't planned on this conversation right now, but I suppose this is as good a time as any."

Sarah detected a slightly strained look on his face. "Are your parents both all right?"

"Yes, they're both fine. This isn't about them."

"Well, what then?"

Kenny expanded his chest before continuing. "Sarah, we've known each other a very long time now, and I know you've always known how I feel about you. I'll only have two years remaining at law school by the end of this coming May, and Dad's already polished off the brass plaque with my name on it, ready to nail it on the door of the office as soon as I graduate. I've got a pretty damned good future ahead of me, with only one exception." He paused momentarily, staring at her while he composed his thoughts.

"What are you trying to tell me, Kenny?" she asked for a third time when she heard the seriousness in his words. A creeping feeling of dread washed over her as she suspected this might be the moment she had worked so hard to avoid.

He looked across the table his eyes filled with longing and yet strong. "Sarah . . . I want you to marry me."

Sarah felt a knot twist in her gut as she scrambled inside to recover from the one question she'd always known she'd eventually have to answer. Wide eyed and motionless, she drew three small breaths in rapid succession watching him intently. He reached into his pocket, placing his keys, which were still attached to the brass key ring Sarah had given him years earlier, on the table. Putting his hand back in his pocket, he pulled out a royal blue, velvet ring box and held it in his hand a moment. He slowly moistened the corner of his lip and then continued. "I didn't plan on this place to give this to you, but now that the cat is out of the bag, I suppose you should have it." He placed the box in her hand. "You don't have to answer me right now—only promise me you'll think about it." For the first time, he held a serious expression that contrasted his usual boyish demeanor. She watched him closely, seeing in him something unfamiliar, a strength in him normally missing, but oddly authentic. "I've already got a great apartment close to campus, and with the trust fund set up for me, my income has increased considerably now that I'm over twenty-one, so money won't be a problem for us." He waited for her response.

Sarah swallowed, digesting his every word. His hands were still clasped around hers as she held the small velvet box. *"God,"* she thought, *"I don't want to hurt him"* She tried to keep her same expression. "Kenny . . . I'm still in college, and I couldn't possibly consider leaving Rachael and my father so soon after Mom's passing."

"I'm not suggesting we elope right now. I want you to have time to plan the wedding you always dreamed of. We could plan on next summer after your graduation. If you're worried about the money for the wedding, you needn't be, because Mom and Dad would want to help with that."

"Oh, Kenny, it's not the money I'm concerned about."

"Well then, what? Haven't I always treated you the way you wanted me to? I don't want to wait for you any longer, Sarah. We're both getting older, and we know each other better than anyone else. If we've been able to stay friends this long, we'd have a decent chance at making a marriage work. Besides, you know I've always been crazy about you." His words were more earnest than any ever spoken before.

She didn't answer him and looked back down, trying to consider what to tell him.

"Is there someone else?"

The question hit her like the sudden clap of thunder in the dead of night. How could she answer him honestly? She had only ever really loved one man, but he was only a memory she childishly clung to. How could Kenny compete with that? Sarah sat across the table, unable to tell him what she was thinking. She answered in the hopes of buying herself more time, while also hoping not to hurt him, "Oh Kenny, there is no one else, but this is a big decision that needs a lot of time to make."

Kenny held his hands around hers a little longer before responding. "Sarah, I'll always be good to you, and I promise you'll never want for anything. We'll be close enough to your father and sister that you'll still be able to be there for them." He pressed his hands around hers more tightly, searching her expression. "Go ahead and open it."

She was desperately trying to balance herself emotionally as if she were seated on shaking ground. Slowly, she opened the small ring box, her stomach churning at the sight of the large pear-shaped diamond reflecting the royal blue hues of the box. Her anxiety turned to dread while holding the box, knowing what she had to tell him, but how could she do it? "It's . . . it's beautiful, Kenny, and it's much more than any girl could ever ask for or want, but I… I can't take this from you tonight." She answered him, leaving herself enough room to escape the question temporarily. Kenny stared back at her, one eyebrow raised.

"I want you to take it with you," he said, with more forcefulness than she was accustomed to hearing him use with her before. He straightened himself and continued. "You don't have to wear it till you give me your answer. How about I pick you up next Wednesday for dinner? That will give you some time to talk it over with the family. . . . You know I do love you, Sarah, but I can't keep waiting forever. If there isn't any chance for us, I need to know now so I can move on. You've seen first-hand that life can be cut short, and I don't want to waste any more time without you. I'm not willing to wait any longer."

The determined, new tone in his voice awakened the sudden reality in Sarah that if she turned him down, she might loose his friendship which she had worked so hard to keep. In that moment, she feared turning him down as much as she feared accepting his proposal. To say "no" was to let something she cherished between them die. Would she ever be ready to make the decision? She had run out of time, and she knew Kenny deserved an answer. With a mirthless smile to her lips and a heaviness pressing her heart, she finally replied, "All right, Kenny, I promise to think about it, and we'll plan on dinner together Wednesday."

Kenny's face suddenly lit up as he drew a deep breath through smiling lips. It was the expression of relief for him, but only represented a temporary reprieved for her. Sarah watched him feeling torn, not knowing how to answer him knowing her heart belonged to another. Biting her inner lip, Sarah squeezed her fingers around the ring box a little tighter.

When they arrived back at Sarah's home, Kenny slid across the seat and turned Sarah's head to face him. Taking her in his arms, he pulled her close to him and kissed her with an eagerness Sarah wished he could control. For him, it was a kiss of expectancy, and for her, the kiss of Judas. Forcing his own restraint, he let go of her and got out of the car to escort her to the door. Sarah remained silent, going through the motions while her mind was a million miles away. She had always known there would be a time she would have to face this question. The expectation of Travis Hall's return was approaching its fourth year, and with no hope of ever seeing him again, she struggled inside with Kenny's proposal.

Once at her door, Kenny gave Sarah another strong bear hug and then kissed her cheek, whispering in her ear, "I know you'll make the right decision, Sarah. I'll pick you up around six-thirty Wednesday night." He smiled that consummate smile full of pearly white teeth and then took the five steps down from her door with a spring in his step all the way back to his car. Sarah entered her house, not with the joy one would expect at times like this but with a heaviness and sorrow she could not mask.

Charley Thompson was sitting in his recliner when Sarah entered the living room. "Glad to see you home before midnight," he said as he glanced up from a late-night talk show.

"You honestly didn't have to wait up," Sarah told him as she removed her coat and hung it in the front closet.

"I couldn't sleep."

Sarah walked to her father's side, kneeled, and rubbed his hand as Charley stayed seated in his chair. "I guess we'll never stop missing her, will we, Dad?"

"Not likely, but we all have each other. Why the sad eyes? Didn't you have a good time tonight?"

Sarah sat down on the couch, still thinking of Kenny's proposal. "It was a good movie, and I guess it was a good time," she answered with an edge of melancholy.

"What do you mean 'you guess'? Did Kenny say something to upset you?"

"No, Dad, it's what I have to tell him that will hurt."

"What are you talking about? What do you have to tell him?" he asked, sitting upright.

Sarah reached into her handbag and pulled out the blue velvet ring box. She handed it to her father.

"Sarah! This is wonderful," he exclaimed at opening the box. "Why the gloomy face? Isn't this what you wanted?"

"I'm not sure, Dad. I don't think I can marry him."

"What are you talking about? You've known Kenny most of your life. He's been a great friend, and you know you could never do better with anyone else. He's got a promising future ahead of him, and he comes from a solid family. You can't tell me that you don't love him!"

Sarah paused briefly, thinking about how to respond, and with a less-than-enthusiastic reply, answered her father, "It's not that I don't love him, Dad. It's that I'm not in love with him. There is a difference, isn't there?"

Charley took on a pensive expression raising his shoulders with a deep breath. "I wish your mother were here for this conversation Sarah, but I want you to listen and think about what I tell you. Love isn't a perpetual high you maintain in life. You grow together over time. Marriage is filled with ups and downs, and you have to work at it. But if you're married to a real friend, it deepens and matures into something much more meaningful. Having a friend and partner is a good start, and if you find a man who can provide a secure financial future, that relieves a lot of stress on the marriage. That's what Kenny would be offering you, Sarah. You might look a long time before someone like Kenny would ever come along again, and there might never be anyone who could offer you what he can. Besides, you already know him pretty well." He paused a moment, wondering what Sarah was thinking as he took in her somber and placid expression.

"You know, Sarah, marriage doesn't mean you would have to give up a career, if that's your concern. You could always pursue your career and still have a great partner to share your life with. Freelancing from home is an option also, if you decide to marry him. It isn't an "either", "or" proposition for you. I can tell you, there is a lot of risk in dating strangers who might not be what you assume them to be, only to find out after the marriage that they are not at all what you were expecting. Kenny is offering you something that might never come along again, and I think you're old enough to put fairytale notions of prince charming on a white horse aside long enough to think this through, keeping your long-term future in mind. You've got to decide if you want a real partner with whom you can share a life together or not. That's a choice only you can make. If you decide you do, then you might seriously consider Kenny's proposal. Why don't you sleep on this, and we'll talk more about it tomorrow."

Sarah slowly raised herself from the couch, still feeling haunted inside by the ghost of a man she would never see again. How could she hurt Kenny when he was the one who had been there all along?

"I will think about it. I promise, Dad."

Charley handed the ring back to Sarah, patting her hand as she took the small velvet box back from him. "I know you'll make the right decision."

Sarah kissed her father goodnight and headed for her room, closing the door behind her. Sleep evaded her, and like most nights before, it was Travis Hall's image beckoning and drawing her, holding her until sleep's final refrain. Ever since that first day of their meeting in September of 1962, Sarah had walked a solitary path, unable to share the lovesick longing of her tortured heart. She was foolishly living in the naive hope of his eventual return, though that dream proved hollow of any real promise. Intellectually, she understood how absurd her fantasy was after so much time had passed, yet her heart always held sway, allowing her the dream and possibility that reality denied. Her repeating thoughts of him remained her constant companion, and she fed the flame that stayed hidden from the world. Sarah ran to it, stoking it secretly where no eye could taint or ear distort it. A life of good fortune with someone else would never extinguish the smoldering embers of passion she held for Travis Hall. Only his memory finally lulled Sarah to sleep.

CHAPTER THIRTY-ONE

MAY OF 1969

Travis was tired and weary as he parked the car in the driveway of his city townhouse. For the first time in weeks, he had managed to get away from work early. He took note of a motorcycle parked across the street in front of his residence as he made his way to the front door. His life had taken a sudden change in course since that fateful night Mary Cavanah had called him asking for their meeting in late October of 1964. In addition to his job at Honeywell and trying to run the ranch, his responsibilities now included a wife and daughter. Jessica had turned four years old a month ago, and she was the only glue that held together a marriage that had always been a sham. The only thing he got out of the marriage was to be with his daughter, while Mary exploited her meal ticket, unencumbered by the need to work. There was nothing he wouldn't do for Jessie, but Mary tried his soul time and again. His effort to get along for the sake of his daughter was proving a wasted trial, while Mary's constant need for thrills bordered on the precipice of illegality, which he found contemptible. His job required long hours, but his sacrifices hadn't come without rewards. He was moving swiftly up the corporate ladder of success with several major contributions in designing weapons systems and other aerospace technologies as the war in Vietnam heated up. Those contributions quickly earned him recognition, but the real war he found himself fighting was at home.

Approaching the front door with his keys in hand, he was surprised to find the door open. Stepping inside, Travis was halted by the silence; not hearing Jessica at play was unusual. A quick glance around the living room brought him to a stand still. A trail of clothes was strewn across the floor, leading down the long hall back to the master bedroom. The noxious smell of cigarette smoke lay heavy in the air, and Travis grew more concerned and suspicious with each passing moment. The sudden laughter of both a man's and woman's voices stood the hair up at the back of his neck. Restraining himself, he quietly proceeded down the hall, tucking his head into Jessica's room first, but she wasn't there either. The laughter took on a rowdier tone as he continued down the hallway, pushing the clothing on the floor aside with his foot. The master bedroom door remained partially open as he peered into the room in utter disgust.

Lying beneath the sheets of the king-sized bed, Mary frolicked and tossed in the arms of a long-haired, tattooed stranger. A motorcycle helmet was lying on the floor at the foot of the bed. Several empty beer bottles rested haphazardly across the end tables, and there was no mistaking the telltale scent of marijuana. Standing silent for a moment watching them, Travis found himself strangely calm, not surprised in the least by Mary's latest depravity.

A brief moment passed before he pushed the door open, forcefully slamming it against the wall, and then folded his arms casually across his chest, waiting for their response. The startled couple threw the sheets off their heads and bolted back up to a seated position, shocked and panicked at the sight of him calmly standing there.

"Well now . . . isn't this just the picture of domestic tranquility?" The corners of Travis's mouth formed a twisted semblance of a smile as he took in their shocked expressions. The hard, cold look in his eyes broadcast a self-imposed discipline that warned not to test him.

"Who the hell are you?" the naked tattooed man questioned from beneath the sheets.

"That seems a strange question coming from a man in my house who's in my bed screwing my wife!"

The man took another long look at Travis and his face took on a colorless pallor. He slowly started to reach for his shorts lying at the side of the bed. "Hold on now, mister, she didn't say nothin' about any husband."

"Mary, love, it seems you've left your newfound friend in the dark. Perhaps you'd care to introduce us?" Travis shot a look of disdain and loathing at her as she pulled the sheets to her neck. Fear glazed over Mary's face as she watched her companion scramble desperately to gather his things while trying to put on his shorts.

"Listen, mister, this whole thing is a big mistake, and this is between you and her; so let's just stay cool, and I'll get the hell out of here." The sound of panic came across loud and clear as the startled stranger tried to exit the door of the room. Travis grabbed the straggly ponytail at the back of the biker's neck and threw him up against the door, putting one hand around the neck of the half-naked man. He held him tightly, forcing his head back hard against the wide open door. With tightly clenched teeth, Travis thrust his knee to the biker's groin bringing steady pressure to bear. Pain and fear swept across the man's face.

"If you ever so much as think of coming into this house again, you'll never hear the word 'daddy' spoken to you in your lifetime. Do you get my drift?" Travis raised his knee, applying more pressure as the stranger groaned in agony.

Mary started screaming as she sat up in the bed, gripped in fear. Travis released the biker abruptly, causing him to fall to his knees. With an unspoken plea for mercy in his eyes, the surprised man crawled out of the bedroom and down the hall, gathering his clothing as he made his way to the front door, moaning weakly as he went. Travis slowly turned back to Mary, his face turned to stone as he listened to her tantrum.

"You son of a bitch! Why did you have to hurt him? He didn't deserve that, you bastard," she yelled as Travis walked ever closer to the bed.

"You're right, Mary. He probably didn't deserve it, but you sure as hell do."

"Who do you think you are?" she screamed at him. Mary's voice faltered, taking in the cold, hard glaze in his eyes. "You don't own me, Travis. . . . You . . . you have no right to tell me who to see and what to . . . to do." Mary's voice slowly trailed off into silence as she watched him take each deliberate step closer. His face grew dark and hardened, causing her to suddenly cower, fearful that he might take his rage out on her next.

Travis stopped short of the bed, taking in the ashtray resting on the nightstand with its two yellowed joints, ashen and spent in the hollow of the clear glass receptacle. Staring back down at Mary, his face took a twisted, hateful look. "You disgust me!" he told her as she crouched at the headboard.

"Don't," she screamed, raising her arms, fearing he might strike her.

Travis stood looking down at her with complete contempt, and then snorted. "Don't flatter yourself, Mary—you're not worth the effort. Now, where is Jessica?"

"She's next door," Mary answered immediately, still gripping the sheet tightly at her chest.

"Get up and put your clothes on before I change my mind."

Mary slowly got off the bed on the opposite side from him and quickly started dressing. Travis went to a closet, pulling two suitcases from the shelf, and then headed to Jessica's room and started filling one of the suitcases with her clothing. Trying to button her blouse, Mary followed him, still filled with an anger tempered slightly by her fear of him. "What the hell do you think you're doing?" she yelled at him as she watched from Jessica's bedroom door.

"Something I should have done a long time ago. Stay out of my way." He continued to pack his daughter's clothes.

"You can't take her. I'll never let you have her. You owe me, you bastard."

"It never was about Jessica, was it Mary? It was always about what she could buy you. You're about to get half of what you wished for, freedom from all her responsibility and lots more time to devote to your insatiable appetite for self-indulgence. It's over, Mary. You're on your own. You can plan on a letter from my attorney in the mail." He hinged the suitcase shut.

Mary's face contorted into an ugly and hate-filled expression as she tried to block his path to the door. "We'll just see about that, you no good son of bitch. I'll take you for all you're worth."

Travis grabbed her arm and threw her up against the wall, restraining himself as he brought his face close to hers. Unable to prevent the spit from spewing through his clenched teeth, he spoke, "I've already told you once to stay out of my way, Mary. I don't intend to tell you again. Save your expletives for somebody who gives a damn." He released her arm with a swift thrust, forcing her hard against the wall a second time as she held her arm close to her side, afraid to move. Travis turned and walked quickly back to the master bedroom.

Once he had put a safe distance between them, Mary cautiously turned and stomped off to the kitchen where she restlessly paced back and forth, trying to determine what to do next. Unable to think clearly, she finally reached for the door of the refrigerator and helped herself to another beer while Travis filled a second suitcase in the master bedroom.

By 2:00 p.m., Travis walked out the front door, placed the bags in the trunk of his car, and then went next door and picked up Jessica from the neighbors. Strapping his daughter in the car, he got behind the wheel and backed out of the driveway without looking back. Mary Cavanah Hall stood at the window, beer in one hand and a cigarette in the other, as she peered through the blinds of the living-room window, mumbling to herself, "We'll just see about that, Travis. You haven't heard the last from me."

CHAPTER THIRTY-TWO

1968–1974

The ten years after Sarah graduated from high school melted away faster than ice cubes in a glass of tea in mid-August. Her life changed dramatically after she relented and accepted Kenny's proposal. Their wedding opened the social season in June of '68 and was the event to attend, making it the highlight of the summer. The talk of the north shore, the Birks' home and estate provided the backdrop for their nuptials. In an instant, Sarah was whisked into a social world reserved for very few, with many of the "who's who" of local politics in attendance. Their wedding was a grand and magnificent affair even though Sarah knew very few of the many dignitaries and guests who were invited.

Charley Thompson wore his pride on his sleeve that day, escorting his sweet Sarah down the long red carpet. Elizabeth flew home from California for the wedding to take her allotted place as maid of honor. Rachael looked positively enchanting as she scattered rose petals down the red carpet, marking the path for Sarah to follow. To have all of his daughters together again gave Charley a level of happiness he hadn't felt since before Lily's passing. He held a heightened sense of joy that Sarah would never suffer a day's want; that happy thought overcame the feeling of loss he was dealing with at her parting.

The Birks insisted on bearing the brunt of the expenses. Nothing was too lavish for them to exclude, although Sarah would have much preferred a more intimate, close friends and family affair in a more reverent church setting. Her wishes quietly took a backseat at the Birks' urging.

The sun-drenched day was made to order with its cottony, billowing white clouds pinned on the clear blue sky. Guests strolled happily on perfectly manicured grounds and took their cocktails under the huge white tent sprawled on the emerald green lawn at the rear of the Birks' stately home. The live band provided entertainment with a large wooden dance floor positioned in front. The stage was set with cascading flowers draping the stone balustrades at the back veranda as well as the backs of the slip-covered chairs that lined the red carpet down the sweeping lawn to the stone wall grotto in the garden. Two large gardenia-filled urns marked either side of the lavish, floral-covered canopy where Kenny and Sarah swore their vows.

Sarah captivated all in attendance with her designer gown in sumptuous ecru-colored silk shantung. It was tailored perfectly, hugging her mid-frame and accentuating her curvy though slender figure. Flaring slightly beneath the dropped waist, the gown carried a lengthy train edged in exquisite lace. Sarah's hair was swept back and formed heightened curls at the crown of her head. The soft plump pillows of her ash blonde and silver-streaked hair were surrounded by a small pearl-crusted band that helped to support voluminous layers of sheer tulle. With the dress's scoop neck highlighting her mother's pearls and its short sleeves trimmed in the same delicate lace as the train, Sarah presented an image of refined elegance fit for royalty. Her eye-catching beauty brought the sighs of the crowd as she made her way down the red carpet supported by Charley and squeezing his arm tightly.

Kenny had managed to stay out of the way during the planning, happy to show up on their wedding day and collect his prize that had been too long in coming. If this was the only way to have Sarah, he was ready, willing and able to walk her down the aisle. He was the envy of all who knew him, and, with Sarah on his arm, he was unable to keep his well-fed self-esteem from taking a giant leap forward. Sarah was exhausted from the work and all the planning involved in the wedding while she finished up the last half-semester of her senior year at college. She made an effort to live her life the best she knew how, trying to conform to the expectations of Kenny's family while also doing her best to fill Kenny's constant need for attention. Little time was left for her father and Rachael.

Their wedding night brought the realization that whatever intimacy she had hoped they might share would be relegated to a wifely obligation that left her wanting. She soon learned if Kenny's needs and demands weren't met, he pouted like a sulking child, as if sex on demand constituted the sum total of love's expression, and without it, he felt completely rejected. He behaved like a spoiled toddler wanting his ice cream, demanding of her a precipitous response, never stopping to savor its flavor. She recalled their wedding night with heartache. In her innocence, she had come to his bed wearing a delicate peignoir ensemble, hoping to please him, but in his eagerness, he quickly laid himself over her, lifting her gown. His long-suppressed appetite ignited at the tantalizing site of her and brought a heated response that demanded immediate consummation as he excitedly positioned himself, quickly spilling his seed without the least bit of ceremony. The whole affair was over in a matter of minutes. Sarah lay on her back and looked up at the ceiling, feeling removed as he quickly finished and rolled off of her like dead weight. She remained silent and wounded, asking herself if this was all she could ever expect from him. She soon learned it was far easier to acquiesce to his demands than to tolerate his boyish sulking and tantrums.

Although she found him more a child than a man, in his own way, Kenny did love her to the degree he was capable. Despite his lack of sexual sophistication and refinement in the bedroom, he would do anything for her if she made her requests known. But Sarah wished he was better able to sense those things without having to be asked.

The first few years of their marriage were not the happy days she had hoped for, although Kenny seemed pleased; Sarah found herself running on empty much of the time while taking on more obligations simultaneously.

Being away from her father and Rachael during those early months of marriage was difficult as Kenny continued at law school. The fact that she had gotten pregnant so soon after the wedding only added to her sense of sorrow, knowing her course in life was now firmly set despite the emptiness she came to live with inside. Rebecca was born the following year, and Sarah did her best to share her attention between their new daughter and Kenny while they lived in their Manhattan apartment.

The following year brought relief when JD and Katherine announced they had acquired property in Muttontown, settling on the perfect place for Kenny and Sarah to build their home. With the architects already hired, Sarah remained out on Long Island with more frequency the second year of their marriage, overseeing the home's construction while Kenny finished up at law school. By this time, Sarah was beginning to understand that Kenny's father pretty much ran the show, and all anyone could do was stand back and hold on for the ride. JD seemed to have laid out the road map for Kenny's future. Sarah wondered if JD ever really knew his son at all, other than what he planned for him to become. She wondered if there would ever come a time when Kenny would take back the reins from his father and find out what he truly wanted for himself in life. The reality was that Kenny preferred a happy-go-lucky lifestyle and would've been content to fill his days with sports and sailing. He lived his life on the surface, never knowing or suspecting the depths of Sarah's heart. Although his frat house days were now behind him, he still carried the same exuberant and youthful playfulness into manhood. He was a charming little boy who never grew up, and Sarah wished he were stronger.

Sarah knew she was Ken's trophy, not so much because she was attractive, even if that were true, but primarily because she was Kenny's choice for a wife, and fortunately for him, his father had approved. Sarah did her best to fill the role everyone expected her to play, but the cocktail parties and politicking, along with the questionable banking practices by some of the firm's wealthier clients, all caused Sarah to turn within to find the happiness and joy she longed for in what to others appeared to be a "picture-perfect life."

Many of Sarah's friends vested tinges of envy regarding her good fortune in marrying Kenny Birk, but none walked in her shoes. She had always been a hopeless romantic, longing to respect and look up to the man she married, but she found something far less appealing in Kenny. She didn't want to look down on him for being spoiled, or for being a puppet of his father, but the truth tore away the respect she had hoped to have for him. Where was the partnership in a marriage when respect was lost? She resented being his substitute mother, yet that was precisely how she viewed their relationship. Whenever those thoughts came to mind, she blamed herself for not being more like the women of her generation who delighted in wearing the pants, many aggressively pursuing careers and climbing their way up corporate ladders. Loveable, less-sufficient men who were dependent on them emotionally didn't seem to bother those women. Sarah found no joy in being a modern, liberated woman. She cared for Kenny at home, keeping his calendar and managing the household, while his father orchestrated his every move at work. At the end of the day, Kenny showed up in bed, ready for dessert, while Sarah persevered, planning what to lay out for him to wear in the morning.

Sarah secretly held the dream of love for years for a man who haunted her like a shadow. His words at their parting still carried a profound meaning, and she was never able to fully accept the fact that her interpretation could have been totally wrong. She replayed his words in her mind, savoring his delivery and wondering: What if she hadn't been mistaken? His memory never died to her, even though some of the details of their time spent together were fading. Sarah fed the flame, regardless of the knowledge Travis was only a misplaced fantasy. She found herself running repeatedly to the one place where the gift of love was always free, untainted, and wholly hers.

By June of 1970, Sarah had birthed a second child. With Rebecca and new son Keith to keep her busy, she spent little time pursuing her own interests, although she did maintain her commitment to a few children's charities that were still dear to her. With two toddlers at home, Sarah spent her days nurturing her children. She did find time to finish decorating their beautiful new home as well as tend her garden. Kenny's need for attention continued, though his time spent under his father's tutelage within the law firm kept him busy with longer hours spent away from home. By then, Sarah had all she could handle and took advantage of the newfound freedom the use of the birth-control pill provided. The peace of mind the pill brought her couldn't be measured, considering Kenny never felt the need to share in such responsibilities.

Financially they enjoyed a much more prosperous lot than most, but Sarah wondered if they might have been happier out from under JD's constant direction. At times, she suspected JD was grooming Kenny for a political office, which he himself was never able to hold. The years moved steadily forward, and Sarah felt like a passenger on board a ship in full sail, moving speedily ahead with strangers at the helm and no way for her to trim the sails.

CHAPTER THIRTY-THREE

SPRING OF 1974

The viewing stands at the Payson Rodeo were slowly emptying after a long day of competition at the nation's oldest continuous-running rodeo. The week-long event brought cowboys and cowgirls from across the nation and Canada to the Rim country in mid-August for the chance to win a title and handsome purse for calf roping, bronco busting, bull riding, and barrel racing. Travis Hall rode his quarter horse from one of the holding pens to his parked pickup and cattle trailer on the opposite side of the arena. He had just finished feeding the calves and securing them for the night. Edgar Sims was on his way back with his horse trailer to meet Travis at his truck, where they would load their horses and saddles and head back to the ranch. Travis's mother had already left for home with nine-year-old Jessica.

Several long-time residents of Payson nodded politely as they walked by Travis, making their exits from the fairgrounds. An old friend and fellow rancher stopped to talk as Travis tied the reins of his horse at the back of the cattle hauler. "We sure liked Cody Dermot's tie time, Travis, and we liked the look of your calves this year."

"Thanks, Frank. I appreciate the kind words. Guess we still had lady luck on our side this year with plenty of healthy cows."

"It's more than luck. What's the average weight you got on hoof out there this year?"

"They're running anywhere from 265 to 275, but we threw in a few stragglers for the youngsters."

"They're good, clean, healthy-looking stock, Travis. Glad to see the herd expanding." Frank brought two fingers of his right hand to the tip of his straw cowboy hat and nodded as he turned to gather his family and move on to their car in the distant parking lot.

Travis threw one stirrup over the horn on his saddle and then loosened the knot at the girth to remove the saddle from his horse.

Stepping out from behind one of the trailers parked adjacent to Travis's, Mary Cavanah Hall sauntered slowly toward Travis from behind with a well-rehearsed and worn sway in her hips. "I see you haven't had your fill of dirt yet," she said with an edge of sarcasm.

Travis turned to see her leaning up against the horse trailer parked next to his. Her brown hair still framed her face with sharp points but was longer now than it had been since Travis last saw her. The straggly appearance of her hair emphasized the noticeably pronounced lines on her aging face. She wore a low-cut, tightly fitted, sleeveless tank top tucked into a skintight pair of blue jeans, leaving nothing to the imagination. Mary always demanded attention any way she could get it, and her efforts were usually rewarded, with everyone except Travis. The mere sight of her standing there brought nothing but revulsion to Travis. It had been five years since their separation and at least a year and a half since he had last seen her. He took note of the darker circles under her heavily lined eyes and didn't hide the look of disgust on his face. "Hello, Mary. What brings you to Payson?" he said with a restrained tenor.

Mary brought the cigarette she held back to her lips and took a long drag before answering. "I figured I'd still find you up here groveling in the dirt and cow shit. Some things never change."

"You didn't drive up from Phoenix to recount your philosophical differences in lifestyles with me, so what do you want?" He folded his arms across his chest.

Mary blew a straight line of smoke from her tightly pursed lips. "That's what I like about you, Travis. You always were one to be direct and get right to the point." She paused, watching the forced restraint on Travis's face. "It's been a long time since we've talked, and things have been changing." Mary twisted her feet on the gravel repositioning herself, fidgeting as she weighed her words under his intense stare. "I'm sure you've noticed the rise in the cost of living, even up here in the sticks. Inflation is higher in the valley, and it's harder to keep up. We need to talk about an increase in the monthly allowance." Still propped against the adjacent trailer, Mary nervously took another drag of her cigarette.

Travis eyed her from her feet to her head, showing little emotion while taking in her dissipated looks. "It seems to me we've already had this conversation and settled this years ago, Mary."

"You bastard! How do you expect me to earn a decent living on my own without more money for more schooling?"

Travis readjusted his Stetson on his head and calmly replied, "I guess just like all the rest of us. We go get a job and earn it."

"Listen, you son of a bitch, I need more money to continue to go to school. How the hell do you expect me to get by without a degree?"

"It's been five years now since our separation, and it doesn't appear that the money you've already received from me was well spent up to this point. You don't have anything to show for it but a few good times. What you do with the money is your choice, and my choice is not to throw good money after bad." Travis turned his back to Mary and removed the saddle from his horse, throwing it over the side of the cattle rack.

Mary flipped her cigarette to the ground and grabbed Travis by the arm. "You no-good son of a bitch, you owe me!"

Travis grabbed her arm from his and turned, pulling her closer to his face with a forcefulness that suddenly seized Mary with fear. Clenching his teeth tightly, he quickly spoke, looking her directly in the eyes, "It's wonderful to see what an education is doing to improve your vocabulary, Mary. Unfortunately for you, the trip up to Payson won't be so fruitful. Now, I suggest you go find yourself another cowboy to entertain you." He released her arm with a forcefulness that jerked Mary back several feet from him, and she stood unsteady on her feet, holding her arm where Travis had gripped it.

Yelling back at him, she countered, "I've got news for you, Travis. There are plenty of other ropers up here who would give their eye-teeth to be with me, just like you once did."

Travis turned back to remove the blanket from his horse, doing his best to ignore her. Mary ramped up her voice, trying her best to get his attention. "You aren't even a good cowboy, and you never did know how to have a good time!"

Travis turned one more time to face her as she continued to berate him. In a calm and measured tone, he replied, "You're absolutely right. My roping and bull-riding days are long gone. One more thing, I don't ride whores anymore either. I can't say it's been good seeing you, but I'm glad we had this little talk anyway . . . and just for the record, Mary, you might like to know that Jessica turned nine this year and is doing quite well. . . . Enjoy your visit to Payson." Travis blew a short burst of air through his flaring nostrils when he finished, unable to disguise his contempt. He turned his back on her for the third time, and Mary hurled several more expletives his way.

Not able to elicit any further response from him, she finally turned away and stomped off, hoping to attract a kindred spirit who, like herself, knew how to let the good times roll. There would be plenty of cowboys to choose from back in town tonight at the Ox Bow Saloon, where her drinks could easily be purchased with assets not held in currency.

CHAPTER THIRTY-FOUR

By 1974, Sarah and Kenny had settled into a respectable routine and, by all accounts, were living an ideal and covetous life. Rebecca was now five years old and Keith was four. The children were more easily able to entertain themselves by playing together, without the demanding need of her total attention. With her sister Rachael now seventeen, Sarah had a trusted sitter whenever the need arose.

One such occasion loomed on the horizon that spring when Sarah received a letter announcing a ten-year class reunion for the 1964 North Shoreline High School graduates. Her thoughts immediately went to the possibility of finding out what had happened to Travis Hall, and perhaps even learn why he had left and where he might have gone. Considering it too much to expect his appearance, she did assume a few of the older teachers would be there and that they might offer some information. Sarah lived the next few months in happy expectation till the reunion that June.

As it turned out, the weather was not as cooperative the weekend of the reunion, despite Sarah's happy anticipation. She and Nonie had maintained a close friendship over the years, still living in near proximity to one another. Nonie, along with her mother, now handled the daily operation of the restaurant. Her father had suffered a massive heart attack, passing away several years earlier and joining Nonie's grandmother on the other side. His untimely death had come as a shock, but not before he was able to walk

Nonie down the aisle and place her hand in Abe Kaplan's. Abe was her father's pick, which worked well for everyone. Once finished with his schooling, Abe Kaplan became an accountant, taking over the books of the Gorman family business. It was a match made in heaven, and as it turned out, on earth as well—just as her father had surmised. Nonie couldn't wait to catch up with her old classmates, and it didn't hurt that she would have Abe at her side when she made her entrance. The rainy skies didn't dampen the enthusiasm she and Sarah shared at the chance to catch up with old friends.

"You look beautiful tonight," Kenny said as they pulled into the parking lot of the hotel, both anxious to join their old classmates. Sarah wore a simple, short-sleeved black dress with a set-in waist and straight skirt that punctuated her still-slender figure. With her hair pulled neatly back and turned in a tight, low knot at the back of her head, she kept the pristine elegance inherent in her nature. A set of pearl earrings and single strand of pearls were her only adornment, and with Sarah's striking natural beauty, she needed no other glitz to attract attention. She still carried herself with a sophisticated and refined simplicity that could easily draw the eyes of those in attendance.

Their arrival at the reunion was unavoidably delayed. Kenny took the opportunity to surprise the crowd by making his entrance wearing his old, letterman's sports jacket. Kenny always thrived in the spotlight, and the reunion proved an opportune stage to draw the crowd. With all the swagger and boldness of a strutting peacock, Kenny entered the hotel ballroom with Sarah on his arm. Wearing a broad smile that exposed his bright white teeth, Kenny puffed up his chest and extended his arms as he gave a shimmy to his shoulders and boldly proclaimed his arrival, feeling at the top of his game. Sarah quickly scanned the crowd for Nonie.

"Sarah, we're over here!"

Sarah left Kenny to his admiring and rowdy former classmates and made her way to Nonie's side. "Nonie, I'm so sorry we're late. Kenny was delayed in court today."

"Can you believe some of these people? I'd hardly recognize many of them. Look over there, Sarah, against the wall. Guess who that is."

"I have no idea. Was she one of our classmates?"

"Would you believe that's Fran Johnson?"

"Oh! It couldn't be. That girl's hair is black as coal."

"Well, it's Fran all right. She lives in Islip and is a hairdresser there."

"Well, it's nice to see Fran in a profession where she can still practice her first trade."

Nonie was stumped. "What do you mean her first trade? Did she work in a different profession before this one?"

"I think we both know Fran's expertise was always gossip."

Nonie laughed heartily in agreement.

Kenny returned to Sarah's side, carrying a glass of wine in one hand and a scotch and soda in the other. After handing Sarah the wine, he gave Nonie a hug. "You look terrific tonight, Nonie. Where's Abe?"

"Would you believe he ran into someone he knows and is off mingling? It's a good turnout—if I could only recognize half of these people! You look like you're ready for the coach to put you back in play!"

Kenny's smiled widened as he received the response he had hoped the jacket would elicit. "Coach Morris could throw me in right now, and there's no doubt we'd win another one for the team."

"I believe you could, Kenny."

Several former classmates and team members called out to Kenny, and he quickly turned, anxious to rejoin them. "Go ahead, Kenny. See how many of the old team members are here and if you can still recognize any of them," Sarah suggested. He quickly turned, leaving Sarah and Nonie to wander without him. Sarah scanned the crowd as she and Nonie pointed out old friends, surprised at each new revelation.

"Who do you suppose that is?" Sarah asked as she called Nonie's attention to a slightly overweight girl with a haggard look.

"You'll never guess who that is."

"I really can't tell, so who is she?"

"Would you believe that's Susan Anderson?"

Sarah didn't try to hide the stunned look on her face. "I never would have guessed!"

"Neither did I, and I was shocked when she finally had to tell me who she was. It seems she married right out of high school and now has four kids. Apparently, things didn't work out well between her and her husband. She mentioned that she's separated now."

"You never know where life is going to take you, do you, Nonie?"

"I guess we're both pretty lucky from the looks of things," Nonie offered with her big brown eyes now scanning the crowd.

"I suppose we are," Sarah answered with a twitch in her heart. "Nonie, look over there—it's Dean Watson. She looks marvelous. I wonder how old she is now."

"I don't know, but she hasn't changed a bit in ten years. She even has the same pageboy hair comb!" Nonie commented in surprise.

"Come on—let's go say hello."

"Okay, but you knew her better than me, so you do all the talking."

"All right, come on," Sarah agreed as she made her way to the dean's side. "Miss Watson, what a pleasure to see you again," Sarah said as she extended her hand.

"Why, Sarah Thompson, it's wonderful to see you also." Taking Sarah's hand in her own, Miss Watson patted the top of her hand affectionately. "You're still the same picture of the lovely young lady I remember so well."

"Thank you. I'm sure you remember Nonie Gorman, now Nonie Kaplan?"

"Of course, it's good to see you too, Nonie." Miss Watson answered, offering her hand in response. "Tell me, Sarah, where has life taken you—to a happy place, I hope?"

"Like many of the others here tonight, I'm married with two very special children. I have a girl and a boy, four and five now. They keep me busy, though I'm still involved in the Children's Center for needy children and do my best to help raise the funds to keep it operating every year."

"That's a very worthy cause. I take it you're still living nearby then?"

"Yes, as a matter of fact we built our home in Muttontown, and I still manage to see a few of my old classmates every now and then, although most have moved on, as you probably have discovered tonight. Perhaps you remember Kenny Birk? After we married, Ken finished law school and is now in practice with his father, not far from our home."

"That's wonderful, Sarah. I'm happy for both of you. It is troubling and painful to know your class lost so many young men to the war, but I suppose with the conflict in Vietnam lasting so long, it's not surprising."

Nonie and Sarah agreed, remembering several of them with fondness, including Mark Stevens.

"Tell me, Sarah, have you pursued your writing?"

"I think about it every now and then and promise myself that when the children get a little older and I have more free time, I might want to try my hand at a novel."

"Don't put it off too long, Sarah. Life slips by so quickly."

"I'll remember that, Miss Watson. I suppose I should have asked if you ever married."

"Heavens no, I haven't! After finishing my doctorate, I was offered the post of principal at the North Shoreline High School, where I'm still in their service."

"Congratulations. They couldn't have chosen a better person for the job!"

"Thank you, but times are changing, and the students are much more rebellious than they were in your day. It's a much more difficult office than it once was, but I've been married to my work for so long now that I don't know any other way to live."

"I suppose in your new post you keep close contact with the teachers, then?" Sarah asked as her heart began to race in anticipation.

"As much as the office calls for, but the job doesn't allow a lot of extra time for socializing."

"Tell me, did you ever learn what happened to Mr. Hall? Did he ever return to teach math after the class of 1964 graduated?"

"No, Sarah, I'm afraid I don't recall. The best I can remember is that he taught only that one year, although that didn't surprise me."

"What do you mean?" Sarah asked, trying not to show in her expression the deep disappointment she felt in that moment. Hiding the wound of not being able to learn his whereabouts, she buoyed her hope for the slightest bit of information concerning him.

"It just seemed to me that he might have been more suited to a different line of work. He was quite intelligent, as well as being a math wiz, and I suspect his talents might have been put to better use in a more lucrative and challenging field. And, if I remember correctly, most of the students were quite intimidated by him."

Nonie nodded in total agreement. "That certainly was true for me."

"I think you're probably right about that," Sarah agreed, hoping not to reveal her utter disappointment in that moment. She had looked forward to this reunion for weeks, secretly hoping she would learn something more about Travis. The dean's lack of information came as a crushing blow. At the very least, she thought, someone else had recognized how extraordinary he was, even if the students never did. Sharing that same belief, Sarah continued, "But he was still able to help me, despite his iron exterior." Two other girls approached Dr. Watson, hoping for a word with her, and Sarah quickly took her leave. "It certainly was a pleasure to see you again Dr. Watson, and I look forward to another visit in the future, perhaps the next reunion?"

"That would be my great pleasure, Sarah. It was so good to talk with you, and perhaps you'll have a novel to share at our next visit."

Sarah nodded politely. "I'll do my best. Thanks for the encouragement."

Dr. Watson turned, greeting the others who were waiting as Sarah and Nonie moved on, glad to have shared a moment of her time.

"Funny you should remember him after all these years, Sarah," Nonie commented.

"I don't know how anyone who took one of his classes could ever forget him, do you?" Sarah questioned with directness.

"That's got to be the understatement of the day!"

Sarah and Nonie slowly made their way from group to group around the ballroom, conversing and catching up with many of their old classmates. Kenny reveled in the limelight, happy to be together again with more than a few of his old teammates. After dinner, their MC called for a moment of silence for all those class members who had died.

Sarah thought it was odd that no one thought to give special tribute to the young men who were killed in Vietnam, those who had paid the ultimate sacrifice on behalf of the nation. She mentioned to Nonie the least they should have done was to read their names out loud in their memory, not just a brief moment of silence with no mention of them individually or of their service. She hadn't forgotten Mark, or the tortuous life he had been exposed to in his youth. She listened to the ways many of her contemporaries had proudly avoided the draft, including hiding out in Canada for a time, gladly leaving others to their nation's call. Their hubris in such admissions in the face of so many others' losses was stunning. Kenny was never called, possibly because he spent extra years in school and was always deferred, or maybe JD Birk had something to do with his luck as well. Kenny, at least, didn't brag about his good fortune.

After dinner, Nonie and Sarah mingled again, leaving Kenny with Abe. They joined another small group of classmates standing not far from them. "John Medford! How are you?" Sarah asked in surprise, realizing who the slightly balding fellow standing to her side was.

"Sarah Thompson, my God, you're still the same beautiful chick you always were! Did you and Kenny ever get together?"

"As a matter of fact we did. We've been married for six years now," Sarah answered quickly.

"I figured as much, since he chased you all through high school! I heard he's with his father's law firm now."

"He is, but what are you up to these days?"

"You know me. I'm in sales and dabble a little on the side, still playing the ponies. I sell cars out in Patchogue nine to five, and spend the weekends at the track."

"Tell me, Johnny, did you ever marry, or did the war take you from home like so many of the other guys?" she asked him, finding his gambling habit dislikable. 'Making a living' and 'gambling' didn't seem mutually suited together in the same sentence.

"Yeah, I was drafted, but I spent two years in the supply corps out at Fort Riley, Kansas, a God-forsaken place in the middle of nowhere! I married a girl out there, but it lasted for less time than my service did."

"I'm so sorry, John," Sarah responded sympathetically.

"She did me a favor with the divorce. The girl didn't share my vision about how to make a buck. Besides, she wanted kids and a house on the prairie. At least I gave her one kid before I left, so she got part of her dream answered! I ask you, what would a good old New York boy like me be doing living on the prairie with a house full of screaming kids?" John facetiously asked with a look of misplaced satisfaction and relief.

"I suppose it was for the best then, John." Sarah replied, slightly sickened by his confession. "You did know that Mark Stevens was killed in Vietnam and was later awarded the Silver Star?"

"The guy always was a jerk, and I guess that just proves it. He picked a hell of a way to make a name for himself. It wasn't my war. You gotta know how to play the angles. I've got a few big deals in the pipeline that I'm working on that are going to make me a real bundle."

"Well, I certainly hope that works out for you, Johnny. It was good to see you again. Would you please excuse me? I see a few others I need to say hi to before they leave." Turning away from him in disgust, Sarah looked for Nonie as she moved on. She couldn't help but think that the once-gregarious boy had turned his charm into a depraved way to feed his own ego. Ever the salesman and deal-maker, Johnny Medford appeared to have sold himself a lie.

Sarah could understand the objection to the war, but the choice to treat those who paid such a heavy price with disrespect drew her contempt.

She made it a point to tell any of the others who had an ear to listen that Mark Stevens had died a hero. Along with the Silver Star, he was posthumously recommended for the Congressional Medal of Honor. His story had taken a back page in the papers several years ago, and Sarah wondered if the nation had learned to turn their backs on their own, forgetting those who fought so valiantly. Protests and campus marches were the norm, while those who suffered the consequences of every political decision knew first-hand the reality and got no recognition, receiving ice-cold shoulders upon their returns. Mark's heroism came as quite a surprise to many in attendance, but those who knew seemed only glad they had avoided the draft, and that the call to arms had finally ended the year before in 1973. To Sarah, their lack of caring at the loss of so many was shocking. So long as it hadn't affected them, they were free to condemn anyone who had served as though they personally made those political decisions and were only murderers, not defenders of freedom. The attitude was a sad commentary regarding the mood of the nation's citizenry and went hand in hand with the times.

Kenny was in his glory that night, reliving old victories and polishing a dulled star in hopes of regaining its former luster. The child in the man was in full bloom, and Kenny was riding high, enjoying the whole affair. Sarah watched him out of the corner of her eye, happy for his joy but somehow overshadowed with sadness, knowing her love for him was void of the passion she had always hoped to share. The subtle, chafed feeling that she was forever tied to a man who had failed her dreams washed over her as she watched him from afar. The guilt brought an immediate, disciplined denial, and she reconsidered her attitude; after all these years, they were still the best of friends. Sarah took solace in that, despite a deep emptiness inside her that she learned to ignore. She came away disappointed not to have learned anything regarding Travis Hall, knowing it was a childish hope. She also felt troubled by the need many of her old classmates had to gloat over their accomplishments. Sarah was glad to have shared a few minutes with a handful of people as each shared their journeys, while plenty of others left her dry.

A few viewed her skeptically for the usual reasons at such affairs, such as Susan Anderson, whose comments Sarah found telling. She had casually suggested that Sarah had it easy in high school because she didn't have to work in order to get a date, or later, a husband with a secure financial future. Like many others there that night, a few of Sarah's friends conveniently blamed their disappointments and lack of happiness on chance. In their misguided judgments someone else always got a lucky break while good fortune had mysteriously passed them by, as though their happiness were somehow outside their own control and, more often than not, predicated on good looks, chance, or wealth alone. Blaming the luck of the draw, or the rich for their varied troubles created an easier pill for them to swallow. They were unable to see the irony in their flawed thinking that allowed them to believe the affluent man's success was only at their expense. After such shortsighted assessments, Sarah marveled that they craved the same circumstance. She wondered who they might blame if the well-heeled shoes of the wealthy man were suddenly fixed to their own feet. Both Susan Anderson and Fran Johnson viewed Sarah questionably, through envious eyes, and joined a host of people unable to cut their own path without excuse or blame.

As the evening progressed, Sarah grew tired listening to their tales. Between the boasters and those who suffered unfulfilling jobs or bad marriages, everyone had their stories, but most left Sarah uninspired. Several had never entered the real world and talked nonstop about their Woodstock adventure back in 1969, feeling positive that peace loomed on the horizon while they were barely able to come out from under the cloud of smoke that enclosed them. The list went on, ad infinitum, as Sarah and Nonie made the tour from group to group.

Ten years marked a milestone in Sarah's maturation. The innocence and goodness she saw everywhere in her youth had parlayed itself into a harder wisdom. Whatever the issues the others carried, happiness wasn't always predicated on what others do to you, but rather how you receive it. She understood where to find happiness in her own life, and she never expected to pin that hope on anyone's sleeve but her own.

CHAPTER THIRTY-FIVE

1974

Robert Baxter glanced at the clock on the wall and took note of the hour as he made the brief calculation that with the two-hour difference in time zones, it would be 7:00 p.m. mountain time. Reaching for the phonebook beside his telephone, he opened to the H's and dialed the long-distance number for Travis Hall.

On the third ring, Travis answered, "Hello?"

"Travis, you old SOB, how in the hell are you?"

"Well, I'm not dead yet if you're checking. Good to hear from you, Baxter. How's the family?"

Bob smirked at hearing his old friend's straight-shooting voice on the other end of the line. "Couldn't be better, although the wife's taken a job in order to 'keep up with the Jones's' around here. I guess the teacher's salary isn't paving the bricks to matrimonially heaven in gold yet."

"It can't be all bad since Katherine hasn't taken the notion to leave you yet," Travis commented with a playful sarcasm.

"What—leave this Casanova? Not when they're still lined up around here to get a hold of me!" Bob countered, still locked into the male game of bravado that had captured their long-time friendship.

"Keep dreaming, friend," Travis joked.

"Are you still holding your own at Honeywell?"

"Funny you should ask. I made the decision to venture out on my own with the help of a few of my old classmates from West Point."

"How's that, Travis?"

"A couple of them were moving up the chain of command and were assigned to the Department of Defense. They knew I was at Honeywell, and they knew my background with some of the top-secret weaponry there. So they contacted me to see if I could secure a few weapons systems that met their specifications, on time and on budget. I became the liaison between Honeywell and the DOD."

"I guess you had about ten years at Honeywell, if I'm counting correctly."

"You guessed about right. The timing of the build-up in Vietnam coincided with my early Honeywell years, and the sales and terms I was able to negotiate turned out to be quite profitable for Honeywell."

"If you're not selling military hardware and arms directly, then what are you doing now?"

"Ever since 1972, when the B-52s started bombing Hanoi, the industry was all competing for those lucrative government contracts. With my old classmates still in procurement at the DOD, they let word get around that I might be the 'go to guy' to land the sale for them, because I knew what they were looking for and had the technical knowledge to bring it together for them. Everyone in the aerospace field was clamoring to get a leg up on the competition for those government contracts. I gradually started to see the bigger picture."

"So when did you pull the plug and finally part ways with Honeywell?" Bob asked with surprise in his voice.

"It took a while for me to make the decision, but I finally left about twelve months ago. I kept getting calls from Boeing, and Lockheed Martian, trying to entice me to jump ship. When that failed, I found out they were willing to pay me on a commission basis as an independent consultant between the DOD and their companies. I'm sort of half industry 'techie' and half military procurement officer. It turns out to be a much more profitable venture than a nine-to-five job. Besides, this way I get to stay put and build that log home I've always wanted on the old homestead. Don't tell me you called just to find out if I was still gainfully employed or not."

"Somebody has got to check up on you and keep you out of the ditch! How is Jessica?"

"She is the light of my life, Bob. You know, she is nearly ten years old now and can ride a horse as well as any man," Travis answered.

"It's hard to believe that much time has gone by already!" Bob paused before he continued. "Listen, Travis, I went to a state teachers' conference yesterday and ran into an old associate of mine from when I worked at North Shoreline High. Maybe you remember the dean, Betty Watson?"

"Yeah, I remember her. Didn't she also teach a few English classes?" Travis asked.

"That's her, a blonde gal in her late thirties back then and all business. Well at any rate, we ran into one another the other day at the meeting, and she happened to tell me she went to a ten-year class reunion last month for the North Shoreline High School class of '64." There was dead silence on the other end of the line as Bob waited to hear if Travis would ask the question he knew he wanted to ask. After a lengthy pause, Bob continued, "Say, Travis, did you know that Sarah Thompson worked for Watson for four years?" he asked, with a slight wavering in his voice.

"I don't think you called to share that bit of old news with me. Where is this going, Bob?" Travis questioned, with a tightening tone.

"All right . . . I asked her if Sarah was at the reunion."

"Well, was she there?"

"Yeah, she was there . . . with her husband. I wasn't able to get her last name now, but I did learn she is still living on the north shore, maybe up in Muttontown. I guess she did pretty well for herself and married an attorney there. I just thought I'd pass that on for whatever it's worth to you."

"I hope she's happy, although the bastard married up." His delivery was sharp and curt.

"At least you know she's well and still living on the island," Bob added.

"Anything else?"

"Nothing much, except that she is involved with a lot of charity work, especially children's charities. Apparently, she can still turn heads when she enters a room, not that you didn't already guess that." Bob could tell by Travis's silence the news had hit him hard, and that he had just opened a wound that cut deep. Nothing he could say would change the way Travis felt and he decided it best to let him process the news on his own. Travis had to appreciate hearing from him about Sarah, regardless of what that news contained.

With those thoughts in mind, Bob decided to close the conversation. "One of these days, I'm going to load up the family in the van and head west, my friend. Who knows, maybe you'll have that log home built by then, and we'll all come for a visit on the way to the Grand Canyon.

"I've got two screaming kids here, so I've got to go, but we'll talk again soon. You take care of yourself, and Jessie too."

As he was about to hang up, Travis caught him and finally responded, "Baxter," Travis stopped with another pause, "thanks, buddy . . . I'll keep you posted on the cabin."

CHAPTER THIRTY-SIX

NOVEMBER 1986

John Douglas Birk appeared resolute as he stood with his son and campaign workers, surrounded by spent streamers, balloons and confetti strewn across the empty auditorium. The banners and signs lay motionless, propped against walls and resting in vacated chairs, adding to the sudden lifelessness of a losing campaign. With only a few stragglers remaining in the hall, Sarah Birk sat in a chair on stage, quietly waiting as Kenny's campaign manager, JD, and a handful of other campaign workers analyzed Kenny's defeat in his run for Congress in the third congressional district. It had been an exhausting two years, and the campaign had taken a lot out of Kenny. He had lost the jubilant boyishness in his step that had always been part of his nature. The long campaign had been difficult for everyone, but more so for their son, Keith, who was now fifteen. He missed time spent with his father in sporting pursuits like sailing and golfing, which were unavoidably put on the back burner during the long and grueling campaign.

Although Sarah would never confide in anyone, she was relieved Kenny had lost the election, not happy to be in the public eye. Over time, she had become disillusioned as she was surrounded by political workers, campaign managers, and handlers who were all vying for attention as they busily concocted press releases, speeches, and strategies—none of which bore any resemblance to the truth. The phoniness and theatrical nature to all of it could easily bring out the worst in people. Too many candidates, as well as their political operatives, were hungry for power and fame. Even those with the best of intentions could be called to corruption over time with the need to placate one group or another. At its best, politics was always a pact between scoundrels.

Sarah watched, as if in a distorted dream, the handful of campaign workers now surrounding Kenny. None of it suited him, as she had rightly known from the start. She recalled her father's expression, which best described her thoughts in that moment: If you lay down with dogs, you're likely to get their fleas. Although Kenny always loved attention, the constant posturing brought him no happiness, and Sarah thought it ironic he should hold office in the hopes of making decisions to improve the lives of others, when he never took the time to discover what was best for himself. He looked tired and had lost weight over the last six months. Sarah had insisted on a complete physical, despite his protestations. She wondered that Kenny had any original thought of his own left with so many people preparing his speeches and telling him what to discuss and when.

JD Birk brought his hand to Kenny's shoulder. "We're going to take a closer look at the numbers, Kenny. We had them on the ropes till the votes from the southeast part of the district started contradicting our own internal figures."

Kenny shook his head. "I worked that area as hard as anybody and don't know what else we could have done."

"I know you did, but I'll get the stats and concentrate on the demographics so we'll know how to reach them next time." JD was ever the fighter, ready to make use of lessons learned and turn on a dime to face the next election.

Kenny stood at his side, wearing a worn expression. Sarah watched him, thinking to herself that he wasn't able to keep his father's same persistence or optimism. The sudden weight of his loss was likely the culmination of many gnawing doubts she suspected he had always had regarding a run for Congress. She knew it never was a direction he would have chosen for himself, and for the first time, Kenny's demeanor verified the fact that he wanted out. In that moment, she saw in his expression a level of disgust for his father's rapacious political aspirations for him. She wondered if Kenny had finally asked himself what had happened to the happy, carefree days of his youth and at what point he had lost them.

"I don't know about a next time, Dad."

A look of obvious objection spread across JD's face. "What are you talking about? You're just worn down from the long campaign. You'll feel rested in the morning."

Kenny backed away from him, and turned to the others. "Let's call it a night. We've all had a long day. I'd like to thank each of you, again, for your tireless effort on the campaign. Go on home and get some rest, and I'll be in touch." The group reluctantly dispersed, promising to return to the office in the morning as Kenny shook a few hands and took a final hug goodbye as they all left the stage. When the last man and woman vacated the hall, Kenny turned back to face his father.

"There isn't going to be a next time, Dad."

JD raised his chin, not happy at hearing those words. "Stop talking like that. That's a defeatist attitude, and I didn't raise a quitter. Besides, we've already got name recognition, and you need to think of this race as just a stepping stone . . . a means to winning the next election. The groundwork has already been laid, and we've got our organization pretty much in place."

With more forcefulness than Kenny had ever used with his father before, he angrily replied, "For Christ's sake, Dad, you're not listening to me. How many more hoops do you want me to jump through in life before I meet your approval? You never once asked me what I wanted."

JD furrowed his eyebrows, expressing a look of shock as Kenny leaned on the podium. "I thought we both wanted the same thing, Kenny. Am I missing something here?"

Kenny coughed slightly, holding his head down, and then looked back up at JD. "You don't take the time to notice if you're missing anything because you're too damned busy laying the tracks down for the rest of us to travel. Did it ever occur to you that I don't really give a damn about being the white knight for the masses? Hell, I was never there for my own family because you've had me so busy chasing your dream."

His father stood erect, chin held high with lips tightly sealed. Placing his hand on the podium, JD finally spoke up. "I never thought it was just my dream, Kenny. You always agreed to the direction your life has gone, and it is a pretty damned good life. You went to the best schools and live in beautiful home with everything you could ever want or need at your fingertips. Most people would give their eye teeth to live your life, so what's come over you?"

"You just don't get it, do you? Sure, I have everything I need, with only one exception."

"What is it? Maybe we can work on getting it."

"Your money has pretty much bought everything you want, including some elections, Dad, but it can't make me the son you want me to be. I'm finished trying to be something I'm not, in the hopes of winning your approval. I'm not running again, and I plan on spending more time with my kids."

JD was taken aback at Kenny's forcefulness, and he paused, assessing the situation.

"Don't look so disgusted, Dad. You may be losing a candidate, but you'll still have a son, even if it isn't the one you wanted."

His words were cutting to JD as he stood there stunned into silence. Kenny turned his back on his father and walked over to Sarah, who stood up, totally surprised by Kenny's confrontation. It was a long time in coming, though this conversation was better late than never, and she was proud Kenny had finally taken a stand. Kenny slid his arm beneath Sarah's as they headed for the exit door offstage without looking back.

JD called out to them as they departed, "Kenny, we'll talk more tomorrow at the office. You'll have a different perspective on things in the morning after you get a good night's sleep." The metal exit door slammed hard behind them as JD watched them depart. Gathering a few loose papers from the podium, JD folded them and tucked them neatly into the interior breast pocket of his perfectly tailored Hickey Freeman suit. He quietly surveyed the now-vacant auditorium, contemplating his son's words. After a moment's pause, he shook his head as though this too would pass and picked up his cashmere overcoat, which was lying on an empty chair. After slipping it on, JD brushed a small speck of lint from his shoulder and slowly buttoned it, straightening his lapel as the janitor moved toward him with a broom, pushing the trash from the floor. *Tomorrow is another day,* JD thought as he finally headed for the exit with his head held high.

~~~~~~~~~~~

Kenny slept in later than usual on Monday morning, and Sarah was glad to have coffee together with him, which had been rare for them in recent years. She offered to fix breakfast, but Kenny refused, taking a seat with her at the kitchen table. He looked at Sarah through tired eyes surrounded by darker circles. It seemed strange to have him home, and she wondered what he was thinking, never seeing him so quiet before. "What is it, Kenny?" she asked him after a moment.

"I haven't always made the right choices, have I?"

"We're all guilty of that, aren't we? You did the right thing putting your foot down with JD last week, and you don't need to second-guess your decision not to run again."

"I don't mean about the decision not to run again."

"What then?" she asked, noticing the strained and pensive look in Kenny's expression.

"You know, when I was young, all I ever wanted was to be involved in sports, and I spent my youth chasing an unrealistic dream. With no hope of a sports career, I let my father direct every
~~~~~~~~~~~

step of my future. It's been a rough ride for all of us. In my whole life, I only made one decision for myself that I never regretted and was always certain of."

"What was that?"

He reached across the table and took Sarah's hand in his before continuing. "You've never disappointed me, Sarah, and I want you to know I've always loved you."

Sarah was surprised at hearing Kenny express that sentiment with a depth not ordinarily seen in him. "I've always known that, but I'm happy to hear you say so," she answered gently, squeezing his hand in return.

"We've had a good life together, haven't we?" He'd never taken the time for circumspection before, and Sarah had noticed a change in him since he had lost the election. She wondered if the loss hurt him more than he was willing to admit. She intuited something wasn't right, but what was it?

"You know we have! Why all this reflection this morning? Are you disappointed you lost the congressional seat? Because I think we're both relieved you won't have to spend time in DC away from home."

"No, I'm not sorry about the election. I just need to know that I didn't disappoint you. I haven't always been there for all of you, and I wish I could change that. Sometimes we don't see our mistakes in life until it's too late." Sarah felt a sudden tightening in her chest, convinced there was more meaning behind his words. Had he looked else ware in life for what she could never give him? The sudden thought was shocking, but in that moment she refused to hurt him.

"You haven't disappointed me, and now that you've made the decision not to run again, you'll have more time to spend at home doing the things you want to do. Besides, it's never too late to follow a different path if that's what will make you happy."

Kenny stared out the kitchen window as they sat at the table together, his eyes drawn and glassed over as if he were still grappling inside.

"I don't know what's come over you, Kenny, but I think you're being much too hard on yourself. We have a full life ahead of us, and maybe with more free time, you can get back to doing some of the things you put off doing in recent years. I know Keith would be happy if you could find more time to spend together with him, now that the election is behind us."

Kenny turned to face Sarah again. A thin smile crossed his lips. "Time . . . that's right, Sarah. We'll make the time," he said slowly and then stood up and walked to Sarah's side of the table. He bent down and kissed her gently before heading back to the bedroom to dress for work.

Sarah sat at the table, bewildered by Kenny's behavior of late. Relieved from campaigning, she thought all of them would be happier. She might even return to her writing since she had developed an idea for a novel several years ago but had to lay it down as the campaign heated up.

Kenny left for work late that morning but not before embracing Sarah one more time on his way out. "You've always stuck by me, Sarah, and I've never told you what that's meant to me."

"I don't know what's come over you this morning, but if I didn't know better, I'd think you were guilty of something you're not sharing." She knew Kenny better than anyone and felt strongly that he was hiding something. The thought of another woman briefly cross her mind again, but somehow even if that were possible, she remained strangely disconnected, feeling instead a deep empathy, sensing a vital wound in him she could not accurately identify.

The corners of his mouth rose slightly as he looked back at her. "You were always able to see things the others miss. You're right—I'm guilty of not appreciating you enough." Kenny kissed her goodbye and left Sarah in the hall, still standing in her robe.

She stood quietly staring at the closed door, contemplating if Kenny had recognized her inward disappointment in their marriage, and like her, the words were never spoken, but his conversation exposed the dark cloak hiding the secret they quietly shared.

Failing his father was hard enough to come to terms with, but having failed Sarah and his marriage would be an admission he wasn't willing or strong enough to make. In that moment, she felt his anguish as well as her own.

Checking the time, Sarah returned to the bedroom and spent the next hour readying herself to leave for a meeting at the children's center to plan their next fundraiser. By 10:30, Sarah was ready, and with a few minutes left to spare, she returned to the kitchen for a second cup of coffee. Passing the center island, she glanced at the counter and noticed that Kenny had left the keys to the house behind. Sarah picked them up, pausing for a moment to look at the key ring she had given him over twenty years ago. Turning it over, Sarah read the now scratched and worn inscription "Friends Forever Sarah." She smiled to herself, remembering with nostalgia earlier years and thinking Kenny had been a friend despite the absence of the deep, encompassing love and passion she had always hoped for. The phone rang just as she poured a second cup of coffee.

"Hello."

"Good morning, is this Mrs. Birk?"

"This is she. Who's calling please?"

"Mrs. Birk, this is Doctor Parker's office calling. We've got Mr. Birk's appointment set up for his first treatment this week on Thursday at 10:45 a.m. He'll need to go to the Glen Cove Medical building adjacent to the hospital, on the third floor, suite 301." Sarah's heart started racing. She was not quite sure she was hearing the caller correctly, and panic crept over her as she tried to make sense of the call.

"Can you tell me again exactly what these treatments are?" Sarah inquired, assuming Dr. Parker and his staff couldn't possibly have confused Kenny with someone else since he had been their family physician for years.

"Dr. Parker feels that radiation is the most effective means available in treating Mr. Birk's late-stage pancreatic cancer. At this point, chemo would take too long." Sarah's hand started to shake.

"Mrs. Birk, it seems advisable to have someone accompany him to be able to drive him home. These treatments can weaken him further."

Desperately trying to regain her composure, Sarah finally responded. "Yes . . . yes, of course. We'll be there at ten-forty-five on Thursday. Thank you for the call."

Bringing the receiver down to the phone as if in slow motion, Sarah started weeping as she realized why Kenny was behaving the way he was. She had suspected something wasn't right with his sudden weight loss, but she'd never guessed anything like this when she insisted he see the doctor for a physical. He probably knew about the cancer the night of the election and had deliberately kept that information from her, as well as from his father. She was hurt that he hadn't confided in her, but he probably needed time to come to terms with it in his own way.

Sarah needed to be strong. She would see to it Kenny's wishes and time would be spent from now on the way he chose. Time would indeed be the one commodity JD Birk couldn't buy, and it was the only thing that had power over all of them—even him.

PART III

In the silent depths of soul's rich soil,
A seed is dropped with little toil.
With whispered thoughts her gentle touch,
A vision fed with love so much.

The picture drawn with unseen hand,
Reveals her heart and dream so grand.
In secret does the vision hold,
The dreamer stands with strength so bold.

Gently watered from above,
A thousand hours held her love.
Till time does birth her heart's desire,
The soul responds with burning fire.

The flame was fed with care so dear,
The universe answered, "I am here."
The flower opens from above,
Darkness withers in light of love.

CHAPTER THIRTY-SEVEN

FEBRUARY 1990

Sarah Thompson Birk sat on the family-room floor beneath the built-in shelving amidst a stack of papers, old journals, and books removed from the cabinets and shelves. More than three years had passed since Kenny had lost his bid for Congress and was diagnosed with cancer. The six months following Kenny's diagnosis had brought his rapid decline, with no relief or remission after extensive treatment. By May of 1987, Kenny's battle ended before anyone had a chance to come to terms with his departure. At the time of his passing, Sarah was forty one years old, and Rebecca and Keith were still in high school, making his death a painful shock for everyone. With those dark days past and both children now in college, Sarah was finally able to clear the house of unneeded papers, periodicals, and journals with Kenny's name on them that were gathering dust.

Kenny had prepared well for such an eventuality. The insurance policies ensured them the ability to keep their same quality of life while the Birks' trust guaranteed an income for the children, assuring their education would not be compromised. Lowenstein, Hammond, and Birk law firm was of great assistance to Sarah through the most challenging days the first year after his death.

Sarah was grateful for the assistance JD had given her, but she was aware of the change in him after Kenny's death. Without his son, he lost the vision and zeal he had once carried in life, spending less and less time at the law firm. JD spent his days on the water, sailing Long Island Sound, or at Martha's Vineyard during the summer months. They held fewer parties at their home, and JD slipped into an early retirement, taking no interest in his former political pursuits. The untimely death of his only child was the caustic solvent that cut away the false heights he had foolishly demanded in life.

Nonie Kaplan stood at Sarah's side throughout the ordeal, and at her insistence, Sarah returned to her writing early in 1988. Along with the passage of time, writing the novel was just the creative outlet she needed, helping her through her grief.

Now that her novel had been completed, Sarah felt free to move on to the next chapter in her life. Pulling several more books from the cabinet, Sarah stumbled upon a copy of Kenny's 1963 North Shoreline High School yearbook. She paused for a moment, picking up the book as she leaned against the couch and opened its cover. Turning the pages slowly, she smiled to herself as she perused each page, remembering fondly those happy, carefree days from long ago. Each face brought back fond memories of the events shared together twenty-seven years earlier. Several pictures featured the basketball team and football team, where Kenny happily posed alongside his teammates; all shared smiles, but none as broad as Ken's. Sarah rested a moment on each picture, able to remember the good times now, without the pain so prominent immediately after Kenny's passing. *He was happy then*, she thought to herself as she scanned every picture of the athletic department along with all the different team members. Repositioning the diamond and wedding band on her left hand, she wondered where life might have taken Kenny if his father hadn't directed every aspect of his life. It hadn't worked out well for either of them.

Sarah turned a few more pages of the yearbook and suddenly stopped, slowly tracing her fingers across the page. Her heart skipped a beat at seeing a picture of Travis Hall standing in front of a blackboard, writing an equation in one of his classes. His eyes were fixed on the board, his chiseled jaw firmly set, chalk still in hand. Sarah caught her breath. How curious that seeing his face in a picture after all these years could still evoke such a strong emotion and response in her. Although thoughts of him had never fully left her, they came with far less frequency as time went on, especially after Kenny took ill. She lingered several minutes, staring at the page and recalling their time together all those years ago, wondering where life had taken him and if he was happy. She could still remember his words at their parting and how she had clung to them in a naive and childish hope. It seemed like a lifetime ago when the feeling of love she bore for him could bring her to soaring heights unattainable anywhere else. *How sad that life should demand so much of us*, she thought, *robbing us of that sweet, innocent feeling and hopeful joy*. She was looking back over her shoulder at what once was, tempered now by the harsher realities that befall everyone over time. Sarah closed the yearbook, placing it to the side. Both Travis Hall and Kenny were now only part of her past. The present and future demanded her attention. Before she could reach for another stack of books, the doorbell rang out. Sarah rose to her feet and went to answer.

"Come on in, Nonie." Happily surprised, Sarah gave Nonie a hug as she entered the foyer. Nonie's arrival lifted Sarah's somber mood allowing the present to take center stage.

"I can only stay a few minutes. I have to beat the dinner crowd back to the restaurant." Sarah hung Nonie's coat and then led the way to the kitchen, pouring each of them coffee as Nonie showed a few of her purchases, pulling them from a bag.

"Did you have any luck finding something elegant to wear on your cruise, besides just sports wear?" Sarah asked as she brought the coffee to the table.

"Well, not exactly, but I still have time to hunt. What in the world are you up to in there? It looks like a hurricane ran through your family room!"

"In a manner of speaking, it has. I've decided it's time to clean up and clear out around here, especially since I've received good news today, and I'm celebrating."

"What good news?" Nonie asked with a squint to her brows.

"I was hoping you would drop by so I could share it with you. My agent called yesterday to tell me they have arranged a book-signing tour for me in order to promote my novel. They'll be calling with the dates and details and wanted to make sure my calendar remains open next month."

"Sarah, that's wonderful! Did they tell you where they're sending you?"

"It all seems so surreal, but they want to reach as wide a market as possible and are planning a nationwide marathon for me. I think they have six or seven cities lined up over a one-month timeframe. They mentioned Boston, Atlanta, Chicago, Dallas, Phoenix, and LA, ending back in New York. I'm so excited. I still can't believe they wanted to publish the book, let alone want me to do the tour!"

"What's not to believe? I've always said you could write the pants off of anyone I ever knew. Besides, the book really is good. You should be very proud of yourself."

"Thanks, but I think if you hadn't been there to encourage me, none of this would be happening."

"That's nonsense. It was in you all along. You just needed a little push like a good Jewish grandmother would give." Nonie's face took on a comical twist.

"What's so funny about that?"

"Oh my God, Sarah, it's just that I suddenly realized I'm about to become one! Tell me something—how in the world did we get here?"

"Interesting you should ask that question, since I was clearing out lots of old papers and journals this morning and had an attack of nostalgia myself. Do you think we've changed that much, Nonie?"

"Heavens no! We haven't changed a bit. Everyone else has."

They both broke out in laughter, and for the first time in months, Sarah was starting to allow herself to enjoy life again.

"When do you and Abe leave on your cruise?"

"The ship departs from Miami on the fifteenth of March, so I guess you and I will be gone about the same time. What do you say we plan a shopping trip together before we both leave? I think I can trust one of the kids to fill in for me at the restaurant another day."

"That sounds great. I could do with some new warm-weather outfits myself before the tour starts. Just give me a call and let me know when you can work it out with the kids."

"That sounds good, Sarah. I better get a move on, or they'll be sending out a search party. I love to feel needed!"

Sarah walked Nonie to the door, hugged her goodbye, and then headed back to the pile of papers and books on the family-room floor, feeling freer to part with more stuff than ever before.

~~~~~~~~~~

By the fourth week in March, Sarah was beginning to wear down from the whirlwind pace of the book-signing tour. Fortunately, each of these events were scheduled for Thursday or Friday afternoons, allowing time for her to fly back home and regroup over the weekend into the early part of each week. The one exception was the second week of the month when she spent Thursday in Chicago and then flew from there to Dallas the next day for a signing on Saturday. She was grateful to finish two of these events in the same week, leaving only Phoenix and LA on the remaining tour before the last event in New York at the end of the month. The book sales were up, and everyone, including the publishers, seemed pleased. Sarah had little knowledge of the business-end in publishing or of promoting a book, and she was grateful for a good agent who helped her negotiate her way through the unending maze in the industry. The only positive thing overriding her exhaustion was that the remaining cities were all in sunshine
~~~~~~~~~~

states, and Sarah was happy to see the sunny skies in light of the long, drawn-out winter still lingering in New York.

Phoenix was not at all what she was expecting with its awesome landscape and colorful, exotic desert plants lining the roadways from the airport to the Biltmore Hotel. The dramatic difference in terrain brought the strange sensation she had landed on another planet. She felt like a kid again, seeing the world as if for the first time. Her flight arrived late in the afternoon on Wednesday, and she was scheduled to be at the Borders Book Store, located in the upscale Biltmore Fashion Park, adjacent to the hotel, at 1:00 p.m. on Thursday. After a light dinner and long, hot bath, Sarah nestled in to catch some much-needed rest. The following morning, she ventured out and strolled along the flower-laden walkways and meandered past the variety of shops in the shopping center next door, stopping for coffee in an open-air café. The picture-perfect, rejuvenating sun-drenched morning left her with a sense of optimism about her life she hadn't felt in many years. For the first time, Sarah had no one to care for but herself, an indulgence never afforded her before.

Arriving a few minutes early for the event, she was surprised to see a line already forming. She was caught off-guard as the manager of the bookstore, a young man wearing wire-rimmed spectacles, came up to greet her. He looked like one of the many yuppies graduating from the universities nowadays. "Are these people here to see me?" she asked in disbelief.

"Oh yes, they most certainly are. We have quite a few members of our community who read books in your genre, and if the reviews are good, we can't always meet the demand. I guess a good love story is something none of us can get enough of!"

"Well, I'm terribly surprised and flattered by the turnout. I suppose this is good for your business as well."

"Everyone wins, Ms. Birk, when books sell as well as yours is apparently doing."

"Thank you. I suppose I shouldn't keep them waiting."

Sarah made her way to the table set up for her. A few copies of her book were on display off to the side with a life-sized poster behind the table, depicting her main characters in an embrace. She took her seat and started greeting the patrons, exchanging pleasantries as she signed each book presented to her.

Returning from his office to the storefront with additional pens, the store manager headed straight back to the table where Sarah sat autographing copies of her novel. With all the politeness of a well-schooled gentleman, he begged Sarah's pardon, "Please excuse the intrusion, Ms. Birk, but I nearly forgot this note. I was asked to deliver this personally to your hand and to no one else." He handed her the envelope and then excused himself a second time, leaving the additional pens resting on the table as he walked to the registers at the front of the store.

Sarah paused, examining the envelope that had her name printed plainly by hand on its face. There was no return address, which piqued her curiosity. Before the next patron arrived at the table, she quickly tore the envelope open pulling the note out. Like the envelope, the letter was printed by hand on a plain piece of white paper:

Sarah,

I'm hoping you might have an extra hour to indulge an old friend with the pleasure of your company again. Although I know it's been nearly twenty-seven years since we've last seen one another, time hasn't robbed my recollection of the one student I promised to always remember.

Please come, Sarah, 5:00 p.m.–Cactus Flower Restaurant, Lincoln and Palo Christie Road, Paradise Valley.

I have a meeting late in the afternoon and will do my best to be on time. Congratulations on the success of your new novel.

Hope to see you there,
Travis Hall

Sarah read the words again, stunned and hardly able to believe what she was reading as her eyes rested on his signature a second time. Her hand started to tremble as she folded the paper and did her best to slide it back into the envelope.

"Is everything all right, Ms. Birk?" the lady next in line queried, as she approached the table.

"Oh yes. . . everything is just fine, thank you. Hearing from an old acquaintance caught me by surprise," Sarah answered, while forcing a smile as the lady stood at the table. "Now, to whom shall I dedicate this copy?"

"Beverly . . . Bev Wilson, Ms. Birk. I'm a big fan of your novel."

Sarah did her best to concentrate on each person who brought a book to her, autographing each one for the duration of the afternoon. Her thoughts were racing all the while. She wasn't sure if she should accept Travis Hall's invitation. Hearing from him after all these years was a shock, and she barely knew what to think. She wondered how old he was, and if he lived in Phoenix. Was he married? Did he have any children? How did he know she was here? The questions kept coming, but the answers were all unknown. What would she have to share with him, and how could she possibly have a casual visit with the one man who had haunted her all her life? Her mind raced as she visualized a dozen different scenarios, all leaving her ruffled in a state of apprehension and anxiety. The tempo of her pulse increased as she wore a smile, pretending to be calm with each new customer while also checking her watch far too frequently over the next few hours. By 3:45 p.m., the last of the books were signed, and Sarah was ready to make a graceful exit.

Stopping for a few words with the store manager before she left, Sarah asked, "I wonder if you might recall when Mr. Hall left this note for me?"

"I almost forgot about it, though I gave my word to the gentleman I would deliver it to your hand and no one else. It's been sitting on my desk since the middle of last week, and if I hadn't returned to the office for more pens, I might have forgotten it completely! I do hope it wasn't a prank letter. He didn't seem the type, and he told me you knew one another a long time ago."

Sarah smiled politely. "Yes, we did know each other years ago, and it was kind of you to deliver the note. Thank you so much."

"It was my pleasure, Ms. Birk. I do hope to see you in the future for another book signing with your next novel."

Sarah extended her hand and thanked him once again before she left. She was still unsure whether to meet with Travis Hall or not, and wondered if he would arrive unaccompanied. With little more than an hour left to decide, Sarah nervously walked back to the hotel, anxious as a cat on a hot tin roof, her mind and pulse still racing.

CHAPTER THIRTY-EIGHT

The Biltmore Hotel limo pulled up at 5:06 p.m. at the front door of the Cactus Flower Restaurant. The driver jumped out and ran to the passenger doors, opening them wide while extending his arm to Sarah Birk as she made her way down the step.

"Just call any time you want to be picked up, Ms. Birk," the young driver said as he held the door open for her.

Sarah placed several dollars into his hand and graciously thanked him for his service. The driver quickly ran to the restaurants ornately carved, wooden front door and opened it for her as well. Smiling broadly, he continued to watch Sarah from behind as she walked into the restaurant. She wore a sleek, fitted shirt-waist safari-styled dress with dark brown wooden buttons on her hip pockets as well as down the length of the placket. The dress kept the same tailored elegance that came naturally to her, and her appearance held the drivers extended attention. The short-sleeved, form-fitted cotton dress had a sewn-in waistband with bodice darts that highlighted her slim silhouette. Opened slightly in front at the hem up to the bottom button just above the knee, the dress exposed the taupe stockings that accentuated the long line of her shapely legs down to her brown leather pumps. Wooden hoop earrings punctuated the crisp, clean lines of the dress, and it was a style that was well suited to her.

She asked herself again why she had accepted Travis Hall's invitation and thought how childish it was to still be drawn to him, despite the number of years that had come and gone since they had last seen one another. For the past few hours, she had convinced herself that at nearly ten years her senior, he might be infirm. She would be polite, and most important, she would remain in control and not allow him an opportunity to lead or intimidate her as he was so easily able to do all those years ago. At one time, several years back, she had convinced herself he might have died, which helped to tamp down his memory whenever thoughts of him returned.

Regardless of the methods she used to dismiss him, his face and the year their lives had been intertwined would come to the foreground of thought when least expected. For better or for worse, Travis Hall had been the only man in her life whom she ever thought of with an intense passion and longing. His memory could not be forgotten, only endured. A deep inner chasm still remained that refused to be washed clean of him. Although the intensity had subsided over the years, spontaneous thoughts of him had never left her, and she was certain the reality of his life was more than likely far less appealing than the fanciful dreams of her youth. In the real world, people age, which often brings the loss of vitality, weight gain and balding. Those realities might destroy the illusion of the perfect man she had loved so intensely for all those years. Confronting her fears, this face-to-face meeting would finally bring an end to that childish and persistent desire in the shadows beneath her well-ordered and proper life.

With the major changes occurring in her life recently, she was ready to be free of the past and embrace a new sense of independence. Where that new life would lead her, she wasn't sure, but the door would eventually open in front of her, just as her writing had opened a new chapter when all else seemed hopeless. This was her chance to relinquish all of the past and to start anew.

Stepping inside the restaurant, Sarah approached the maitre d' at the guest podium. "Good evening, I'm Sarah Birk and am meeting Mr. Travis Hall. The reservation was for five o'clock."

With efficiency and promptness, the maitre d' acknowledged her, "Of course, Ms. Birk. We have your table ready for you. Would you please follow me?"

A sudden flurry of nerves fell over her as she steadied herself. The host led her past a '40s-styled bar with high-backed, tufted red leather booths and teardrop lights ensconced in swirled-colored glass that gave off a mellow amber lighting, setting a nostalgic mood. They moved past the bar and several other dining areas reserved for smaller groups and parties.

The larger dining room had a slightly more formal feel, with several crystal chandeliers spread out over the expansive space, and crisp white tablecloths with linen napkins in the shape of fans at each place setting on every table. Upon entering the dining room, she was immediately drawn to the wall of windows across the entire width of the room. The view of the open courtyard outside with the shading of the purple and pink mountains in the background was spectacular. Located in the center of the courtyard, a three-tiered fountain was surrounded by exotic-looking flowers and plants. Several Palo Verde trees and orchid trees provided shade and added color, while white mini-lights were strategically wrapped around their trunks and up through their branches, allowing for alfresco dining well into the evening. The perimeter of the courtyard showcased meticulously sculptured flowerbeds that added waves of colorful displays in shades of blue, white, and lavender, while giant planters and pots were laden with draping vines and blush pink rose trees, placed thoughtfully between tables to offer added privacy for diners. The iron tables each cradled a large umbrella in a neutral shade of clay so as not to detract from the stunning backdrop of brilliant colors in the early evening sky. The beauty of the lush and colorful garden was breathtaking.

To the side of the main dining room facing the courtyard, two booths provided a more private space. The maitre d' placed two menus at the farthest booth from the main dining area, while simultaneously removing a small "reserved" card resting on the table. The view of the garden and the angular peeks of the mountains in the background were framed perfectly from this vantage point.

To her surprise, Travis Hall had not arrived yet, and she wondered if she had made a mistake by coming. As if reading her thoughts while catching Sarah's questioning expression, the maitre d' continued, "Mr. Hall called moments ago and asked us to inform you he has been delayed but should be arriving within a few more minutes."

In that moment, a waiter approached the booth. "May I bring you something to drink while you wait?" the waiter asked as Sarah stood beside the booth.

Feeling too self-conscience to leave, she slid into the booth without further delay. "Coffee for me, please. Thank you," she said, hoping it would help her to think more clearly. With the high backs on the leather booths, Sarah was unable to see anyone approaching, and she suddenly felt a slight loss of advantage. Her pulse began to race, and it took a moment for her to calm down as she reminded herself how childish it was to be so ill at ease. This would soon be over and just another memory she would have of a closed chapter in her life. The waiter returned with her coffee, and Sarah was grateful for the moment alone to be able to rein in her emotions.

She wondered if Travis Hall had grown up here as she thought of the rugged and hostile nature the desert fostered. The beauty of the garden calmed her as she took in the dramatic juxtaposition of the stunning desert terrain behind the lush and well-tended garden presented by the view from her booth. The majestic mountains cut out jagged shapes against the azure blues and sweeping pink streaks of the early evening sky. They jutted up off the desert floor as if by some mystical power, orchestrating their awesome shapes and colors, leaving men to pick their perfect names to match their images, like Mummy Mountain, Camel Back, Praying Monk, and

Twin Peaks. They all played an integral part of everyday life in the valley of the sun where residents of Phoenix used their names as location markers the same way buildings acted as landmarks back on the East Coast. The amethyst and crimson strokes of color at sunset and sunrise, along with the azure blue of the midday sky were surreal in their pristine beauty, and Sarah couldn't help but think the sky looked much larger and expansive here.

A harshness to the desert belied its beauty; it could be so unforgiving with the high heat of summer, along with the wildlife unwilling to relinquish their territory to newly developed neighborhoods. Avant-garde buildings and lush plantings positioned in such harsh and rugged surroundings seemed a mismatched yet stunning contrast. To Sarah, something was still vital, raw, and untamed about the Southwest that she found intrinsically attractive.

Arizona was truly magnificent in its majesty with its awesome mountains interspersed with emerald green golf courses now dotting the formidable and hostile landscape. The newer Southwest-style homes perched on the sides of the mountains fit into the landscape seamlessly, allowing the giant saguaros, ocotillos, and yucca plants magnificent backdrops for their beauty. She admired the pioneering spirit that brought people to this inhospitable place over a century ago and the sacrifices they made to live here and bring the desert to life in all its glory after many years of toil with Mother Nature. The Arizona desert seemed a fitting place for Travis Hall as she remembered his unwavering ability to dominate every situation with ease. His disciplined mind covered an unknown power that he kept in check. Some measure of difficulty had to have been levied against him during his life for him to have exercised the inner strength she recalled. Whatever the level of testing was, it produced the perfect temperament and character needed in order to embrace life's difficulties, as well as the ability to endure the arid and rugged terrain of the desert Southwest.

Sarah wasn't the girl she used to be, and Travis Hall was sure to have changed as well. She turned her wrist to check the time. It was now fifteen minutes after five, and she wondered how much longer she should wait. No more than a minute passed when Travis Hall finally made his appearance, standing beside the booth and resting a knuckle on top of the table as he looked down at Sarah, just as he had done the first day they met.

"Hello, Sarah. It's been a long time," he said with a faint smile across his lips.

Sarah's heart raced at the site of him standing there, those same piercing, emerald green eyes directed intently at her own. For a moment, she was a teenager again falling under his spell, incapable of controlling her emotions. His deep-set eyes were still compelling, although etched with deeper lines on a much ruddier and sun-worn face. The same chestnut hair was still cropped shorter at the sides and temple but was decidedly gray now, with additional intermittent graying at the crown where he still sported a full head of hair. The navy blazer with gold buttons was set off with a pale-blue dress shirt and a rich-looking silk print tie with various shades of blue that had a slight shimmer to its appearance and bounced the light back to his face, enhancing the gray at his temples. His understated yet distinguished look, right down to his gray trousers and polished black leather loafers, was unanticipated. Although he did appear slightly older, time had not minimized those broad shoulders and well-defined chest that had punctuated his authority way back in Sarah's high-school years. She was taken aback at his appearance, and there was absolutely no mistaking him, despite his more polished attire. She could have spotted him in a crowd with ease. She swore to herself she would keep control, and she quickly fought back old emotions.

"Mr. Hall, it's so good to see you again," she said without offering her hand, not wanting to risk his touch.

"Please, call me Travis. I apologize for being late. It's always difficult to gauge these meetings exactly." He paused momentarily as if taking in her reaction to him. "You look fabulous, Sarah, and you haven't aged a bit!" he said without batting an eyelash. He slid into the opposite side of the booth without taking his sight off of her.

She felt the weight of his stare and forced herself to respond, "Thank you, and I see time has been kind to you as well."

"I've taken a few kicks, but can't complain," he said as he leaned on the table. His eyes scanned her and then rested on her left hand which still bore her wedding band and diamond. "I wasn't sure you'd come," he said in a softer tone.

"I wasn't sure if I would either," she answered immediately with an honesty that even surprised herself.

He remained expressionless and then asked her, "Why did you decide to meet with me, Sarah?"

"I suppose the fact that you neglected to leave a number where I might reach you in order to politely decline, for one reason," she responded quickly hoping to keep an equal footing, but immediately regretting her negativity. The corners of his mouth turned upward, indicating to Sarah he knew exactly what he was doing by not leaving a phone number for her to call.

"And the other reason you decided to come?"

"Perhaps plain old curiosity, particularly wondering how you knew I was in Phoenix, since I have a different last name now." She met his eyes directly, establishing a defensive boundary.

"Your public relations people did a wonderful job of providing advance notice of your book-signing event at Borders. It was published in the *Arizona Republic* last Sunday."

"But how would you have known it was me since my name has changed since we last knew one another?"

"That's what made it so easy—they included a beautiful picture as well, and you haven't changed a bit in twenty-seven years."

"I suppose I should be flattered, although I know better," she said. The waiter arrived and asked if they were ready to order. Before Travis could speak, Sarah raised her hand and interjected, "Only coffee for me, please." The response spilled from her lips defensively, guarding against being cornered into a situation she might not be able to extract herself from easily.

"Bring a black coffee for me as well, and check back with us later," he said, laying the menus aside, leaving the issue of dinner open.

"He was still in control," she thought, and he was able to use it covertly so as to go unnoticed—if she hadn't been paying such close attention to every detail in his actions.

"I suppose you must live in Phoenix then," Sarah commented as the waiter left them.

"I don't actually live in Phoenix, but about two hours north, on the Rim."

"What do you mean 'on the Rim'?"

"The Mogollon Rim is a six- to seven-thousand-foot-high escarpment that runs for two hundred miles across the central part of the state of Arizona. It has some of the most beautiful scenery in the country and some of the oldest stands of ponderosa pines anywhere on earth."

"It sounds fabulous but also remote. Are you teaching there?"

Travis laughed. "No, I gave teaching up when I left New York. I never went back to it again."

"Somehow that doesn't surprise me," she said. "What do you do so far from the city?"

"You make it sound like a penalty to live there, when in fact it is a privilege. Besides, with today's technology and transportation, one could live almost anywhere and still not be totally isolated. That being said, it would be tough to raise cattle in the city."

"So, you're a rancher?" Sarah asked with surprise.

"Yes, I ranch, among other things, but you seem surprised." He leaned back in the booth as the waiter arrived with his coffee.

"I don't know how many ranchers come to town wearing suits and attending meetings," Sarah replied with an inquisitive look on her face.

He took a sip of his coffee, placed the cup back down and, reminiscent of his demeanor all those years ago, he gave Sarah a three-word response that was direct but still revealed nothing, "This one does.

"That's enough about me. I seem to recall a young man named Birk back at North Shoreline High. Did you marry him?"

Sarah couldn't hide the sudden pain his question brought her as she recalled the love Kenny had for her all those years ago when they were in high school together and the loss she had suffered when he passed away. The wound was still so fresh. "Yes, we were married for nearly nineteen years," she answered with a slight wavering in her voice while she avoided looking directly at him in answering.

Travis let a moment laps, allowing her some space. "You said you 'were' married, Sarah; are you divorced?"

"No," she paused, slowly regaining control of her emotions. "Ken died almost three years ago now," she answered softly. One of Travis's arms was resting on the table. His hand opened slightly, then slowly closed again as if he were about to touch her and then thought better of the impulse.

"Sarah, I'm so sorry," he said, with a genuine tenderness she hadn't expected him capable of expressing.

"Thank you," Sarah continued, "but I'm learning to take each day as it comes. I started writing again to keep from falling into a depression, and I had no idea it would be successful. It's been a blessing for me."

"I'm happy for the success of your novel, Sarah. Tell me, do you have children?" he asked in hopes of changing the somber mood.

"Yes, I have a daughter, Rebecca, and a son, Keith, who are both in college. My daughter plans on teaching, and my son wants to go into graphic arts. What about you? Did you ever marry and have children?"

"My wife and I parted ways in '69, but she did leave me with a terrific daughter, Jessica, who lives here in the valley with her husband and two sons."

"Somehow, I can't picture you as a grandfather," Sarah said with a gentle smile across her face.

"Life is full of unexpected surprises!" They both smiled happily at each other. "You know, Sarah, you have an absolutely beautiful smile," he said. "Tell me something, how come you never smiled much when you were in high school?"

The question caught Sarah completely off-guard. "I don't recall that I didn't smile. Whatever makes you ask a question like that?"

"To be more exact, I meant you hardly ever smiled when you were around me."

A sudden flash of insight crossed Sarah's mind. "It's funny you should ask such a thing because I recall a comment written in my yearbook made by a friend of yours regarding my smile that I thought was odd."

"Really, who was that?"

"Mr. Baxter."

"And exactly what did Bob write?"

"As I recall, something about keeping my nose up and not smiling. I wondered what in the world he meant by that, especially since he was never my instructor and he picked up my yearbook and signed it without being invited to do so!"

Travis chuckled and shook his head slightly. "That sounds like something Baxter would do. He could walk out on a limb where he didn't belong and worry about the consequences later. He also did too much talking."

"Where is he now?" Sarah inquired.

"I'm afraid Bob died several years ago from lung cancer. The cigarettes finally got to him. He was a good man and great friend. I miss the guy. But you still haven't answered my question. Why didn't you smile very often?"

Sarah drew in her breath, trying to garner enough time to formulate a response. "Perhaps I was afraid of failing. I really can't recall; it was so long ago," she said, not wanting to reveal the attraction she had felt for him then, and the recurring fear she had in those days he might regard her as nothing more than an unintelligent child.

He listened to her answer intently, and then spoke with a serious expression Sarah found unnerving, "Funny, I still remember it like it was yesterday."

His words cut to Sarah's heart, and she was left speechless. They remained locked in each other's eyes, Sarah unable to respond while she tried to digest what he had just said and why.

The silence was suddenly broken as the waiter came to the side of the table, carrying a telephone and then plugged it into a jack at the side of their booth. "Excuse me for the interruption, Mr. Hall, but there is a caller, a General Hacket, expressing the need to talk with you right away."

Travis nodded and then turned back to Sarah as the waiter left the phone resting on their table. "Normally I wouldn't answer this, but I have to make an exception in this case. Please excuse the interruption." He answered and then took a pen and small piece of paper from inside his breast pocket. "What are the numbers, General Hacket?" Travis wrote down several numbers on the paper. "Have you received the ETA on the first shipment?" Another pause eclipsed his speaking. "Good, I'll be getting back to you the first of next week. Give my regards to Hank Evans back at DOD, General." He hung the phone back up, raising his hand slightly for the waiter to come retrieve the phone, and then replaced the paper and pen in his lapel pocket.

Sarah's curiosity was heightened, wondering if it were indeed a military general with whom he had been speaking and what the numbers he had recorded meant. She was too polite to ask and only remembered how he excelled in math and how that too had intimidated her years earlier.

"I apologize again for the interruption and bad timing," he repeated, and then posed a question she was totally unprepared for, "Sarah, I'd love to show you the Arizona I know and love. Would you consider spending a few extra days in Phoenix and let me be your tour guide to some of the most beautiful country you'll ever see?"

The invitation was surprising, especially coming on the heels of what appeared to be an important phone call. She took note of how quickly he was able to set aside the call and continue as if there had been no interruption. "I . . . I . . . don't think that would be possible," she said, feeling awkward at his suggestion.

"It will be spectacular, and very much above-board. You can stay at a hotel in Payson, and I'd have you back early every night. You'd have the chance to see the real Arizona that few ever get to see. Two days isn't a lot of time to set aside for a once-in-a-lifetime adventure—besides, you'd be in good company," he added with a bit of humor.

Sarah was resting her fingers against her forehead while looking down as he spoke, trying to protect herself from his ability to coerce her. He tilted his head down and then to the side, looking at her with that half-smile she remembered so well. He seemed almost playful in his approach. Sarah was torn, wanting to know more about him but also not feeling comfortable enough to be alone with him.

"I . . . I have to be in LA on Wednesday, and I really do need to check back in at home before then," she said, with a hesitancy she was unable to hide.

"Sarah, you can always come up with a million reasons why you shouldn't take the time to stop and smell the roses in life, but considering our age, we should take every opportunity we have to enjoy the time allotted to us. Surely you can check in by phone. Besides, a change of scenery might do you good." She was struggling to find a way to decline, suspecting he would try to prevent that from happening. "What's two days in the grand scheme of things?"

"I'm afraid I don't have a car rented, and I'm scheduled to leave tomorrow anyway," she said.

Travis quickly replied, "I'm sure your publicist can have your ticket changed, and you won't need a car. I'll pick you up and return you safely to the airport on Sunday."

Sarah was waffling under the pressure of making a hasty decision she didn't want to regret later. After all, what did she really know about him?

Travis leaned forward and spoke with a tenderness that touched her for the second time. "Sarah," he started out slowly, with an imploring expression that caught her attention, "do you have the heart to disappoint an old friend at the chance to share the country he loves so much?"

His comment seemed so genuine and heartfelt that Sarah gave in. "All right, Travis, I'll accept your invitation with the understanding that I must leave on Sunday." She had stepped headlong outside her comfort zone entering the unknown with trepidation—and amazement that she had agreed. The pleasure reflected in his mischievous smile was slightly unnerving although she suspected his reaction was in part the fact that she had addressed him using his first name.

"I promise you won't regret this, Sarah," he said, with sincerity.

"What hotel do you recommend?" She asked.

"It's already taken care of. You're booked at the best hotel in Payson for tomorrow and Saturday night," he answered with a glint in his eye that caused a slight shiver in Sarah.

"That's twice you've assumed I would agree. How did you know that I would?" she demanded with her head suddenly held higher and her eyes drawn closer together.

He kept that half-smile and gleam in his eye, sitting as steady as a rock. Without flinching, he answered immediately. "I've never made a dime or closed any deal without a gamble, Sarah!"

She couldn't help but wonder what category he placed her in with such a comparison and instant answer. "Well then, exactly what did you intend to gain with this gamble?"

He leaned back in the booth, unable to hide the mild sense of satisfaction on his face. "Do you want the long or short answer?"

"I want the truth!" Sarah demanded.

The slight upturn at the corners of his mouth gave away his notable pleasure at her ability to spar with him, free of the old role of teacher and student. She was now an equal, and Sarah interpreted his Cheshire smile to indicate that he also liked what he saw. "The simple answer, Sarah, is happiness."

Travis left her without argument. She remembered he had always been direct without ever laying all his cards on the table or giving away his thoughts. It was one of the reasons she was drawn to him. He was still able to distill everything to its simplest and shortest form while remaining very much in control. Travis Hall had an air of mystery about him that could move her in a direction she might not want to go. He was dangerously attractive to her, even after all these years, and she hoped she wasn't making the wrong decision in spending the weekend in his company and hometown. Yes, their roles were different now, but so was she. Besides, what did she really know about him, except for the little she had known as a lovesick teenager who was swallowed up in his bigger-than-life presence? He would be on his turf, putting Sarah at a distinct disadvantage, yet the idea that she might get to know more about him was too irresistible for her to refuse. She had spent secret hours thinking of him, imagining where he was and what his life might be like, but over the years, life had eroded the dreams and innocence of such an untested love, and although he had never left her heart, she recognized the passion for what it was through more reasoning eyes. To have the sweet image and passion of her life discredited by a less-than-respectable truth all these years later would be an unwelcome heartbreak. This was a risk that, with anyone else, she would never take. This gamble was definitely out of character for her and the life she had always led. She was the one who stayed between the lines of moral and ethical standings and who was always counted on to do the right thing while holding her virtue. She refused to be an easy mark, if that was indeed his intention. She had her children, and regardless of his insufficiencies, Kenny had been a good father. That meant something to Sarah, and she would not betray all of that in a moment of weakness. Besides, assuming such a motive in Travis would be presumptive. The last thing she wanted was to play the fool with him a second time by assuming he wanted a relationship with her, though the fact remained that she was still vulnerable with him. Honoring her life when around him would take strength. She watched him carefully as he reached for the menu.

"I happen to know the food is much better here than at your hotel, Sarah. I would consider it a pleasure if you might reconsider, now that it is past six o'clock. I'm ready to eat. I suppose you'll have to have dinner sometime tonight anyway. I'll get you back to the hotel as soon as we're finished."

He knew she would finally acquiesce, the same way he had known she would agree to the weekend and their meeting. Trying to decline after he had maneuvered her into his plan so quickly would be a wasted effort. Travis Hall was proving to be a much more formidable challenge than she was prepared to handle.

By the time they were ready to leave, he surprised her again when the valet arrived, driving a glossy new silver BMW. Somehow, owning a BMW didn't fit the image of a rancher living in the high country. She chose not to fall into the trap of mentioning it to him, lest he use it for another opportunity to shock or challenge her perceptions. He held the door open for her as she slid into the passenger seat, which was covered in supple, stone-colored leather that bore the scent of newness. Sarah was self-conscience of the slit in her dress at the center between her knees, and she managed to force the opening closed after negotiating the bucket seat. She looked back up at him, her face suddenly washed pink. Travis looked down at her keeping his roguish smile, saying nothing with one eyebrow slightly raised. Closing her door, he returned to the driver's side and headed south to Camelback Road on the way back to the Biltmore Hotel, adjacent to the Borders Book Store where her book-signing event had taken place.

"How early can you be ready in the morning?" he asked her as he drove.

"How early would you like to leave?" Sarah countered. He smiled at her response, evidently enjoying their time together.

"Would eight a.m. be too soon for you? We could grab a coffee, and by nine-thirty or ten, be up in Payson in time for breakfast at the Beeline Café."

"Eight a.m. it is then," she said.

"By the way, you did bring a pair of blue jeans with you, didn't you?"

"I'm not sure. Does it matter?"

"For tomorrow it does," he said with conviction.

"Well, I'll see what I can come up with before then. What do you have planned for us?"

"Let's just say it may involve some hiking, and it's best to be prepared."

Sarah didn't know what she had gotten herself into, but for all the organizing and scheduling her life revolved around, the not knowing was exhilarating. Just being with Travis for two hours had filled her with an excitement she hadn't felt in years. She made every effort to deny what she was feeling, hoping to find some reason to dislike him. The fact that she couldn't predict what he would say or do next made him all the more exciting to be with, and she found that as intriguing as the mystery that surrounded him.

He remained two steps ahead of her at every turn, and she still perceived latent untapped willpower just below the surface. It gave him an uncommon strength she could sense but not grasp in physical terms alone. She wished she knew what he was thinking, but he was so difficult to read. He could be charming in one moment and in the next so direct and challenging he could instantly make her feel undone. Then he could melt her heart with a sensitivity she judged to be totally genuine and endearing. He left her with more questions than answers.

Arriving at the hotel, Sarah watched him thoughtfully, still weighing their time spent together and wondering if she would ever feel as if she knew him. "Thank you so much for the wonderful dinner, Travis, and for your invitation for the weekend tour as well. I appreciated the geography lesson on Arizona, and I'm looking forward to seeing the countryside tomorrow," she said sincerely, as he glanced back at her with a faint smile.

"The pleasure was all mine, Sarah." Travis got out and walked to her side of the car, opened the door, and put his hand out to help her up out of the bucket seat. Sarah looked up at him and hesitated. He was so sure of himself, but she wouldn't let him faze her. She reached up and took his hand as he held it firmly, pulling her up to her feet. Once she was standing, he kept her hand locked in his for a protracted, deliberate moment, and she shook inside at his temerity.

He released her hand only after their eyes had locked once more and Sarah shivered a second time, knowing his timing was definitely intentional. "I'll be in the lobby at eight a.m. sharp. I've enjoyed this evening very much, and I look forward to seeing you tomorrow," he offered in parting.

Still slightly off-balance at his self-assured behavior, Sarah turned to leave and couldn't resist using his words from his letter. "I'll do my best to be on time," she said with a penny's worth of sarcasm and a twinkle in her eye. She caught his slight grin out of the corner of her eye as she looked back at him from the door of the lobby, then turned leaving him standing along side his car.

Travis watched her as she crossed the lobby and headed to the elevators. Something elegant and graceful in her movements stirred a fire in him like no other woman ever could. Returning to the driver's side of his car, he gripped the handle of the door and then looked back in the direction of the lobby. Undeniably happier tonight than he had been in years, Travis was still wearing his smile.

CHAPTER THIRTY-NINE

FRIDAY
MARCH 23, 1990

Travis Hall entered the lobby of the Biltmore hotel at exactly 7:55 a.m. The brilliant early morning sunrays shone through the southeastern entry doors, illuminating a magnificent floral arrangement on a large, round marble-top table in the center of the foyer. The increasing sunlight flooded into the lobby, welcoming another spectacular, sun-drenched day. The consistent number of sunny days brought tourists to Phoenix with regularity all winter long—until the hotter days of summer when its intensity turned the Valley of the Sun into an unforgiving inferno not fit for the faint of heart. A small number of patrons were busy at the front desk checking out, while others waited for their limos to the airport. Several porters negotiated luggage onto wheeled carts, and with their exception, the receiving hall remained relatively empty.

Making a quick pass through the lobby, Travis finally took a seat facing the direction of the elevators, waiting for Sarah.

He sat patiently, reflecting on their reunion. Checking his watch one more time, Travis slowly smiled, taking note that it was now five after the hour; he wondered if Sarah would visit upon him the same delay in her appearance he had subjected her to the day before. *A woman's prerogative*, he thought to himself, knowing full well he would wait for Sarah no matter the time or delay. He couldn't help thinking how she had kept her refinement and ladylike character, as if the hardships and disillusionments of life had passed her by or were somehow unable to harden her. *You don't reach your forties unscathed, without experiencing a few hurtles or setbacks*. She still maintained the indestructible virtue wrapped in an elegance and beauty that had drawn him with such force at first sight. Sarah was the one woman he could never forget, and she could still light the flame of his heart after all these years.

The elevator opened again, and several people exited simultaneously, a woman in a business suit followed by a man wearing a suit and tie who was holding a briefcase. The gentleman held the door of the elevator open with a wide smile, and Travis watched as Sarah exited, pulling a wheeled suitcase and carrying a garment bag. Sarah thanked the gentleman holding the door and then turned toward the lobby. Travis stood up and was charmed by the sight of her in a pair of blue jeans; he was totally absorbed by her absolutely stunning figure. Her short-sleeved white blouse was open at the neck and fitted neatly beneath the blue jeans held securely by a smooth, black leather belt with a bright silver buckle. With one side of her collar slightly raised to accommodate her shoulder bag, the deep v-neck blouse fitted perfectly, highlighting her well-proportioned and still-slender frame. Her ash blonde, silver-streaked hair was pulled neatly back and fastened with a navy bow at the nape of her neck. He had to smile when he saw she was wearing sandals and wondered if they were the only shoes she had brought with her. Walking down the hall to meet her, Travis caught her arm and took the garment bag.

"Good morning, Sarah. Glad to see you could make it!" he said, with a tinge of humor as he reached for the roller bag in her other hand. Sarah looked into his eyes directly with a small smile and a slight raise of her eyebrow. She held her tongue, letting him enjoy his play with her regarding her few minutes' delay.

"It's a beautiful morning, thank you," she said, noticing his well groomed but casual clothing. He was wearing a freshly laundered pair of wranglers, a fitted Western-styled plaid shirt with snaps on the breast pockets, and a pair of worn, but dirt free black cowboy boots. One more time, his appearance was not what she was expecting, and he continued to turn her assumptions upside-down. To be surprised and mildly shocked was turning out to be the norm, and Sarah made an effort not to react to the unanticipated in him. To see him this morning in a completely different image than the blazer and dress slacks of yesterday kept her intrigued.

"Travis, I'll have to stop at the front desk to turn in the key."

"While you're doing that, I'll put your bags in the car. I'll meet you at the front entrance when you're done."

"Thanks, I'll be right with you," she said.

Sarah waited for one of the clerks to become available. A sudden rush of nervousness coursed through her body, anticipating the day ahead, and she continued to ask herself why she had so easily agreed to meet and be with him. His offer to take the time to show her the beauty of the state was generous and kind, but could he possibly expect something more of her in return? The thought gripped Sarah with a wave of unease. She hadn't had much experience with dating, or men in general, and she hoped she wouldn't make a fool of herself. She chastened herself for being so presumptuous in her thinking to even assume he might feel that way toward her. Sarah signed her bill and handed in her card key, then headed for the door where Travis was waiting with the passenger door of his BMW opened wide for her. She slid into the seat, and Travis closed the door behind her, before making his way back around the car to the driver's side.

Once underway, he turned his head toward Sarah. "Could I interest you in a cup of coffee-to-go before we leave town? AJ"s Café and grocery store is just ahead."

"That sounds good to me," Sarah happily responded.

Travis headed north to Lincoln Road, passing neatly manicured yards with lush, colorful plantings and landscapes surrounding the beautiful homes and condos along the way. The compelling colors of the bougainvillea and roses draped freely over fences and archways capturing Sarah's attention and made her feel as if she were in a fairytale. Patches of green grass were highlighted by blooming oleanders, bird of paradise plants, colorful lantana, and stone walkways. She was happily mesmerized with the visual extravaganza passing by her window.

"The flowers and plants are stunningly beautiful!" Sarah exclaimed as they drove, fixing her gaze out the windows as they turned toward the east. "It's so delightful to see the way they have landscaped the medians with such colorful plants. What are those beautiful silver-green bushes covered in purple flowers called?" she asked him with delight in her eyes.

Travis smiled as he watched Sarah's reaction to the desert plants, remembering the way she had always found joy in simple pleasures. He turned toward her, his eyes slightly creased at the corners while sporting his smile. "That's called 'Texas Sage.' It grows quite easily here in Arizona since it doesn't require a lot of water."

"And the trees with the smooth green bark and yellow flowers, what are they called?"

"Those are Palo Verde trees, which essentially translates to 'green trees.'"

"I never thought the desert could be so utterly beautiful!" Sarah exclaimed as they continued down Lincoln Road. Camel Back Mountain jutted up off the desert floor to their right, and Mummy Mountain to their left. Magnificent homes were nestled into the sides of the mountains, some appearing as though they were a natural outcropping suspended above boulders, or happily balanced on protruding ridgelines. They dotted the mountainsides randomly, drawing the eye in wonder at their architectural feats and dazzling locations, some positioned so precariously as if on a precipice of a cliff, daring a deep and sudden fall. The staggering elevations of the homes, along with their cantilevered walled patios and balconies, were accentuated by the cascading waves of magenta and violet bougainvillea that dangled freely over their edges. The brilliant and colorful hanging flowers brushed the shards of rocks below them, paying homage to the inaccessible cliffs that supported them. Studded across the jagged mountainsides, the saguaro cacti stood with their stout arms open, pointing heavenward as if in worship of the sun. The scenery from the car windows was breathtaking, highlighting the spectacle of man's intercourse with nature. Some homes begged the question of what the views from those lofty residential perches would offer in return.

"Don't let it fool you. The danger is still out there if you're not careful," he reminded her.

"How do your cattle survive in such hostile desert conditions in the summer months?"

"The Rim doesn't share the exact same climate conditions that the valley does, although it has its own set of problems to contend with."

"Just how far away is Payson from Phoenix?"

"About a hundred miles, give or take a few, but it's not the distance, it's the elevation that causes the dramatic climate changes. Payson is relatively dry, being a high desert region, and fires are always a threat, but depending on snowfall amounts and reservoir levels, it's less likely to suffer from the extended dry spells and heat that the valley does. I still wind up feeding my cattle by late summer and through most of the winter, but the pastures and clearings are always green and healthy come spring. At least we don't have to contend with the intense heat of the valley." Travis turned into AJ's parking lot and brought the car to a stop close to the entrance. Walking to Sarah's door, he opened it and took her hand, pulling her up as he had done the night before. Sarah didn't hesitate this time to accept his hand.

"How do you take your coffee? Or would you rather have a cappuccino?" he asked on their way in.

"Black with a bit of sweetener would be fine." Sarah smiled back as she took in the array of delectable pastries and sweets displayed neatly in glass cases; they rivaled those back east in their presentations and varieties. One more time, Sarah was discovering the virtues of being happily surprised and shaken out of her limited and generalized expectations of the West. Every new discovery matched the seemingly endless and unanticipated aspects to Travis Hall's astonishing life. Neither Arizona nor Travis was what she was expecting, and both were charming her.

"Would you care for a muffin or scone to go along with your coffee?" Travis asked.

"No, thank you. The coffee will be plenty for now."

Travis paid for their coffee, and then they headed back to the car. "It will take us a while to hit the Beeline at this time of day, but it should be clear sailing once we're past Fountain Hills and we head north."

"I don't mind at all. I'm really enjoying the ride and scenery," she responded and turned to face him, catching his eyes resting on her. Sarah quickly turned away, unable to hold his glance at the onset of another rush of sensations combined with anxiousness. The old feelings came bubbling up so unexpectedly and remained totally outside her control. The question flashed through her mind of how she would be able to get through the weekend with him.

"I take it you've never been to Arizona before?"

"No, but if I had known how beautiful it was, that might not have been the case!"

"Where did you venture for a vacation then?"

"The East Coast mostly. I had family in the Carolinas, as well as New England, where it was always breathtaking to visit in the fall. The lure of the beaches and sunshine in Florida during the long winters became an attraction, in addition to Disney World when the children were young. Never being able to find more than a week's worth of time to spend away, the Eastern Seaboard seemed close enough not to rob the length of days allotted for vacations. I've always wanted to visit the West but never found the time to take the trip." Sarah paused, wondering what questions would be fair game for her to ask him but not wanting to sound too inquisitive or intrusive into his personal life. She hoped he would share more about himself on his own. "What made you settle in Arizona?" she asked, a general enough question not to sound overly curious.

"I was raised here," he said, glancing back in her direction. Travis caught her expression and then added, "You hadn't guessed that?"

"No, I really wasn't sure where you were from, only I did suspect you weren't from the East Coast. Why did you ever decide to teach in New York of all places?"

Travis chuckled under his breath before answering. "Now that's a long story I'll save for another time." Sarah turned her attention back out to the magnificent terrain, sensing Travis wasn't one to talk endlessly about himself. They drove past several golf courses with their well-cared-for greens smack in the middle of the stark desert terrain infiltrated by rock formations, ocotillos, and saguaros. The dramatic contrasts had a mystical quality and feel. The traffic was slowing, and the stoplights were impeding their speed, but Travis took the extra time to identify landmarks and points of interest along the way. Sarah took note of the extensive canal system stretching across the valley; it was one of the first things she had noticed when her plane made its approach into Sky Harbor Airport. Travis looked at his watch and then asked her to look out of the left side of the car. Much to her surprise, a huge gush of water rocketed skyward in the morning light, pushing higher and higher into the sky. "Oh! What an absolutely fantastic sight to see out here in the desert. Is that a geyser, or is it a man made fountain? I wonder how high it pushes the water."

"It is a man-made fountain. They say it reaches up to five hundred sixty-two feet, and is the fourth tallest in the world. It's quite an eye catcher, but I think the town council had it built to attract more residents to their growing community."

"How did you know it was about to go off?"

"They've timed it to pump once every hour at precisely the same time. Nice engineering, and catchy! For me, it signals a clear passage home from here."

Sarah smiled back at him, taking in his sense of place and recognizing the love of home implied in his statement. It was a side of him totally unknown to her.

"Tell me more about your children, Sarah. How old are they?" he asked as they turned north onto Highway 87. They are both good kids, but very different from one another. Rebecca is the oldest at twenty-one and Keith will be twenty in June. He toyed with the idea of following in his father's footsteps and initially planned to attend law school, but he eventually opted for a graphic-arts career instead. Rebecca is more like her mother, I'm afraid, which can lead to a few interesting challenges at times. She loves children and hopes to start teaching kindergarten this coming fall. All things considered, I suppose I'm very lucky to have the self-motivated and loving children I've been blessed with."

As they pulled farther away from Fountain Hills and the city, the broad expanse of the open desert had a more desolate feel. The sudden thought crossed her mind of what it must have been like for those early settlers making their way across such foreboding terrain in Conestoga wagons with the desert's myriad dangers of torturous cactus needles, rattlesnakes, scorpions, and lack of water. How odd that Travis felt so at home here, while she carried a sense of foreboding with a slight edge of fear and isolation at facing such dangers. In many ways, the desert was exquisitely beautiful—particularly in spring when in full bloom, and the arresting colors of the pink and white cactus flowers, orange blooms of the willowy ocotillos, and desert daisies all wowed the senses; but venturing out into its wild and untamed harshness carried a danger even Sarah recognized with impunity.

"What is your daughter like?" Sarah asked Travis.

"Jessie is quite a gal. She can ride a horse with the best of them all day and be ready for dinner by five, never missing a beat! I wouldn't have guessed she'd have gotten involved in interior designing, although she always could draw pictures and colorful cards as a child. I somehow thought she was too much of a tomboy growing up with me for her to ever get involved with designing, but she makes a point at delighting and surprising me most of the time! Jessica turns twenty-six this year. She married her college sweetheart three years ago. I have to say, taking care of twin boys and working full time is quite a challenge, but she handles it with ease. She still manages to come up to the ranch at least every other weekend. She tells me she comes up to ride, but I think she comes to keep tabs on me and make sure I'm keeping the place up to her standards."

A happy expression lit Travis's face as he spoke about his daughter, and she wondered how the "dreaded" Mr. Hall of North Shoreline High School fame had managed to soften enough to raise a daughter. Jessica had clearly stolen his heart. *Life does have a way of smoothing out our rough edges.*

"I've noticed an almost instant end to the city, with no buildings—as if a line in the sand marks a change. Is there a reason for that?" Sarah asked.

"I'm surprised you noticed that. We've just passed over the Rio Verde on the Fort McDowell Indian Reservation, and like a lot of Arizona territory, the Indian lands are not open to development, which is just fine with me."

"I don't know how they eke out a living out here," Sarah commented as they continued north.

Travis broke a smile. "It isn't as bad as you might think. The desert can grow most anything with enough water, and they have found a way to bring in money with the newly constructed casinos popping up around the state. Regardless of what you and I may think, we can't offer them more than the intimate contact and reverence they already have for the land. Money and a cushy life don't always make men happy. They have their own police force and tribal councils that govern them, free from our reach."

"I suppose you're right. I guess my perceptions are filtered through my own experience." Looking out of the windshield,

Sarah pointed to the northeast. "Travis, what's the name of those mountains with the snow-capped peaks?"

"They're called the four peaks and are part of the Mazatzal Mountain Range," he told her.

"They certainly get your attention and make a striking presence against such a crystal clear and beautiful blue sky! What a different place this is, with the heat here in the valley and snow-topped mountains on the horizon. How do you spell that mountain range? Because I don't think I could pronounce it."

"Just say 'mad-as-hell' as fast as you can, and it'll sound close enough," he suggested with a slight grin.

Sarah laughed out loud at his sense of humor and down-to-earth approach to life in general. He didn't ramble on about anything and offered enough information for her to make of it what she would, and then he remained silent as if absorbing life, not participating until necessary or called upon to do so. How different he was from Kenny, who could give a soliloquy on any subject, as if he enjoyed hearing himself talk! Travis was able to keep the mystery about himself, despite the time they were sharing together. His strength was in the background, never openly displayed but a step back from the threshold, ready to use if needed. Kenny wore his accomplishments on his sleeve and boasted of his successes in court and out, leaving no surprises or guesses about what came next. His hand was always out in the open and exposed. Travis Hall was on the flip side. He seemed to find no glory in exposing himself to another, remaining silent about his past, making the next moment dangerous in its supposition. He made it a point to divert attention from himself, as though discussing his life was not useful and would be profaned by another's assessment. She thought back to high school, when he never told the students who had challenged him to chess that he knew the game very well. His silence allowed the students to make a fatal error in presumption and ego not found in him. Sarah longed to know more about him but still remained apprehensive and challenged while in his company. The unnerving thought crossed her mind that if the veil covering him were suddenly dislodged, it might not reveal what she presumed to find.

Sarah turned her attention back to the changing appearance of the terrain as they steadily gained altitude up the highway on their way to Payson. "Somehow, I feel like I'm in a Wile E. Coyote cartoon, witnessing all these strange and unusual rock formations with slabs of stones resting on top of boulders!"

A broad smile crossed Travis's face at her description. "You're right—he's out there. If you turn around and look back toward the valley, you can see a good part of the city now."

Sarah turned and took in the awesome view from their higher elevation and distance, a thrilling excitement in her chest at the glistening sight of Phoenix sprawling out far below them back down in the valley.

"Oh, Travis, this is a grand vision a person could never grow tired of seeing. How magnificent all of this is," she answered with a genuine sincerity. He enjoyed reliving the now old and familiar trip up the Beeline Highway through her eyes, as if seeing it again for the first time.

The first hour passed by quickly, and they were making good time, but the four-lane highway hadn't been completed fully yet, and narrowed into a two-lane road. As they climbed higher, cedar trees began dotting the mountains alongside the cacti, and a few open areas sported patches of green, as if grass were slowly starting to flourish where before there had been none. The changes were becoming more dramatic as the once-prominent saguaros were becoming fewer in number, with more distance between them. The BMW shifted gears automatically, smoothly accommodating the steep inclines and turns through passes casting dark, penetrating shadows, only to be greeted instantly with the searing, mid-morning light around each sweeping curve. Every new mile and turn framed a view more spectacular than the one preceding it, and Sarah remained in awe. The repeated need to yawn in order to open her ears increased as they drove north, gaining altitude with every passing mile.

The town of Sunflower lay just ahead and brought a new feel to the changing landscape. The bubbling, rushing waters of Sycamore Creek came into view and paralleled the roadway on the east side, watering thirsty and stately sycamore and cottonwood trees along its banks. The sycamores shared space with larger cedars interspersed amongst the newly appearing pines, as if only they could now lay claim to the mountains' loftier heights. The deep, twisting canyons and passes brought an interplay of darkness and light that cut like a knife with precision and intensity, drawing Sarah's wide-eyed attention as if she were a spectator in a 3-D theater. How surreal the awesomeness of the mountains and terrain seemed to her as she drank in the rapidly changing and dramatic landscape with its pristine and treacherous beauty. Sarah reminded herself she might have missed this thrilling and breathtaking scenery if she had declined his invitation, and in that moment, she was glad she had accepted.

"Are you working up an appetite?" Travis asked as they took another gentle turn around the winding roadway.

Sarah smiled back at him and his directness. "Ready when you are."

"Good. Then we'll stop off at the Beeline Café before taking you to your hotel, if that's agreeable to you?"

"I'm along for the ride, and happy to be here," she said as she caught that subtle upturn to his lips that let her know he was pleased but had other thoughts that he deliberately kept to himself.

"How much farther is it to Payson?" Sarah asked a few minutes later.

"It's only about ten more miles past Rye, which is just ahead. Do you need to stop?"

"No, just curious, hoping it doesn't end."

"It's just beginning," he responded. Sarah looked back in his direction, but Travis kept his eyes straight ahead, not adding another word.

Within a few minutes, they were heading up another steep incline with much taller pine trees now embracing both sides of the highway.

"Look straight ahead out the front windshield as we approach the crest of the next incline," he directed her.

Sarah turned her head back to the front, and at the moment they reached the crest, she fell breathless at the glorious sight that greeted them. There in the distance, the sun illuminated a long, snow-capped ridgeline running for miles with deep walls dropping dramatically to depths unknown, as if they had been cut with an enormous backhoe at the hand of heaven. The reflection of the dancing and twinkling sunlight against the distant and awesome rim left Sarah in awe. The escarpment was a dramatic, unexpected sight to behold as it filled the sum of the horizon. Never before had any vision demanded all of her with such force.

"Welcome to Payson," Travis announced casually as he tilted his head in her direction.

Sarah couldn't take her eyes from the scene in front of her and finally swallowed, taking a breath of air. "That's truly the most magnificent sight I've ever been privileged to witness. I'm blown away, Travis! How lucky you are to live so close to this visual paradise!"

"Glad you approve . . . It comes with a price!"

"Do you care to elaborate?"

"Nope, I care to eat."

Sarah laughed, realizing he was going to continue to be the mystery she found so enticing. She wouldn't push him and go where she wasn't invited. With nearly a day sharing his company, Sarah had garnered little more about him than what she had known before. He was expert at staying unknowable. Travis was like a puzzle with each piece delivered separately, segregated by long stretches of time that kept the big picture just out of reach.

They pulled into the parking lot of the Beeline Café among older pickup trucks that all appeared to have been worked hard.

Travis led Sarah to the entry and held the door for her as two older men, dressed in Western-styled work clothes, were making their exit. Immediately, they both stood to the side to allow Sarah to pass, tipping their cowboy hats simultaneously as she walked by them. Travis continued to hold the door open for the departing men and one of them offered a word on his way out the door. "A little late for breakfast, isn't it, Travis?"

"Morning, Henry," he responded while nodding. "That depends on who you're eating with, I suspect."

"Maybe your breakfast will be a might bit better than ours. They're at each other this morning," one of them shared with a smile as they continued out the exit.

A counter with fixed swivel stools in front formed a horseshoe around the centered kitchen, while booths ran down both sides of the restaurant's outer walls. Sarah was surprised at how relatively small the overall space was, considering the number of trucks and cars filling the lot. The cafe had a homey "Mom and Pop" feel, and several more locals extending their first-name greetings to Travis cinched the hometown essence. No frills of the city were evident here, but the place was inviting nonetheless, functional and friendly, with the scents of bacon and fried hash browns and onions lingering in the air.

Travis led the way to an empty booth, stopping briefly to acknowledge several more Payson residents. Sarah wondered if he knew everyone there. Most of the men had hats with wide brims hanging on hooks alongside their tables, and the majority was wearing boots. Black cowboy hats, straw cowboy hats, and even a leather cowboy hat made it appear to be the unspoken and indispensible accessory for men. The women were all dressed casually, most wearing pants, and one or two in simple jumpers. Sarah had entered a different world, far removed from the East Coast diners with their diverse patronage of mixed ethnicity and eccentric clothing that could shock the senses. She saw no jewelry or gold chains, commonplace among the young men back east. No overt extravagance and showy glitz here. The customers were natural, honest-looking, and totally unadorned. When she spoke to someone here, there was nothing to distract her from the meaning of his or her words. Perhaps that was why Travis never found it necessary to use more than a few words when he spoke, never having to compete for attention. This was the first time Sarah sensed an insight into the real Travis Hall, capturing something about his nature that, by virtue of his environment, extended to him. This place felt comfortable, unpretentious, and real.

"Travis, what did that gentleman leaving the café mean when he said they were at each other?".

Travis laughed under his breath. "It won't take long for you to figure that out," he said, just as the waitress approached the table.

Casting two menus down on the table with a heavy hand, the slightly overweight, older waitress placed her hand directly down on top of Travis's menu, preventing him from opening it. "Now, Travis, do you want to make this easy on both of us, or am I going to have to do the ordering?"

Sarah remained silent, mystified by the woman's familiarity and coarseness. Looking directly back at Travis, Sarah waited to hear what he would say.

"Rita," he started out slowly, "we both know we still have till eleven a.m. before breakfast ends. From where I sit, the clock on the wall reads ten o'clock, so I'll make this half as quick by ordering my usual, and you can come back with two black coffees, at which time you can take the lady's order."

Staring back down at Travis sternly, Rita replied, "I'm glad we understand each other!" She then walked off to get the coffee.

"Is Rita always this brusque?" Sarah asked, half-whispering.

Travis brought a full smile across his lips before answering. "Don't let her intimidate you. She's actually quite fond of me."

"Well, she sure has a strange way of showing it!" Sarah opened her menu.

"It's really not me she's troubled by."

Deciding on oatmeal, Sarah asked, "Who is she troubled by then?"

"You might guess if you visited once or twice."

Rita returned with two black coffees and immediately turned to Sarah, pad in hand. Without waiting to be asked, Sarah spoke up quickly, "I'll have the oatmeal with raisins, and milk on the side, please."

Rita gave Travis a funny look. "You ought to be ashamed of yourself, Travis! Can't you afford to buy this wisp of a woman some real meat?"

"Maybe next time, Rita," Travis played along.

By now, Sarah could see this was part of a usual dance the waitress played, and Sarah took note of the service rendered to the other patrons, some of whom took far worse ribbing, all with smiles, as if it was expected and enjoyed.

Across the other side of the café, a younger waitress in her mid-thirties yelled across the room, "Hey, Mom, did you forget Lefty, or am I suppose to do my tables and yours too?"

Rita quickly turned, airing the family feud right back, "Well, if you didn't stay out so late last night, you might have the energy to pour an extra cup of coffee around here, the same way I always do." Walking back behind the counter, Rita's voice boomed, "Order up. One oatmeal with raisins, hold the milk."

Sarah brought her hand to cover her lips, hoping to hide her need to laugh. Raising her eyes to meet Travis's face, she reflected his smile.

By 11:00 a.m., Travis and Sarah headed out the door of the Beeline Café, leaving Rita and her daughter to both entertain and do battle in front of the assortment of cowboys and local business trade for the now-growing lunch crowd.

"I thought I'd drop you off at the hotel and let you get settled, while I run a few errands. I'll be back in an hour to pick you up and show you the sights. By the way, what size shoe do you wear?"

"Seven and a half, but I already have a pair of tennis shoes I could wear," she insisted, trying to guess the implication of his surprising question. "Exactly where are you taking me?"

"A place very few people have visited, and I'll leave it at that for now," he stated with a sense of authority and mild enthusiasm. "By the way, if you have a jacket, you might want to bring it along also."

Sarah wondered what he was planning, although she could tell from his comments it would likely be an outdoor excursion. While cooler than the valley, the temperatures felt comfortable, and she couldn't foresee the need for a coat. Travis knew how to keep her in suspense.

Once at the hotel, he pulled up in front of the lobby, and then got out and opened Sarah's door, extending his hand as before. His warm, strong hand encompassed hers, and with a comforting steadiness, he gently pulled her to her feet. Returning to the trunk, Travis gathered her bags, and they entered the lobby.

Sarah turned to Travis. "Why don't you go on ahead? I can manage things here and get settled in on my own. That will give you a few extra minutes to run your errands, and we won't miss a minute of the remaining day that way."

"I like the way you think!" Travis said with a wink of his eye. "I'll be back in fifty minutes, at exactly high noon."

As Travis handed Sarah her garment bag, she glanced up at him with a slight smile. "I'll be in the lobby waiting for you."

After checking in and making her way to her room, Sarah was glad to have a few minutes to freshen up and make a call back home to let her daughter know about her change in plans and where she was staying. She drew in a deep breath. The air felt so much cleaner and crisper here with the scent of pine wafting in the dry, cooler air. A subtle, tingling sensation rushed over her as if the mountain air itself invigorated her. Sarah felt truly alive here and was happily anticipating their adventure together.

CHAPTER FORTY

At 11:50, Sarah made her way back to the lobby, making sure she would be there with minutes to spare. She would be able to claim punctuality, robbing Travis of the right to poke fun at her tardy arrival for a second time. Although he no longer carried the authority that being her teacher once had, at forty-four, Sarah still felt a tinge of his commanding influence over her, even after all these years. How odd, she thought, particularly because he hadn't treated her in any other way than an equal.

Wearing the same jeans and tailored white blouse, Sarah now sported a pair of tennis shoes and held a lightweight navy raincoat in her arms, along with her shoulder bag. Travis hadn't arrived yet, and she took a seat facing the main entrance to wait. The entire ride up to Payson from the valley had been spectacular, and Sarah remained overwhelmed at the beauty and grandeur. But she also felt shaken inside at how easily Travis could arouse old feelings of attraction in her. He still exuded a masculinity that was hard for her to ignore. That small shock of chestnut hair at his forehead occasionally fell forward, just as she remembered, and Sarah was still humored at the way he brought his hand to his hair, running all five fingers up through the loosened lock to push it back into place. *Some habits never die*. She wondered how such a handsome man had remained unmarried all these years, and once again, she found herself wondering if he had any female companions with whom he kept frequent company. To be near him caused her heart to skip a beat, and she had to remind herself that this was a different time; she was no longer the naïve school girl she once was, and yet she found herself working to keep her balance around him.

Traffic at the front desk started picking up as guests made their way in and out of the hotel. Sarah checked the time—11:57 a.m. A few men in Western-styled clothing made their way into the lobby from the parking lot and walked past Sarah, tilting their heads as they passed. A late-model, dual-wheeled, silver pickup truck hauling an enclosed trailer pulled up under the portico at the entrance. Sarah didn't expect to see Travis Hall walk around the front of the pickup and enter the lobby. Wearing a felt cowboy hat, he took Sarah by total surprise. She stood up immediately as he walked toward her. "I'm afraid you surprised me showing up in a different vehicle, or I would have come right out."

"I guess that makes two of us who are surprised," he countered.

"How is that?"

"It seems our watches are finally synchronized!" he professed to her with that telltale smile on his lips. Sarah let that comment rest on its own legs.

Travis went to the passenger side of the pickup and opened the door for her as she pulled herself up into the light-colored leather seat. At first glance, the pickup was definitely used as a work vehicle. Although not dirty, the signs of use included bits of hay and grass on the floor mats, an empty coffee cup in the cup holder, and a few receipts and papers on the dash as well as on the console. It was still fairly clean for a hard-working utility vehicle. Travis took his seat behind the wheel and headed north out of the parking lot.

"Do you always bring your live stock with you when you're out for a drive to see the sights?" Sarah asked, perplexed.

Travis kept his eyes focused on the curving road. "That's not cattle, Sarah—that's our transportation."

"You're not serious—are you?" she questioned, too stunned to believe him.

He turned his head toward her, wearing a boyish grin. "I've never lied to you."

A gripping fear suddenly overtook her and Sarah hardly knew what to say. "If that's what I think is back there, you should know that I've never been on a horse in my life! There is no way I can do this, if that's what you're planning."

"All the more reason for you to try. Besides, we can't get to where we're going any other way, not to mention horseback is the best way to see the real Arizona up close."

Sarah brought her hand to her chest as panic crept over her. "My God, Travis, I can't do this."

Travis looked back at her with a gentle smile, shaking his head slightly. He reached out and took her hand in his, squeezing it lightly. "I promise you, Sarah, you'll do just fine, and besides, I won't let you get too far from me. You never can tell. You might just decide you love it."

Sarah swallowed hard, feeling as though she were a child who was given the keys to the car and asked to drive to the store during rush-hour traffic. How was she ever going to make it through this adventure? He was so sure of himself, and now of her too. His confidence felt totally misplaced—one that escaped her unconditionally in that moment. Trying hard to regain her composure, she scrambled to think positive thoughts in the hopes of overcoming her sudden fear. After all, he was always expert at everything he did; why would this be any different? He had saved her from her own inabilities once before, but this was a completely different situation. Whatever had possessed him to think that a suburban girl from the East Coast would be able to get on the back of a horse and ride through the wilderness? The only animals Sarah ever had any contact with in her life were several coach-potato family-friendly dogs, and a goldfish living in a visible, but separate, enclosed environment. This adventure would take more courage than she could conjure up in the next few moments.

Traveling only a few miles, they quickly left the town of Payson behind, and the winding mountain road brought the beauty of the terrain into focus for the first time. The majesty of the taller pines provided canopies for the cedars and scrub bushes Sarah was unfamiliar with. Outcroppings of granite rocks and small cliffs added layers to the changing terrain and increasing altitude. The winding roadway cut through the mountains, forging a path beneath the towering canopies of ponderosa pines. The scenery was breathtaking, and for a few moments, Sarah lost all thought of her upcoming challenge. Travis turned off the main drive onto a dirt road and followed its winding path beneath the denser pines, leaving all signs of civilization behind. After fifteen more minutes, he turned to Sarah and took in the wonder in her expression. "You might like to put your window down," he suggested. "We're getting closer."

"Closer to what?" she asked.

"Listen carefully, and you'll hear it." Driving much slower now, a faint roar rose over the grinding of the pickup's engine.

"What is that sound?" she asked him.

Travis cocked his head in her direction, pointing out the windshield to the right side. "Look as we take the next turn."

The roaring sound grew louder and louder as they wound their way around the sweeping curve. Much to her delight and awe, they came to a clearing adjacent to a rushing river, forcing its way down the mountains over slabs of rocks, coursing powerfully downstream with such force its droning could be heard from a great distance away. Travis brought the truck to a stop as Sarah remained mesmerized by the untouched and primal beauty of this magnificent and isolated location. The rushing river had a melodic tone that drew Sarah with its intensity.

Travis got out and went to her side of the truck, opening her door. "This is where we start." He offered his hand, as he had done so many times before. Sarah quickly laid her hand in his while her gaze remained fixed on the river.

The rushing waters tumbled and churned fiercely, cascading over rocks and boulders. The rippling and swirling eddies of water formed pockets that would circle momentarily as if to leave a greeting, and then the water continued its forceful play downstream on its journey into the unknown. Drawing in a deep breath, Sarah caught the sweet, clean scent of the pines invigorated by the mist of the pure waters flowing from the mountains' magical heights. Pine needles softly cushioned beneath her feet, and a tingling sensation caused goose bumps to race up her arms. Life here was untamed and raw, powerful in its zeal. The towering pines, the river, the clear blue sky, and the air she breathed had a living, moving existence of their own that swept her away into their primal essence, as if claiming her as prey by mere proximity. She lingered in the all-encompassing arms of a mighty power, hitherto kept secret.

As if to waken her from her reverie, Travis gently touched her arm. "Don't wander too far while I unload the horses," he cautioned before he made his way to the back of the horse trailer. Sarah headed to the water's edge, still hypnotized by its potency and forcefulness as it cut its path through the mountain's flesh.

Travis opened the doors at the rear of the trailer and backed each horse out with ease, indicating he had performed the same task hundreds of times before. Both horses were already saddled and ready to ride. The first to exit was a sorrel gelding, which was a larger animal than the buff-colored mare that was smaller in overall size and height.

Tying the reins of both horses to the back end of the trailer, Travis made his way to the river's edge to join Sarah. There was wonder in Sarah's eyes, and it thrilled him to have her in his company again, free from old restraints. Time hadn't robbed her of that joy she was able to find in simple things, as if the innocence and wonder of her youth remained in her heart, no matter the trials and disillusionments of life. She hadn't become cynical or hardened, and her tender heart and alluring body drew him like a magnet he struggled to keep in check while he was with her. He had had his fill of savvy women who could play hard and enjoyed pushing the envelope, experimenting with their newfound sexual freedoms or drugs, always reaching for some new high, as if life couldn't provide them enough happiness without help from an artificial and phony substitute. As if they had all gone mad, and in order to feel anything, they had to be shocked harder and harder in life to find any joy in living. Educated women were no different than the uneducated, and in some cases, far worse since their incomes allowed for more abuse. Living out West hadn't insulated them from the excesses of the '60s and '70s, where virtue had become a thing of the past. Sarah was much wiser now, but still maintained the strength of character that allowed her to keep her virtue by choice. She was a woman he could love in every way. Watching her closely, he could see she was struggling to deny the same feelings, and he promised himself not to press her until she recognized it was a mutual attraction and always had been. He saw in her the fact that she was still unable to separate him from the post he once held, and he hoped that their time together would allow her to accept him outside of that role.

Reaching down to the river's edge, he picked up a few rocks and threw one to the far side of the swiftly moving river. It landed in a darkened pool with a splash accompanied by an echoing clunk. It was the first time Sarah saw Travis do anything that didn't have a purpose or plan behind its action. She looked back up at him with a small smile. "I guess that's a boy thing to do when standing so close to a body of water. What's the name of this river?"

"It's the East Verde River, but I don't think fun has a gender. If it had a smooth surface, it's fun to skip them too." He looked down at her with a smile and handed her a stone. "Here, you throw one. It makes you feel happy."

Sarah took the stone from his hand and cast it out into the moving waters, and together, they watched as it splashed into the river's depths. She felt like a kid again. The face of the boy inside the strong man made himself visible, and suddenly the tension present until this moment eased. Travis bent down to gather several more rocks and handed half to Sarah. They stood silently, side by side, for several more minutes, happily lobbing the stones into different parts of the river. A simple happiness descended on Sarah; standing beside Travis in those shared moments carried more meaning than anything she had done in her entire life.

When the last stone was cast, Travis turned to Sarah, and then tilted his head toward the trailer. "Let's get you ready for a ride."

Opening the door on her side of the pickup, Travis pulled a large canvas bag from behind the front seat. "Come sit up here, and you can wear these," he told her as he pulled a pair of cowboy boots from the bag.

"What's wrong with my tennis shoes?"

"You need the added protection and strength of the boots. Besides, Trixy might not feel the rubber of the tennis shoe on her side as well as she would the hard leather of the boots. We want to make her move, not tickle her," he said knowingly.

"What size are they?"

"Seven and a half, just like you told me."

Sarah removed her sneakers, and Travis handed her a clean pair of long, cotton socks. "These will help keep you from any blisters." He gave her the left boot first, and Sarah did her best to pull it on. Seeing her difficulty, he instructed, "Swing your legs outside the truck. I'll push, and you pull." Together, they eased each boot into place.

With both boots securely on, Sarah stood up and couldn't help but laugh out loud. "I'm afraid I can't even walk in these, let alone try to ride a horse in them!"

"You'll get the hang of it—just give yourself time to warm up to them," he cajoled. Reaching back into the canvas bag, he pulled out a pair of leather chaps. "You might appreciate wearing these as well."

"And exactly what are they for?"

"We'll be riding through some taller brush, and you'll need to protect your legs from thorns."

"Travis, I really don't think I'm ready for all of this."

Travis took her shoulders and turned her around so her back was facing him. "Trust is a wonderful thing, Sarah. You should try embracing it. Hold your arms out."

Feeling out of her comfort zone, and duly chastened, she brought her arms up slightly as Travis wrapped his arms around her waist, centering the chaps evenly over both legs. As he tightened the chaps with a buckle at her back, Sarah felt the urge to laugh but held her stance as directed. Starting with her left leg, Travis tied the leather cords of the chaps at the back of her leg, and Sarah shook inside, feeling his hands tighten the strap at her thigh.

"Move your right leg further to the right," he told her. He tied the chap at the bottom of the right leg first. His hand moved up the inside of her leg, and she nervously jerked at his contact. His steady smile gave away the fact that he easily anticipated that reaction in her as he finished securing the chaps in place. He turned her around to face him directly again. "Is this the only coat you brought with you?" he asked, as he looked back into the seat of the pickup.

"What's wrong with my coat?"

"Well, for one thing, it's too long, and it has no slits in it to be able to straddle the horse, and for another, it might not be warm enough. I've brought an extra Carhartt jacket along, just in case you needed it." Reaching back into the cab behind the seat, Travis pulled out a jacket and a straw cowboy hat, which he placed on her head. It was slightly larger than her head size and came down lower on her head, touching her ears.

"Is this really necessary? I don't usually wear a hat."

"You will up here, unless you like the feel of a bad sunburn."

"I hardly think it could be any worse than being at the beach!" Sarah exclaimed, not convinced his certainty was accurate.

"It is, at this altitude."

Jumping into the bed of the pickup, Travis raised the lid of a storage chest and pulled an assortment of gear and bags out of the box. Sarah watched him as he strapped another pair of chaps over his jeans, all seemed second nature to him. Standing with his long legs spread apart, he quickly tied and buckled them into place. When his gray felt Stetson and chaps were in place, Sarah suddenly thrilled inside herself recalling how she had wondered about him and where he might have been raised. The last thing she would have ever guessed was that he was a modern-day rancher and cowboy, raised in the mountains and surrounded by all this beauty.

An inborn wisdom reflected in him permitting him to recognize life was not to be placated out here and there was no putting off till tomorrow what mandated being done today. Mother Nature waited for no man, and you either learned to live with her, or she would forcibly take you, ready or not. Travis appeared to know how to live with her. Locking the storage trunk, he then carried the saddlebags and jacket to the horses and tied them onto the back of each saddle.

"I think we're ready. Come on over and meet Trixy."

Feeling apprehensive, Sarah made one more attempt to stall. "May I take my purse?"

Travis shook his head and then he continued, "Why don't you take what you need out of it and put it in the saddlebag? It will make it easier that way."

Sarah followed his suggestion realizing that Travis saw through her ploy to stall and she reluctantly went to the cab. She removed a few personal items from her purse, and then stowed her bag beneath the front seat before making her way back to the horses.

"The buff colored mare is your mount, Sarah. She's a pretty gentle old girl, and the only problem you might have with her is getting her started. Trixy, meet Sarah!" he said, as if the horse understood every word. He brought Sarah's hand to Trixy's forehead and, placing his hand over hers, he gently moved it side to side, showing Sarah what Trixy liked. Trixy snorted a friendly puff of air through her nostrils, letting Sarah think she might have made a friend. "Come on over to the left side of the horse. This is the only side you mount and dismount from, or you will confuse her. It's always best to avoid the hind quarter and approach her from the left side so she knows you're there. You don't want to startle her, or she might react by kicking." Sarah made her way to Trixy's left side where Travis stood ready to give her a few more pointers. "She's trained to turn in the direction you lean the reins. If you want to head right, you move your wrist to the right, and to go left, move your wrist to the left. To stop her, you lightly pull straight back on the reins with a steady, even hand, leaning back in the saddle slightly. The first mistake many new riders make is they tend to jerk and over-enforce their directions. That's not very kind to an animal whose services you need. Like with most women, it's best to win their affection by respecting them and treating them kindly. You don't want to confuse them about what your intentions are."

Sarah looked at him after hearing that analogy, slightly amused.

Travis caught her glance. "It's good to see you're paying such close attention," he said with a subtle glint in his eye. "Are you ready to give it a try?"

Sarah was still apprehensive, but Travis was doing a good job of putting her at ease, and she didn't want to disappoint him. Somehow, in that moment, she was so glad he had training as a teacher. "Ready as I'll ever be, I guess!" she nervously replied.

"All right then, put your left foot in the stirrup and grab hold of the horn on the saddle, pulling yourself up, and then, once standing, swing your right leg over the saddle to the other side."

Sarah was having a great deal of difficulty trying to pull herself up. Travis stood back with his arms folded, a restrained smile across his lips as he watched her. She needed a boost to get the leverage she needed to mount. Still standing at her side, he asked her to take her foot out of the stirrup and he would help her. "Put your left knee in my hands and reach for the horn, swinging your right leg over the saddle." Sarah faced him and put one hand on his shoulder for balance and then brought her left knee to his cupped hands as directed. In one fell swoop Travis lifted her as she threw her right leg over Trixy and was in the saddle in a flash. Travis brought her left foot to the stirrup. "Remember, keep your heels down close to Trixy's side. Put your other foot in the stirrup and then raise yourself up off the saddle."

"You mean you're not supposed to sit down when you ride?"

Travis started laughing, thinking just how green she was. He wondered if there was a pre-beginner's class before the beginner's instruction that covered the obvious. "No, you don't stand up in the stirrups the whole time you're riding. If your horse changes his gate or suddenly bucks, you might want to ride it out above the saddle to ease the impact on your hindquarter. So long as you maintain control of the reins, you're the boss. It will be less painful on both of you that way. Let's just see if these stirrups are adjusted right to give you the clearance you need." Sarah raised herself up, and Travis gave her the okay. Untying the reins from the trailer, Travis handed them to Sarah, one on each side. "Try to keep enough slack in them to make Trixy comfortable, but taught enough to react with small amounts of movement."

"I think you're putting way too much confidence in me, Travis! What if I can't keep up?"

"Trixy won't let Big Red get too far out of her sight, and I promise a nice, slow walk with no trotting. Besides, I intend to keep you very close."

Sarah felt slightly unnerved at the delivery of his comments, particularly the emphasis placed on his last sentence, but she offered no response.

With Sarah mounted, Travis locked the truck and closed the trailer securely, then took the reins of his horse in hand, passing the right rein under Big Red's neck and tossing it up over the horn of the saddle, catching it with his other hand. Firmly grasping both reins in his left hand, he took one quick hop into the stirrup, mounting the sorrel effortlessly. Big Red made a complete turn as Travis adjusted himself in the saddle, twisting a bit while standing hard in the left stirrup.

"What's wrong with your horse?" she asked.

"There's nothing wrong with the horse, only a slight adjustment needed to the saddle." Travis had a rifle resting inside a tooled leather sleeve strapped to his saddle, and she thought that was strange to see but didn't ask him about it, much too anxious to think about anything else but staying on the horse. Once Travis had his saddle positioned correctly, he readjusted his Stetson and then looked back at her. "Tap Trixy with your heels, and just follow

Big Red. Let's go see some of Arizona." Travis coaxed Trixy and Red with a clicking sound, encouraging them to move, and Sarah held the horn on the saddle with one hand while firmly grasping the reins in the other, leaving Trixy the slack Travis indicated. Much to Sarah's surprise, Trixy responded and walked forward right behind Big Red.

CHAPTER FORTY-ONE

The clean, fresh scent of the cool mountain air pervaded Sarah's awareness as she followed Travis's horse further away from the East Verde River. The canopy formed by the stately ponderosa pines cast moving shadows that mingled with occasional flashes of golden sunlight as it pierced through the swaying pine bows and licked the forest floor. With every lumbering step of her horse, the rocking lull eased the initial tension Sarah had felt. The sound of creaking leather from the saddle was comforting, and the feel of moving muscles beneath her legs imbued a sense of power that, by extension, she shared with her newfound friend. The occasional waft of the horse's scent was distinct and earthy, adding another layer of sensual delight in their journey up the mountain. Her grip on the horn gradually loosened, and she was better able to focus on the serene and beautiful surroundings.

Fifteen minutes into their ride through the forest, the sound of silence gave way to subtle yet still-audible sounds of living movements coming from all directions: a shrill whistle from an unseen bird to her left in one moment, followed by a subtle creaking of pine branches gently rubbing against each other while caught in a chance breeze. For the first time, Sarah was hearing the audible and faint undertones of the wilderness up close, as though she were party to its music in a chair in the center of a great and holy orchestra. The hoofs of the horses were muffled on beds of pine needles but still detectable, along with an occasional snort, as if the horses were clearing their noses to make room for more heavenly air.

She heard a cracking in the distance. "Are there people living near here?" she called to Travis.

"No, we're actually crossing part of the Tonto National Forest, but the noise you heard could have been from any number of creatures that live here. They can easily break a branch as they walk through the old growth of the forest, and there is always an occasional rockslide. The keen ear of a hunter listens for such things," he told her with a turned head as they continued. An unexpected owl maneuvering his way through the slumbering bows of the mighty ponderosa trees was magical to watch, and Sarah felt she had just entered a different world, one far-removed from the hustle and bustle of life in the city. This place enchanted her; never before had she felt so close to nature and the glorious beauty that abounded here. In that moment, to be alive and present was enough, not thinking of tomorrow or remembering yesterday. Her mind was at rest, and she was the silent witness to something extraordinary that could not be explained or comprehended with words or sound bites. If this was Travis's world, Sarah could kneel at the same altar and rejoice.

Travis brought Big Red to a halt and rose up in the saddle, turning to face Sarah. Without speaking, he brought two fingers to his lips, indicating to her not to speak and then pointed to the far left. There at a distance several hundred feet from them and disguised by the encompassing stand of pines, a small herd of elk were making their way south. The sudden sound of cracking branches accompanied the elks' passing, and Sarah felt privileged to witness such a sight. She smiled broadly, looking back at Travis as he balanced himself with one hand on Big Red's hindquarter, still turned to face her. After a few minutes elapsed, Travis urged Big Red on, and Sarah coaxed Trixy with a few light kicks to her flanks. Not wanting to lose Big Red, Trixy happily obliged, and Sarah was feeling much more comfortable than at first. They pressed on, making their way around smaller mounds of rocks jutting up along the path or passing around steeper inclines as they moved to higher elevations.

Sarah held the horn of the saddle slightly tighter as Trixy put forth more effort to negotiate a steeper and rockier pass. Once they passed the incline, Sarah rested easier again in the saddle.

Thirty minutes into their ride, Travis brought Red to a standstill under an assortment of evergreen trees. He quickly dismounted and tied the gelding to a smaller pinyon pine tree. Trixy stopped behind him, and Travis came to her side.

"I wanted to show you my favorite getaway spot that I often come to when I want to think or just be alone," he told her.

Sarah brought her right leg over Trixy's back but couldn't quite reach the ground. Standing back with arms at his side, Travis watched in amusement, totally entertained at her feeble and comical attempt to dismount.

Still struggling to reach the ground, Sarah finally asked, "Are you just going to stand there and watch me, or do you intend to help?"

"I thought you'd never ask!" he teased her as he tied the reins on a tree limb next to Big Red. "Throw your leg back over the saddle, and then bring your right leg back across the front of the saddle over the horn. Now, just slide to me, and I'll catch you."

Sarah bit the corner of her lip in anxious anticipation of how this was going to work but did as he instructed, and Travis caught her as she slid down off the saddle and fell against his chest. His body felt strong and warm, and his grip was tight. He didn't release her instantly, and they caught each other's eyes. Travis stood straight-backed, just smiling down at her, while Sarah was too startled to move as she rested against him. She felt a sudden flush and pushed against his hardened chest, hoping to regain her footing. He slowly loosened his hold. Sarah brushed herself off, deliberately hiding her eyes from his. Walking back to Red's left side, he untied his saddlebags, and then threw them over his shoulder and reached for his rifle.

"What do you intend to do with that?" Sarah asked.

"I don't intend to use it unless I need to. You seem uneasy. Is there something else on your mind, Sarah? You look like you're fidgeting."

"Well, I can't believe you're not!"

Travis knew immediately that she was too self-conscious to tell him she needed to relieve herself. "If you've got to go, pick a tree and go hide behind it."

Her eyes grew wider and her face flushed pink at his suggestion, but her need was greater than her pride in that moment. Travis offered reassurance, "It's okay, I'll stay over here till you return. Only don't stray too far."

"Why do you keep telling me to stay close?"

"There a lot of creatures out here that aren't always friendly, and since you're invading their home, they might not take too kindly to you. Better to be safe than sorry."

"What kind of creatures are you talking about?"

"Mountain lions, for one, bears, coyotes, and rattlesnakes also. None of them are friendly."

Sarah turned, nervously surveying her surroundings that, until that moment, had appeared so peaceful. With a watchful eye, Sarah cautiously headed toward a cluster of pines not far from the horses, trying to locate the widest tree in sight. Travis turned back to Trixy and gathered a blanket and a few more supplies from Sarah's saddlebags while he waited.

Finding reassurance behind a stately ponderosa pine, Sarah lowered her jeans, bracing herself with her arm against the massive tree. The awkwardness of what was normally a natural act suddenly took on an obstacle in balance and exposure never experienced before. *"This might work if I were a boy,"* she thought, as she struggled to maintain her emotional equilibrium and balance. Pulling a tissue from her pocket, Sarah quickly finished, and then stood up tucking in her shirt before fastening her jeans. Raising her head, she looked up at the huge ponderosa pine she hid behind, and noticed peculiar markings where the bark had been scraped away. Running her fingers slowly over the surface of the markings, she tried to make out the carvings that appeared to have been made there long ago. The symbols were difficult to decipher, but the carving looked like an equation with numbers and letters faintly visible. She could vaguely make out the letter "L" followed by an equal sign and then the letters "TT" and possibly an "S." Others were carved in several lines above it that were difficult to decipher. She identified the number "2," but most of the other markings were too difficult to interpret since the growth of the tree impinged on its space and form. How curious to see such a thing so far removed from man's passage. After buckling her belt and positioning it securely, Sarah felt comfortably ready to face Travis again.

Travis had gathered the saddlebags and was leaning against a rock with his rifle cradled across his chest in his arms. Coming to a stand, he waited for Sarah to join him.

"That large tree over there has something carved on it. How strange it is to see that out here so far from everything."

A sudden look of surprise crossed Travis's face as he squinted at hearing her comment. After a slight pause, he raised his head and then nodded as if his memory had returned. "It's not strange at all, Sarah. What you saw was carved by me."

"Really, what does it say?"

"It was a long time ago, I'm afraid," he casually answered while waving his free hand slightly.

Still not satisfied with his answer, Sarah pressed him further, "I couldn't quite make it out. Exactly what does it mean? It appears to be an equation of some sort." He stared back at her as she waited for an answer. Inhaling slowly he finally explained.

"It is . . . I always used to think that, someday, I'd build a small cabin here since I'd often come up here to think. Then, I could stay here long enough to watch the sun set and rise from this vantage point. I carved out the equation to try and figure the amount of logs and timbers it would take to produce the right number of studs to complete the project."

"Oh, that accounts for the letters 'L,' 'T,' and 'S' that I thought I was able to make out. I'm sorry you were never able to build your cabin," she offered him with a feeling of sympathy.

"It's never too late, and I still might build it in the future," he stated assuredly in a deep resonate tone, while smiling back at her. Sarah found his confidence in all things uplifting and admirable.

He cocked his head to his left indicating it was time to move on. "Stay close behind me, and follow me up this incline," he told her as he hoisted the saddlebags to his shoulder. Sarah did her best to keep step with him as they took the steeper incline around the rugged rise. She found it difficult to negotiate the steeper path wearing cowboy boots, the smooth soles slipping on stones. Travis turned to see her sliding on the loose granite stones and came back to offer his hand. "Just a little farther, and I promise you, it will be worth the climb."

She gladly took his hand, and he gently pulled her up as they negotiated the slender path together. Sarah suddenly felt a sharp sting at the rear of her right leg and stopped cold, wincing in pain. A momentary sense of panic overtook her fearing a snake bite. Travis turned and instantly saw what the problem was.

"Don't move or try to break free. Just stand still."

"What is it?" she asked, looking back over her shoulder and seeing a branch of a bush still attached to her jeans.

"Just one way the mountain tries to keep you when you get here. It's called 'cat claw.'"

"Those thorns are awfully long."

"Take a small step backwards so I can ease the thorny bush from your blue jeans," he told her. Taking out a pocketknife, he cut the branch from the bush and threw it away from the path.

Sarah could now appreciate the chaps and wondered why they hadn't made them into pants to protect all of the leg.

"Travis, is this your land?" she asked as they continued up the path.

"No, not all of it—only a few hundred acres here belong to me. Most of it is part of the Tonto National Forest. The nice thing about my property is that no one will ever be able to build around it, keeping the views just as they are now. We're just about there. Give me your hand again and step up onto this ledge."

Stepping up with his help, Sarah got her footing. When she raised her head, the awesome sight of the Mogollon Rim greeted her, spanning more than a hundred miles in both directions. Her heart skipped a beat at the grandeur and scope of the vision. Billowing clouds cast their ever-changing shapes and shadows across the Rim's boundless face. Patches of snow on the Rim's crest hinted that winter was ending but the blue-white snow still clung to the loftier heights, allowing the Rim's sovereignty to tarry and perpetuate its crowning glory. The vision was more spectacular here than at first sight when they'd arrived in Payson.

After a moment of spellbound silence, Sarah finally found her voice. "What an unbelievable view this is, Travis! I can see why you like to come here. It would be difficult to tear yourself from such a vision."

"I'm glad you like it. The Rim has a way of putting everything else into perspective."

They were standing on a large ledge backed by a higher rock formation. Travis took the small blanket he had brought with them and laid it down. Placing the saddlebags on the blanket, he invited Sarah to make herself comfortable. "I've brought a couple of sandwiches and some bottled water. We probably need to eat them. They won't last much longer without refrigeration."

Sarah sat down on the blanket next to him, and Travis handed her a bottle of water and a sliced-turkey sandwich. She hadn't anticipated this level of thoughtfulness in him. "Tell me something, how were you able to trailer the horses and then get back to the hotel so quickly this morning?"

"I had help from my friend, Edgar Sims. He planned on being at the ranch today anyway and volunteered to get the horses ready for us."

"That was very kind of him. How far is the ranch from here?"

"Not far. Maybe five miles as the crow flies."

The sudden loud whistle of a bald eagle pierced the still air above and brought their attention to the azure sky. The eagle lazily circled, riding the heating air currents, spiraling higher and higher with every pass. Sarah was once again drawn into the magic of the moment, escaping time, and fell totally absorbed into the scene playing out above them with its dramatic backdrop for a stage. Travis leaned back against the rocks for support, his eyes focused on her as she became lost to time. A subtle smile formed on his lips as Sarah took part in his world, basking in it with an intensified joy she couldn't seem to get enough of.

A few silent minutes passed before Travis swallowed a long drink of water. Still staring at her, he was taken with her flawless beauty, even after all these years. Breaking her seeming trance, he asked her, "Has anyone ever told you that you have a gift of seeing the beauty in everything, Sarah?"

She turned in surprise staring back at him. "I hardly think anyone could miss the beauty in this place, but I suppose I have been accused of something similar without it being framed just that way."

"How then?" he asked her.

Sarah laughed. "You'll probably find this humorous, but I'll share it with you anyway at my expense. One Christmas, when the children were still in their teens and we took them to Florida for the holiday, it occurred to me I hadn't ever seen Christmas lights in palm trees before. I suggested we all take a drive around the local neighborhoods to see the lights decorating the palm trees and the boats in the canals, which were also lit up for Christmas. Anxious to see the sights, I insisted it would be a fun thing to do after dark. My son, Keith, was not as entertained as I was, and like most teenagers, I suspect he was bored to death, being confined to the car without the excitement he craved. Within the first few minutes of our drive, he spontaneously called out to me, telling me that he guessed I must have been a 'cheap date.' It hadn't occurred to me till then that not everyone would find the same level of happiness in looking at the lights as I did," Sarah relayed, with a gentle smile across her lips.

Travis listened carefully. He fully understood both points of view, and the incident perfectly captured her essence, which her son was apparently able to surmise in his own way as well. It didn't take much to please her, and she carried an unknown joy within herself that was real and genuine. Sarah didn't need an adrenalin rush or the forgetful effects of drugs to catapult her to happiness that so many of her contemporaries demanded in life. She was a rare jewel, and he was exerting more effort in will to keep from embracing her.

"That was very observant of your son, though not very tactfully communicated," Travis offered. "Do you see many of your old classmates, still living on Long Island as you do?"

"I see a few every now and then, but not as many as you might guess. Our class lost quite a few young men to the Vietnam War, and many others just moved on to other places. I still maintain close contact with Nonie Gorman. She and her husband now own the delicatessen and restaurant her parents once owned and operated." After a slight pause, Sarah continued to share information about someone else he might remember, "Do you remember Mark Stevens?"

"You mean the guy who liked showing off his bravado?"

"Yes. He was a neighbor of mine. I always felt sorry for him when we were kids. You probably guessed he didn't have a very happy home life, and after his alcoholic father murdered his mother, Mark joined the military. He wound up in Vietnam and died in an act of heroism, saving five other marines during the Tet Offensive in 1968. . . . It's funny, you think you know someone pretty well, and then they can surprise you in an instant and do something so extraordinary—something never expected of them!" she said pensively, still moved by Mark's bravery.

"I suppose a man never knows what he's made of until he's tested. All that pushing back allowed Mark to think for himself and toughened him up, enabling him to stand in the face of danger and do the right thing when he needed to most. As I recall, he wasn't afraid to face a challenge head on. Most men move the books around on top of a desk and think themselves accomplished. Mark thought for himself, doing the heavy lifting, eventually carrying the desk the others played on. I suppose, like his troubled life, the last moments of any man's life can erase his past and change his epitaph for all eternity." Travis spoke as if he, too, had empathy for Mark, as well as many other friends, especially several old class mates he had known who chose to put themselves in harm's way. Like Mark, they shared similar fates.

"Well, that's certainly true of Mark's life," she agreed. Sarah turned her head from him, as if she were thinking of something she was hesitant to share.

"What is it Sarah?" he asked, noting her pensive expression.

She dropped her eyes suddenly and then thought better than to share her thought. She wanted to ask him why he never returned for the 63'-64' school year, but suddenly felt unprepared to hear his answer or to give herself away and make a fool of herself. Looking back at him she smiled. "I was just thinking how happy I am to see this place." Travis returned her smile.

Another long pause in conversation happily entertained them as they finished their lunch and continued to take in the spectacular panoramic view from their vantage point. Time was absent its usual drumbeat here, and Sarah was comfortable with the frequent interludes in conversation many would find disconcerting. They shared a reverence of the mighty Rim together a few more moments until Travis readjusting his Stetson, bringing himself to sit upright, away from the rock incline behind him.

"I think we need to finish up, or I'm afraid with the thirty-minute or more ride back down to the truck, we won't make it back to the ranch before sunset. I'd really like to get the horses unloaded before then."

Sarah obliged and helped to gather their belongings. There was a comfortable simplicity between them that wasn't hurried or forced, making itself evident by the absence of idle chatter. The volume and noise in life were turned down, and peacefulness pervaded the atmosphere here. Sarah was keenly aware of the difference. It was a far cry from the life she had shared with Kenny, who could always make an entrance and assure that his presence was known by everyone—even in a large room. He had always demanded attention, a result which, she considered, stemmed from his privileged birth, and Ken sought that attention in public as well as in private. He could strut like a peacock, and only adulation appeased him.

But something much more meaningful emerged when words weren't over-used and when silence was considered enough, as if being present was complete in itself, not thirsty for bells and whistles in every moment. Why hadn't she understood this attribute in Travis before? It had always been there; the fact that he didn't waste much time talking allowed his words much more authority. That might have accounted for the feeling of intimidation around him back in high school. Her childish interpretation was totally misplaced then but so obvious to her now.

With the saddlebags tied back in place and the rifle secured, Travis went to Trixy's left side to help Sarah mount her horse. Just as before, Sarah brought both hands to his shoulders and placed her left knee into his joined hands, and in a flash, she sat reassured back in the saddle.

Halfway back to the truck, Travis halted his horse and slowly turned to Sarah. In a whisper, he told her to hold Trixy's reins tightly and not to move. With as little movement as possible, Travis gently eased his rifle from its leather sleeve and brought it up to his shoulder, sighting it while still holding the reins in his hand. Sarah looked in the direction he was aiming and saw nothing out of the ordinary. In a split second, the rifle rang out with a loud echo leaving her ears ringing. Trixy jumped, raising Sarah off her saddle then slamming her hard back down again as she kept a tightened grip on the reins. Able to keep herself in the saddle and Trixy from bolting, she looked back in the direction Travis had taken his shot. Much to her astonishment, Sarah caught the full length of what looked like a mountain lion with a cub, hurtling down off rocks and into the cover of the woods.

"You weren't intending to kill them, were you?"

"No. I was intending to scare them off since we were about to ride beneath the rocks where they were perched. No sense inviting trouble. If I had intended to kill them, they'd already be dead," he said with a surety that didn't sound like bragging, but much more like stating the obvious.

Sarah felt relieved, never before witnessing the actual carcass of any hunted animal, and she thought of the lion's cub as well. "I'm so glad you didn't shoot her!" Sarah exclaimed. Travis waited a moment before sliding his rifle back into its carry case. Turning his horse, he brought Big Red to Sarah's side.

"That lion you just saw with her cub isn't too choosy about what to feed her offspring. During the springtime when they are birthing, it takes a lot of hunting to keep her family fed. Anything that moves and looks like meat is fair game to her. I'd much rather keep you on this side of the rifle than have you served up as dinner for that cat."

Sarah shuddered at his words, understanding his concern. He untied a strap at the back of Sarah's saddle and handed her the jacket he had brought for her.

The shading of the forest was becoming more pronounced as the sun was beginning to lower. The many turns in their path hid them from the sun's direct light. Feeling much more comfortable with the jacket on, Sarah was able to pay closer attention to the differences in the pines. One in particular interested her. "Travis, what type of pine tree is that one with all the wrinkles and scales in the bark?"

"It's called an alligator pine. They don't get as tall as a ponderosa pine, but they definitely have more character," he called back to her.

How happy she felt, invigorated by her surroundings and the newness and excitement of this place, but also thrilled to be with him again. He was turning out to be everything she had loved and then some, making him more desirable than before. She hadn't felt the pangs of passion so strongly since the year they spent together in the early '60s. What a fool she was to assume she could be in his company again and not want him. But why now, when her life was turning a page and starting to finally fall into place? What would she do if he expected something from her? It was too far out of the realm of possibility, and besides, she didn't want to think about it and spoil their time together or behave like a smitten child. She refused to give in to the demanding wave of compelling desire now washing over her. Where was the fault in him that she expected to find to clear him from her memory once and for all?

It took them over thirty minutes to trek back to the parked pickup, and the sound of the rushing East Verde River let her know they were nearing the truck. Arriving back at the river, Travis quickly dismounted leaving Big Red to drink at the waters edge. He walked to Sarah's left side just as the bay came to rest next to Red. Taking the reins from Sarah, he asked, "Do you want to try and dismount on your own again?"

Feeling surer of herself and wanting to appear capable, Sarah threw her right leg over Trixy's back and then pulled her left foot from the stirrup while leaning against the smooth surface of the leather saddle. She suddenly started sliding much too speedily and found herself racing to the ground. Travis was there behind her to catch her before she landed on her backside. Holding her beneath both arms just above the ground, he started laughing, and a strong sense of embarrassment flooded over her at her inartistic dismount. With a swift pull up, Travis brought her to her feet.

Sarah turned, red-faced, to meet him head on. "I hardly think it was that funny!" she snapped at him.

"That depends on where you were while viewing it," Travis countered, still holding a semblance of a smile across his lips.

She managed to offer a muted thank you, despite the sudden flash of heat now rising to her face. They stood at the rivers edge watering the horses, and then returned to the trailer tying Trixy and Red to hooks on its side.

She gathered her things from the saddlebags as Travis hopped into the bed of the pickup. He removed his chaps and then unlocked the storage box, placing the chaps inside. Lured by the river again, Sarah returned her things to her purse in the cab and then made her way to the water's edge. Travis untied the saddlebags, stored his gear, and then returned to load the horses. Bending down beside the rushing waters, Sarah looked for a stone from its edge, not to throw as before, but to save for a tangible reminder of the river's sublime beauty. Taking her time, she scavenged more than a few stones for several minutes, examining each closely before returning them. Not satisfied, she continued her search.

Standing quietly by the open trailer doors, Travis glanced back at Sarah as she knelt down by the waters edge. Then closing the doors to the trailer with both horses securely inside, he made his way to the river and then bent down beside her. "What are you looking for?" he asked, his brows slightly furrowed.

Sarah looked back up at him with her bright blue eyes and a tender smile. "I'm looking for the perfect stone to always carry with me to remember this place," she told him with an expression that seemed to say, *Doesn't everyone do this?*

His heart melted at hearing her words. He remembered how his wife had hated it here, and how she had found nothing to like or that was worth remembering. He took his gaze from Sarah's sweet smile to help her search. He looked back into the swiftly moving current, and something caught his eye. As he reached for the sparkling rock, Sarah brought her hand to the exact same spot, and Travis brought his hand to rest on top of hers as the water danced happily over their joined hands. Sarah brought her head up to meet his gaze as he held her hand over the sparkling stone beneath the racing waters. Just like the last day of school back in '63 when he had rested his hand on hers, Sarah didn't move or speak but remained silent, fixed on his eyes.

"It appears we both found the same attraction," he said slowly, keeping a steady gaze on her face. Sarah said nothing, frozen in place, waiting to see what he would do next. He slowly lifted his much larger and stronger hand from hers, and Sarah quickly retrieved the shining stone from the river's rushing waters. Bringing herself to a stand, she held the small stone close to her chest, watching Travis as he, too, stood back up. Her heart was racing, and for the first time, she was certain he meant something more. *No, it can't be,* she told herself, trying to deny what his eyes were clearly saying.

"Are you going to look at it, or should we search for another?" he asked with a penetrating look. Sarah was lost, nervous and shaken, totally unsure of herself. Still dazed, she unfolded her hands and looked at the small rock more closely. "It's . . . it's . . . perfect," she half-whispered, hoping he wouldn't detect her insecurity. He smiled back at her without a blink, as if he were reading her thoughts, and Sarah felt uneasy, totally under his spell, just as she had been all those years ago.

He stood at her side, taking in her expression. *She wasn't very good at hiding her same feeling of love,* he thought to himself. Though, it was obvious to him that she still hadn't recognized it was mutual. Until she was certain, he kept himself in check and her from any misgivings or apprehension about him. He also knew not to move to quickly with her so soon after the death of her husband, wanting to leave her the space she needed to come to terms with both. Keeping close watch on her as she turned the stone in her hand, he thought it uncanny that she kept the same unblemished nature he remembered so well. To be with her was to recapture the wonder and beauty of life that escaped him in maturity. Sarah had returned to him many years late, but he was so glad to be with her again. She could make his spirit dance and expose the melody in his soul. It was more than how she wore her hair or held her eyes when he looked at her. Travis knew what she remembered, and those memories were his memories as well. They played on the strings of his heart, and the chords were the music that fed him. Being in her company allowed him to see the world as if new again, without the tarnish that previously darkened it. He longed to embrace her and make her part of himself but he would wait till she held the same certainty.

"Let's get you out of those chaps and head back to the barn before the sunlight vanishes behind that ridge."

Sarah gladly agreed, struggling to regain her calm and to escape the intensity of the moment. She turned and started walking toward the truck, her heart still pounding in her chest. *God,* she thought, *could this really be happening?* She didn't know how to handle any of this. What if she were wrong? Sarah was in a state of panic, second-guessing her every thought.

"Turn around," he told her when they reached the truck.

"What?" she asked, still dazed and frightened at the implication of her sudden awareness, not knowing how she should behave.

"The chaps, Sarah, I'll unbuckle them."

Sarah slowly turned her back to him, anxious, confused and vulnerable. Travis untied the chaps and unbuckled them, reaching around her waist to pull them to her side. She closed her eyes as if to hide from the sensation his closeness caused in her, while a tremor moved like quicksilver up her spine, shaking her slightly as he removed the chaps from her waist and legs. She remained silent, not sure what to say, and not wanting to look back into his face for fear of finding the truth she wasn't yet able to believe.

He threw the chaps into the box in the bed of the truck, closed it and then opened the door of the pickup, waiting for Sarah to enter. She swallowed and bit her lower lip, still grasping her shiny silver stone as she quickly slid into the front seat. Travis closed the door behind her and then walked to the driver's side, taking his seat behind the wheel. Sarah turned her head, looking back out her window as they slowly pulled away, trying to keep the memory of this place alive with the sound of the rushing waters of the East Verde River nearby. A strange sense washed over her, as though she were leaving part of herself behind. But she wondered whether she was leaving a small part of her heart at the river's edge, or if she was leaving behind the fragile, unknowing, and innocent teen who had been so madly in love with him. Hauntingly, the youthful image of her old self took release, remaining at the river's bank. The ghost from days gone by waved mythically back to Sarah with an innocent smile as they slowly drove away.

Travis sensed her tentativeness, and after a few minutes riding, he tilted his head in her direction. "Do you want to share your thoughts?"

Looking back at him, she could only think how much he had always been a part of her life despite his physical absence. Travis had always been the one she ran to in memory when life became hurtful or lonely or when she needed the thrilling feeling of love that only his memory could provide. Choosing not to expose her thoughts to him, Sarah finally answered, "I was just thinking . . . how much I've enjoyed today, so much so I don't want it to end."

He looked back at her intently with little expression to give himself away. "It's not over yet," he stated simply with a compelling directness Sarah knew had more meaning beneath its surface. She always suspected Travis had the ability to take life as it was delivered to him, and then make the most of it, never second-guessing what was evident. It was just the facts, and he could accept those facts on the merits, without adding to or subtracting anything from them.

Although the ranch was not a great distance from where they started their ride, the road was unpaved as it wound its way through the mountains, and they arrived twenty minutes later. The sun was still up as they turned off the gravel road and approached the ranch's entrance. Two huge, stripped ponderosa pine logs stood guard on either side of the long entry drive, with a third log straddling above the roadway. They fitted together with large notches, allowing the cross log to extend several feet on both sides beyond the vertical logs. Cross-bracing at the corners enforced the overall powerful and substantial presence. Fixed and centered on top of the cross log, hand-hammered iron lettering spelled out the word "Tonto," followed by a circle with an "H" centered inside and then the word "Ranch."

"I assume the 'H' stands for 'Hall'?" Sarah questioned as they pulled through the entrance.

"'Tonto Circle H Ranch,' if you put it all together. The circle with the 'H' in the center is the brand used on all our cattle, and the 'Tonto' is a simple designation of the ranch's location in the Tonto National Forest."

They continued driving past a green grass clearing with barbed-wire fencing that enclosed at least fifty head of cattle. The road followed a winding path, lazily making its way around the base of a loftier hill to their left. As they crossed a creek with a built-in cement ford, Sarah could finally see the barn ahead of them off to the right. It was painted white and had a four-rail fence attached to its side, forming a large corral. As Travis pulled up in front of the barn, a tall, thin man walked out from inside. He was cleaning his rugged hands with a rag that he quickly stuffed into his back pocket when the pickup came to halt. His long, lanky legs sported a well-worn pair of blue jeans, topped at the waist with an oversized, tarnished brass buckle. Between his black felt Stetson and his "Wilford Brimley" mustache, it was difficult to see his face. Travis jumped out of the pickup and met Edgar Sims in front, giving him a friendly slap on his shoulder. They exchanged a few words and then Travis walked to Sarah's side of the truck, opening the door for her.

"Sarah, I'd like you to meet Edgar Sims, a good friend and neighbor."

Sarah put out her hand to shake Edgar's, but he was hesitant. "I'm afraid these hands have been in a place that a lady like yourself best not gets acquainted with," he said, quickly removing his hat in a gesture of greeting. "I'm happy to make your acquaintance, Sarah."

Sarah smiled broadly at him. "That's very kind of you, Edgar, but I think today my hands have been places they've never been before, and I'm not too sure about them either. I'm very happy to meet you." Sarah detected a smile somewhere under that mustache, and she found Edgar a delightful soul, worthy of friendship with Travis.

"Let me give you a hand with the horses, Travis, and we'll get them unloaded in no time a-tall," Edgar eagerly offered, moving to the back of the trailer.

Sarah looked at Travis, and without her having to say a word, he suggested exactly what was on her mind.

"I suppose you'd like to wash up a bit and brush some of the horse off, so why don't you head on up to the house? The guest bath is the first door down the hall to the left from the foyer. It will take us a little while to feed and water the horses once we put up the saddles, so make yourself at home and put your feet up." He pointed to the house behind her.

Sarah turned around and looked back up at the top of the steep hill. She was stunned to see a massive log home occupying the entire crest of the higher rise across from the barn. The front entrance was marked by a massive drive under portico, supported by enormous vertical pine logs fixed atop stacked stone bases. She hadn't even noticed the house when they pulled up—its much-higher elevation allowing it to remain out of her line of sight. The huge structure constructed with massive logs appeared much more reminiscent of a dude ranch than a private home. Sarah looked back at Travis with a look of utter shock on her face. "Are you sure that's not a hotel?" she questioned jokingly.

"If it were a hotel, I probably couldn't get you to go in with me!" he stated emphatically with a faint smile. Sarah felt the sudden sting at his overt and comical implication but kept silent, still digesting it, wondering if her interpretation of his subtle meaning were correct.

She headed up the long drive, and with each step closer, the logs appeared larger and larger in size. She marveled at the home's massiveness as well as the beauty of its construction. She had never been in a log home before and was anxious to see its interior. Why in the world would Travis have built such a formidable-sized home with only one daughter and himself living there? He was definitely difficult to know and a continual source of surprises. *The only way to really know him would be to live with him,* she thought, and even then she suspected he could easily keep someone in the dark if he chose to do so. She recalled how little everyone knew about him when he taught at North Shoreline High, and even the class busybody, Fran, could find out little about his life outside of school. The fact that none of the students knew where he went or why he left after the '62-'63 school year ended served to make Travis Hall the only visible, invisible man she ever knew.

Back at the barn, Travis helped Edgar unload Big Red and Trixy from the trailer. Bringing them each into separate stalls, Travis unsaddled Big Red, throwing the saddle over the front slat wall of the stall, while Edgar did the same with Trixy's saddle in the adjacent stall.

"Travis, How come you didn't tell me it was a female friend you were planning on riding with this morning?" Edgar asked as he continued to work, removing the blanket and then the halter from the mares head and mouth.

Travis kept working, hanging Big Red's halter outside the stall on the opposite wall, with all the other tack, in its allotted space. "There's a lot I don't tell you, Edgar," he said without skipping a beat.

Edgar brought Trixy's halter out of the stall and hung it on the wall close to Big Red's, then casually looked over at Travis again. "You could start now by telling me how an old rancher like you knows a classy lady like Sarah," Edgar pressed him.

Travis brought a restrained smile to his face but continued to tend his chores by removing the lid to a steel barrel containing the horse feed and then scooping four scoops into a bucket. Edgar edged closer, bringing the sole of his boot to the back wall and slowly leaned against it. Travis turned and out of the corner of his eye looked back at him. He readjusted his Stetson slightly. Edgar was quick to catch a hint of a smile and a glint in his eye as Travis offered up his answer, "I could . . . but I won't."

Taking the bucket in hand, Travis entered Red's stall first, dumping the feed in the corner trough and then went on to feed Trixy next, leaving Edgar to assume what he would.

~~~~~~~~~~

Sarah reached the portico and approached the massive front door. The thick, wooden door bore a large, black iron back plate beneath a burly, twisted iron handle. Centered on its face, a matching doorknocker that looked almost too weighty to lift held prominence. The door was much taller than eight feet, and with its hefty and oversized proportions, she could only anticipate with interest what lay behind. Assuming the door would be difficult to open, she was utterly surprised when it swung open effortlessly with hinges not set to the side, but slightly off-center, pivoting so the left side of the door pushed into the house while only a third of the door's width remained outside. Stepping into the foyer, Sarah was amazed at the sheer volume and open spaciousness that greeted her.

Above her head, an enormous iron chandelier hung from a long, black chain. The ceiling was constructed with tongue and groove boards forming a peak to the A-shaped entry hall. To the right of the door, a Western-styled hall tree with pearl-colored horns for hooks took its place and held several cowboy hats, as well as a canvas jacket. Beneath the coat rack on the wide-planked dark-wood flooring, a bootjack lay next to a pair of cowboy boots and loafers. Not wanting to track any dirt into the house, Sarah quickly removed her boots and socks resting them on the floor next to the hall tree. She stood for a moment, taking in the grandness. The openness of the space allowed her spirit to soar, as if nothing could hem her in—the way so many of the houses back East with their much lower ceilings could make her feel. She followed the hall to her left, and the Native American motif of the
~~~~~~~~~~

wool carpet runner caught her attention. Markings and designs spoke in an unknown language, and she found its simple geometric patterns with three basic colors exquisitely beautiful, too lovely to walk on. Hanging from the wall to her left, a Native American dress was displayed in a Plexiglas case, showing off its intricate blue and orange beadwork against the gray leather. Its long, leather fringe at the sleeves hung gracefully down from outstretched arms, highlighting the intricacy and skilled craftsmanship in its construction. Other artifacts were spotlighted down the length of the hall, and she was moved by the elegant presentations, which were much better than an East Coast gallery.

Entering the bathroom, Sarah turned on the light. Bronze lamps on each side of the sink were shaped like hefty, hanging pinecones, and light spilled out of their slots around the circumference, casting a warm, golden glow. Matching bronze-colored towel racks shaped like branches held freshly laundered off-white towels. The rectangular mirror was framed in a wood unknown to Sarah. Its smooth finish contained both light and dark coloring and had a luster as if just polished. The faucets were bronze and were large with a heavy feel to the handles, and when turned on, the spout cascaded water from its lip as if from a flat slab of stone at a waterfall.

Sarah made use of her time by removing her blouse and washing herself as well as she could without the use of the shower. After rinsing her face she took down her hair and brushed it, releasing a few stray pine needles still clinging to the back of her head. Brushing her lengthy sun-streaked hair back from her face, she clipped it smartly to the rear of her head with the same navy bow and then powdered her nose, finishing by adding a swath of color to her lips. It wasn't the best she had ever looked, but it was the most she could offer in such a short amount of time, providing her a more comfortable and relaxed presence. Sarah slipped back into her blouse, tucking it into place beneath her jeans, wishing she had brought a clean change of clothes as she took a final look in the mirror.

~~~~~~~~~~~

Back at the barn, Edgar and Travis were finishing their chores, and Travis thanked Edgar for his help before turning to head for the house. Travis took only a few strides before Edgar called him back, "Travis . . ."

Travis turned back to Edgar.

"It's good to see you with your boots polished again," Edgar offered with a slight hint of a smile beneath his rusty gray-white, full mustache.

Without another word, Travis made an about-face and headed back up the hill to the house, sporting a half-smile apparent to only himself.

Returning to the foyer, Sarah placed her handbag down on the hall tree bench. Standing along side of the massive entry door, she glanced out the sidelight window back down toward the barn. She watched as Travis spoke to Edgar and then turned to make his way back up the hill to the house, leaving the truck and trailer parked by the barn. She stood nervously along side of the door, watching him—hoping she wouldn't make a fool of herself. She lacked experience with men in general, and she was still uncertain of Travis's motives. Kenny had always made his intentions obvious, and Sarah was never surprised at his open and aggressive manner in his call to love. His need for intimacy was always devoid of subtlety. "God," she prayed, "please help me get through this visit and help me behave with some degree of sophistication!" To be a fool twice with him would be an agony she couldn't stand.

She watched as he made his way up the long drive and removed his hat; brushing the sides of his jeans with it, he knocked the hay from his pants and then replaced the hat on his head. Almost to the door, he stomped his feet several times, dislodging clods of dirt and debris from his boots, and once under the massive portico, he removed his Stetson again, this time running all five fingers up through the wayward chestnut lock at
~~~~~~~~~~~

his brow, forcing it back into place. Sarah stepped back from the large sidelight window, not wanting him to see her watching him.

The door swung open and Travis went directly for the bootjack lying to the side of the hall tree and removed both boots in a matter of seconds. Sarah stood behind him and announced herself, so as not to take him by surprise. "Are the horses all right?" she asked for lack of anything better to say.

Travis turned and gave a slow lingering smile before he spoke. "Never been better! They don't like being separated, and taking a nice, long stroll together suits them both just fine. They'll sleep well tonight." Sarah was happy hearing those words, although... his subtle smile aloud her to think he might have had a double meaning. Why did she always feel that it was what he wasn't saying that carried the most weight when he spoke? "I hope you found everything you needed," he said, looking directly back at her. "The mountain air suits you well, Sarah—you look beautiful!"

"Thank you," she replied instantly, feeling a slight flutter in her stomach at his complement. "I didn't know it would have that effect on me."

"Would you mind if I take ten more minutes to wash the trail off myself?" Travis asked politely.

"Not at all. Take all the time you need. I'm enjoying your wonderful home. Would you mind if I have a look around?"

"Make yourself at home. Off to the right is the kitchen, if you care to help yourself to something to drink, and the living room is straight ahead."

"Thanks, but I'll wait on the drink."

"Suit yourself. I'll only be gone a few minutes." Travis headed to the rear of the house, and Sarah stood in the grand foyer, unable to decide where to head first. *When in doubt, put one foot in front of the other*, she told herself, and then walked straight ahead to the living room.

Entering beneath the cross-beamed arches from the hall to the living room, Sarah turned in surprise as she took in the spectacular space with its floor-to-ceiling wall of windows that offered an unobstructed view of the mountains lying to the southwest. She remained momentarily immobile, as if the awesome sight were too much to comprehend. The glorious view was framed perfectly by the twenty-foot-high windows, as if the outdoors were part of the environment within.

Moving slowly into the room, her eye was drawn to the stacked stone fireplace with its massive split pine log mantel. The focal point was a large oil painting depicting a Native American chief, wearing a full, feathered headdress, on horseback. The colors were dynamic and arresting, with a waterfall in the background that captured the translucent effect of the sun beaming through the falling water. The chief's arms were raised up, outstretched in prayer as the sunlight laid claim to his headdress, illuminating it from above as though in answer to his call. The painting captivated Sarah with a mystical quality that spoke to her heart. She leaned closer to read the artist's name and could make out the name "Pabst."

The dark, wide-planked floors continued into the great room from the foyer and gave the entire space continuity. They were partially covered with larger and slightly more colorful Native American rugs, each with their own individual designs. The great room was divided by a separate seating area in front of the fireplace, with two other smaller seating areas to the side and rear. A fourteen-foot-long rustic dining-room table was positioned close to the expansive windows. Two elk-antler chandeliers hung above the massive table. The interlocked, woven antlers pyramided up, supporting three full circles of candlestick lights.

All the furnishings had a masculine feel, many covered in rich leather, some in shades of burgundy and others in deep mahogany. The tables were varied and none were matched, giving the room a look that had grown over time, but all were well crafted with splendid patinas. A generous-sized coffee table caught Sarah's attention with its heavy glass top; its clear surface revealed twisted wood branches beneath it as support. With its bark removed, the unusual wood presented red, brown, and tan coloring all in the same branch. It was quite unique, and Sarah had never seen anything like it before.

The leather sectional was grand in scale; its rich mahogany color gave it a warm and inviting feel. An assortment of pillows added interest with their Native American motifs as well. Sarah was struck by the beautiful artwork around the space, including several bronze sculptures and more than a few pieces of Native American pottery displayed in lighted niches to the right of the fireplace. The designs on the pottery were strangely contemporary in feel and blended well with the clean lines of the seating throughout the space. Sarah never expected to see this level of design excellence, and she was particularly impressed with the order and cleanliness of the overall space.

Retracing her steps, she returned to the rear of the great room, intrigued by a set of etched-glass entry doors. Opening one of the tall doors, she entered a large office/study that had an important presence, with plaques and photos displayed in proportionate groupings around its paneled walls and shelving. Deep crown moldings added to the strength and substance, emphasizing the room's sphere of influence. Stretched across the dark ebony-colored, wide-planked wood flooring, a brown and white hide offered lighter contrast and kept step with the Western heritage. The built-in shelving behind the desk presented an artfully displayed mix of leather-bound books, various artifacts and photos with what looked like a pile of manuals stacked above built-in file cabinets that were custom-fitted to match the shelving. An impressive burgundy-leather-topped desk with intricately carved panels depicting indigenous wildlife—elk, coyote, and mountain lions—was centered prominently in front of the built-in bookcases. The handsome, wingback desk chair appeared well worn and was covered in some type of hide Sarah was unfamiliar with.

What interested Sarah most were the photos and plaques, and she marveled at how many there were. Several pictures were of a young woman with shiny brown hair and light green eyes, one in particular of her wearing a cap and gown. Sarah surmised the young lady to be Travis's daughter—with the same color eyes and shining hair as him, it was an easy guess. Staring at her picture a moment longer, Sarah thought with regret, Jessica was *his* daughter, and that she was never able to share the possibility of parenthood together with him. Her thought was presumptive and one sided, though she found herself at a loss in preventing it as she touched the frame.

Working her way around the room, she was intrigued by the many plaques hanging from the walls. She paused to read several of them. One engineering and technology award, as well as several sales awards, all presented by the Honeywell Corporation. She continued, reading further across the wall; there appeared to be one accommodation and award after another. Stopping in front of what looked like a picture of a stately old limestone building covered in ivy reminiscent of many of the older buildings on the East Coast, Sarah took the time to read the plaque below it. "For academic excellence and successfully achieving the highest numerical grade-point scores as Brigade Commander of the Class of 1959 United States Military Academy at West Point, Travis Hall is hereby presented this award in recognition of his achievement." Sarah stood dumbfounded, and reread the words. Moving her gaze further along the paneled wall, she read one plaque after another, each recognizing another high achievement while attending West Point Military Academy. The many awards ran a gauntlet, including academics, marksmanship, athletics, and even one for winning a collegiate chess championship in 1958! Sarah was taken aback by the sheer number of them and wondered if there was anything he couldn't master. She felt as though she had suddenly fallen headlong into the life of the mystery man she had secretly loved but who only now was being revealed to her in all his true greatness. He had always been compelling to her, but she could never have imagined the depth to his life. Here in his study, Sarah touched the essence of his character, driven by achievement and the meeting of one challenge after another successfully. Her attraction to him was in part the fine distillation of a life richly lived, filled with accomplishments and excellence. His many achievements, no doubt, had been hard-earned, skilled, and disciplined, devoid of falsity, and strong in character. That essence had resonated powerfully with her, regardless of the fact that she had known so little about him.

Sarah turned to the desk and picked up a silver-framed photograph sitting slightly off-center on its surface. She recognized Travis immediately, standing between two other cadets, all in uniforms, with their arms over each others' shoulders. They were happily smiling as if good friends. There was no mistaking Travis's determined, square jaw line, straight-backed posture, or broad shoulders—and that smile easily gave him away. He was just as she had always remembered him, looking the same as he did when he taught her algebra so many years ago: handsome, highly disciplined, intelligent and strong, a force to be reckoned with, who somehow all made sense to her now. She ran her fingers over the surface of the picture, as if to drink in the feel of it. The revealing implication of his beginnings, combined with the place he was raised, put the many pieces of the puzzle together for her now, and a tear welled up in her eye, wondering why he hadn't shared anything about his past with her. Sarah wiped a single tear from her cheek as she stood there for a protracted moment, lightly caressing his photo and contemplated days now long gone. How sad that he had remained so far out of reach to her when he had always been the only man she had ever truly loved. With a heavy heart, she questioned why life had taken them in opposite directions. She placed the photo back down on his desk and turned, only to see him standing there, leaning against the door, arms folded, watching her with his still-damp hair falling forward at his forehead. Sarah shook slightly, startled by his presence.

"How long have you been standing there?" she asked him.

"Long enough," he answered in his usual style of five words or less.

"Do you ever speak using complete sentences, or is everyone else supposed to know what's going on in your head?"

He stared back at her with his unassuming smile and brought himself to her side. "I don't think it would be good for either of us if that information became public."

Sarah blushed, and she turned to the desk again to change the subject, asking him about the photo and West Point.

"It was a long time ago. I started in nineteen fifty-five and left in fifty-nine."

"What do you mean you 'left' in fifty-nine? Don't you mean you graduated that year?"

"Not exactly. I was due to graduate in May of that year, but I was involved in an auto accident the month before graduation." He paused for a moment, a look of strain still detectable in his expression. "My injuries were too extensive to allow me to return and finish out my last month, although I fulfilled all the requirements for graduation. But because I was no longer able to pass the physical exam for commissioning at that time, I had to forfeit my military career."

That accounted for the scarring Sarah had observed on him the first day of class back in 1962, though it was not now as visible or as pronounced as it had appeared back then. "I'm so sorry, Travis. That had to be very difficult for you with only a month left till graduation."

Shaking his head slightly, he continued, "Not as difficult as losing both my best friends." He looked down at the photo Sarah had been holding; he meant the cadets in the picture with him.

"Were they involved in the same accident with you, then?" she gently asked him. An intense yet far-away expression washed over Travis's face as he stared down at the photo. He didn't answer right away, taking time, still lost in memory. She waited, not pressing him, unsure whether she should have broached the subject.

"I was driving the three of us back to the Point from a weekend trip to Manhattan. It was a stormy night, and a tree fell in front of us, forcing the car off the side of the road into a ravine." He paused a moment with eyes still fixed on the photo and drew a breath. "Gunner and Wade were both good men, and we shared a lot together, good times and hard times."

"I wish it could have turned out differently, Travis," she offered, moved and affected by his reaction.

"It didn't, and for whatever reason, I'm still standing here." He brought his gaze back to Sarah. "Since you're here standing beside me, perhaps we need to enjoy that fact with a glass of wine." Taking her arm, he gently led her from the study back through the foyer to the kitchen.

"Do you prefer white or red?" he asked as he made his way to the wine cooler in the huge center island. Sarah was taking in all the gourmet appointments, asking herself exactly what the nature of his work really was. After her short perusal of his office, ranching alone was obviously not the sole source of his income. Whatever he was involved in must have accounted in part for his being able to build such a large and luxurious home. She was feeling much more comfortable with him, but was unable to bring herself to dig too deeply; besides, he would eventually tell her if he wanted her to know, just as he shared with her the accident.

"Whatever is open will be fine for me, or your choice. I like either," she answered him.

"Merlot it is then," he announced as he pulled a bottle from the wine cooler. Sarah watched him and her heart skipped a beat as she took in his long line and handsome form. Unconsciously, she started making mental calculations about his age, thinking that if he had graduated college in '59, he might have been twenty-two years old, depending on when he started. Three years later, he would have only been twenty-five. There was the possibility that he was only eight years her senior when he came to teach at her school in New York in 1962. He still looked remarkably fit for fifty-three, if her calculations were correct.

Travis handed her a glass of wine and suggested they take a few snacks out with them to the deck. He wanted her to see the sun set, and it was already making its rapid decent into the western sky and would soon disappear behind the Mazatzal Mountains. Sarah gladly agreed, cupping her wine glass in hand as he led the way.

Greeted again by the sweet pungent scent of the pines, they walked out on to the covered deck. Sarah drew in a deep breath for the hundredth time as she viewed the forest spread out below them with the Mazatzal Mountain range looming in the distant western horizon.

Travis rested his glass on the rail and balanced himself partway on it with his back against one of the huge pine columns that supported the roof of the deck. "Tell me about your novel, Sarah, and how long it took you to finish."

"I worked on it off and on over a period of several years, and then laid it down when Kenny was first diagnosed. By then, he was already in stage four of the disease, and for the next year and a half, I didn't touch it. It took me some time to pick it back up after Ken's passing." She paused a moment. "I've always loved history, as well as writing, and thought I'd combine the two with a historical romance of sorts, though I think there's a bit of mystery to it also. It isn't exactly *The Great Gatsby,* but the time period and setting is similar." She took a sip of her wine and suddenly felt deficient with her meager talents by comparison to all his accomplishments. Her world seemed like child's play and fantasy compared to his. For a brief moment, she felt as though she were his student again, still overwhelmed realizing how much more accomplished he was than her. He had left his mark on the world while she toyed in her fantasy and writing.

She turned from him glancing out at the distant mountains, and Travis could tell she was thinking something. "I always believed you had the gift to write, Sarah, as well as a beautiful heart."

Sarah brought her eyes to his once more, surprised by his comment, wondering how he knew about her writing ability back then, since she had never shared any with him. She also wouldn't have guessed his assessment of her, other than his possible opinion that she was totally inept when it came to math. But then, that was a fact that was well known to both of them.

Changing the subject, Sarah brought their attention to the lights now appearing at a great distance in the deepening shadows of the long valley stretched out below them. Several pastures were surrounded by the mighty pine forest, each with cattle dotting the green open spaces, but the great distance and fading daylight made counting the number of heads difficult.

"I wonder what the man who owns that property far below yours is thinking when he looks back up here at the lights in this huge home so high above everything else."

Travis sipped his wine and rested his glass back down on the rail, tilting his head up and scratching his chin, looking back at Sarah with a funny little smile on his face.

"Well, haven't you ever wondered that?" she asked him.

"Nope. . . ." he said quite casually still holding his slight smile, restraining himself from laughing.

"I can't see how you find that question humorous, since it was one of the first thoughts to cross my mind at seeing this fabulous sight! Haven't you ever tried to put yourself in his shoes just once?"

With a slightly bemused look on his face, Travis finally answered, "They'd be a perfect fit if I did!" Travis chuckled under his breath. When Sarah gave him a puzzled look, he explained, "It hadn't crossed my mind, Sarah, since I'm the man who owns that property!"

He couldn't have made that bit of information more shocking in its delivery if he had tried, she thought. "Just how far is that from here?" she asked him.

"It's somewhere between a mile and a half and two miles."

Sarah gulped her wine, not able to calculate the amount of acreage but fully cognizant of the enormity.

Travis kept smiling as she suddenly fell silent. "It will only take another couple of minutes for the sun to disappear," he said, pointing to the western sky. Sarah turned around with her back to Travis, still nursing her wine. She couldn't put into words what she was feeling, and the whole day tracked through her memory with the sweetest visions, each following another in ecstatic succession more glorious than the one before. No matter what tomorrow would bring, she would carry this day with Travis Hall in her heart forever.

CHAPTER FORTY-TWO

The brilliant display of pink and purple colors that washed across the early evening sky began fading in the diminishing light of the setting sun. Sarah held her glass of wine, fixed in adoration of the majestic closure to an awesome day. From early morning till sunset, the day had been filled with unforgettable scenery and grandeur unlike any she had ever been exposed to before. She had never felt so alive and completely part of the sacredness of nature. She now understood why Travis called the Rim his home. Neither one of them spoke in the waning moments of the day's last light. Sarah watched the setting sun play out its quiet and magical ritual as it had done ceaselessly from the dawn of time. Her joy and reverence in that moment mirrored his as Travis watched from behind.

His home and life filled her with wonder at the extraordinariness of him and this unspeakably beautiful place. The hours spent with him only served to expand her bigger-than-life perception of him, his strengths and abilities, and the unpretentious nature that belied his accomplishments. What a fool she had been to try and convince herself that he was probably not like she remembered. By now, he would likely be an aging and declining man, she had told herself. How could she have been so woefully wrong?

To Sarah, Travis was a million miles ahead of the many social climbers she had found herself forced to deal with during Kenny's tenure at Lowenstein, Birk and Hammond law practice. Attending the frequent social functions and dinner parties that Ken's career mandated had always been difficult for Sarah, and she was often at odds with many of his peers. For all the supposed integrity and ethical oaths they were to have taken, their lives were rife with infidelities and corruptions, all glazed over behind their perfectly beautiful homes in the right neighborhoods with all the right friends. The New York social scene wore thin on Sarah, and she dedicated herself to her children, charity work, and, later, her writing. Somewhere in the background of her thoughts, the recurring question of what her life might have been like had Travis Hall ever been a part of it continued to beg her attention throughout her marriage. Everything she had ever loved about him was suddenly magnified and heightened. The idea that she would be able to find some deficit in him, allowing her to finally put an end to thoughts of him, was fast becoming her folly.

She turned to face Travis in the darkening light as he leaned against one of the sizeable log columns. A sudden feeling of shock and panic arose within her at the sight of him.

"What is it Sarah?" Travis asked.

Too embarrassed to tell him what she was thinking, she turned away from him and shook her head, "It's nothing," she said, trying discretely to hide her thoughts.

"It must be something. Why were you looking at me like that?" Travis questioned her.

"Really, it's nothing," Sarah insisted, as her thoughts raced.

Sarah, I would have to be both dumb and blind to believe that it was nothing. I'd really like to know what you were thinking."

Feeling self-conscience, she hesitated and then responded to him with a slow cautiousness, unsure of herself. "All right . . . I'll tell you if you insist. It's just the way you're standing there leaning against the column with your arms folded and the sole of your foot pressed against the log."

Tilting his head while squinting he responded, "I tend to take advantage of the support in order to take the weight off old injuries." He searched her expression and waited with a questioning look for her to clarify further.

"It's . . . it's . . . just that it brought back a memory of you from high school when I went back to my locker late one afternoon. It was already turning dark in the project area. I remembered having the distinct feeling that I wasn't alone, and when I turned around, you were standing across the PA in the shadows, exactly as you're standing right now. Do you remember that day?"

"Yeah . . . I remember it," he said with a slight nod of his head.

With no further elaboration or even explanation for his silence on that day all those years ago, she asked, "Why didn't you say something to me?"

Travis remained expressionless, holding the same stance, still propped against the log column. He kept his silence a moment longer, watching her carefully. "I didn't have conversation on my mind, so there was no need to say anything."

Sarah swallowed hard, not totally sure of his meaning and still unable to believe he might have had the same compelling attraction for her that she had held for him. He was difficult for her to read, yet the intensity in his eyes let her know he was telling her the truth, without any other expression to give him away. "Didn't you at least want to know what I was thinking when I saw you standing there in the shadows that day?"

Without moving a muscle, Travis answered her, "I already knew what you were thinking, Sarah."

Sarah's stomach dropped, and she was unable to speak. Embarrassed that she had confided in him her thought and shocked at the idea he might have known her hidden desire for him, she turned away, feeling the intensity of his knowing eyes too difficult to bear. A sudden chill coursed through her body. "It's gotten quite a bit cooler out," she said, holding both arms closer to her torso and rubbing them, hoping to change the subject.

"It can drop as much as forty degrees after the sun goes down up here on the Rim. Let's get you back inside." He took her arm and led her back into the living room. A shock wave of emotions washed over her feeling embarrassment by his words and at the same time thrilled by his touch. A mild sense of fear bubbled up to the surface of her thoughts, not sure what to expect next from him.

Travis had been the perfect gentleman all day, and Sarah was more confused and uncertain of him than ever. He would answer her questions directly, but his meaning could be taken one of two ways, and her mind hesitated to believe what her heart and his eyes were plainly sharing. Her emotions and feelings were in the way, obscuring a clear understanding of him. She couldn't let go of the idea that he must have thought of her as a naive schoolgirl for whom he had felt pity all those years ago. Sarah wasn't sure what he expected from her now, and more importantly, even if his interest in her were certain, was she prepared to accept him on his terms without disappointing either of them. She wasn't willing to play the fool again like she had in the past, believing he would return.

She was carrying the weight of her own self-imposed guilt, still trying to remain loyal to Kenny and unable to break the bonds of a marriage that had ended at his death. She had never completely been able to let go of Travis, and his memory had filled her life during her nineteen-year marriage to Ken. She wouldn't have the courage for a casual affair if that was Travis's intent; he was the only man she had ever truly loved. He was the flame that never died. She had allowed secret thoughts of him while outwardly living the ideal and consummate life with Kenny. To her friends and family, she and Kenny were the perfect "happily ever after" fairytale couple and the paragon of loyal matrimony. The secret duplicity had marred Sarah with a deep sense of perceived infidelity that went against every moral value she believed in. Travis was always there in the background, haunting her. She had loved Kenny, but that love was void of the passion she had always felt for Travis.

Standing there in front of him after all these years was a form of penance. She had always secretly wanted him, but now her guilt demanded contrition in the cruelest way. Being this close to him was overwhelming for her, and just as a mental fog encompassed her when she was his student, she couldn't think clearly. She never fully believed her faint suspicions that he might have wanted her as much as she had desired him, counting those thoughts nothing more than youthful fantasy. Despite Sarah's gift with words, she was inexplicably unable to interpret his meanings or motives with any clear understanding without getting caught up in her own guilt, doubts, and troubled emotions.

She was straining to deny the same passion he was so easily able to ignite in her all over again. Everything about him now only served to solidify the compelling attraction she had felt back then. To be with him another day now was to want him, but just like during her high-school days, he didn't do anything to directly indicate that same sentiment. She had remained in love with him, and the torturous, denied passion of her youth had resurrected itself in less than twenty-four hours. He gave only innuendos and small gestures that she dare not take as conclusive evidence or she risked being wounded all over again. He had exited her life all those years ago as simply as the closing of the last page of a book, with no fanfare, and this reunion would more than likely end the same way.

Placing his wine glass down on the coffee table, Travis walked to the fireplace. A cavalcade of thoughts and emotions raced through Sarah's mind, all beginning and ending in a deep-seated longing that had never left her—even after twenty-seven years of separation.

Why did he ask her to be with him and then bring her to his home? Was she still that same inexperienced schoolgirl who read into everything he said only what she wanted to believe, or was the obvious too much for her to accept after a lifetime of repressed desire? What did he expect of her now, and could she dare to think she could fulfill his desires after so many years had gone by? She was no longer the innocent and youthful girl she once was. She also lacked the sexual sophistication he might expect of a woman her age living through the sexual revolution of her generation. Kenny had been the only man in her life, and although she loved him dearly, it was a sisterly love, lacking the passion a man like Travis Hall might expect of her. She couldn't face the most difficult question of all. If he made any advance toward her, would she walk away from the only man she had ever truly desired? Sarah was uncertain of everything, especially herself.

Travis bent down and lit the gas logs in the massive fireplace. The glow of the fire added a warmth and flickering light to the expansive space, taking the chill off the cool night air. Sarah rested her glass on the coffee table and walked to the fire, extending her hands to warm them. Standing by the glowing flames, she contemplated how different Travis was from Kenny. He never wore his emotions on his sleeve or wasted his words. When he said something, he meant it, but she was always left to try and fill in the blanks.

"Do you still love music?" he asked her, after standing and taking another sip of his wine.

"Yes, I'll always love music. I'm surprised you remember that," Sarah responded, touched by his regard for something she loved.

Travis set his glass back down and picked up a remote control from the built-in shelving to the right of the fireplace and asked if she had any preference.

"I love most anything except hard rock."

He tuned to a smooth and sultry sound, then turned to face her again. She wondered what he was thinking as he stood silently watching her.

"Come dance with me, Sarah," he said, as he put the remote back down on the shelving.

"I don't think that's a good idea," Sarah answered, half-surprised that he asked her and much too nervous to get that close to him.

"Come with me. It's just a dance, not a test," he said, a small dent visible at the corner of his mouth as he held his hand out to her with a steady calm.

"It's just that I . . . I . . . haven't danced in such a long time," Sarah explained, squeezing her hands together a little too tightly.

Travis reached out and took her hand in his, coaxing her to follow him as he walked backward, pulling her forward toward him.

"That's a problem you have that you really do need to work on," he said as he pulled her gently to the space alongside the seating area where the wooden floor was no longer covered by the area rug.

"What do you mean?"

"You think far too much. This is the easy part," he answered her in a matter-of-fact tone.

Sarah's heart began to race as he gently put his arm around her waist and cupped her right hand with his own, turning it to lie on his chest. She stood straight and couldn't bring herself to get any closer to him, but Travis gently tightened his hold and brought her body closer to his as he moved with the music. She could feel his heart beating beneath her hand as it rested on his chest, and she prayed he couldn't hear her heart beating so rapidly. The heat from his body brought waves of inflamed tingling, and she became lost in the strength of his arms and the sensation his nearness caused in her.

Gradually, Sarah started to relax and found herself totally absorbed in the simple act of moving together with him to the rhythm of the music. Her will lessened with each step as she swayed in unison with him. She delighted in every new sensation the nearness of him brought to her. Travis pulled her closer and brought his head to rest at the side of her face, and she felt his breath with every exhale at her ear. She was enthralled by him and the ecstatic feeling of being in his arms after a lifetime of wondering what such a moment as this might be like. The tension in her body slowly relented, allowing her to mold perfectly in his arms as effortlessly as a truffle melts on the tongue. Being in his arms felt surprisingly right, with no pretense, and as natural as breathing. Neither of them spoke a word as they embraced each other, caught up in something so deep no words could explain what she was feeling. No time or distance came between them, and twenty-seven years of unanswered longing was being pulled into the abyss of oneness they were now sharing. As if both of them together had always been this way. Sarah finally stopped thinking and marveled at the change that occurred in her at the closeness of him.

The music slowly came to an end and Sarah took one cautious step back from him, then leaned against the wall behind her for support, shocked at how unmistakably genuine and perfect being with him was and how totally at home she felt in his arms. Travis brought his hand to the wall on Sarah's right side, supporting himself with his arm extended as he stared into her glistening, aqua blue eyes. In the flickering shadows of the darkened room, he waited to see what her reaction would be as he brought his face closer to hers. Sarah met his eyes, catching her breath, but couldn't turn away. She loved him desperately and was certain she couldn't refuse any further advance he made. He tenderly stroked the side of her face with the back of his right hand, running it down the length of her neck. She shut her eyes and tilted her head back with a slight shudder at the thrilling sensation his touch instilled in her. Leaning forward, Travis whispered her name in her ear and then gently kissed the side of her face as a tear rolled down Sarah's cheek. He cupped her face in his hands and tenderly brushed his lips over hers so delicately that, with her eyes still closed, it felt like a warm summer breeze seductively urging for more. Breathless and immobile she slowly opened her eyes. Travis watched her expression closely, waiting a second time, but still saying nothing. She stared back into the depths of his penetrating deep green eyes. He cocked his head and raised his brows slightly while holding his intensity, as though he were questioning her. In the stillness of his pause Sarah's eyes suddenly grew wider as she drew a quick breath. The truth of their mutual longing hit her like lightening as she clutched at the wall to keep her balance. Instinctively, and without another word Travis leaned into her, pressing his body against hers, and kissed her mouth passionately as Sarah surrendered willingly, returning his passion with her own, wrapping her arms around him, responding with his same wantonness. In the heat of the moment, Travis pulled back slightly and then took her by the hand a second time and led her to his bedroom on the far side of the expansive great room. The sun had long ago set, and the full moon rose above the Rim, allowing its light to filter through the ponderosa pines flooding the expansive floor-to-ceiling windows of his room with a clear, white light. It cast a soft glow over the king-sized bed, illuminating the entire space.

Sarah went freely with him, letting him lead her to his bed where she sat down on the edge and watched him as he stood in front of her and removed his shirt, all the while keeping his attention fixed on her. He continued undressing in the soft white light of the moon, as Sarah sat perfectly still, hands in her lap, facing him.

God, he is so beautiful, she thought. Even at his age, with the broad expanse of his chest and arms, his muscles full and strong, with a few gray hairs on his chest catching the moonlight, Travis surely owned her heart. He stood naked in front of her as she admired his long legs, flat stomach, and his perfect composure. Travis knelt on the floor in front of her, picked up both her hands, and slowly brought them to his lips, kissing each of her palms. Sarah closed her eyes as he brought her hands to his face, and she arched her neck back at the sublime tenderness of this simple act of love. Reaching out to her, Travis removed the clip from her hair at the nape of her neck and ran his fingers through the length of its velvety softness. The silver strands highlighting her ash blonde hair shimmered in the moonlight as they fell around her face and spilled to her shoulders. With an almost imperceptible touch, he slowly brought his hand to her blouse, unbuttoning it, one button at a time, while Sarah remained motionless, in awe of him and his gentleness with her. She was vulnerable with him, still tainted by her modesty and afraid she might fail him as a woman. But his tender expression as he laid her blouse aside thrilled her beyond words. Taking her hands in his once more, he pulled her up to stand with him and then continued undressing her with a sensitivity that Sarah found both rapturous and caring, something she'd never expected him capable of. He unfastened her belt and unzipped her jeans, letting them fall to the floor. Bringing her body closer to his, he removed the last of her undergarments and then embraced Sarah, holding her against him. Sarah's breath let out a sigh as their bodies touched, sending an electrifying sensation through her unlike anything known to her before. Travis brought her gently back down to the bed and slipped between the sheets next to her, cradling her once more in his arms, and delicately brushed the loosened strands of her silken hair from her forehead. His body felt hard while his touch was featherlike, tantalizing and seductive mingled with the manly fresh scent of his soap. He traced a path down her neck and along the curves of her body as his hand lazily explored her womanly beauty cupping the fullness of her breasts. Sarah thrilled to his touch and the ravishment he was creating in her. The delicate curve at the small of her back gently moved beneath the pressure of his exploring hand, and in her response, the softness of her flesh pressed against his powerful torso, molding to his form. The heat from his body washed over her and Sarah was consumed by him, not thinking of what was next, just existing in the moment, responding bodily to him without thought. Her night had become day, as the brilliance of the sun now burned inside of her. She had always lived for this consummation, reality now wedding her to the moment, perfectly reflecting what her heart witnessed within.

Travis held her body close to his now, but still seeing her in his minds eye when she had sat quietly on his bed with her hands in her lap. He was struck in that moment with the certainty that he was the only other man she had ever allowed herself intimacy with. Moved by her willingness to give herself to him, he couldn't erase the unblemished nature she carried, even after all these years. It excited him through and through that her reluctance had given way so easily. It heightened his passion for her at a deeper level than he could conceive. The longing and aching he had suffered over the years to be with her and to touch her was at long last being fulfilled. There was something enthralling and passionate in the way she moved against him at his lead, and it carried him in heated expectancy. The thought raced through his mind that there was nothing forced, harsh, or contrived in her movements as she instinctively molded to the contours of his form, intoxicating him with her bodily intuitiveness. He brought his lips once more to hers and took in their sweetness, thirsty for all of her but restraining himself to bring her to his fervor, savoring the warmth in them and then moving down to the hollow of her neck, tracing a moistened path to the soft pink crests of her breasts. The desires that had been denied release for so many years were surfacing now, growing stronger with each passing minute, and he sensed they were both experiencing a passion previously unknown to either of them.

He continued to savor the feel of her flesh, kissing her shoulders and then moving down slowly, exploring every inch of her, crimping the creamy white flesh of her belly between his lips. He covered her body fluidly, like a river seeking out its natural course, caressing and devouring everything in its path, leaving no stone unturned. He pressed against her knowingly, bending and shaping in her the response he thirsted for. Wittingly and gently, he brought her to reoccurring heights of rapture loftier than the moment before, and she responded with abandon to his demands. He was spellbound by her latent sexuality, and it brought his ardor to a heightened pitch. Demanding more of her, he wrapped himself around her tasting her hungrily now with his mouth, no longer restraining his blatant need. Sarah clung to him and moaned his name faintly as Travis brought her to the edge of her desire. Instinctively, he brought his full weight to bear as Sarah wrapped her long legs around him, pulling him down, deeper and deeper into the enveloping softness of her flesh to an invisible luminous sea. His need was her need as well, as her silken legs and thighs encompassed him meeting his thrust with her own. Drunk with passion for her, he moved against her slowly and deliberately, stirring her again and again as she clung to him. "Oh God." she pleaded under her breath. With uncanny perception, Travis screened her senses by quickening and then slowing his motion repeatedly, bringing her to soaring heights of ecstasy, unifying her insurmountable pleasure with his own. His mind fell submissive to passion as he lost himself to a living, breathing compulsion. He became a driving, repeating force, blindly leading to one final act of convulsive release and collapse into the sweet valley of satiation. Sarah simultaneously arched her neck back, clinging fiercely to him at the pinnacle of their desire, trembling, falling, falling into waves of brilliant, intense rapture. She clutched at his back, their bodies mingled, spent in the sweat of lovers' work that endlessly attempts in desperation to stay the hands of time. It was in this ecstatic moment that their long quest to find the happiness that had eluded them gave way to a fountainhead of uncontainable joy and bliss.

For a while, he held her trembling body beneath his own and tenderly stroked her flushed and joy-filled face. They remained uplifted, woven in quiescence, embraced in body and spirit, totally emerged in the euphoric peace that neither could have anticipated or understood after years of separation and suppressed longing. It was the ultimate communion that had been denied them their whole lives, and Travis knew, in that moment, that she was the only woman who could ever bring him this much happiness. For this one moment, he would have gladly lived another ten lifetimes. It was Sarah he had desired for all those years, and no one could ever replace or satisfy him the way only she could. The wound he carried at not being able to be with her but for the sake of another year's difference in her age—till she was eighteen—had cost him a lifetime of happiness, which had escaped him at their parting. He had known he loved her then, and that she would forever be the only one for him, first, last, and always.

Sarah leaned against his chest, breathless and dazed, aware that this was the first real fulfillment she had ever known. The joy she felt at finally knowing that Travis wanted her added to the euphoria, and she was shaken at how easy it was to be with him and how remarkably natural their lovemaking felt. Kenny had always been in love with her, but his need to have her was always filled with an immediacy and harshness that left Sarah cold and only able to meet him on his terms. Travis asked nothing more of her than what she was willing to give, and he delighted in giving all of himself to her, even denying himself for her full and complete gratification. Neither she nor Travis could have known the extent of the bond they had forged with one another all those years ago, but the certainty of their mutual love was now and forever sealed in their hearts this moonlit night high atop the Rim where Travis made his home.

Travis felt reborn, receiving his second chance. Sarah was finally on his side of the equation, and he would do everything in his power to make it work for them this time.

CHAPTER FORTY-THREE

The early morning sunrays wove their way through the gently rustling pines, filling Travis's room with a subtle dance of flickering light. The pine bough's images skipped across the bed in rhythmical flutters as Sarah woke up and caught its play on the sheets through her sleepy eyes. Looking toward the expansive floor-to-ceiling windows, Sarah pulled the sheet up closer to her chin, unnerved at the thought of exposing herself to the openness the massive windows invited. After turning to look for Travis and finding him missing, she sat up in the bed and, for the first time, surveyed her surroundings in the morning's light. It occurred to her how foolish her concern was regarding the lofty and undraped windows. On second glance, nothing but all of Mother Nature's grandeur was visible as far as the eye could see. Travis's log home was built on a high ridge above everything else, with the exception of a few taller ponderosa pines to one side of his home and a long line of mountains on the far distant horizon. The expansive view from the massive windows was breathtaking, and Sarah was awestruck at the beauty and openness, as well as the slight feeling of isolation it evoked in her. She was sitting on top of the world.

His bedroom was equally as grand in scale as the rest of the log home, and she marveled at the beautiful works of art displayed proportionately around the room. Most were original oil paintings by different artists, while a small bronze sculpture of a cowboy on horseback held a place of prominence on top of the left side of a large chest. All of the art shared similar subject matter reflecting the Western way of life. Two of the walls exposed the log timbers to the peak of the twenty-foot-high ceiling, giving the appearance of a much larger room than its already spacious proportions. The exposed log walls added to the rustic feel, while two other walls were sheet-rocked and painted a neutral tan, allowing the artwork to take center stage. Somehow, Sarah hadn't even noticed that the king-sized bed she slept in had four massive, dark-stained pine posts at each corner, with a tall, rich sienna-colored tufted leather headboard between the two posts at the head of the bed. The minimal furnishings were sizeable, although not obtrusive, and in keeping with the overall scale of the space. The dresser and furnishings conveyed a masculine feel while at the same time bore a richness and sheen usually reserved for fine antiques lovingly cared for over time. A small smattering of family photos rested on the furniture around the room, and Sarah recognized Travis's daughter, Jessica, in several of them—one in particular at the nightstand next to his bed. They offered a sense of home, personalizing the space without looking cluttering or distracting from the calming and natural influence the room imparted.

Two oversized, stuffed, comfortable-looking leather armchairs sat on either side of a small, square table facing the massive windows. Two red plaid wool blankets with fringe on their ends hung over the backs of both chairs, adding color to the room's rustic and natural appearance. With the exception of the woven wool Native American designed rugs topping the dark, wide-planked wood floors and a few paintings, the blankets were the only bright pop of color in the calming space. Another fireplace took the wall opposite the bed, and it too had a smaller, split-log mantle like the one in the great room. The hearth was raised up off the floor and afforded perfect viewing from the surface of the bed. Stacked stones continued to the ceiling, reinforcing the overall earthy and masculine feel of the room. The sizeable painting above portrayed a man and a young female child on horseback together. On the opposite wall from the windows, a beamed archway led to what looked like a master bath. Searching for her clothes, but unable to find them on the bed or floor, she wrapped herself in one of the smaller throws resting on the back of a chair and made her way to the bathroom.

She continued down the passage way to the bath passing a large walk-in closet to her right opposite a closed door on her left. Much to her surprise, the master bath was enormous and kept a grand feeling with its higher beamed and vaulted ceiling. The limestone flooring was set on the diagonal, with small darker brown squares of granite inserted like diamonds intermittently across the flooring. The focal point was an enormous jetted bathtub that could easily accommodate two people comfortably, with rolled headrests built in on either end. It was centered beneath a large arched window that provided a spectacular view of the snow-topped mountains off in the distance toward Flagstaff. A three-tiered iron chandelier hung from a lengthy chain fixed to a cross beam above the tub. Two separate vanities on opposite sides of the room gave the open space a balanced feel, while the center of one had a lower counter height and bench neatly tucked beneath. The rich-umber-colored granite counters gave a depth to the room, matching the tiny diamond-shaped squares in the flooring, adding contrast to the lighter-colored limestone floors and light russet walls. Two large mirrors hung over the sinks on opposite sides of the room, each framed in rich dark chocolate leather, continuing the sense of rugged earthiness, while, strangely, providing an elegant feel to the bathroom. A glass-block shell entrance with pebble-stone flooring, reminiscent of tumbled and washed river rocks, led to a spacious, multi-headed, two-person shower with jets on all sides of the walls. A lengthy, built-in bench held court at the rear wall of the spacious shower.

Sarah was struck at how well-kept and clean the entire space was, and she wondered why Travis had gone to the expense of building such a grand and luxurious master bath, obviously meant to accommodate a couple, while he had remained single for all these years? She marveled at the symmetry throughout his home and how well designed every detail and aspect of its furnishings and accessories were. The log home held a feel of reverence and respect for nature and the Southwest history, while at the same time, the open, clean lines and straightforwardness reflected a refinement in the art and overall design that held Sarah spellbound. With its openness and connectedness to the broad expanse of the western skies, it perfectly reflected Travis's bigger-than-life demeanor, unable to be hemmed in or fully known.

She quickly found the commode room, tucked to the side of the luxurious bathroom, and availed herself of its use. Returning to the bath, she hesitated to use his shower, but finding clean towels she hastily managed a Texas shower over the sink. Once finished, Sarah made her way back to the bedroom wrapped in a towel and returned the small woolen lap blanket to the back of the chair. Throwing the bed covers aside a second time, her search for her clothes remained fruitless. Turning back toward the bathroom again, she stopped at the open door of the walk-in closet, and then entered the large space, surveying the impressive array of neatly hung clothes in two tiers around the room's circumference. Jackets and sport coats were neatly aligned in one upper section, while trousers were color coordinated below. Shirts and jeans shared billing, with built-in shelving, tie racks, and shoe storage all filling out the sides. She brushed her hand lightly across the neatly hung shirts, then gathered their sleeves and brought them to her face, lingering in their scent. A subtle tingling washed over her at his scent and she asked herself how it was even possible that she found herself standing in Travis's closet. After a momentary pause, she took one of his more casual-looking cotton sport shirts from a hanger and quickly put it on, buttoning it from the chest down. Although Sarah felt a bit awkward taking the liberty to do so, the shirt felt less cumbersome and uncomfortable than the blanket or towel. She managed to find a brush and comb and did what little she could to make herself presentable, rinsing her mouth with the tooth paste resting on the counter. Without a clip or binder for her hair, she combed it to one side, letting it fall free but tucking it behind her ear.

Sarah found herself dazed thinking about the last twenty-four hours and how she had been so unsure of Travis. The night she had just spent with him was surreal, as if from a dream, and she could hardly process the events of the last few days and how he had appeared back in her life so unexpectedly. Two days ago, she was at a book signing starting a new single life and never would have guessed she would come face to face with Travis Hall again. She could not conceive being this happy, and she was certain Travis was the only man alive who could make her feel this way. For the first time in her life, she knew the true joy of loving someone completely and receiving the overwhelming happiness and joy that their love afforded them. For years, she had deluded herself into believing what she had with Kenny was the best life had to offer anyone, and she tried to convince herself life wouldn't have been any better if she had been able to be with Travis. She now understood clearly that, to love someone completely, there had to be something more than what she had shared with Ken. There had always been something missing, and to have been with Travis was to realize the thrilling passion and tenderness that had escaped her in her marriage. She had discovered a side of herself she never knew existed, and felt a new sense of wholeness.

She headed back to the master bedroom and took the iron handle of the heavy bedroom door in hand, pulling it open. The scent of freshly brewed coffee filled the air as Sarah walked across the great room toward the kitchen, admiring the subtle and different feel of the space in the early morning light. The broad expanse of the wall of windows captured the intense and dramatic display of light and darkness set against the majestic heights of the distant mountains paying homage to the rising sun. She stopped to catch her breath at the seeming newness of the vision by comparison to yesterday's compelling play of late-afternoon color, brooding purple shadows and inexpressible beauty. A constantly changing kaleidoscope of living colors moved ceaselessly from dawn till dusk, creating a fresh canvas at every hour, beckoning the eye to witness. Sarah sensed a great and holy majesty here in this place, demanding her reverence and constant adoration. The Rim was indeed Travis's place of worship, and she felt its awe-inspiring power.

She turned the corner and stood in the arched entry to the kitchen, but Travis wasn't there either. Making her way to the coffee pot, she found a note resting beneath a clean cup. It read: "Be back soon, checking stock. Hope coffee isn't too strong! T." Sarah smiled to herself. *He couldn't have shortened it any more if he tried.* The very thought of him brought an excitement inside, accompanied by an electrifying sensation, and Sarah wondered how, after all these years, he was still able to make her feel like a lovesick teenager. She poured her coffee and savored its richness as she surveyed her beautiful surroundings.

The gourmet kitchen was a delight to sit in, and she took in all of its appointments. The center island surface was constructed of hard maple, serving as a chopping block, and stood beneath a combination iron pot rack and decorative light supported from the tall ceiling by heavy chains. The rack's large oval circumference sported mini metal castings shaped like shadow portraits of cattle, horses, Indians, and teepees, with horseshoe hooks beneath carrying pots and pans of various sizes. Granite counters capped the polished alder-wood cabinetry, and a hammered, metal hood with metal studs and straps stood guard above the restaurant-sized commercial gas range.

Sarah made her way to the deep double sinks to admire the view from the arched window above. The view from the log home's elevated vantage point allowed her to see down toward the horse barn and small corral, as well as part of the road from the lengthy driveway. A silver pickup drove up to the barn and parked near its entrance. She watched as Travis exited the truck and headed to the faucet and watering tank sitting adjacent to the fence. He took off his dusty and sweat-stained straw Stetson, wiping his brow on his sleeve. Removing his shirt and hanging it on a post, along with his hat, he turned the faucet on and held his head beneath the running water. After soaking his head, and splashing his arms and chest, he shook his head, releasing the excess water droplets from his drenched hair. Sarah couldn't help but admire his sculptured and well-defined physique, understanding that he was still very much acquainted with physical labor and that it helped to keep him in such good shape. She suddenly wondered if her brief calculations about his age were correct and reminded herself to find the appropriate time to broach the subject. The truth was, she was still wildly attracted to him, regardless of how old he was. He still maintained that same rugged and manly appearance she cherished so much, despite the more weathered look, including the deeper lines etched across his face and the graying of his hair.

She loved everything about him, including his direct and uncomplicated way of expressing himself, as well as his genuine humility—never drawing attention to himself or looking for accolades despite his accomplishments and successes in life. He could be playful, but at the same time, he had a more sensitive side that he could articulate, unexpectedly, when he felt moved to do so. His inner strength and determination, expressed in his deep-set green eyes, were what Sarah felt most strongly, as if he could bear anything, regardless of the weight or pain it carried. The ability he displayed in being able to prioritize according to order of importance allowed him to simply bypass life's little annoyances without letting them affect him, while Sarah always found herself bogged down in those details. Combined with his willingness to give of himself so freely, Sarah could only remain in love with him as well as in awe of him. Travis was everything she was not, and her heart could not contain the admiration and love she bore for him. His thoughts were always difficult to guess, but that added to his intrigue and mystery, and if she asked or pressed him, he would always share them in his own direct way. Her heart pounded faster as he put on his shirt and headed to the house.

Standing in the archway leading to the kitchen from the hall, Sarah held her cup in hand, hesitating to enter the foyer; she still felt awkward without her own clothing. Travis made his entrance and immediately hung his Stetson on one of the horns of the hall tree. Using the bootjack, he removed his mud-crusted boots and turned to see Sarah standing in the archway leading to the kitchen, watching him. He smiled back at her with that quiet, unassuming smile she treasured so much, and she found herself at a loss of words.

"Good morning!" he said, with a rakish smile, as if he were thoroughly entertained at seeing her wearing one of his much-too-large shirts. It was hanging so loosely on her that it practically fell off one shoulder, requiring her to hold it closed when she walked. "Did you sleep well?" he asked as he walked over to join her.

The sensation of fluttering butterflies grew in her stomach as he approached her, and she thought how silly of her to still have that same reaction to him after the intimacy they had already shared. His affect on her was powerful and overwhelming. "A little too well, I'm afraid," she answered, still feeling off-balance, pulling the shirt closed at the neck. She had never before allowed herself such a departure from her normally proper and chaste behavior. "I'm . . . sorry about the use of your shirt, but I couldn't find my clothes."

"That shirt never looked that good on me, and I must say, I much prefer it on you. I hung your clothes up this morning on my way out," he said with a telltale smile and twinkle in his eye. "I see you found the coffee," he commented as he made his way into the kitchen and picked up his cup from the sink. Pulling the pot from the coffeemaker, he turned to offer to fill Sarah's cup first, but suddenly stopped, his eyes fixed on her. Sarah stood barefoot in the archway between the foyer and kitchen trying to decipher his sudden halt. She could feel the heat of the sun rays grazing her back as it spilled into the foyer. Watching him closely, Travis slowly wetted his lower lip forming a lazy upturn at the corners of his mouth while staring at her. His devilish expression gave himself away.

Until that moment she hadn't considered that the sun light might be casting a silhouette of her body against the thin cotton shirt she wore, and she immediately moved into the room holding the neckline of the shirt a little tighter, feeling slightly off balance at her sudden awareness. Travis held his thoughts, still sporting his grin. He slowly raised the pot with a twist of his head in an offering gesture, keeping his playful smile. Sarah walked toward him holding her cup in one hand and the shirt closed with the other. He took the cup from her hand and placed it down on the counter, then placed the coffee pot back on the hot plate. Saying nothing, he reached out and brought his hand to the back of Sarah's neck and wrapped the other arm around her waist, pulling her to him. Without restraint, he brought his parted lips to hers kissing her passionately, forcing her tender body against his hardened chest. It was a long, languorous kiss, tender and undulating, thrilling in its heated and unexpected delivery. Sarah molded to him like putty yearning for its impression, wrapping her arms around him and relishing the feel of the taught muscles across his broad and dampened back. Being so utterly carried away by him in an instant was almost madness. She was overcome at how easily he could stir her, as well as at her own willingness to accept him so unconditionally. His need was her need as well. Nothing ever felt so compulsively unified or perfectly shared in all her life.

Travis slowly released his hold on her, keeping in check their passions, then tenderly brushed the strands of Sarah's hair to the side of her forehead with his fingers. Turning back to the counter again, he filled her cup and then his own, handing Sarah her coffee.

Together they made their way to the built-in table and bench seating in the alcove, at the side of the kitchen. The large windows surrounding the nook offered a good view of the small pasture next to the corral, and several horses, including Trixy, enjoyed the freedom and grass the pasture provided. Sarah slipped into one side of the cushioned bench seating, crimping her eyes shut with a slight grimace. Travis pulled up a chair sitting next to her on the open side watching her as she slowly eased herself down on to the bench. A subtle knowing smile formed on his lips accentuating the mischievous look in his eyes as Sarah blushed in embarrassment. "I don't know what you have planned for us today," she said, "but I do hope it doesn't include the need to see anything from the back of a horse!"

Laughing out loud, Travis didn't try to hide his amusement. "The day is ours, Sarah, and I'll do my best to make it enjoyable," he said while still smiling. "We could try a few tourist sites from the seat of the car, like the natural stone bridge, or head to Christopher Creek for lunch, or maybe you'd like to see Zane Gray's old residence where he lived for a time writing many of his novels. After that, we could come back here, hang out, and grill a couple steaks. I thought we'd play it by ear today and just take it slow and easy."

"I'd be happy doing any of that, only I've got to get back to the hotel for a change of clothes and shower," Sarah pleaded.

"All right, I'll take you back right after breakfast. I'll run a few errands and finish up here with a few extra chores I've been putting off doing for far too long. How much time do you need?"

"Would three hours give you enough time to finish your chores?"

"Perfect! I'll drop you off after breakfast and pick you back up by noon." Travis went to the refrigerator and pulled out a slab of bacon and some eggs as Sarah got up to help. He knew his way around the kitchen and was certainly used to fending for himself. *How could he be more perfect?*

After breakfast, Travis retrieved Sarah's clothes from the second master bedroom closet and left Sarah to dress while he went to get his pickup and bring it back to the house. On the ride back to the hotel, Travis took her hand in his and brought it to his lips, gently kissing the back of it and then telling her how happy he was to have shared the last day with her. Sarah was genuinely moved at how free he was in expressing his love, and she wondered how she could have missed his signals all along. She couldn't remember when life had ever felt so good. The expression "walking on air" didn't adequately describe what she was feeling, though it was as close as she could come in that moment.

Travis pulled up under the hotel portico, parked the truck, and got out to open the door for her. He offered his hand just as he had done the first night they were reunited. Sarah slowly left the seat of the truck with his aid, and she could still detect the slight grin as he was reminded of her discomfort. When she stood with both feet firmly on the ground, he whispered in her ear that he had a remedy for her problem and would be happy to share it with her later. *His timing for sharing his sense of humor is impeccable,* she thought, noting that the public place did not dissuade him from sharing his playful banter. He gently kissed her cheek, and then reminded her he would be back at noon to pick her up. Travis held the door open to the hotel for Sarah and then returned to the truck as Sarah entered the lobby.

Stopping off at the front desk, Sarah caught the attention of the slightly overweight, middle-aged woman in attendance. "Good morning, I'm Sarah Birk in room 107, and I wondered if there were any messages left for me."

"No, I'm afraid not, Ms. Birk. Travis told me to take special care of you, and I'd remember if you had a message."

Sarah realized the clerk knew Travis well enough to be on a first name basis.

Curiosity got the best of her. "If you don't mind my asking, how long have you known Travis?"

"I guess I've known him ever since I was a kid growing up here. Everyone around these parts knows the Halls," she said emphatically.

"So, you know Jessica as well?"

"Sure, she's one of the best barrel racers around this part of the country, and I know his wife, Mary, too."

Sarah's heart felt like it had just been penetrated by a twelve-inch dagger. The pain was swift and acute. In a state of semi-denial, Sarah brought herself to finally ask, "What do you mean his wife? I thought he was divorced."

"I guess a lot of people think that because she stays down in the valley and hardly ever comes up to Payson. Word has it Travis bought her a real nice place in Phoenix. She always said she hated it up here. Mary only shows up around here once in a blue moon, usually to raise Cain. Come to think of it, I can't say I've seen her in Payson in a very long time, though I'm not sorry about that, if you'll pardon me for saying so. It's really too bad, because they just don't make 'em any better than Travis Hall. He's the salt of the earth. Can I do any thing else for you, Ms. Birk?"

Sarah was numb and wanted desperately to refuse belief. Her insides had just been ripped out of her and she could hardly think. A ghostly white pallor enveloped her face as she could feel the blood draining from her cheeks.

"Are you all right?" the friendly desk clerk suddenly asked.

The clerk's concerned question shook Sarah out of her sudden stupor. "Just a little too much sun, I think. I'll be fine. Thanks for your help."

Sarah turned to walk to her room, feeling the sudden urge to vomit, but gulped, swallowing twice forcing bodily restraint. Using sheer will power alone, she pushed on to her room as quickly as possible. Once inside her room, Sarah fell back against the closing door as a volcano of repressed emotions erupted to the surface. With the flood gates now open, she clutched at her chest and sobbed uncontrollably—deep, heaving sobs, painful in their force, and uncontrollable. She slid down to the floor while pressed against the back of the door, unable to hold her weight in a standing position. Sarah's pain was total and consuming, reaching into a deep chasm never tapped before. She sat on the floor, weeping for at least ten minutes, till she had no more tears left to cry. How could she have been so naive? The hurt she felt was unbearable. Travis had meant everything to her, and she gave to him all that was hers to give. She had emptied herself like a vessel of wine at a symposium until she was completely drained, exposing her earthen essence. Over the course of her life, she had felt extreme longing and desire, inexplicable ecstasy and passion and, now, unbelievable heartbreak with sorrowful shame, all at the hand of the one man she now knew she could never hope to have or fully understand. She sat there, dazed and blank, empty and lost. The betrayal had been so complete, and she, like a lovesick child, fell totally under his spell, as if the die had been cast all those years ago.

How was she to live from this moment forward? Sarah looked at the time, and then pulled herself up. She never wanted to see him again! She would not put herself in harm's way by having to confront him. Sarah made her way to the bathroom, took off her clothes, and stepped into the shower, letting the heat of the water roll down her back for a protracted period of time, hoping to wash away the layers of emotion she was experiencing. Travis would be returning in another two and half hours from now. Sarah quickly dried her hair, donned her clothes, and packed all her belongings. She dialed the front desk and asked for the number of a local car-rental company, and then informed the desk clerk she would be checking out. After making arrangements to be picked up in thirty minutes, Sarah retrieved her airline ticket from her purse and called to change her departure from tomorrow to the earliest available flight today. She would need at least three hours to make the trip back down to Sky Harbor Airport, allowing enough time to turn in the rental car and get checked in. Fortunately, she was able to secure a seat on a 3:30 p.m. departure. Moving quickly now, Sarah finished packing, then headed to the lobby to meet the car-rental sales representative who would pick her up and bring her back to their office to fill out the rental agreement and assign her a car. Once in the lobby, Sarah went to the front desk and requested the bill to check out from the same lady she had spoken with earlier. The look of surprise on the clerk's face was noticeable. "I do hope everything is all right, Ms. Birk, since we had you booked through tomorrow?"

"Everything is fine—I've just had a sudden change in plans. May I please have my bill?"

"It's already been paid for, Ms. Birk."

"Do you have an envelope please?"

"Certainly," the clerk responded politely, and then handed one to Sarah.

Sarah took a card indicating the rates for the room off the counter and then took out her checkbook and wrote out a check for the amount of the room's rental, adding enough for what she thought would cover the miscellaneous taxes. She scribed the words "hotel room expense" in the lower left corner of the check's remark section. Sticking the check into the envelope, she sealed it with no other note included, and addressed it to Mr. Travis Hall. Handing it back to the clerk, she asked, "Would you be so kind as to make sure to deliver this to Mr. Hall when he returns at noon?"

"Sure thing, Ms. Birk," she replied. "Will we be seeing you in Payson again anytime soon?"

Sarah bit her tongue and tried to respond without showing the sting the question had brought. "As beautiful as this part of the country is, I'm afraid I won't be returning anytime soon."

The rental company arrived right on time at 10:45 a.m., and Sarah left, not looking back, hoping to put as much distance as she could between herself and Travis Hall.

The long drive back down to the valley of the sun had Sarah operating on autopilot, unable to rejoice in the dramatic and glorious beauty that abounded the entire distance. She was wrapped in a cocoon, gone within to hide from the world of the living, unwilling to be exposed to any further sensory perception, having been whipped into non-feeling. She drove by sheer rote memory, brooding inside, replaying the signs she had missed and vowing never to allow herself to fall victim to such again.

Why had he already made the hotel reservation in advance of their meeting when he didn't know she was now a widow, or did he just assume he could lure her to his place, thinking she was an easy mark, regardless of her marital status? Perhaps he thought that she, like so many others of her generation, could simply do their own thing without conscience and enjoy an open marriage, like he apparently shared. And then, when she had asked him if he was married, he implied he had been divorced for years without actually saying so. How deceitful, cunning, and convincing he had been. She had heard only what she wanted to believe. When she questioned in her thinking why Travis had built such a grand master bath with his-and-her amenities, it never occurred to her that he still had a wife who might be sharing his home, even if only infrequently. It hadn't felt exactly right, but she never brought herself to question it any further. How stupid of her not to have looked into the second closet, which was closed at the time, allowing him to retrieve her clothes which he was careful to return himself, and she, like a fool, respected the privacy the closed door implied. It was all becoming so clear to her, and because she loved him so desperately, all of it was missed. How would she ever heal after a lifetime of living with his memory engraved in her heart? She had the sickening feeling she had become another inconsequential conquest on a broad list of names whose faces he might very well be unable to recall. The pain was unbearable and cut to the heart of her because she had loved him so completely.

Sarah remained as if in a trance, finally boarding the aircraft and at last leaving behind the one place on earth awesome in its pristine beauty and the place where she had suffered her most grievous pain. It was the perfect reflection of the dichotomy and incongruity of her walk with Travis Hall. She went from sublime ecstasy to sheer heartbreak all in the space of a day and a half. She watched as the vision of Phoenix and Arizona disappeared beneath the clouds, and vowed it was the closing of the last chapter of a very long and torturous novel.

~~~~~~~~~~

Travis drove his BMW to the hotel, anxious to pick Sarah up while reflecting on his good fortune. He asked himself how he had been able to live this long without her. She was still ravishingly beautiful, totally oblivious to that fact, and she remained untainted by the shadier side of life. She was filled with an uncommon
~~~~~~~~~~

virtue still bordering on innocence but was also able to give and receive love openly with genuine sincerity and, he now knew, with unbridled passion as well. He knew her to be kind and caring, full of empathy—though she could easily exert her will when necessary or when provoked. She was a real woman, and a true lady in every respect. Sarah was everything he had ever wanted in a woman, and his opinion and assessment of her was the same now as it had been nearly thirty years ago. *God, I love her*, he thought.

At 12:00-noon sharp, Travis Hall pulled up to the hotel and parked the BMW not far from the front entrance. He had finished his chores at the ranch in plenty of time to shower, and even had time to stop at the package shop for a bottle of his favorite merlot. He couldn't hide the spring in his step, feeling the joy of anticipation at being with Sarah again. Entering the lobby, he could see that Sarah was not yet there. He walked to the front desk and tapped the bell, hoping to get her room number. The clerk came out from behind a wall that camouflaged the office and gave Travis a friendly smile. "Hey, Travis, how's it going?"

"I couldn't be better, Becky! How are the kids?" He smiled back at her.

"Like everybody else's I guess, getting into trouble and eating us out of house and home!"

Travis nodded with a slight grin and then asked, "What room number is Sarah Birk in? She is expecting me to pick her up about now."

Becky had a look of concern on her face and said, "I guess she didn't call you. Ms. Birk checked out this morning."

"You must be mistaken and have her confused with someone else," He stated definitively.

"Oh no, I'm quite certain it was her, and she even left this envelope for you," Becky said as she reached beneath the counter, retrieving the sealed envelope addressed to him. Travis ripped it open, hoping for an explanation but only finding her check, covering the cost of the hotel, inside. He suddenly felt as if he had just taken a sucker punch to the gut.

"I do hope everything is all right. I thought she looked a little pale when she came in this morning, but she insisted she was fine."

"What do you mean she looked a little pale? I was with Sarah earlier this morning, and there was nothing wrong with her. Exactly what did she say to you?" he demanded in a stern tone.

"Well . . . I don't know, Travis. It was just everyday chitchat and nothing out of the ordinary."

"I want to know everything she discussed with you," Travis requested again forcefully.

"Okay, let me try to remember. . . . She wanted to know if there were any messages, and I told her there were none, and that I would have remembered since you had asked me to pay her special attention."

"What else did you say to her?"

Becky strained to recall the rest of the conversation. "She asked me how long I knew you, and I told her since I was a child and that most everyone around here knew your family."

"Go on," Travis prodded.

"I'm trying to remember exactly. Oh yeah, she asked if I knew Jessica, and I told her I knew both Jessica and Mary."

Travis pursed his lips as the blood drained from his face. Doing his best to control himself, he pushed her for more information. "What did you tell her about Mary?"

"Gosh, I don't know, Travis. I may have mentioned how she doesn't like it up here and stays down in Phoenix, and that I hadn't seen her in a real long time. I hope I didn't divulge anything I shouldn't have. I only did my best to answer her questions. I figured I didn't tell her anything everybody up here didn't already know anyway."

Travis drew in a deep breath and rubbed the back of his neck with his hand. He felt as if a freight train had just hit him, and he couldn't hold Becky responsible for his own screwed-up life. Totally drained, he continued in a calmer tone, "I'm sorry, Becky—you haven't said anything inappropriate, and I'm sorry for behaving so out of sorts. What time did Sarah leave?" he asked, checking the time.

"I suppose it was still within checkout time, so I'm guessing a little before eleven a.m."

No way could he catch up to her with more than an hour's head start, and even if he could, what could he possibly say to her now to make her understand why he hadn't told her the whole truth from the beginning?

Travis left the lobby and headed to his car, totally defeated and wounded, unable to stop the pain in his heart from growing stronger with each passing minute. He had waited a lifetime to finally be with Sarah and didn't want to do or say anything that might jeopardize his chance of realizing his dream to be with her. He had planned on telling her everything but couldn't risk doing so until he was certain she felt the same way and was willing to start a new life with him. How could he make her understand she was the one he had always loved, and could he even get her to listen, knowing what she must be thinking and feeling in this moment? He had no one to blame but himself, and he would have to think long and hard about how to repair the terrible damage and pain his defensive actions had caused. Travis could not accept the thought that he might not ever see her again; he would never let go of her. How could he? She was in him and was part of his very soul. They had been bound together from the beginning, and no time or distance was ever able to put out the burning light of his love for her that even years of separation had failed to squelch. If he had waited this long for the possibility of them to be together, he would hold on to hope longer and somehow try to repair the damage his silence had already caused. Wounded and discouraged, he was headed back home, and it would never be the same there again, unless Sarah was at his side.

Once back in his truck, Travis pulled her check out again from the envelope and noted that the upper left-hand corner conveniently recorded her address; it would make getting her telephone number an easier task. He would give her some time and space before attempting to contact her, hoping the wound he had caused wouldn't be as raw with a few weeks' separation. It would also give him the time to think of a way to present his reasoning for withholding all his history and at the same time convince her that he had always loved her.

Travis folded the envelope and put it back in his shirt pocket, then started the truck and headed back to the now empty and lonely ranch.

CHAPTER FORTY-FOUR

SEPTEMBER 1990

The days felt weighted and lengthy, and Sarah bore her disillusion with a melancholy and brooding, unable to rise from the valley she found herself forced to walk in. She was grieving inside for all that would never be, and all she had longed for, as if part of herself had died. If only she were able to think back on her time with Travis as just a casual and pleasant sexual diversion, like so many of her generation were able to do. She never could separate the physical from the emotional, and with him, it was impossible. Nothing was casual about her feelings for Travis Hall. She had been deeply in love with him, and he was the never-ending flame she turned to time and again when life's burdens were heavy or when she needed the happiness that only thoughts of him would provide.

That retreat was now gone, burned away by the man himself.

It was difficult to remember the feeling of youthful love, when she had been carried away by him as if by soft billowing clouds floating effortlessly in the clear blueness of a new sky. The purity and innocence of the unknown added to the exhilaration of love when it had been a thing dreamt of and wondered about. Just as the clouds had the inevitable way of bringing rain, so too had the realities of life taken on a cruel realism that cut deep with pain, hurt, and betrayal.

The time and distance between them now allowed her to see the uncovered truth without the raw emotion of their last encounter. Sarah thought how long ago her love for him had been planted in her heart, and how she had been drawn to him from the first moment they met. He had captivated her with his powerful presence, his unmatched intelligence, and his inner strength. But his unassuming smile, his willingness to endure to the finish line with her when she lost hope in herself as his student, and his tender gentleness filled with passion in their lovemaking brought Sarah back, over and over again, to that hidden place of love she held for him. In so many ways, he was her life. She had grown up with him in her heart. He was there first when she was still a young, inexperienced teen, and he taught her what it was to feel the pangs of love. He had meant everything to her, and she gave to him all that was hers to give in return. Its death, like a long obituary in the making, tarried to grasp the past, clutching at the essence of what once was. Sarah's love for him was an unrequited love, resembling a rosebud whose fullness of blossom was denied at the hand of a pruner's harsh sheer. What was left was only a hint of color, a glimpse of what might have been.

She could not erase him or the imprint his life had left on hers, but she would continue on, despite his consuming absence now. She had refused his calls time and again over the past five months since her return, until they ceased to come any longer. Although she had much to be grateful for, the knowledge that he could never be a part of her life shrouded her heart with such sorrow that she mourned the loss of the innocent hope she had always secretly carried. She had her children and her writing, though that too had suffered since her return. The fundraisers and charity work helped, even though it meant moving in the same old social circle of climbers and status seekers. The money raised went to those in need, and Sarah found peace in that, tolerating the excesses of others and their need to brandish and pontificate their generosity. To see and to be seen was a burdensome duty for Sarah, who much preferred the quiet solitude of her writing.

It had shocked and disturbed her that, after Kenny's death, many of his so-called friends had considered her fair game for the taking, as if their infidelity was some sort of badge of honor one was expected to earn in life. How sad if Kenny would have known the depth of their depravity. But then she cautioned herself to consider that if the tables had been turned the other way, perhaps Ken too might have succumbed to such a temptation. Travis Hall had played that role, and she never would have suspected him of such duplicity. To be awakened to the prevalence of human weakness and infidelity only served to push Sarah away from the life she once lived before Ken's death. Had her marriage and their fidelity all been a lie as well?

She had been as guilty as the rest, marrying Ken because he came from the right family and her father thought it was the right match, while she had always loved Travis. Trying to do the right thing, she had followed a path others chose for her, hoping to please them. The guilt of her own duplicity hurt her the most. The only difference between her and the others was she never crossed over the fine line of fidelity, even though that was only by God's grace since Travis had vanished without a trace.

It was her own wishful thinking, but the mere thought of him had always brought her to a thrilling high that captured the essence of love, and she could no longer be without the feeling that only thoughts of him could provide. He was always there, beckoning her to a time and place when love was strongest and he had captured her heart. It had mattered very little to Sarah that her love for Travis would never be anything more than a childish memory. Travis Hall was her refuge and happiness she could find nowhere else.

In her sadness now, Sarah asked herself whom she could run to when she needed the feeling of love or sense of joy only he had always provided her. The truth was she had always been madly in love with him, and their recent time spent together only served to solidify that fact. He could make her tremble inside with a glance, and his smile brought her every defense tumbling down in happy surrender. His touch lit a thousand torches across her captive body, and his tender kisses gave way to a sublime loss of all thought. The deception and heartbreak, knowing they could never be with one another, was more than she could bear, no matter the fact that he hadn't lied outright to her. It was a deep betrayal unworthy of him. Just as before, an insurmountable wall rose between them. In her youth, his position as teacher and her as underage student disallowed any thought of relationship, and now, it was too late for them since he had a wife, and Sarah, once again, was to remain off-limits to him and he to her. A cruel twist of fate had brought them so close yet so far from one another twice in their lives. What act of fate would repeatedly light such a flame and then allow it to die such a painful, untimely death without it reaching its full potential? Sarah could not conceive of her life without him, for he was a part of her, and she knew no way to rid herself of him in her heart. For better or for worse, Travis Hall would remain the love of her life.

Lifting herself from her chair, Sarah checked the clock and walked to the hall, donning her coat and scarf. She made her way out the door, heading for the mailbox, going through the motions of her daily routine. Returning to the house, she hung her coat and walked back to the kitchen, throwing the mail down on the kitchen table. The damp chilliness sent Sarah back to the stove, where she turned on the water for tea. With her cup in hand, she returned to the table, sat down and started sorting through the pile of mail, weeding the junk from the bills. Toward the bottom of the pile, Sarah picked up a plain white business envelope with her name and address printed by hand on the front. There was no return address on either side, and Sarah thought the printing looked vaguely familiar. After closer examination, her eyes widened, and her heart started to race. Knowing full well whom it was from, she placed the letter back down on the table, her face inflamed by rising heat. She wasn't sure she should open it, afraid to hear what Travis Hall had to say. Even if his separation back in '69 were true, as he had implied, the hotel clerk plainly stated they were still married. If they truly "parted ways" twenty-one years ago, why was he still married now, and what type of relationship did he and his wife really share? Being separated or merely estranged didn't equal a divorce and short of that, he was off limits and unavailable. Travis conveniently neglected to share those details. If she had been privy to that information the first day of their reunion, her moral compass would never have allowed an affair. She had refused his calls and was not yet ready or strong enough to come to terms with the role he had played in her life. She was still wounded, trying to move past him.

With her pulse racing, she stared down at the envelope for a few more minutes, fingering it intermittently, wavering between wanting desperately to read it and, at the same time, contemplating tearing it up and throwing it away. Another minute passed before Sarah finally composed herself, and then took the letter opener in hand and cut open the envelope's edge. Grinding her teeth, she slowly drew a deep breath while sliding her hand into the envelope, unfolding the letter tucked inside. Sarah read his words slowly, holding back her tears.

My Dearest Sarah,

I hope this letter makes its way into your hands and that you would find it in your heart to read what I'm about to tell you. If these words are never read, I can't say that I would blame you. I am deserving of such treatment as you see fit. There is so much I need to confess to you but would like to start at the beginning and hope you will recognize the truth in what I'm about to tell you.

The first day I laid eyes on you in 1962 changed my life forever. You must believe me when I tell you that I fell in love with you then, as I remain to this day. To be with you, day in and day out, that year was a very great challenge I freely admit to failing. Forgive me if I speak for you when I say that I knew you, too, felt the same way. There was little I could do to change the predicament we both found ourselves in, other than to hope we might meet again when your schooling was complete and you had graduated.

Life doesn't always take us down the road of our own choosing, and after I arrived home at the end of the '62-'63 school year, my father suffered a stroke. I want you to know that it was my plan to return as soon as possible or at least before your graduation. Sadly, my father lingered for a long time until his death many months latter. During this time, it became evident that the family ranch had taken on more debt than any of us realized. In order to keep the ranch, I took a job with Honeywell down in the valley and spent my weekends up on the Rim to work the ranch and help bring it back to profitability. I want to tell you the rest in person, but I need to share this much now for you to see the truth of my enduring love for you and that our brief time together earlier this past spring was not a casual or one-time thing.

Do you remember you once asked me to write down an equation expressing Love? After I returned to Arizona, I tried to do just that, as I was feeling your absence in my life very strongly.

Last March when you were here with me, I brought you to my getaway spot where I told you I would often go to think and where I had hoped to build a smaller cabin in the future. Of all the trees you could choose to hide behind that day, you went to the one where I had carved a crude attempt at an equation expressing my love for you some twenty-seven years earlier when I first arrived back home. It was not meant to indicate the Logs, Timbers and Studs needed for the cabin as I told you when you asked about it. This is the key to its meaning.

L = Love

SS = Sarah Student

TT = Travis Teacher

2 = Second Chance

$>$ = greater than

∞ = infinity

This is what I carved in a very unrefined and simplistic way:

$$2L - 2SS = 2TT$$

$$2L = 2TT + 2SS$$

$$\frac{\not{2}L}{\not{2}} = \frac{\not{2}TT + \not{2}SS}{\not{2}}$$

$$L = TT + SS > \infty$$

I knew, in order for it to work out between us, I had to get both of us on the same side of the equation, and that required a second chance at love. Once that chance was made possible, the 2s would cancel each other out, leaving both of us on the same side. If I could somehow make that happen, I believed that the equation expressing love was as simple as "Love equals Travis Teacher and Sarah Student, a love greater than infinity." Little did I know then the number of years it would take to bring about my desire to have the equation proved. I believe in my heart, Sarah, that we were always meant to be together, and I'm asking you for the chance to let me explain the rest of the story to you in person. I did not lie to you. My wife and I separated twenty one years ago. If you have it in your heart to listen, please let me explain.
No man knows the number of his days, but I do know that whatever that number is for me, I want to spend all of them I have left with you, Sarah. Please, let me see your face once more and allow me to explain to you that what appears to be a lie is, in fact, something quite different. If you believe nothing else, know that I do love you, now and always.

Forever yours,
Travis

Sarah wept uncontrollably as she held his letter to her chest. The fact that he had loved her all those years ago and never forgot her deeply affected her, but how could it work out between them now? She was more upset than ever and didn't know what to do.

Checking the clock one more time, she returned to the hall for her coat and grabbed her handbag on the way to the garage. His words required more thought than she was capable of expending in that moment, and Sarah needed a lifeline thrown by another who was not caught in the same turbulent sea.

CHAPTER FORTY-FIVE

Sarah pulled into the parking lot of the Plainview strip mall and parked in front of Morty's Delicatessen and Restaurant. The best time to catch Nonie to steal a few minutes to talk with her was between the lunch and dinner hours. When she entered the second set of double doors, a few patrons were still at the counter with a smattering of customers seated at the tables interspersed around the room. The scent of corned beef and cabbage filled the air and mingled with the smell of freshly baked breads and pastries. The hostess stand was unoccupied, and Sarah made her way to the baked-goods showcase. Bent down behind the colorful pastry display case, two women were restocking the extravagant sweets, presented in perfectly even rows. Leaning over the showcase, Sarah caught sight of Nonie.

"What does a person have to do to get a table around here?" Sarah called out jokingly, trying to hide her apprehension.

"Good God, Sarah, where did you come from?" Nonie exclaimed.

"I'm sorry I didn't call first, but something important has come up. Have you got time to talk?"

Nonie assessed the look on Sarah's face determining it was time to head to the chairman's booth. "I'll be in back, Sylvia. I'm sure you can fill in without me," Nonie directed her assistant as she made her way back around the case to Sarah's side. "Well, this must be important for you to show up in the middle of the afternoon like this." They made their way to the last booth in the rear of the restaurant, Sarah sitting restlessly in her seat. "I haven't seen you like this in years. What in the world has come over you, Sarah?"

Sarah took a deep breath, reigning in her emotions, though her demeanor and restlessness gave her away. "Nonie," she started out slowly, "I don't know what to do."

"You don't know what to do about what?"

Sarah tried her best not to get emotional and continued, "I got a letter in the mail today, and I'm more confused than ever. I honestly don't know how to handle this."

"Who is the letter from?" Nonie asked with a puzzled look.

"Travis Hall."

Nonie leaned back in the booth, her mouth falling open at hearing the news. "Well, he certainly has a lot of chutzpah; I'll give him that! Just what did he have to say for himself?" she asked after the look of shock wore off her face.

"I thought I was through with him for good, and then he sent this." Sarah reached into her purse and pulled out his letter, handing it to Nonie. Sarah remained silent as Nonie opened the letter, leaning back in the booth as she read. Sarah watched Nonie carefully, hoping to gauge her reaction through her facial expressions. Nonie's large brown eyes widened as she turned the page, then, stopping halfway through, she caught her breath before continuing. When she was finished, she put the letter down on the table and looked directly at Sarah, sighing.

"My God, Sarah . . . I was right; he did have a thing for you all the way back in high school! For a man of so few words, he sure knows how to use them when he needs to," she exclaimed, fanning her face with the envelope.

"Nonie, I don't know what to believe or what not to believe. Should I trust him and go back out there to let him explain?" Sarah questioned with a heavy heart.

Nonie reached across the table and patted Sarah's hand affectionately. "You know, Sarah, we have been friends for far too long for me to ever tell you what to do, but I think you already have the answer you're looking for."

"No, I don't. I just can't think straight when it comes to him. What if I go back out there and I discover I was just another notch on his bedpost of naive women he's been able to corral over the years with the tidy little arrangement he has with his wife?"

"Sarah," Nonie started out thoughtfully, "it seems to me he did the right thing when he walked away from you all those years ago, knowing he had the opportunity and the advantage his position held over you. And, as I recall, it was only on account of him pulling out extra points from your Regents math exam on second review that you were able to pass that important test. Didn't you say he let you set the pace this last time also? You told me yourself he didn't force anything with you that you didn't agree to. He doesn't appear to be the kind of man who would deliberately take unfair advantage of another person for his own selfish ends. Nothing he has ever done regarding you would indicate that in his character."

"I just don't think I can face him again or . . . or I'll . . . "

"Or you'll what?

"I can't imagine what he could possibly say to me that would make any of this right, and I don't want to leave myself vulnerable to him again," Sarah said, shaking her head.

"I think you have to ask yourself if you really love him or not."

Sarah paused briefly, then confessed, as her eyes welled-up as she spoke, "I've always loved him, Nonie. No one has ever made me feel the way he does."

"You're a lot stronger than you think you are. Why don't you call him?"

"No... I don't want to do that," Sarah said, as she shook her head. "If I decide to let him explain, I need to see him face to face so I can gauge his truthfulness in his body language. This isn't something that can easily be resolved over the phone. He means far too much to me and this discussion deserves more than just a phone call could provide."

"You're probably right. It makes better sense to see him in person, and besides, what's the worst that can happen?" Nonie asked, shrugging. "If you don't believe his story, you can turn yourself around and come right back, knowing you gave it the chance it deserved. Wouldn't that be better than not going and always wondering if you should have? After all, he has left it in your hands, giving no ultimatum. He only asked if you would be willing to hear him out," Nonie reminded.

The knot in her stomach loosened as she realized Nonie was right. "I guess deep down inside I already felt that. It will take me a while to clear my calendar before I can leave, but I needed to hear it from someone else to make sure. Either way it goes, I guess I can't really lose something I never had to begin with!"

"It sounds like the right attitude and a good plan, if you ask me."

"You've always been there for me, Nonie, and I am so grateful for your friendship," Sarah said thankfully.

"That goes for both of us, and besides, we don't go this far back through thick or thin without learning a few things about each other!" They both laughed, knowing the chairman's booth had played its hand one more time across life's journey. Nonie didn't miss the opportunity to add, "I guess this calls for Bubbe's matzo ball soup!"

CHAPTER FORTY-SIX

Three weeks after receiving Travis Hall's letter, Sarah Birk boarded a plane headed to Phoenix. With all the commitments on her calendar finally cleared, Sarah was able to leave town. She hadn't called him, preferring instead a face-to-face meeting. A phone call couldn't convey the same understanding that being with him in person would reveal. Sarah had prepared herself for the worst, assuming little he could share would encourage further relationship, so long as he was still married, but she was convinced that hearing him out was the right thing to do. Of greater concern was whether she would be strong enough to withstand his power of persuasion, despite his marriage. She was vulnerable around him, and she didn't want to give him advanced warning of her arrival. If the hotel clerk had told her the truth about his wife rarely coming up to Payson, then her surprise visit would at a minimum, verify his separation. But even so, his explanation for that omission would still be standing on shaky ground. The fact that she couldn't recall knowing anyone who had remained "separated" after twenty one years, made all of this questionable at best. Still, his words from his letter filled her with hope.

Landing in Phoenix late that afternoon, Sarah rented a car before taking a hotel near the airport. She needed time to regroup and rest before heading to Payson the following morning. With her plan to leave no later than 11:30 a.m., she estimated her arrival in Payson at 2:00 p.m. Saturday afternoon. The long day and lengthy flight time was tiring, but sleep evaded her nonetheless. She lay awake in the dark, anxious about seeing him, and unsure how their meeting would resolve itself. Several different scenarios crossed her mind; none envisioned the ending she hoped for. Lying awake, thinking about tomorrow's visit, she began to realize how connected their lives had always been. Travis Hall stamped a deep and lasting impression on her, carrying her into womanhood. To finally know that he, too, had carried her memory for all those years encouraged her to return. No amount of time or distance had erased each other from both their memories. Whatever the outcome of their meeting, Sarah would always keep his words that he did indeed love her. Reliving moments shared together, she lulled herself into the darkness of sleep.

Sarah took her time getting ready to leave the following morning, still apprehensive as she put her bag into the trunk of the rental car. The sun was shining brightly, and the heat was extreme compared to her earlier visit back in March. She wore a floral-patterned, white sundress well suited for the heat, with a pair of thin-strapped sandals that offered airy, unrestricted comfort. The square-cut neckline and perfectly fitted bodice flared at the waist, while two wide straps crisscrossed over her back. Preparing for cooler temperatures in Payson, she carried a lightweight cardigan in a pale pink hue that highlighted the shades of pastel pink in the floral print of the dress. Pulling her hair back to the rear, she clipped part of it at the crown of her head, letting the rest fall free. The climate was much drier in Arizona, and it took much less time for her hair to dry. It was one of the pleasant observations she recalled from her first visit that helped to seal her fondness for the desert Southwest. Remembering to take along extra bottled water for the long drive, Sarah was ready to head north.

The scenery was equally grand as her earlier visit, though the desert was no longer in bloom. The dramatic and breathtaking landscape helped to pass away the more than two-hour drive, taking her thoughts away from what she might say to him. Arriving in Payson earlier than expected, she stopped for a few minutes at a fast-food restaurant for a much-needed break before proceeding on to the ranch. She had come a long way, and there was no turning back. She was marking a change in her life, one way or another, concerning him.

The road to the ranch was unpaved and off the beaten path. The crushed granite gravel provided a sound roadway surface, but Sarah wasn't used to the dust that the much dryer climate produced as she took her time negotiating the winding curves through the rugged, pine-topped mountains. There was no traffic out here, though she did pass one old pickup truck heading in the opposite direction, probably back to town. It wasn't the same model or same color as the pick-up truck she remembered Travis driving. This place was stunningly beautiful, but still untamed, the perfect place for Travis.

The entrance to the ranch came into view as she checked the time once more. She passed under the majestic log entrance at just after 2:00. Proceeding down the winding road, she eventually passed over the ford, which was now bone dry. The pasture was empty of cattle, and its springtime, deep green color gave way to large patches of rust-colored grass beneath the dryer skies of the ending summer. Approaching the barn, Sarah didn't see his pickup, and she was concerned he might not be home. She had planned for such an eventuality and reserved a room at the same hotel as before. Either way, it would be too late in the afternoon to make the long drive back down to the valley before nightfall. Continuing past the barn, she drove up the steep driveway to the massive log house, parking under the portico at the front entrance. Her pulse began to increase as she set the brakes, and then raised her shoulders, drawing a breath before stepping out of the car. With her straw hat, sweater, and handbag in hand, Sarah went to the oversized front door and rang the bell, waiting nervously.

A moment passed before a shadow flickered at the sidelight. The large entry door opened, revealing an attractive young woman. With a questioning look of surprise, the young woman stared back at Sarah from the now open door. Sarah was taken aback by her as well, but after a brief moment, Sarah recognized her from the many photos displayed around Travis's home.

"Hello, you must be Jessica," Sarah said, smiling slightly. The young woman's expression still carried a puzzled look, and Sarah continued, "Forgive me, I should have introduced myself."

Before Sarah could continue, Jessica spoke up with the startled look now vanished from her face. "Yes, I'm Jessie, and you must be Sarah."

"How . . . how did you know that?" Sarah asked, quite shocked Jessica knew who she was. The awkward hesitation on both their parts gave way once they both made name recognition.

"Would you like to come in?" Jessica asked.

"I really don't want to intrude but was hoping your father might be here."

"He isn't here at the moment. I was about to stop and make tea, and I'd be happy if you'd care to join me. Won't you please come in?"

"That's very kind of you, if you're sure I'm not interrupting."

Jessica held the door wide open, motioning with her arm toward the foyer as Sarah joined her inside. Leading the way to the kitchen, Jessica offered Sarah a seat at the table, then went to the stove and turned on the water.

Jessica was quite beautiful with her long, shining, chestnut-colored hair, and her small and perfectly straight nose. Her green eyes were a lighter shade of green than her father's and were set on a much fairer complexion, though her freckles added to her youthfulness. She was shorter than Sarah, perhaps five-foot-four or -five, but was trim and appeared quite physically fit with well-defined muscles in her arms and legs. Jessie wore no makeup and had a natural wholesomeness about her that was a far cry from the appearance of so many young women on the East Coast who showed little restraint in their use of cosmetics. She bore a resemblance to her father, though she definitely had much more refined features.

Bringing the cups to the table, Jessie sat for a moment, waiting till the water boiled. "Do you live in Arizona?"

"No, I actually live in New York. Tell me, Jessie, I still don't understand how you knew my name. Did your father tell you about me?"

Jessie fashioned a modest smile before continuing. "Heavens no, he didn't!"

A look of confusion spread to Sarah's face.

"I suppose I should explain. Uncle Edgar mentioned he met you last spring, and he wanted to know if I knew you. After he described you to me, I told him I didn't think I'd ever met you and had no idea how Dad knew you. We talked for a while, and he told me he suspected my father held a special place for you in his heart. It was probably just a hunch, but Edgar knows my dad pretty well, even if he doesn't talk about himself very much."

"I see. Well I suppose Edgar must have done a good job providing my description then," Sarah offered, still surprised at Jessie's recognition of her.

"I could have picked you out of a lineup. You're even lovelier than he described."

"I'm flattered, thank you, Jessie, and you too are more beautiful than your pictures."

A small pause opened between them before Jessie continued, "How do you know my father, if you don't mind my asking?"

Sarah didn't know how much she was willing to share, if Jessica's father hadn't spoken about her, and not knowing what Jessica's relationship was with her mother or between Travis and her mother. "Your father and I knew each other many years ago when he was living in New York. We had occasion to meet each other again in Phoenix last spring, and he was kind enough to offer himself as a tour guide, knowing I'd never visited Arizona before. I'm afraid I'd never been on a horse before either, and I don't know who was worse for wear the next day, Trixy or me!"

Jessica laughed along with Sarah as the water finally came to a boil. Jessie returned to the stove and brought the hot water to the table, pouring it over the tea bags in each of their cups. "Do you take anything in your tea?"

"Sugar would be fine, thank you."

Returning with the sugar, Jessica joined Sarah at the table again.

"I recall your father mentioning you have twin boys," Sarah said. "Are they here with you today at the ranch?"

"Not today. They're with my husband back in Phoenix. He gives me the time to come up and check in with Dad, as well as ride, which I miss if I don't get my fix. Most of the time they come along, but my husband enjoys his time bonding with them, doing boy things together. Besides, I make better use of the time around here when I'm by myself. Dad's expert at organizing and picking up after himself, but doesn't always keep up with weekly cleaning, and I try to keep up for him!"

"Not many daughters are as thoughtful or as talented as you are, Jessica. The house is decorated beautifully and I think your dad mentioned you were behind most of that."

"Thank you. He is organized, but as I mentioned, not overly concerned with the house cleaning or the decorating department of home ownership. For a long time, we lived in the old homestead without much to work with until Dad finally finished the log house. We eventually tore down the old ranch house after Grandma died, and I loved combining the older furnishings with the newer things. A mix of old West meets new West appeals to me in designing, and Dad's house was the canvas that allowed me to do that."

"The home is absolutely beautiful, and I can appreciate how anyone would want to spend time here, thanks in part to your talent in decorating. I suppose your mother must be equally proud as I know your father is." She waited to hear what Jessie would say.

Jessica's face took on a peculiar expression before she turned her head, looking out the window. Turning back to face Sarah again, she answered, "I guess my father hasn't shared anything about my mother with you . . . That's just like him to leave well enough alone."

"I'm afraid I don't understand," Sarah responded, a puzzled look on her face.

"I would have thought he might have said something to you about her, but she's not a topic of conversation he would ever bring up freely. Besides, if it isn't important, he tends to ignore it, especially if the topic is harmful without purpose, and I suppose that's the way he deals with my mother for my sake. The truth is my mother couldn't care less about my interests or talents in life."

Sarah was shocked to hear such an assessment of one's own mother. "I'm so very sorry, Jessica. Your father hadn't explained to me what the family dynamics were, and I certainly didn't mean to bring up anything painful."

"There is no need for you to apologize. I have a terrific life, and I'm happier without my mother taking any part in it. I can thank my dad and my grandmother for the fact that I don't feel deprived in the least without her. If there was any sadness in it, I suppose the fact that Dad was never happy, not because he was without her, but because he never had anyone to share his life with whom he loved." Jessie stopped a moment, her gentle green eyes resting on Sarah.

"My father was never one to wear his feelings on his sleeve. He always kept anything meaningful or important to him close to his chest. I suppose I always suspected he had loved someone other than my mother somewhere in his past, but I wasn't the one for him to share that with. What I do know is he always loved me and did everything he could to protect me from the unvarnished truth about my mother. He never spoke one negative word about her to me, even to this day, but I knew as a child what she was." Jessica paused slightly before continuing, as if she were considering what to share.

"My very first memory of her was seeing her rolling around on the floor with a strange man I didn't know, and when I cried because I thought he was hurting her, she yelled at me and called me 'a dirty little shit ass' and sent me back to my room. That was my first real memory of her, and it went downhill from there." Jessica spoke with a stoic look on her face, as if she had overcome the hurt from her past.

The painfulness of Jessica's memory was mirrored in Sarah's expression as she listened, believing that Jessie's strength was like her father's, though her openness and way of expressing herself carried a depth of detail missing when Travis spoke.

"I'm so sorry you were hurt by her," Sarah responded, empathetically.

"It was a long time ago, and I've been able to move on, but I wanted to share with you my history so you can perhaps understand my father in a way he would never express to you himself. When I was four, my father finally packed his and my clothes, and we drove up to the Rim to stay at my grandmother's house permanently, not just for the weekend. It was the first time I ever really felt safe and protected with the people who loved me, away from my mother. I saw her periodically after that whenever she needed more money or was in some kind of a jam and needed Dad to rescue her from some calamity. Most of my memories of her revolved around her screaming and cursing, calling my father all kinds of awful names. I can remember trying to hide when she showed up here, not long after Dad and I left, because I thought she would try to take me away to live with her again. I hid in my grandmother's closet and wouldn't come out even after she had gone. As I grew older, I heard the stories and rumors people told about her up here in Payson. They talked about her drug use under their breaths, and the same question always got asked: Why didn't he divorce her? He had every reason to, and no one understood why Dad kept to himself, never living with her again while providing generously for her when she treated him so badly." Jessica brought her cup to her lips, sipping her tea slowly before continuing, as if thinking how to proceed.

"I used to think maybe he didn't want me to think badly of her or if he completely abandoned her I might somehow blame him for her absence in my life. His way at least, I didn't have to wonder if I even had a mother, or one that gave a damn anyway. So I thought he did it in the hope I might not feel the sting of rejection and that it was his way of protecting me from a sense of abandonment. The truth was I didn't give a damn about her. My Grandmother Clara was the only mother I really ever had, and that was fine with me because I loved her." Jessica stopped to look out the window again before continuing, her bright green eyes open wide with insight. Sarah remained silent, not wanting to hinder her from sharing, allowing her the space she needed to go on.

"As time went on, we saw less and less of her, and she continued to spiral downward into a living hell of drugs, alcohol, sex, and abdication from life in general. Then in 1982, when I was seventeen and only saw her on rare occasions, I was busy packing boxes, getting ready to sort through years of collected junk so we could be ready to move into the new log home Dad had been working on for so long. While working my way through papers and files, I came across a few old legal files of Dad's and opened them to see what they contained. I always knew how depraved my mother was, but for the first time, I finally saw what my father had agreed to, legally, regarding my mother and why he stayed married to her. In the file was a letter from her attorney addressed to my father's attorney in response to his having filed papers for divorce. She threatened to keep custody and fight in court, dragging it out as long as possible, knowing that the courts at that time favored the mother's right to maintain custody. The letter stated that if he pursued the divorce, there was a very real possibility of losing permanent custody of me, but if he opted for legal separation with no divorce, she would relinquish all rights to custodial care, agreeing never to see me again without my father being present. She would agree to that, but only so long as the marriage stayed intact, citing her religious belief that divorce was forbidden. I had to laugh when I read that, since I could never remember her attending church and couldn't conceive how adultery and drugs were apparently acceptable . . . Anyway, she would get to keep the

Phoenix home, and he would continue to provide her support till I was eighteen. In essence, she sold me back to my father for a price!

"I should have been shocked, but somehow it was the sanest thing about their entire relationship I'd ever heard. It all made sense in some convoluted way. She got what she wanted—the house in the valley, money, and the right to keep his name, which in her vengeful way kept him from future happiness—while my father got me. I guess my father felt there was no price too big to pay for the guarantee she could never hurt or have me again. I haven't seen her in years now, but I know she still lives in Phoenix, probably in the same house my father bought and paid for."

Sarah listened intently to Jessica's painful memories with an aching heart and couldn't prevent the tears from welling up in her eyes. She now understood why Travis couldn't bring himself to mention anything about Mary. She wanted to ask Jessica one more question and hoped she might be able to give her a better insight into Travis's thinking.

"Jessie . . . why do you think your father didn't eventually divorce her once you came of age and could make your own choices?"

"Don't you know?" she said, surprised at Sarah's question.

"No, I can't see why he would allow her that vengefulness all those years later."

Jessie brought a slight smile to her lips and tilted her head to the side as she continued, "You know, Sarah, my father's life didn't afford him the two things I believe he wanted more than anything else, although he never talks about either. The accident he suffered at the end of his senior year at West Point robbed him of what promised to be a stellar military career. He had worked very hard toward that dream, and it was taken from him in an instant. My grandmother said it devastated Grandpa too, and he never was able to get over it, although Dad carried on.

"Remember I told you I always believed my dad had loved someone else, even though he never mentioned her by name to me? I always knew he never loved my mother. I just assumed whoever he did love had died or moved on and took part of Dad's heart from him when they parted for whatever reason. Right before my marriage to Kirk, I remember asking Dad if I should marry him or not. He asked me if Kirk was the first thing I thought of every morning when I woke up and was he the last thing on my mind before I went to sleep? When I said he was, then Dad told me to follow my heart and don't let one day go by without his company, because if I let him go, even for a short while, there was a chance I might not ever get to be with him again. I asked him how he could be certain of that. Dad said he had made that mistake in his life and, as a result, had to live with the loss of someone he had loved very much. He didn't want me to make that same mistake. I never asked him who it was or whatever had happened to the woman, knowing how private a man my father is. But losing her was the second greatest disappointment in his life. I always assumed she had died or vanished and it was too late for him by then. Dad never mentioned it again, but I always felt bad that he remained alone in life and unhappy, without the woman he had really loved long ago.

"Anyway, I guess what I'm trying to say is what was the point of him getting the divorce after all those years if the woman he had really loved was already gone? He had lived his life that way for so long a divorce wouldn't affect him or change the way he was living. It never occurred to me the woman from my dad's past might still be alive somewhere, until Edgar told me about you having been here and how Dad had known you a long time ago before he married my mother. Edgar knew right away you held a special place in my Dad's heart, and that's why he told me about your visit."

Sarah was speechless at Jessica's assessment and intuition, surprised and overwhelmed Travis might have felt the same way all those years. The confirmation pierced her heart. Sarah remained silent, wounded as she tried to fully digest all Jessica had shared with her, all the pain and guilt she now harbored at hearing the truth of Travis's life, and how selfish she had been in not understanding or reading his signals correctly. Jessie's story left a sense of sorrow she could not overcome.

Jessica sat quietly for a moment, paying close attention to the wound in Sarah's expression. "Edgar was right about you, Sarah. You are every bit the lady he said you were!" She searched Sarah's face for her thoughts before continuing, "May I ask you something?"

"Of course, ask me whatever you want, and I'll do my best to answer, if I can."

"Do you love my father?"

Jessica's perception and straightforward inquiry pulled at Sarah's heart, and she could only respond with the same honesty and openness. "Yes, Jessie . . . I do, very much. I wish it could have been different for your father and me."

Jessie leaned forward, looking at Sarah directly. "Then why don't you tell him that now?"

Sarah raised her head and looked back at Jessica, all the while thinking how wrong she was not to have trusted Travis enough to let him explain. "Jessica, I hope I haven't made the same mistake your father warned you not to make. I don't know if it is too late for us or even if your father would want to accept me back. I'm afraid I may have hurt him. I want you to know I do love him with all my heart and have loved him deeply all of my life. Whatever it takes for us to be together is what I'm willing to do, if he'll have me." Sarah sat motionless, thinking how selfish she had been, unsure anything she could say or do would heal the breach she had put between them.

Jessica reached out and patted Sarah's hand as it rested on the table. "I suppose there is only one way to find out." Looking back out the window, Jessica continued, "Don't waste any more time on the past, Sarah. He's back unloading hay at the barn."

Sarah turned to look out the window and watched as Travis lifted a bale of hay from the pickup and stacked it under the eave of the barn with the others. Looking back at Jessie, Sarah exchanged smiles with her.

CHAPTER FORTY-SEVEN

Without another word, Sarah rose to her feet, put on her sweater and headed for the front door. Pushing the massive door open, she placed her straw hat on her head and started walking down the long hill, watching Travis as he unloaded the hay bales from the pickup. Her heart was racing with each step closer, not knowing what she would say to him, or even if he would listen. To see Travis, even at a distance, brought the same longing she always held for him, and the thought that he might not accept her attempt to reconcile was unbearable. How could she possibly explain why she refused to take his calls? The thought of losing him a second time because of her rigid judgment was too painful for Sarah to accept. She had to find a way to make him understand only her ignorance of the situation between him and his wife had caused her to leave.

Halfway down the long sweeping hill, Travis suddenly looked up and caught sight of her. He came to a sudden halt, fixed on her. Sarah paused, nervously returning his stare from her distance. After a momentary standstill, Travis tilted his Stetson back slightly on his head, and then he removed his leather gloves, placing them on top of one of the fence posts of the corral. He stood, watching her. That he made no effort to acknowledge her or even try to meet her part-way stabbed her heart, but instead he leaned against the corral post with folded arms across his chest, waiting to see what she would do next. Her heart sank in her chest. This was the second-longest walk forward she had ever taken, with the exception of having to face him once before when she had received her final grade at his hand in algebra so long ago. Just as before, she was at a loss to know what he was thinking, and now, his reaction was not what she had hoped for. Swallowing her pride, Sarah continued down the hill, bearing the weight of his fixed gaze. She came within ten feet of him, stopping short, unsure of herself, wondering if she should have come. She desperately wanted him to hold her but couldn't bring herself any closer, fearing his rejection.

"Sarah," he said tilting his head slightly in way of greeting her. With his arms still folded, the intensity of the moment was palpable and his eyes searing. "Are you just passing through Payson, or did you have a reason for this unexpected visit?"

His voice sounded cold, and his need to keep his distance both physically and emotionally wounded her. She looked down and then brought her head back up to face him again. "I . . . I got your letter and was hoping we could talk, and that you might let me explain why I left."

"I think we both know why you left. What I need to know is why you've decided to return."

Sarah kept her distance, unsure what to tell him as she stood, nervously holding the edge of her sweater. Travis had always been direct with everything he did and said. Believing he would behave any differently now would be a mistake.

"I didn't know the whole truth, Travis, and I'm so sorry for the way I reacted."

He waited for her to continue, watching her struggle while trying her best to answer him. She seemed unable to go on.

"You refused my phone calls for five months. My letter was mailed almost a month ago. After six months you decided you want to hear the truth?"

"No . . . I mean, Jessica shared with me the real story about her mother, and I'm so sorry I didn't let you explain." Attempting a way to bridge the gap she had put between them, Sarah's words weren't coming out the way she wanted. "In your letter, you explained the equation you had carved on the tree. That you carved an equation attempting to express how you felt about us moved me. . . that is, that you remembered my question. I . . . I mean you took the time to carve an equation to express love." She was stumbling, trying to tell him what he meant to her and how much in love with him she had always been, but for the first time in her life, the words wouldn't come out right.

"Sarah," Travis spoke up, keeping his eyes fixed rigidly on her, holding his distance. "That's not the equation up there on that tree. It never was. Don't you see? You and I are the equation and have been all along. We were from the beginning because it was written inside of us, not with symbols, words or even numbers in equations. It doesn't need to be written down, but only lived. There can be nothing outside of us that wasn't already inside ourselves."

"I don't understand," she said, wanting desperately to hold him in her arms again, hoping it wasn't too late to tell him how sorry she was for not trusting him enough and for leaving him that day in Payson. He stood back up, away from leaning on the fence post as he spoke to her.

"Do you remember that day when you saw the equation carved in that pine tree up there on the Rim?"

"Yes, I remember it clearly," she said, hoping he could see how much she cared.

"It had no meaning to you. So you felt nothing. But every time you looked at me, you felt something because it came from within you. It was the same for me also. Every time I was with you, even to see you at a distance, I had the same feelings you did. Do you see the difference? Not until we came together with the same intent, feeling, and understanding would the equation be complete, and the only place it is written down is right here, where it matters." Travis thumped his chest with his fist.

Sarah swallowed over the lump in her throat. She was right to come back and hoped he would forgive her. Travis removed his Stetson, wiping the sweat from his brow with his sleeve, and then placed his hat on top of his gloves now resting on the fence post.

He took several steps closer to her. She watched him cautiously while her heart skipped a beat. She was unable to read his expression, not knowing what to expect from him. Taking another step closer without saying a word, he reached out to her, slowly removing her straw hat from her head as they stood facing each other, surrounded by the ponderosa pines next to the corral. High above the Rim, an eagle circled, riding the heating air currents, and in that moment, gave a piercing whistle as if to call his mate to the same majestic heights.

Travis looked down into Sarah's eyes with the intensity only he could express and whispered through smiling lips, "You never could do the math, Sarah, but if you decide to stay this time, it won't be for just the weekend."

Sarah brushed a tear from her cheek then looked up, nodding slightly, and added, "I hope you like lots of lights in pine trees at Christmas."

Travis took her into his arms and kissed her passionately in the brilliant, midday Arizona sun.

Sarah finally understood that they had always been communicating their love, but she had missed it, resting her understanding in words alone, which had failed to completely express the love she had been searching for all her life. Even the equation itself was inadequate and missed her understanding when she saw the symbols carved on the tree. The equation had to be known from within, and that knowledge was out of reach unless experienced from within. Every attempt to communicate love in writing was only a poor facsimile meant to point to what they already shared. To speak it or to write it did not capture the essence of love in those in whom it had been born. Sarah fed the flame as Lily had encouraged, until its light consumed the very reality of her world.

The words of Sarah's world fell silent and the numbers in Travis's world disappeared into a mysterious union of both as they discovered they were one and the same, part of the glorious shining light of love known only to themselves.

That light of love was the equation, and they both proved it.

What seeds we plant, if only we knew,
Whose fruit to have in future view.
Though time does steal our hope from hand,
The soul will work its secret plan.

Keep thy dreams in slumber's rest,
Until the world it does confess.
To you this day the fruit is given,
Because the lover held her vision.

∞

ACKNOWLEDGEMENTS

There is much we can learn with every new venture, and writing *The Equation* has added considerably to my storehouse. The axiom "No one reaches the finish line without help from others" certainly applies in my case. While any imperfections within the work itself are solely attributable to the author, any favor has the imprint of many talented hands. To have crossed the finish line is first and foremost due to the support of my husband, Andy, who spent countless hours listening to rewrites, encouraging me when impasses surfaced, and who, above all others, believed in me. My heartfelt gratitude and love will always belong to him.

For their expertise and thoughtful suggestions, I remain ever grateful to contributing editors Miranda Henley and Kelly Lynne. Thanks to Barbara Cook, for her typing skills. Without their talents, this title might not have seen the light of day.

Special thanks to my daughter Jennifer, who helped to facilitate the cover photo shoot. Her enthusiasm is infectious. For my stepsons, Andrew and Matthew, who gave inspiration while fulfilling their dreams. My gratitude and hugs extend to each of their spouses and children, who light our hearts and color our days.

Every story has its beginning, and this one would never have come to light if the true life experiences of friends and family hadn't emboldened me to put pen to paper. "Thank you" seems a paltry expression in light of their contributions. To Revela, for sharing her heart, and to Cousin Mike and his bride, Linda, whose real-life story reads like a "love lost and then found" novel. All inspired me greatly, in addition to countless others who renewed my faith in the power of love to make dreams come true.

Kudos to photographer Mike P. Nelson for his excellent cover photo, because everyone knows, "A book is only as good as its cover." Thanks also to Ramsey Middle School, Minneapolis, MN, for allowing us the use of one of their classrooms, which provided the perfect setting.

Thanks to my sister Kim, for her cherished feedback. To my niece Maddy, for her beauty—inside and out! To my brother, Drew, and my sister Linda too, who had the stamina to tolerate the sibling among us who is occasionally referred to as "the one who was vaccinated with a phonograph needle!"

In addition, my heartfelt thanks belongs to dear friend Dora Lee, who never failed to uplift and encourage me when I needed it most.

Above all, to my readers who have allowed me to enter their lives and, hopefully, for a time, entertain and uplift them.

Finally, my everlasting gratitude rests with my parents, Lorraine and Whitney, who defined the light of love and placed that light in the hearts of all their children.

JUDITH I. HILL

Born and raised on Long Island, New York, Judith and her husband reside in a rural setting in the mid-west. Her former work in public relations and protocol within the travel industry and the US Department of Commerce has given her a broad perspective from which she draws inspiration. Along with their three children, the family farm has sheltered a wealth of wild life including horses, ponies, four dogs and two cats. ***The Equation*** is her debut novel.

Made in the USA
Monee, IL
27 May 2023

34071236R00267